Revolution's Dawn

Edward Spiller

Copyright © 2024 Edward Spiller
All rights reserved
ISBN: 9798340903167
Imprint: Independently published

Other Books in this series

Revolution's Dawn
Revolution's Echo
Revolution's Seeds

Disclaimer

This book is a work of fiction. Names, characters, places, and incidents either are the product of the author's imagination or are used fictitiously. Any resemblance to actual persons, living or dead, events, or locales is purely coincidental.

Contents

- Prologue 7
- Chapter 1 The Gathering Storm 13
- Chapter 2 Boiling Point 24
- Chapter 3 The Unlikely Allies 37
- Chapter 4 The Government Strikes Back 49
- Chapter 5 Seeds of Revolution 71
- Chapter 6 A Call to Arms 85
- Chapter 7 The Cost of Rebellion 101
- Chapter 8 A Growing Flame 116
- Chapter 9 The Rising Tide 130
- Chapter 10 Operation Unity 142
- Chapter 11 The Enemy Within 157
- Chapter 12 A Nation Divided 165
- Chapter 13 The Betrayal 180
- Chapter 14 The Darkest Hour 194
- Chapter 15 Regroup and Rebuild 206
- Chapter 16 The Government Counteroffensive 215
- Chapter 17 Turning the Tide 227
- Chapter 18 A New Dawn 240
- Chapter 19 The Gathering Storm 254
- Chapter 20 The Battle Begins 277
- Chapter 21 Aftermath 294
- Chapter 22 The Silent Resistance 311

Chapter 23 Love and War 333
Chapter 24 The Government's Last Gamble 343
Chapter 25 The Underground 367
Chapter 26 Betrayal and Loyalty 383
Chapter 27 The Turning Point 398
Chapter 28 The Final Push 414
Chapter 29 The Battle for Freedom 435
Chapter 30 Victory and Sacrifice 449
Chapter 31 A New Beginning 462
Chapter 32 Revolution's Dawn 479
Author Biography 487

Prologue

The country had once been a place of quiet order, of slow-moving politics, and carefully managed stagnation. For fourteen long years, Britain had endured a government that did little to provoke change but even less to inspire hope. There had been frustration, of course, grumblings in pubs, angry letters to editors, and discontent simmering beneath the surface, but nothing that ever truly boiled over. And then, in the blink of an eye, everything changed.

It started with a snap general election. No one had expected it, least of all the people. But after years of mediocrity, the government had grown complacent, confident in the apathy of the nation. They were wrong. The opposition, a left-wing party that promised radical change, seized the moment, using the growing disillusionment to fuel their rise. They spoke of justice, of a brighter future, of tearing down the old systems and building something new. They captured the imagination of a tired nation, a nation that had grown weary of inaction, of being ignored. In a landslide victory, they took power.

For a brief moment, there was hope. People believed that change was coming, and that this new government might finally be the answer to years of neglect. But that hope didn't take long to curdle into something darker. Within weeks of taking office, the new government showed its true colours.

It started with the pensioners. The most vulnerable, the elderly who had worked their entire lives and depended on the modest benefits they had earned. The government, citing budget concerns, stripped away the winter fuel benefit, the lifeline that helped pensioners survive the harsh British winters. When the cold came, so did the deaths. Thousands of elderly citizens, unable to heat their homes, perished in the brutal frost, their bodies found in their beds, wrapped in layers of blankets that couldn't hold back the biting chill. It was a national tragedy, but the government's response was one of cold indifference. They spoke of "necessary sacrifices," of "balancing the budget," but the people heard something different: 'We do not care.'

The country began to tremble, the first cracks in the façade of control beginning to show. But it didn't stop there. In their zeal to reshape the nation, the new government passed sweeping censorship laws, curbing free speech in ways that hadn't been seen in Britain for generations. What was once a country where open debate and criticism were celebrated now became a place of fear. Social media was monitored with ruthless efficiency, and ordinary citizens, mothers, teachers, and students, were arrested and jailed for something as simple as retweeting a post critical of the government. Online dissenters disappeared overnight, their homes raided, and their lives torn apart for nothing more than expressing a thought. Fear seeped into every corner of life.

Then came the immigration crisis. For years, the borders had been porous, the government unable, or unwilling, to stem the tide of illegal immigrants flooding the country. But under this new regime, it wasn't just an oversight, it was policy. Hundreds of thousands of young men from the Middle East were allowed to flood the cities, and their presence was celebrated by the government as a triumph of humanity and compassion. But the reality was far different. The government spent millions housing them in hotels, paying them living benefits while the citizens of the country struggled to survive. Crime rates soared. Knife crime rose by sixty percent, sexual assaults by seventy, and shoplifting by an astonishing one hundred and twenty percent. The streets, once relatively safe, became dangerous after dark, with police stretched too thin to respond to the rising chaos.

The people had had enough. The dream of a better Britain had become a nightmare. The promises of justice and equality were nothing but hollow words, replaced by fear and violence. The government had turned against its people, prioritising the welfare of outsiders over the lives of its citizens, silencing any who dared speak out against the injustice. Britain, once proud and resilient, was crumbling under the weight of its leaders' betrayal.

The spark of rebellion had been lit in those quiet moments, in the homes of pensioners who had lost everything, in the voices of mothers mourning their assaulted daughters, and in the trembling hands of men and women who had watched their country be stripped away from them piece by piece. It was whispered in the back alleys of London, in the pubs of Manchester, in the fields of the countryside. People began to talk, to organise, to resist. They weren't activists, they weren't revolutionaries by nature, but they had been pushed too far. Ordinary men and women, workers, shopkeepers, teachers, and students, Britain's silent majority, were finding their voice.

The revolution didn't begin with a gunshot or a grand speech. It began in the quiet fury of a nation betrayed. The people had endured too much and lost too much, and now, they were ready to take back what was theirs. Across the country, there were whispers of a new beginning, of justice not dictated by the government but demanded by the people. The fire had been lit in their hearts, and as the cold winter began to recede, that fire would burn brighter than any in British history.

This wasn't just anger. This was a revolution. And it was coming.

PART I
The Spark

Chapter 1 The Gathering Storm

The UK had once been a nation of steady rhythms and predictable patterns, where the daily grind of life moved forward with a certain sense of inevitability. But that was before the cracks began to show before the thin veneer of stability peeled away to reveal the deep fissures beneath. Now, the country was a pressure cooker, its people simmering with frustration and anger, a sense of betrayal coursing through the very fabric of society.

The streets of London, once bustling with the routine hustle of workers, tourists, and shoppers, now felt different. The energy that had once driven the city forward was tainted with an undercurrent of tension that seemed to throb just below the surface. The familiar sounds of traffic and chatter were frequently interrupted by the wail of police sirens, the thud of helicopter blades overhead, and the distant roar of protest marches that had become almost a daily occurrence. The air was thick with an uneasy mix of diesel fumes and the acrid tang of tear gas, remnants of the previous night's skirmishes between protesters and law enforcement.

Graffiti had begun to spread like wildfire across the city's walls, bold and unapologetic. Messages of defiance and anger were scrawled in every available space: "ENOUGH IS ENOUGH," "THE PEOPLE WON'T BE SILENCED," "NO JUSTICE, NO PEACE." Once the domain of the disenfranchised and radical, these words had become the everyman's slogans. The walls themselves seemed to pulse with the collective fury of a population pushed too far.

Across the UK, the unrest was not confined to the capital. In the industrial heartlands of the North, the sense of abandonment was palpable. Once-thriving towns, now left to rot as industries collapsed and jobs vanished, were hotbeds of resentment. The high streets, lined with shuttered shops and pubs barely clinging on, bore witness to the slow death of these communities. Young people, seeing no future in the places where they had been born and raised, had turned to the only outlet left to them: protest.

But these were not the peaceful demonstrations of the past. These were gatherings born of desperation, where the lines between protest and riot blurred. In cities like Manchester, Birmingham, and Liverpool, clashes between police and protesters have become increasingly violent. The sound of breaking glass, the crack of batons, and the shouts of anger and pain echoed through the night, leaving behind streets littered with the debris of a society in turmoil.

The rural areas, too, were not immune to the growing unrest. Farmers, once the backbone of the nation, found themselves squeezed by government policies that favoured large corporations over small, family-run farms. The frustration that had long simmered in these communities was now boiling over. Fields that had once symbolised the stability of the countryside were now battlegrounds, as farmers and rural workers took to blocking roads, setting up makeshift barricades, and demanding that their voices be heard.

The government, bloated with bureaucracy and mired in scandal, responded to the unrest with a heavy hand. New laws were passed at breakneck speed, each one more draconian than the last. Freedom of assembly was curtailed; protests were declared illegal; dissent was met with swift and brutal retaliation. The media, once a beacon of accountability, had been brought to heel, its coverage increasingly sanitised, parroting the government's narrative that the unrest was the work of a few "extremists" rather than the widespread movement it had become.

Yet, despite the government's efforts to stamp out the flames of rebellion, the fire only spread. The crackdowns, the arrests, and the show trials, all served only to fuel the anger of the people. In homes across the country, families sat around dinner tables, discussing the latest developments with a mix of fear and defiance. Conversations that had once been about the weather, or the latest football match, were now about survival, about how to protect themselves, about whether it was time to take to the streets.

Even in the quietest corners of the country, the tension was inescapable. In small villages and sleepy coastal towns, where life had once moved at a leisurely pace, the atmosphere was charged with an unfamiliar anxiety. Neighbours who had lived side by side for years now eyed each other with suspicion, wondering who might be a government informant, who might be a sympathiser of the resistance. The fabric of society, once woven tightly by shared experiences and mutual trust, was unravelling.

Amid this growing chaos, the government's grip on power was beginning to slip. The Prime Minister, once a figure of authority and control, now appeared haggard and uncertain, his public addresses increasingly defensive, his policies increasingly desperate. The cabinet, too, was divided, with whispers of dissent and defection growing louder by the day. The once-unshakeable belief in the government's ability to maintain order was crumbling, and with it, the illusion of stability that had kept the country from descending into outright anarchy.

But for the ordinary people of the UK, the stakes were clear. The country was on the brink, and something had to give. The frustration, the anger, the fear, they were no longer emotions to be suppressed or ignored. They were a call to action, a demand for change that could no longer be silenced. The streets, the fields, the towns, and the cities, were all battlegrounds now, in a war for the very soul of the nation.

And as the tension mounted, as the protests grew more frequent and the violence more intense, it became clear that this was not just a passing storm. This was a reckoning, a moment of truth for a country that had long been content to paper over the cracks in its foundation. The people had awakened, and they were not going back to sleep.

The storm was gathering, and it would not be long before it broke.

The rain fell in a steady, relentless rhythm, a fitting soundtrack to the unravelling of a nation. It was a late afternoon in November, and London was shrouded in a murky twilight that blurred the line between day and night. The streets, once bustling with life, were now choked with the debris of a country in turmoil, piles of uncollected garbage, abandoned cars, and the occasional shattered window, a testament to the unrest simmering just beneath the surface.

John Mason stood on the rooftop of an old, abandoned warehouse in East London, the decaying structure a ghost of the industrial past that once defined this part of the city. From this vantage point, he could see the city laid out before him, a sprawling urban landscape caught between decay and defiance. The skyline was a jarring mix of towering glass skyscrapers and crumbling tenements. The gleaming structures of the financial district rose in the distance, their lights flickering like beacons of a world that seemed increasingly out of reach for the people living in the shadows of this part of the city.

Below, the streets were a maze of narrow lanes and alleyways, snaking through a neighbourhood that had long been forgotten by the city's planners and politicians. What was once a thriving hub of factories and workshops had, over the years, transformed into a patchwork of derelict buildings and hastily constructed shelters for those with nowhere else to go. The air was thick with the scent of rot and damp, mingling with the acrid stench of burnt rubber and smouldering trash that lingered from the latest clashes between protesters and police.

John's eyes drifted across the scene, taking in the details that had become so familiar over the past months. The graffiti covered nearly every surface, the slogans and symbols of resistance and defiance mingling with desperate pleas for help and bitter curses against a government that had failed its people. The boarded-up windows of shops had long since closed, their owners driven out by the escalating violence and economic collapse. The flickering streetlights, many of them broken or shattered, cast erratic pools of light that did little to chase away the encroaching darkness.

In this place, amidst the ruins of what once was, John had found himself again drawn into a fight he had thought he had left behind. The memories of his military service came back to him in fragments, dusty villages in far-off lands, the sharp crack of gunfire, the smell of gunpowder and blood. He had left the army to escape the violence, to find some semblance of peace, but it seemed that fate had other plans. The streets of London were now his battlefield, and the enemy was not some foreign insurgent but the very system he had once sworn to protect.

He lit a cigarette, the orange ember a tiny defiance against the encroaching darkness. John had never been one for speeches or grand gestures, but the gravity of the moment weighed on him. The UK was at a breaking point. The government, bloated with bureaucracy and crippled by indecision, had done nothing to stem the tide of illegal immigration that was tearing the fabric of society apart. The economy was in freefall, with jobs scarce and public services stretched to the brink. As the streets filled with protests and counter-protests, the government's only response had been to tighten its grip, censoring the media, outlawing public gatherings, and cracking down on any dissent.

But John knew the real problem wasn't the immigrants. They were just the scapegoats in a much larger game. The rot went deeper, into the very heart of the system. He'd seen it firsthand during his years in the military, corruption, incompetence, and a complete disregard for the people they were supposed to serve. It was why he'd left the service, disillusioned and angry, and why he now found himself standing on this rooftop, about to do something that would have been unthinkable just a few years ago.

The door to the stairwell creaked open behind him, and John turned to see Emily Carter emerge into the fading light. She was younger than him by a decade, but the lines of worry etched into her face made her look older. Her auburn hair was pulled back into a tight ponytail, and she wore a worn leather jacket that did little to shield her from the cold. In her eyes, John saw a reflection of his resolve, steely, unwavering, but tinged with the same weariness that had settled into his bones.

"Is everything set?" John asked, his voice gruff.

Emily nodded, pulling her jacket tighter around her. "The others are on their way. We're meeting Hassan at the safe house. He's bringing the final piece of the plan."

John took a deep drag from his cigarette, exhaling slowly as he considered her words. Hassan Ali was the last person he'd expected to be working with in this new chapter of his life. An academic by trade, Hassan had been a prominent voice in the fight for immigrant rights, a man of peace who had always believed in dialogue over conflict. But even he had reached his breaking point. The government's refusal to listen, to even acknowledge the growing unrest, had pushed him to a place where words were no longer enough.

"Do you trust him?" John asked, more out of habit than doubt.

Emily looked at him, her eyes narrowing slightly. "Do you?"

John didn't answer immediately. He'd known Hassan for years, though they'd always been on opposite sides of the ideological spectrum. If anything, Hassan's involvement only confirmed how dire the situation had become. "I trust that he knows what's at stake," John finally said. "And I trust that he's as desperate as we are."

Emily seemed to accept that, and they stood in silence for a moment, the wind carrying the distant sounds of the city to their ears, sirens, shouts, and the occasional crack of gunfire. London was a powder keg, and they were about to light the fuse.

"Any second thoughts?" Emily asked, her voice softer now.

John shook his head. "No. It's too late for that."

Before Emily could respond, the sound of approaching footsteps echoed from the stairwell. A tall figure emerged, moving with a deliberate, almost methodical pace. Hassan Ali stepped into the light, his dark eyes sharp and alert. He was dressed in his usual understated manner, a plain black coat over a sweater, his thick beard flecked with grey. There was an air of quiet intensity about him, a man who had long been accustomed to fighting battles with his mind but was now prepared to fight with something more tangible.

"It's time," Hassan said, his voice calm but with an undercurrent of urgency. "The others are waiting."

John stubbed out his cigarette, the last ember crushed beneath his boot. He glanced at Emily, who gave him a curt nod and then turned to follow Hassan down the stairs. As they descended, the weight of what they were about to do settled heavily on John's shoulders. This wasn't just a protest or a statement. This was the beginning of something far more dangerous. A rebellion. A revolution. And once they crossed that line, there would be no going back.

As they stepped out into the street, the rain intensified, drumming against the pavement. The city loomed around them, dark and oppressive, but John felt a flicker of something in his chest. Hope? Determination? It didn't matter. What mattered was that they were ready. They were about to strike the first blow in a fight for the soul of the nation.

In the distance, a siren wailed, its mournful cry echoing through the streets. It was a sound John had become all too familiar with, a constant reminder of the chaos that had become the new normal. But tonight, it felt different. Tonight, it felt like a call to arms, a signal that the time had come to act.

John took one last look at the city, committing the scene to memory. This was the London he was fighting for, not the gleaming towers of the rich and powerful, but the gritty, battered streets where real people lived and struggled. He turned away from the edge of the roof, the rain soaking through his coat, and headed toward the stairwell where Emily and Hassan were waiting. The time for watching was over. Now, it was time to fight.

Chapter 2 Boiling Point

The rain had tapered off by the time John Mason and Emily Carter made their way to the safe house. The wet streets glistened under the dim glow of streetlights, reflecting the fragmented city around them. The night was silent, save for the occasional distant wail of a siren or the rumble of a passing train. Yet, beneath the surface, an undercurrent of tension buzzed in the air, a palpable sense of dread that seemed to hang over every street corner and alleyway.

The safe house stood on a narrow, forgotten street in the heart of East London, a part of the city that had once thrived but was now little more than a shadow of its former self. The townhouse, built in the late 19th century, had once been a modest home for a working-class family, its brick facade weathered but resilient. Now, it was one of the few structures still standing in a neighbourhood that had long been abandoned by progress and prosperity. The street itself was a relic of the past, its cobblestones worn smooth by generations of footsteps, now slick with rain and grime.

As John and Emily approached the safe house, the surrounding buildings loomed over them like sentinels of decay. Most were boarded up, their windows shattered and doors hanging from rusted hinges. The shops that had once lined the street, bakeries, greengrocers, and small corner stores, were long closed, their signs faded and barely legible, remnants of a time when this part of the city had been alive with the hum of daily life. Now, only the occasional flicker of light from a distant window or the soft murmur of voices carried on the wind hinted that anyone still lived here.

The street was eerily quiet, the kind of silence that feels unnatural in a city as vast and sprawling as London. The only sounds were the soft drip of water from broken gutters and the scurry of a rat darting into the shadows. The air smelled of damp earth, rusting metal, and something acrider, perhaps the lingering scent of a fire that had long since burned out. The rain, which had earlier poured down in torrents, had slowed to a drizzle, leaving puddles in the uneven road that reflected the dim glow of the streetlights.

The safe house itself was unremarkable, its appearance deliberately mundane to avoid drawing attention. The brickwork was mottled with age, the mortar crumbling in places, but it held together, much like the people who now used it as a sanctuary. The windows were covered with heavy blackout curtains, their edges frayed from years of use, and the front door, a solid oak slab reinforced with metal bars, bore the scars of countless attempts to force it open. A faded number plate beside the door was the only indication that this building had once been part of a community, a place where families had lived, laughed, and grown old together.

Inside, the safe house was a stark contrast to the desolation outside. The hallway was narrow and dimly lit, the floorboards creaking underfoot as John and Emily stepped inside. The air was cool and still, carrying the faint scent of wood smoke and old books. The walls were lined with shelves filled with supplies, canned goods, medical kits, and stacks of bottled water. A large, threadbare rug covered most of the floor, its intricate patterns worn down to mere shadows of what they once were.

The main room, where the group had gathered, was sparsely furnished but functional. A heavy wooden table dominated the centre of the room, its surface scarred from years of use. Around it were mismatched chairs, some upholstered in faded fabric, others bare wood, each telling its own story of how it had come to be here. The walls were painted a dull, peeling white, adorned only with a few old maps and posters that had been tacked up hastily. A small fireplace in one corner provided the only source of warmth, its embers glowing faintly, casting flickering shadows that danced across the room.

Despite its age and the wear and tear visible in every corner, the safe house had an air of resilience. It was a place where plans were made, where people gathered not just to escape the storm outside, but to prepare for the battles ahead. The table was cluttered with the tools of revolution, maps marked with key locations, documents detailing government movements, and the occasional weapon, a grim reminder of what was at stake. The flickering candles on the table added to the atmosphere, their flames reflecting off the worn surfaces, casting a warm but uncertain light on the faces of those gathered around.

As John and Emily took their seats, the room seemed to close in around them, the outside world fading away as they focused on the task at hand. The safe house, though simple and unassuming, was more than just a hiding place; it was the heart of their resistance, a place where hope was kindled, and strategies were born. Outside, the city lay in ruins, but here, within these walls, there was still a flicker of life, a spark that could ignite a movement capable of changing everything.

The room was quiet, save for the soft crackle of the fire and the murmur of low voices discussing plans and contingencies. The walls, though thin and cracked, seemed to absorb the tension, holding the weight of their conversations within, as if even the house itself was conspiring to keep their secrets safe. The atmosphere was thick with anticipation, each person acutely aware that this small, unremarkable space could very well be the birthplace of a revolution.

Outside, the world was dark and crumbling, a place where hope seemed a distant memory. But inside the safe house, amidst the flickering candles and the hushed conversations, there was a sense of purpose, of determination. The storm was gathering, and here, in this forgotten corner of London, a new dawn was quietly being forged.

John and Emily exchanged a glance before taking their seats. The others, Hassan Ali, and a handful of their most trusted allies were already gathered, their faces set with grim determination. The table was quiet as Hassan began to speak, his voice low and measured, outlining the final stages of their plan. But as the discussion continued, John found his mind drifting back to how it all began, how the UK had spiralled into chaos, and how he had found himself at the heart of a revolution.

John's memories took him back to a time that now seemed like a different life altogether. He could still recall the sense of pride he had felt when he first joined the British Army. Fresh out of school, he had enlisted at eighteen, eager to serve his country, to be part of something bigger than himself. Back then, the world was a simpler place, or so it seemed. The UK was stable, its government a beacon of democracy, and its people, though diverse, were united in their shared sense of identity.

But over the years, things had begun to change. The first cracks in the façade appeared during his deployments abroad. He had served in Afghanistan, Iraq, and later, in the Balkans, witnessing firsthand the horrors of war, the cost of political manoeuvring, and the thin veneer of civilisation that could so easily be stripped away. Each deployment left him more disillusioned, more aware of the rot festering beneath the surface of the very institutions he had once revered.

It wasn't just the foreign wars that troubled him. As he returned home after each tour, John noticed the subtle shifts in his own country. The economy, once robust, was beginning to falter. Jobs were becoming scarce, wages stagnated, and the gap between the rich and the poor widened with every passing year. Immigration, a topic that had once been a point of pride for the UK, became a contentious issue. The government's inability to manage the influx of people fleeing war, poverty, and persecution from across the globe sowed seeds of discord among the population.

The media, once a trusted institution, played its part in fanning the flames. Sensationalist headlines painted immigrants as criminals, a threat to the "British way of life." Politicians, eager to deflect from their own failures, seized upon these narratives, using them to stoke fear and division. Protests became a common sight, on one side, those demanding stricter immigration controls; on the other, those advocating for human rights and compassion.

John had always tried to keep his distance from politics, focusing instead on his job and his family. But as the protests grew more violent and the government's response more draconian, it became impossible to ignore. The tipping point came when he was called in to assist with a domestic deployment, a rare and troubling occurrence that signalled just how dire the situation had become.

The memory was vivid, even after all these years. He had been deployed to the streets of London; his unit was tasked with controlling the crowds during a particularly volatile protest in Trafalgar Square. What had started as a peaceful demonstration quickly descended into chaos. The protesters, frustrated and angry, clashed with the police, who responded with batons, tear gas, and rubber bullets. The air was thick with smoke and the cries of the wounded.

John had found himself in the middle of it all, his training at odds with his conscience. He remembered the moment when he had locked eyes with a young woman in the crowd. She couldn't have been more than twenty, her face streaked with tears and blood. She wasn't a threat, just a student who had been caught in the wrong place at the wrong time. But the orders were clear, disperse the crowd at all costs.

He hesitated, just for a moment, but it was enough. A fellow soldier stepped forward; his baton raised. John's hand shot out instinctively, stopping him. They exchanged a look, one that needed no words. The soldier lowered his baton, and together they helped the woman to safety, ignoring the chaos around them. It was a small act of defiance, but it was the beginning of John's disillusionment with the military and, by extension, the government that had sent them there.

When he returned home that night, he was a different man. The uniform he had once worn with pride now felt like a burden, a symbol of everything he had come to despise. He handed in his resignation shortly afterward, but the events of that day haunted him. It wasn't long before he began to see the same anger and frustration that had driven the protesters in Trafalgar Square reflected in the faces of people he knew, friends, neighbours, and even his own family.

As John sat in the safe house, his thoughts drifted to Emily. Her journey had been different from his but equally harrowing. He had met her several years ago, during one of the many protests that had become a near-daily occurrence across the country. But Emily's story had begun long before that, shaped by her experiences as a journalist.

Emily had grown up in a small town in the Midlands, the daughter of a schoolteacher and a factory worker. From a young age, she had been a voracious reader, devouring books on history, politics, and social justice. Her parents had instilled in her a strong sense of fairness and a belief in the power of education, values that would shape her future career. After university, Emily had pursued journalism, eager to uncover the truth and give a voice to those who were often silenced.

For a time, she had flourished in her chosen field, working for a respected newspaper, and covering stories of social injustice and political corruption. But as the years went by, she began to notice a disturbing trend. The media, once a pillar of democracy, was becoming increasingly compromised. Corporate interests, political pressures, and the relentless pursuit of profit were eroding the integrity of journalism. Stories that didn't align with the prevailing narrative were buried or distorted, and investigative journalism was becoming a rarity.

Emily's breaking point came when she uncovered a government scandal involving the mistreatment of immigrants in detention centres. She had worked tirelessly on the story, gathering evidence, interviewing survivors, and corroborating facts. It was a damning exposé that, in her mind, would force the government to act, to address the horrific conditions and abuses taking place under their watch.

But when she presented the story to her editor, she was met with resistance. The newspaper, fearing repercussions, refused to publish it. Emily was devastated. She had always believed in the power of the press to hold those in power accountable, but now she saw that even the media could be complicit in perpetuating injustice.

Determined to get the truth out, Emily leaked the story to an independent news outlet. It was published, but the consequences were swift and severe. She was blacklisted, her reputation tarnished, and she was hounded by the authorities. Her home was raided, her notes and equipment seized, and she was subjected to endless harassment. The experience left her shaken, but it also ignited a fire within her. If the traditional avenues of change were closed to her, she would find another way.

That's when she turned to activism. She began organising protests, writing manifestos, and using her investigative skills to expose the government's lies and abuses. It was through this work that she met John, who, like her, had become disillusioned with the system. Together, they formed the core of what would eventually become a revolutionary movement.

The safe house was filled with the quiet murmur of conversation as the group finalised their plans. John and Emily exchanged a glance, a silent acknowledgment of the path that had led them here. They were not alone in their disillusionment. The country was teetering on the edge, pushed to the brink by years of neglect, corruption, and oppression.

The government's failure to address the root causes of the crisis, economic inequality, social division, and the erosion of civil liberties, had driven ordinary people to desperation. The streets were filled with anger, and the once-peaceful protests had given way to violent clashes between the people and the authorities. The government's response had been predictably brutal, curfews, mass arrests, and the deployment of military force to suppress dissent. But the harder they tried to crush the resistance, the more it grew.

For John and Emily, the decision to take up arms had not been an easy one. Both had spent their lives believing in the principles of democracy, justice, and the rule of law. But when those institutions became instruments of oppression, what choice was left? They had tried peaceful protest, civil disobedience, and dialogue, but all had been met with violence and repression. The time for words was over. Now, they were preparing to take action, to fight for the future of their country.

As the meeting drew to a close, John felt a sense of resolve settle over him. This was not a fight they had sought, but it was one they could no longer avoid. The stakes were too high, the consequences of inaction too dire. They were fighting not just for themselves, but for the millions of people who had been betrayed by their government, for the future of a country that had lost its way.

Emily's voice broke through his thoughts. "We've all seen where this road leads," she said, her tone steady but laced with emotion. "We've seen it in the faces of the people we've met, the stories we've uncovered, the lives that have been destroyed. But we also know that change doesn't come without a fight. We can't stand by and let this continue. Not anymore."

John nodded, the words resonating deeply within him. He looked around the room at the faces of the people who had become his comrades, his friends. They were a diverse group, men and women, young and old, from different backgrounds and walks of life. But they were united by a common purpose, a shared belief that something better was possible.

As they prepared to leave the safe house and step into the night, John couldn't shake the feeling that they were standing on the precipice of something monumental. The road ahead would be long and perilous, and there would be losses along the way. But for the first time in a long while, he felt a glimmer of hope. They were no longer just reacting to the world around them; they were taking control of their destiny.

Outside, the rain had stopped, and the air was crisp with the promise of a new dawn. The city was quiet as if holding its breath in anticipation of what was to come. John took a deep breath, steeling himself for the battle ahead. The UK was at a boiling point, and they were about to light the fuse that would set it ablaze.

As they stepped out into the street, the first light of dawn was beginning to break on the horizon, casting a pale glow over the city. The storm was no longer coming, it was here. And John Mason, Emily Carter, and their small band of rebels were ready to face it head-on.

Chapter 3 The Unlikely Allies

The city was a pressure cooker, and today the lid was about to blow. London's streets, usually a chaotic but manageable tangle of humanity, were now a battlefield. The protest that had begun peacefully in Hyde Park had spilled over into the surrounding streets, where anger and frustration had collided with a wall of riot police. What had started as a demonstration against the government's draconian immigration policies had quickly escalated into a violent clash, the air thick with the acrid smell of tear gas and the shouts of thousands of people determined to be heard.

John Mason was in the thick of it, moving with the fluid precision of a man who had seen combat before. His military training kicked in instinctively as he navigated the chaos, his eyes scanning the crowd for signs of trouble. He hadn't intended to get involved; he had come to observe, to gauge the mood of the protest and assess the level of unrest. But now, as the situation spiralled out of control, his instincts told him it was time to act.

He spotted Hassan Ali almost by accident. The former university professor was at the front lines, trying to hold his ground against a line of heavily armoured police officers. Hassan had been one of the organisers of the protest, a voice of reason calling for nonviolent resistance. But the crowd's anger was too much for even him to contain. As the police advanced, pushing back the protesters with batons and shields, Hassan was caught in the surge.

John saw the flash of a baton as it swung toward Hassan, and before he could think, he was moving. He pushed through the crowd, his larger frame helping to clear a path, and reached Hassan just in time to intercept the blow. The baton glanced off John's forearm, a sharp pain radiating up to his shoulder, but he didn't falter. Grabbing Hassan by the collar, he pulled him out of the immediate danger zone and into a narrow alleyway, out of sight of the advancing police.

"Are you alright?" John asked, his voice rough with adrenaline.

Hassan nodded, breathing heavily. "I'm fine, thanks to you. That could have ended much worse."

John studied him for a moment, noting the determination in Hassan's eyes. He had heard of the professor before, a man known for his intellect and his unwavering commitment to justice. This was a man who had once believed in the power of words to change the world, but John could see that something had shifted in him, something that resonated with John's sense of disillusionment.

"You shouldn't be out here," John said, his tone bordering on reprimand. "This is no place for a man like you."

Hassan met his gaze evenly. "And what kind of man should be out here? One who knows how to fight? Because that's exactly why I need to be here. This fight isn't just about who can throw the hardest punch. It's about more than that, it's about standing up for what's right."

John couldn't argue with that. The crowd was still surging, the sound of shouting and clashing metal echoing down the alley. They were far from safe, and he knew it. But there was something in Hassan's words that struck a chord within him, something that made John realise that maybe this wasn't just another protest, another skirmish in a city slowly tearing itself apart. Maybe this was the beginning of something more.

"Come on," John said, deciding in that instant. "We need to get out of here before things get worse."

Hassan didn't argue, and together they made their way through the backstreets, avoiding the main thoroughfares where the violence was escalating. John led them through a labyrinth of alleys and side streets until they reached the relative safety of a quiet residential area, far from the chaos of the protest.

They stopped in front of an old, rundown café, its windows dark and shuttered.

"Here," John said, pushing open the door. "We'll be safe for now."

Inside, the café was a relic of a time long past, its walls adorned with faded posters and photographs. The tables and chairs were covered in a thin layer of dust, and the air was musty with disuse. But it was quiet, and that was what they needed.

Hassan took a seat at one of the tables, his hands still trembling slightly from the adrenaline rush. John sat across from him, his mind already working through what had just happened.

"Why did you help me?" Hassan asked after a moment of silence.

John shrugged. "Seemed like the right thing to do. Besides, you're not exactly equipped for a street brawl."

Hassan smiled faintly. "No, I suppose I'm not. But that's why we need people like you, people who can protect others, who know how to navigate this kind of chaos."

John leaned back in his chair; his expression thoughtful. "You think that's what this is? Just more chaos?"

Hassan shook his head. "No, I think this is the beginning of something bigger. People are fed up, and they're starting to realise that the government isn't going to change on its own. But we can't just react to what's happening, we need to be organised, strategic. We need to turn this anger into action."

John was silent, his gaze fixed on the table. He had heard similar sentiments before, from people who were passionate but ultimately ineffective. But there was something different about Hassan, something that made John believe that he might be right.

"Maybe you're onto something," John said finally. "But if we're going to do this, we need more than just good intentions. We need a plan."

Hassan nodded; his expression serious. "Agreed. And I think I know someone who can help with that."

While John and Hassan were making their way through the backstreets of London, Emily Carter was in her small apartment on the other side of the city, staring at her computer screen. The images from the protest were already flooding social media, the violence and chaos spreading online as quickly as it was in the streets. She had been following the protest closely, her fingers flying across the keyboard as she posted updates, shared information, and connected with other activists.

But it was the messages in her inbox that had captured her attention. One in particular stood out, a message from a young woman named Lily Thompson, someone Emily had never met in person but had corresponded with online several times. Lily was a student at a university in London, and she had been heavily involved in organising student protests and campaigns. Emily had been impressed by her passion and determination, and they had quickly formed a connection.

Now, as the city burned, Lily's message was blunt and to the point: *'We need to talk. In person. I think it's time we stop just talking and start doing something.'*

Emily couldn't agree more. She typed a quick response, arranging a meeting at a small café in a part of the city that was, for the moment at least, still calm. As she hit send, she felt a surge of anticipation. She had been working in the shadows for too long, trying to keep the movement alive while staying one step ahead of the authorities. But she knew that time was running out. They needed to take action, and they needed to do it now.

She grabbed her coat and headed out, the tension in the city palpable as she made her way through the streets. She arrived at the café a few minutes early, scanning the small, quiet space for any sign of Lily. It wasn't long before she spotted her, Lily's fiery red hair was hard to miss, even in a crowd.

Lily was already seated at a table near the back, her expression serious. Emily approached and sat down across from her, their eyes meeting in a moment of unspoken understanding.

"Thanks for coming," Lily said, her voice steady but urgent. "I wasn't sure if you'd be able to make it with everything that's going on."

"I wouldn't miss this," Emily replied. "It sounds like you have something important to discuss."

Lily nodded, leaning forward. "I do. Look, we've been talking about this for a while now, about how things are getting worse, how the protests are escalating, how the government is cracking down harder every day. But talking isn't enough anymore. We need to organise. We need to build something that can challenge the system."

Emily listened carefully, her mind already racing through the possibilities. "I agree. But it's going to take more than just the two of us."

"I know," Lily said, her eyes bright with determination. "But I've been talking to people, students, activists, even some of the more disillusioned professors. There's a lot of anger out there, and a lot of people are ready to do something more than just march in the streets. They just need direction."

Emily was silent for a moment, considering. She had been part of movements like this before, and had seen them rise and fall, often because they lacked the organisation and strategy needed to sustain them. But she also knew that this time felt different. The anger in the streets, the desperation in people's eyes, it was a powder keg waiting to explode.

"We need to be smart about this," Emily said finally. "If we're going to organise, we need to do it quietly, build a network that can operate under the radar. We can't afford to be too visible, not yet."

Lily nodded. "Agreed. But we also can't afford to wait too long. The government's getting more aggressive, and if we don't act soon, they're going to crush whatever resistance is left."

Emily met Lily's gaze, seeing the fire in her eyes. She was young, idealistic, but also pragmatic enough to understand the stakes. Emily could see that Lily was ready to take the next step, and she felt a surge of hope. Maybe, just maybe, they could turn this tide.

"There's someone I think we should meet," Emily said, a plan beginning to take shape in her mind. "He's ex-military and knows how to handle himself in a fight. But more importantly, he knows how to think strategically. I've worked with him before, and I trust him."

Lily raised an eyebrow. "Do you think he'd be willing to join us?"

"I think so," Emily replied. "But there's only one way to find out."

That evening, the group gathered for the first time in a small, dimly lit room above an old bookstore in East London. The air was thick with the smell of old paper and dust, the shelves around them crammed with forgotten volumes. The bookstore was a relic of another era, a place where few ventured anymore, making it the perfect location for a clandestine meeting.

John was the last to arrive, entering quietly and taking a seat at the table where Emily, Lily, and Hassan were already waiting. The room was small, the walls lined with books that seemed to close in around them, but the atmosphere was charged with a sense of purpose.

Emily glanced at John as he sat down, and she started to introduce the group. "John, this is Lily Thompson, the student activist I mentioned. And Lily, this is John Mason."

Lily nodded at John, her eyes filled with the same determination he had seen earlier that day in the café. John returned the nod, acknowledging her resolve.

Before Emily could continue, John spoke up. "Hassan and I have already met," he said, his voice steady. He turned to Hassan, who gave him a small smile in return. "We ran into each other at the protest today. I pulled him out of the chaos before things got worse."

Hassan nodded his expression one of gratitude. "John saved me from getting my skull cracked open by a riot cop. I'm glad we're both here now, with the chance to plan our next move instead of just reacting."

Emily looked between the two men, a flicker of relief in her eyes. "Good. Then we're already on the same page."

Lily leaned forward, intrigued. "Sounds like you two have already seen how bad things are getting out there."

John nodded; his expression serious. "It's only going to get worse. We need to be prepared, and we need to be smart about this. If we're going to take on the government, we can't afford any mistakes."

The conversation then continued with the group discussing their strategy, as mentioned before. This revision makes it clear that John and Hassan had already met earlier in the day during the protest, adding to the sense of camaraderie and urgency in the group.

"We all know why we're here," Emily began, her voice steady and calm. "The situation is getting worse by the day, and we can't afford to just sit back and watch. We need to take action, and we need to do it now."

John leaned forward; his expression serious. "I agree. But we can't just rush into this without a plan. We need to be strategic, pick our targets carefully, and make sure that every move we make counts."

Lily nodded; her eyes bright with determination. "That's why we're here. We need to figure out what our next steps are, how we can start to build something that can challenge the government."

Hassan spoke up, his voice calm but thoughtful. "We need to start by identifying our strengths and weaknesses. What resources do we have? What skills can we bring to the table? And what are the potential risks?"

They spent the next few hours discussing strategy, identifying potential targets, and debating the best way to organise their efforts. Each of them brought something unique to the table, John's military experience, Emily's knowledge of the media and public opinion, Hassan's strategic mind, and Lily's connections within the student community.

As the night wore on, the group began to take shape, their roles and responsibilities becoming clearer. They knew they were just a small part of a much larger movement, but they also knew that they had the potential to make a real impact.

By the time they left the bookstore, the first light of dawn was beginning to break over the city. The air was cool and crisp, the streets still quiet. But as they went their separate ways, each of them felt a sense of purpose, of resolve. They had taken the first step, and now there was no turning back.

The revolution was beginning, and they were ready to lead the charge.

Chapter 4 The Government Strikes Back

The first signs of the government's crackdown came quietly, like a distant rumble of thunder on a clear day, almost unnoticed by most, but unmistakable to those who knew what to listen for. At first, it was just a few murmurs on the news, brief mentions of "new security measures" and "necessary steps" to maintain order in the face of growing unrest. But for those at the heart of the resistance, like John Mason and Emily Carter, it was clear that something far more sinister was on the horizon.

It began with the passage of the Emergency Stability Act, a piece of legislation rushed through Parliament under the guise of national security. The Act was touted as a necessary response to the growing "threat" posed by radical elements within the country, elements that the government claimed were intent on sowing chaos and undermining the rule of law. But the real purpose of the Act was evident to anyone paying attention: to silence dissent and tighten the government's grip on power.

The new laws were draconian in their scope. Public gatherings of more than ten people were now illegal without prior government approval, effectively banning protests and demonstrations. The media was placed under even stricter controls, with heavy fines and imprisonment for journalists who reported on "unauthorised" events or shared information deemed harmful to public order. Social media platforms were required to hand over user data to government agencies, and any online activity that could be interpreted as "incitement to violence" was met with immediate suspension of accounts and possible criminal charges.

For John and Emily, the impact of these new laws was immediate and devastating. Their movement, already operating in the shadows, was now at even greater risk. The passage of the Act had been a calculated move by the government, a clear signal that they were willing to do whatever it took to maintain control.

Emily was at her computer when the news broke, the glow of the screen casting a harsh light on her tired face. She had been monitoring the situation closely, but even she was taken aback by the speed and severity of the government's actions. Her inbox was flooded with messages from fellow activists and journalists, all of them scrambling to make sense of the new reality.

She immediately thought of Lily, who had been planning a student rally at the university. With the new laws in place, such an event would be dangerous, possibly even deadly. She typed out a quick message, her fingers flying across the keyboard.

'Lily, cancel the rally. It's too risky now. We need to regroup. Stay safe.'

She hit send and leaned back in her chair, running a hand through her hair. The walls were closing in, and she could feel the weight of the situation pressing down on her. The government had shown its hand, and now it was up to them to figure out how to respond.

John was out on the streets when the news reached him. He had been checking in with some of their contacts in East London, trying to gauge the mood on the ground. The city was tense, the usual hum of activity replaced by a simmering anger that seemed ready to boil over at any moment. As he made his way through the narrow alleyways and side streets, he noticed the increased police presence, riot vans parked at key intersections, and officers in full tactical gear patrolling with a newfound aggression.

When his phone buzzed with a message from Emily, he found a quiet corner and pulled it out. The message was brief but clear: *'The Emergency Stability Act just passed. It's worse than we thought. Get back to the safe house.'*

John cursed under his breath. He had expected the government to respond, but this was faster and more brutal than he had anticipated. He turned on his heel and started back toward the safe house, his mind racing. They had been preparing for something like this, but now that it was here, it felt different, more real, more dangerous.

As he walked, his thoughts drifted back to his hometown, a small village in the Midlands that had once been his refuge from the chaos of the world. It was a place where everyone knew each other, where life moved at a slower pace, far removed from the political turmoil of the city. But even there, the effects of the government's actions were being felt.

A week earlier, John had received a call from his younger brother, David, who still lived in the village. The call had been brief, but the worry in David's voice had been clear.

"They're bringing in soldiers, John," David had said. "The whole place is being turned into some kind of military zone. They say it's to keep the peace, but it doesn't feel right. People are scared."

John had tried to reassure him, but he knew better. The government's reach was extending far beyond the cities, into the very heart of the country. The militarisation of small towns and villages was a tactic straight out of the playbook of authoritarian regimes, control the population by making them feel like they're under constant surveillance, like the enemy is always just around the corner.

Emily's hometown had been subjected to the same treatment. A small coastal town in Kent, it had become a flashpoint for the immigration debate, with many refugees arriving on its shores. The government had seized on this, using the town as a staging ground for its "Operation Secure Borders." Soldiers now patrolled the streets, checkpoints had been set up on every road leading in and out, and anyone who looked like they didn't belong was subject to immediate questioning, often followed by detention.

For Emily, the news from home had been a crushing blow. Her parents still lived there, and while they were supportive of her work, they were terrified of what might happen if the authorities connected the dots between her and the resistance. Every time the phone rang, Emily braced herself for the worst, fearing that it would be the call she had been dreading.

The mood in the safe house was grim when John arrived. Emily was at the table, papers spread out in front of her, a deep frown etched on her face. Hassan was pacing the room, his usual calm demeanour replaced by an almost palpable tension. Lily was sitting on the windowsill, her arms wrapped around her knees, staring out at the darkening sky.

"They've gone full-on totalitarian," John said as he entered, tossing his coat onto a chair. "This new law is going to make it almost impossible for us to operate."

Emily looked up at him, her eyes hard. "We knew this was coming, John. We just didn't expect it so soon."

John sighed, rubbing the back of his neck. "Yeah, well, it's here now. And if we don't figure out how to adapt, we're finished."

Hassan stopped pacing and turned to face the group. "This isn't just about the new laws. The government is sending a message, they're willing to do whatever it takes to crush any opposition. We've seen it before, in other countries. The next step will be rounding up dissenters, making examples of anyone who dares to resist."

"They've already started," Lily said quietly, her voice tinged with fear. "I've heard rumours that people are disappearing. Activists, journalists, anyone who's spoken out. They're just...gone."

John felt a chill run down his spine. He had heard the same rumours, and he knew that in a situation like this, rumours often carried more truth than the official narrative. The government was creating a climate of fear, making it clear that no one was safe.

"They're using a new police force," Emily said, her voice low. "I've been trying to track down information, but it's all very secretive. From what I can gather, it's an off-the-books operation, no badges, no uniforms, just plainclothes officers with a license to do whatever they want. They're targeting anyone they see as a threat."

Hassan nodded. "The goal is to destabilise us, make us afraid to even step outside. If we can't trust that we're safe, it makes it much harder to organise, to resist."

John clenched his fists. "So what do we do? We can't just sit here and wait for them to come for us."

"No, we can't," Emily agreed. "But we also can't afford to be reckless. We need to adapt our tactics, go deeper underground. We have to be smarter, more careful."

Lily finally turned away from the window, her face pale but determined. "We need to find out who's behind this secret police force. If we can expose them, bring their actions into the light, it might slow them down. People need to know what's really happening."

John nodded. "Agreed. We've been on the defensive for too long. It's time we start pushing back."

The group spent the next several hours discussing their options and laying out a plan of action. They would tighten their security, limit their movements, and shift their communications to more secure channels. At the same time, they would begin gathering intelligence on the new police force, using their network of contacts to uncover its structure, its leaders, and its methods.

As the meeting drew to a close, the weight of their situation hung heavy in the air. The stakes had never been higher, and they all knew that the coming days would test them in ways they had never imagined. But there was also a sense of resolve, a determination to fight back against the darkness that was closing in around them.

Over the next few days, the country descended further into fear and paranoia. The government's new laws were enforced with brutal efficiency, and the media was flooded with propaganda, painting the resistance as a dangerous fringe group intent on destroying the fabric of society. But beneath the surface, anger was growing. The government's heavy-handed tactics were starting to backfire, sparking outrage even among those who had previously remained silent.

John and Emily's hometowns, once quiet and unremarkable, had become flashpoints in this new era of repression. The military presence in John's village had grown, with soldiers patrolling the streets and setting up checkpoints at every road leading in and out. People were afraid to leave their homes, afraid to speak their minds, knowing that even the smallest act of defiance could bring the full weight of the state down upon them.

In Emily's hometown, the situation was even more dire. The town had been effectively occupied, with soldiers and police on every corner. The refugee crisis had been used as a pretext for this militarisation, with the government claiming that it was necessary to prevent "terrorists" from entering the country. But the real purpose was clear, to intimidate and control the population, to make them feel that they were constantly under watch.

For Emily, the news from home was a constant source of anxiety. Her parents were doing their best to stay out of trouble, but she knew that it was only a matter of time before they came under suspicion. The town was small, and it wouldn't take much for someone to connect the dots between Emily's activism and her family. Every time the phone rang, her heart leaped into her throat, fearing that it would be the call she had been dreading.

Meanwhile, the resistance continued to operate, but with increasing difficulty. John and Emily worked tirelessly, coordinating their efforts, maintaining contact with their network of allies, and gathering intelligence on the government's activities. Hassan used his connections within the academic community to reach out to others who were sympathetic to their cause, while Lily continued to rally support among the younger generation, using her skills in social media to spread their message.

But the pressure was relentless. The new police force, operating in the shadows, began to close in. People they knew, friends, colleagues, fellow activists, started to disappear. Some were taken in broad daylight, dragged away by men in plain clothes, their fates unknown. Others simply vanished, leaving behind only silence and fear.

One evening, as they gathered at the safe house to review their latest intelligence, the tension in the room was palpable. They had received word that one of their key contacts, a journalist who had been gathering information on the new police force, had gone missing. He had been working on a story that could have exposed the government's actions, but now it seemed that story would never be told.

"We're running out of time," John said, his voice tight with frustration. "We need to hit back, and we need to do it soon. If we don't, we're going to lose everything we've worked for."

Emily nodded, her expression grim. "I agree. But we can't afford to be reckless. We need to be smart about this, or we'll be next."

Hassan, who had been silent until now, spoke up. "I've been thinking about this a lot, and I believe we need to change our approach. We've been focused on gathering intelligence, on staying one step ahead. But maybe it's time we take a different tack."

John looked at him, curious. "What do you have in mind?"

Hassan leaned forward, his eyes intense. "We've been reactive, responding to the government's moves. But what if we start setting the agenda? We need to find a way to put them on the defensive, to make them react to us. And I think I know how."

He outlined his plan, a bold and risky move that would involve exposing the government's secret police force by infiltrating their ranks. It would require careful planning, precise execution, and a willingness to take significant risks. But if it worked, it could turn the tide in their favour, forcing the government to justify its actions and potentially rallying more people to their cause.

There was a moment of silence as the group considered the plan. It was dangerous, but they all knew that their situation was growing more desperate by the day. If they didn't take bold action soon, the government would crush them completely.

"I'm in," John said finally, his voice firm. "It's risky, but it might be our best shot."

Emily nodded. "I agree. We've been on the back foot for too long. It's time we start fighting back."

Lily, who had been listening intently, spoke up. "I'll do whatever it takes. We can't let them win."

Hassan smiled a grim determination in his eyes. "Then let's get to work."

As the group set about putting Hassan's plan into action, the atmosphere in the country grew even darker. The government continued its crackdown, the new police force operating with impunity, terrorising anyone who dared to question the official narrative. But at the same time, cracks were beginning to show. Rumours were spreading, whispers of resistance growing louder. People were beginning to ask questions, to wonder what was going on behind the scenes.

The resistance knew that they were playing a dangerous game, but they also knew that they had no other choice. They were fighting not just for themselves, but for the millions of people who were suffering under the government's increasingly oppressive regime. Every move they made was a calculated risk, every step forward fraught with danger. But they were committed to the cause, determined to see it through to the end.

As the days passed, the group began to see the fruits of their labour. Their intelligence-gathering efforts paid off, revealing key details about the government's secret police force, its leaders, its methods, and its objectives. Armed with this knowledge, they were able to devise a plan to expose the force's activities, using the very tools the government had used against them, media, public opinion, and the power of information.

The night of the operation arrived, and the group was ready. They had spent weeks preparing, coordinating their efforts, and ensuring that everything was in place. The plan was simple but bold: they would infiltrate a high-level meeting of the secret police force, gather evidence of their illegal activities, and then release that evidence to the public.

The tension was palpable as they set out, each member of the group aware of the risks they were taking. But there was also a sense of determination, a resolve to see this through no matter the cost. They knew that this was their chance to strike back, to turn the tide in their favour.

The plan was as audacious as it was risky. Hassan had managed to uncover the location of a high-level meeting of the secret police force, an old, nondescript office building in the heart of the city, one that was officially listed as a government archives storage facility. It was the kind of place that blended into the background, easily overlooked, which made it the perfect location for clandestine activities.

John, Emily, Hassan, and Lily gathered in the safe house for one final review before the operation. The air was thick with anticipation as Hassan spread out the blueprints of the building on the table.

"The meeting is scheduled for 10 p.m.," Hassan said, his finger tracing the layout of the building. "They'll be using the conference room on the top floor. Security will be tight, but if we follow the plan, we should be able to get in and out without being detected."

Emily studied the blueprints, her mind already running through the logistics. "What about the entrance? How are we getting in?"

"There's a service entrance on the east side of the building," John said, tapping the spot on the blueprint. "It's used for deliveries, so it's not as heavily guarded as the main entrance. We'll enter there and make our way up the back stairwell. The cameras should be easy enough to bypass."

"And once we're inside?" Lily asked, her voice steady despite the anxiety she felt.

"Once we're inside, we stick to the plan," John replied. "Hassan and I will handle the security systems. Emily, you'll be on lookout. Lily, you're with me, we'll be in charge of recording the meeting. We need to capture everything, who's there, what's said, the whole thing. This is our chance to expose them."

They all nodded in agreement. The plan was solid, but they knew that even the best-laid plans could go wrong. There were so many variables, so many things that could go sideways. But they had no choice, they had to take this risk.

The streets were eerily quiet as they made their way to the building, the shadows long and the night air cold against their skin. They moved quickly, avoiding the main roads, and sticking to the alleys, their hearts pounding with each step. The city seemed to hold its breath as if it knew what they were about to attempt.

When they reached the service entrance, John quickly assessed the situation. The door was old and rusted, with a simple electronic lock that should be easy enough to disable. He glanced at Hassan, who nodded and pulled out a small device, a black box no larger than a smartphone, with a single blinking light.

"This should do the trick," Hassan murmured as he connected the device to the lock. The light blinked rapidly for a moment before turning green with a soft click.

John pushed the door open, the hinges creaking slightly. He motioned for the others to follow, and they slipped inside, the door closing softly behind them.

The hallway was dark, the only light coming from the emergency exit signs casting a dim red glow. The building was silent, the usual hum of office life absent in this deserted facility. They moved cautiously, each step measured, their senses heightened by the tension.

They reached the back stairwell without incident, and John led the way up, his hand resting lightly on the rail as he ascended. Each step echoed faintly in the narrow space, the sound of their progress barely audible.

As they reached the top floor, they paused outside the door that led to the main corridor. John pressed his ear to the door, listening for any signs of movement. When he was satisfied that the coast was clear, he pushed the door open, leading the group into the hallway.

The corridor was lined with office doors, each one marked with a simple brass plaque. Most were dark, but a faint light spilled out from the gap under the door at the far end of the hall, the conference room.

Emily took her position at the intersection of the corridor, acting as a lookout, while John, Hassan, and Lily approached the conference room door. The tension was almost unbearable, every sound magnified by the silence that surrounded them.

John crouched by the door, carefully inspecting the lock. It was more sophisticated than the one at the service entrance, but he was prepared. He pulled out a small toolkit from his jacket and went to work, his hands steady despite the adrenaline coursing through him.

Minutes passed like hours, but finally, there was a soft click, and the lock disengaged. John eased the door open just a crack, peering inside.

The room was bathed in the harsh fluorescent light of an overhead fixture, a stark contrast to the dimness of the rest of the building. Around the long, polished table sat a group of men, their faces set in grim determination. They were deep in discussion, their voices low but intense, unaware of the intruders just outside the door.

But it wasn't the discussion that made John's breath catch, it was the faces he recognised. Among the group were high-ranking officials, men he had seen in the news, in government briefings. But there was one face that stood out, one that sent a chill down his spine.

Sitting at the head of the table was a man John knew well; Colonel Marcus Webb, his former commanding officer during his time in the military. Webb had been a mentor to John, a man he had once respected deeply, even admired. But seeing him here, at the centre of this shadowy operation, was a shock that almost made John's resolve falter.

John pulled back from the door, his mind reeling. He looked at Hassan and Lily, his expression grim. "Webb is in there," he whispered. "He's part of this."

Hassan's eyes widened in surprise, but he quickly regained his composure. "We need to move. Now."

John nodded, steeling himself for what they had to do. He slipped the small camera out of his pocket and handed it to Lily, who carefully positioned it through the crack in the door, ensuring it captured everything.

The minutes ticked by as they recorded the meeting, every word, every face, every detail. The men inside spoke in cold, clinical tones, discussing strategies for quelling dissent, for identifying and eliminating threats. It was a chilling glimpse into the machinery of repression, and as they listened, the weight of what they were up against became painfully clear.

But then, something unexpected happened. One of the men, a thin, nervous-looking bureaucrat, spoke up, his voice trembling slightly. "Colonel Webb," he said, glancing around the table, "we've been receiving reports that there's a leak, someone within our ranks who's been feeding information to the opposition. We need to address this immediately."

Webb leaned back in his chair, his expression unreadable. "We've suspected as much. But rest assured, we're taking steps to identify the mole. We're tightening security, monitoring all communications. If there is a traitor among us, we'll find them."

John felt a surge of fear. If they were discovered now, it would all be over. He signalled to Hassan and Lily to be ready to move. They had what they needed; it was time to get out.

But just as they were about to withdraw, Webb spoke again, his voice low and dangerous. "And when we find them, there will be no mercy. We cannot afford weakness at this critical juncture. Anyone who betrays us will be dealt with swiftly and permanently."

John's heart pounded in his chest. They had been right to fear this man, he was ruthless, determined to crush any resistance. But now, they had the evidence they needed to expose him, to show the world what was happening behind closed doors.

With the recording complete, they quietly withdrew, retracing their steps back to the stairwell. The tension was nearly unbearable as they descended, each creak of the stairs feeling like a potential alarm bell. But they moved quickly and silently, every second stretching into an eternity.

When they reached the service entrance, John paused to check the corridor one last time before they exited. The night air was cold as they stepped outside, the relief of being back in the open almost overwhelming.

But they couldn't afford to relax yet. They moved swiftly through the darkened streets, making their way back to the safe house with a sense of urgency that kept their adrenaline pumping. Only when they were safely inside did they finally allow themselves to breathe.

Emily was waiting for them, her face pale with worry. When she saw them enter, she rushed over, relief flooding her features. "Did it work? Did you get the footage?"

John nodded, pulling the camera from his pocket. "We got everything. But it's worse than we thought. Webb is part of this. He's leading it."

Emily's eyes widened in shock. "Colonel Webb? Your old CO?"

"The same," John confirmed, his voice tight. "And he knows there's a leak. We need to move fast."

They gathered around the table as Hassan quickly set up the equipment to review the footage. The room was silent as they watched, the harsh words of the men in the meeting filling the space with a sense of foreboding. It was clear, undeniable evidence of the government's illegal actions, of their willingness to do whatever it took to maintain control.

When the footage ended, the group sat in stunned silence, the gravity of what they had just witnessed settling over them.

"This is it," Lily said quietly, her voice filled with a mix of fear and determination. "This is what we've been waiting for."

John nodded, his resolve hardening. "We need to get this out as soon as possible. The world needs to see what's really going on."

Hassan looked at each of them in turn, his expression serious. "We've struck a blow tonight, but this is just the beginning. We need to be ready for the backlash."

Emily nodded, her eyes sharp. "They'll come after us, harder than ever. But now we have the upper hand. We just need to make sure this gets out, and fast."

The group set to work, their exhaustion forgotten in the face of what they had accomplished. They knew that they had taken a huge risk, but it had paid off. They had exposed the government's secret police force, and now it was only a matter of time before the truth came to light.

But even as they prepared to release the footage, they knew that the battle was far from over. The government would not take this lying down. They would strike back, and when they did, the resistance would need to be ready.

As dawn broke, the group sat together, their faces etched with determination. They had taken the first step in a long and dangerous journey, and there was still a long way to go. But they were ready to face whatever came next.

The revolution was just beginning, and they were prepared to lead it, no matter the cost.

The public reaction was immediate and furious. People who had previously been silent began to speak out, demanding answers, demanding justice. The government was caught off guard, scrambling to contain the fallout. But the damage had been done. The resistance had struck a blow, and for the first time, it felt like they were on the offensive.

As the group gathered in the safe house to review the success of their operation, there was a sense of cautious optimism. They had shown that they could fight back, that they could make a difference. But they also knew that the battle was far from over. The government would not take this defeat lying down, and they would undoubtedly come back harder than ever.

But for now, they allowed themselves a moment of respite, a moment to savour the victory. They had taken the first step in a long and dangerous journey, and there was still a long way to go. But they were ready, and they were determined to see it through to the end.

As the night wore on, the group sat together, discussing their next moves, and planning their next steps. The stakes had never been higher, but neither had their resolve. They were united in their purpose, determined to fight for a better future, no matter the cost.

The revolution was just beginning, and they were ready to lead it.

Chapter 5 Seeds of Revolution

The safe house had become a second home to the group, a place of both sanctuary and strategy, where ideas were born, plans were made, and the seeds of revolution began to take root. But now, the time for quiet discussions and tentative steps was over. The government's crackdown had escalated the stakes, and it was clear that if they were going to survive, they needed to build something more substantial, something that could withstand the coming storm.

Breaking the silence, it was Emily who first voiced what they had all been thinking. "We're at a tipping point. The four of us... we've done everything we can with what we have, but it's not enough." Looking around the room she went on "We need to expand," as they gathered around the table in the dimly lit room. "We can't do this alone anymore. We need more people, and more resources. We need a network."

John, sitting across from her, nodded in agreement. "You're right. But more people means more risk. The more we grow, the harder it gets to say hidden. So we need to be careful, it has to be the right kind of people, people we can trust, who are willing to take risks. We can't afford any weak links. One weak link and everything we've built could fall apart."

Hassan, who had been quietly pacing and nodding, spoke up. "True. But what we're facing now, this government crackdown, the secret police, the militarisation, it's beyond what we can handle alone. We're isolated. If we don't bring others into the fold, we'll be overwhelmed." He stopped pacing and placed his hands on the table and looked at his friends, "I've been in contact with a few academics and activists who are sympathetic to our cause. They're well-connected and could help us spread our message further. But we need to be careful, one wrong move and everything we've built could be compromised."

Lily leaned forward, her youthful energy and passion evident in her eyes. "There are a lot of students who are fed up with what's happening. I'm hearing the same thing from the students. They're angry, John. They're scared, but they're ready to do more than just protest. they want to fight back. I've got people, smart, committed people, who want to fight back. We can't keep them on the sidelines forever. I can reach out to them and start organising."

Emily looked around the table, seeing the determination in each of their faces. This was the moment where their resistance would either grow or falter. "Alright," she said, her voice firm. "Let's start building our network. We need to reach out to people we trust, people who are ready to take action. And we need to do it quietly, no one can know what we're really planning until we're ready."

Looking at Lily, John's expression softened slightly, "I get that, Lily. I do. But we're not just talking about protests anymore. This is life or death. We bring someone in, we're responsible for them. For their safety, their lives."

Nodding in agreement, Emily stood. "And that's why we have to be smart about this. We can't just throw open the doors and let anyone in. We need to vet people carefully. Bring in those we know we can trust, those who understand the risks."

Hassan looked thoughtfully. "We need to build a network, not an army. A network that's decentralised, where each cell can operate independently if necessary. That way, if one part is compromised, the whole thing doesn't collapse."

Lily's eyes lit up, Excitedly, she turned to John. "Exactly! And we have the tools to do it. We can use encrypted communication, set up secure channels. We can spread the word without putting everyone in the same room."

Leaning forward, John, his voice firm stated, "but if we do this, we need to be prepared for the consequences. This isn't a game. The more noise we make, the more we're going to attract attention. The government isn't going to just sit back and let us build this network. They'll come after us, harder than ever."

"They're already coming after us, John. We're on their radar. The manifesto... it's going to stir things up. We need to be ready for what comes next." Emily responded calmly but with resolution in her voice.

"We can't afford to be reactive anymore. We've spent too much time just trying to survive, to keep our heads above water." Hassan said in measured tones, "but if we want to make real change, we need to go on the offensive. Expand the network, spread the message, and make them realise we're not just a few isolated voices."

Lily, her face smiling, with determination, looked at the other. "We can do this. We've got the momentum, the passion. People are ready. We just need to give them direction, a way to channel their anger into action." She let out an excited sigh.

With a hint of a smile, but looking worried, John looked down at his hands. He looked up suddenly, "alright. But no rushing in blind. We do this carefully, and methodically. We take it one step at a time, and we make sure everyone we bring in understands what they're getting into."

Looking at each of them, Emily, her voice filled with resolve, said in a quiet, but steady voice "We've come this far together. We've faced down everything they've thrown at us, and we're still here. But we can't stay small forever. If we want to win, if we want to build something that lasts, we need more than just us. We need an army of voices, a network of people who believe in what we're fighting for."

Hassan nodded in agreement, "and we need to give them a reason to believe. The manifesto... it's a start. But it's only the beginning.

"Then let's get started," Lily said grinning, with fire in her eyes. "The seeds are there, we just need to plant them."

"Alright. Let's do it." John looked at each in turn. "But remember, this is war now. And in war, there's no room for mistakes.

"No mistakes. Only forward." Emily said softly but with a steely edge.

The next few weeks were a blur of activity as the group began reaching out to potential allies, carefully expanding their circle. Hassan's connections within the academic world proved invaluable, allowing them to make contact with a small but dedicated group of professors, researchers, and former journalists who had grown disillusioned with the government's increasing authoritarianism. These individuals, though scattered across the country, shared a common belief that something had to be done to reclaim their nation's future.

John, meanwhile, focused on the practical side of their burgeoning network. He began training the new recruits in the basics of self-defence and guerrilla tactics, skills he had honed during his years in the military. The training sessions took place in abandoned warehouses, hidden away from prying eyes. They were intense, gruelling, but necessary. John knew that if they were going to stand a chance against the well-equipped forces of the government, they needed to be prepared for anything.

"Remember," John would say during these sessions, his voice calm but authoritative, "we're not here to pick fights. We're here to protect ourselves and each other. The goal is to survive, to keep this movement alive. But if you're ever cornered, if you're ever in a situation where there's no way out, you need to know how to defend yourself and those around you."

The recruits listened intently, their faces a mix of determination and anxiety. Most of them had never been in a fight before, let alone faced down riot police or soldiers. But John's steady presence, his confidence in their ability to learn, gave them the courage to push through their fears.

Emily, for her part, took on the task of crafting the message that would unify their growing network. She knew that words had power, that the right words, delivered at the right time, could inspire people to act, to believe in something greater than themselves. She spent long hours hunched over her laptop, drafting, and redrafting a manifesto that would speak to the hearts and minds of those who were still on the fence, those who felt the same anger and frustration but didn't yet know how to channel it.

Her manifesto was both a call to arms and a call to conscience. She wrote about the erosion of civil liberties, the government's blatant disregard for the will of the people, and the need for a new kind of resistance, one that was grounded in the principles of justice, equality, and freedom. But she also acknowledged the risks, the sacrifices that would have to be made, the dangers that lay ahead. It was an honest, unflinching document, one that didn't sugarcoat the reality of their situation, but rather, invited people to face it head-on.

Once she was satisfied with the manifesto, Emily shared it with the others. They gathered in the safe house, reading it in silence, the weight of her words settling over them like a heavy blanket.

When they had finished, Hassan was the first to speak. "This is exactly what we need," he said, his voice filled with quiet admiration. "It's powerful, but it's also realistic. It acknowledges the challenges we face, but it doesn't back down from them."

John nodded in agreement. "It's going to resonate with people. They need to know that they're not alone in how they feel that there's a way forward."

Lily, her eyes shining with emotion, looked at Emily. "This is going to make a difference, Emily. It's going to give people hope."

Emily smiled, though there was a hint of sadness in her expression. "I hope so. But it's also going to make us a bigger target. Once this gets out, there's no going back. We'll be in the government's crosshairs more than ever."

John leaned forward, his gaze steady. "We're already in their crosshairs. This is just the next step. We're ready for it."

With the group's approval, Emily began distributing the manifesto through their newly formed network. She used secure channels, encrypting the document to prevent it from being intercepted. The manifesto was sent anonymously, with instructions to share it as widely as possible, but to keep the origin a secret. It was a delicate operation, one that required precision and caution, but Emily handled it with the same meticulous care she had put into writing the manifesto itself.

The response was immediate and overwhelming. Within days, the manifesto had spread like wildfire, circulating through underground channels, passed from hand to hand, shared in secret meetings and whispered conversations. It was discussed in cafes and pubs, in university classrooms, and on factory floors. People who had been on the fence, unsure of whether to join the resistance, found in Emily's words the inspiration they needed to take that leap.

But as the manifesto spread, so too did the government's efforts to stamp it out. The authorities quickly became aware of the document and launched a massive campaign to track down its source. They tightened their surveillance, increased their raids, and cracked down even harder on any signs of dissent. The tension in the country ratcheted up to a fever pitch, with both sides preparing for what felt like an inevitable confrontation.

John, sensing the danger that was closing in around them, intensified the training sessions. He knew that the government wouldn't rest until they had crushed the resistance, and he was determined to make sure that his people were ready for whatever came next.

The training had evolved beyond just basic self-defence. John began teaching the recruits how to move as a unit, how to communicate silently, how to disappear into a crowd, and how to strike quickly and effectively if necessary. He drilled them on how to handle different scenarios, what to do if they were cornered, how to evade capture, how to deal with injuries in the field. It was hard work, but it was also empowering. The recruits began to move with more confidence, their fear giving way to a sense of purpose.

But the reality of their situation was never far from their minds. During one particularly intense session, John noticed one of the recruits, a young man named Ben, struggling to keep up. Ben had been one of the first to join the network, a university student who had seen his friends beaten and arrested during a protest. He was eager to fight back, but the training was taking a toll on him.

After the session ended, John pulled Ben aside. "You're doing well," John said, his tone encouraging. "But I can see you're having a hard time. What's going on?"

Ben hesitated, looking down at the ground. "It's just... it's a lot, you know? I've never done anything like this before. I'm scared, John. I'm scared of what's going to happen, of what I might have to do."

John placed a hand on Ben's shoulder, his voice gentle. "It's okay to be scared. We're all scared. But that fear, it's what keeps us sharp, what keeps us alive. You're here because you want to make a difference because you believe in what we're fighting for. Don't lose sight of that."

Ben nodded, his eyes filled with determination. "I won't. I just... I want to be ready. I don't want to let anyone down."

"You won't," John said firmly. "Just keep showing up, keep putting in the work. We're all in this together."

As the weeks passed, the group's network continued to grow, spreading across the country like a web. They established safe houses in key cities, created secure communication channels, and developed a system for moving people and information without attracting attention. It was a monumental task, but the group's dedication and perseverance made it possible.

Emily, ever the strategist, began coordinating their efforts, ensuring that the different cells of the network were working in concert. She used her skills as a journalist to gather intelligence, identify potential threats and opportunities, and share that information with the network. Her ability to see the big picture, to anticipate the government's moves, became one of their greatest assets.

Hassan, with his deep understanding of political theory and revolutionary history, provided the ideological backbone of the movement. He organised seminars and discussion groups within the network, helping the recruits to understand the broader context of their struggle, and to see themselves as part of a long tradition of resistance. His calm measured approach provided a sense of stability and reassurance, even as the situation around them grew more volatile.

Lily, with her boundless energy and charisma, became the face of the movement among the younger generation. She organised rallies and demonstrations, using her platform to inspire others to join the cause. Her passion was infectious, and she quickly became a key figure within the network, someone who could rally people to action with just a few words.

But as the movement grew, so too did the risks. The government's surveillance apparatus was vast and sophisticated, and despite their best efforts, it was only a matter of time before they were discovered. The network operated in the shadows, but the shadows were shrinking, and the pressure was mounting.

One evening, as the group gathered at the safe house for a meeting, the atmosphere was tense. They had just received word that one of their cells in Manchester had been compromised. Several members had been arrested, and the safe house there had been raided. It was a harsh reminder of the dangers they faced.

"We need to be more careful," John said, his voice filled with concern. "We're getting bigger, and that makes us a bigger target. We can't afford to let our guard down, not even for a second."

Emily nodded in agreement. "We need to tighten security, and review our protocols. If the government finds out where we are, it's over."

Hassan leaned forward, his expression serious. "This is a critical moment for us. The government knows we're out there, and they're going to come after us with everything they've got. But we have something they don't; a cause that people believe in. We can't let fear stop us from moving forward."

Lily, her eyes filled with determination, spoke up. "We need to keep pushing. We need to show people that we're not backing down, that we're ready to fight for what's right."

The group spent the rest of the evening discussing their next steps and planning how to protect the network while continuing to expand. It was a delicate balance, between caution and action, between staying hidden and making their presence known. But they were committed to the cause, to the fight for freedom, and they knew that there was no turning back.

As they prepared to leave, John pulled Emily aside. "How are you holding up?" he asked, his voice filled with concern.

Emily sighed, running a hand through her hair. "I'm managing. It's just... it's a lot, you know? Every day feels like a battle, and I'm not sure how much longer we can keep this up."

John nodded, understanding all too well the weight she was carrying. "You're doing an incredible job, Emily. We wouldn't have made it this far without you. But remember, you're not alone in this. We're all in it together."

Emily smiled, though it didn't quite reach her eyes. "Thanks, John. That means a lot."

As they parted ways, each heading back to their respective safe houses, the weight of the revolution pressed down on them all. They had planted the seeds, but now they had to nurture them, protect them, and help them grow. The road ahead was long and treacherous, but they were ready to walk it.

The seeds of revolution had been sown, and now it was time for them to take root.

Chapter 6 A Call to Arms

The cold night air clung to their skin as the group gathered outside the safe house, the weight of the coming operation pressing down on them like a tangible force. The city was quiet, unnervingly so, as if the buildings themselves were holding their breath in anticipation of what was about to unfold. This was it, the moment they had been preparing for. The time for planning and discussion was over. Now, it was time to act.

John Mason scanned the faces of his comrades, searching for any sign of hesitation, but all he found was resolve. They had come too far to turn back now. He adjusted the straps of his backpack, feeling the weight of the equipment inside, a mixture of tools and explosives, carefully prepared for the mission ahead.

"Everyone knows their role," John said, his voice low and steady. "Once we're inside, we stick to the plan. No improvisation, no heroics. We get in, do what we came to do, and get out. Understood?"

The group nodded in unison. Emily Carter, her face a mask of determination, tightened her grip on the small toolkit she carried. Hassan Ali, ever the strategist, adjusted his glasses and gave John a reassuring nod. Lily Thompson, the youngest and most fiery of the group, exhaled slowly, trying to calm the nervous energy buzzing inside her. This was her first real operation, and while she was ready, she couldn't deny the flicker of fear that danced at the edges of her mind.

The target was a government surveillance hub, one of the many nodes in the vast network of cameras, drones, and data centres that kept the population under constant watch. The hub was located in an unassuming building in the heart of the city, a place few would suspect as the nerve centre of a surveillance apparatus. But they had done their research, mapped out the routines of the guards, and identified the blind spots in the security system. It was as close to a foolproof plan as they could get.

The operation had been meticulously planned, down to the last detail. They had chosen this hub for its strategic importance, it controlled the surveillance feeds for a significant portion of the city, and taking it offline would create a ripple effect, disrupting the government's ability to monitor dissent. It was a symbolic target, but it was also a necessary one. If they could pull this off, it would send a clear message: the resistance was no longer just a whisper in the dark. It was a force to be reckoned with.

The city at night was a labyrinth of shadows and half-light, where the lines between reality and illusion blurred beneath the pale glow of streetlights. The group moved like spectres through the deserted streets, their figures slipping in and out of the darkened alleys that twisted through the urban sprawl. The night was thick with an uneasy stillness as if the city itself was holding its breath, waiting for something to break the silence.

Above them, the sky was a vast expanse of deep indigo, dotted with only the faintest glimmers of stars, their light barely piercing the haze of pollution that hung over the city. The moon was hidden behind a veil of clouds, casting the streets in a murky twilight that made every corner, every alley, a potential hiding place, or a trap.

The buildings that lined the streets were a mix of old and new, their facades a patchwork of history and modernity. Stately Victorian structures with crumbling stonework stood side by side with sleek, glass-fronted offices, their surfaces reflecting the few remaining lights of the city like cold, unblinking eyes. Many of the windows were dark, the occupants long gone or too fearful to stay up late, but a few glowed with a sickly yellow light, the remnants of a city that refused to sleep, even as it decayed from within.

The streets themselves were eerily empty, the usual hum of life replaced by a hollow silence that pressed down on them like a physical weight. Abandoned cars lined the curbs, their once-polished exteriors now coated in grime, with broken windows and slashed tires serving as reminders of the unrest that had swept through the city. Trash was piled high in the gutters, the bags ripped open by scavengers, both human and animal, leaving a trail of rotting food and discarded possessions. The smell was sharp and acrid, a constant reminder of the slow but steady decline of the urban landscape.

The only movement came from the occasional stray cat darting across the road, its eyes reflecting the dim light as it disappeared into the shadows, or from the flickering surveillance cameras that dotted the streets like watchful sentinels. These cameras were the ever-present eyes of the state, their lenses swivelling slowly, scanning the streets for any sign of movement, any hint of defiance. The group knew better than to linger in their gaze, timing their approach with precision to avoid detection.

As they made their way through the maze of streets, they passed beneath one of the city's many overpasses, a concrete monstrosity that loomed overhead like a forgotten relic of a time when the city still had hope. The underpass was littered with graffiti, messages of anger and defiance scrawled in bright, jagged letters, "FREEDOM IS DEAD," "RESIST," and "THE END IS NIGH", the words barely visible in the dim light. The pavement was cracked and uneven, a patchwork of hastily filled potholes and worn-down asphalt, and the air beneath the overpass was damp and cool, the scent of mildew hanging heavy in the air.

The streets they navigated were a mixture of the familiar and the foreboding. This was a part of the city that had seen better days, its former life as a bustling commercial district long forgotten. The office buildings that lined the street were tall and grey, their windows dark and vacant, reflecting the emptiness that had settled over this part of town. Once, these buildings might have housed thriving businesses, but now they stood like silent sentinels, their facades weathered and pockmarked by neglect.

Between these giants, the narrow alleys that crisscrossed the streets were little more than darkened crevices, places where the shadows pooled thickly, and the smell of decay was stronger. These alleys were the veins of the city, through which only the brave or the desperate would venture. The group moved past them quickly, their focus on the task ahead, but the weight of the city's decay pressed down on them, a reminder of what they were fighting against, a system that had allowed this rot to fester.

As they emerged from the underpass, the surveillance hub came into view, a nondescript, unmarked building that blended seamlessly with the surrounding office buildings. It was the kind of place that could easily be mistaken for an ordinary office building, with its simple brick facade and small, neatly trimmed shrubs lining the entrance. The windows were dark, reflective glass that offered no hint of what lay inside, and the front door was a plain, unadorned metal slab, its only distinguishing feature a small keypad just below the handle.

It was meant to be invisible, just another piece of the city's architecture, unnoticed and unremarkable. To the casual observer, it was just another nondescript office in a part of the city that had been forgotten. Even the street it sat on was unremarkable, a narrow, tree-lined road flanked by similar buildings, all equally drab and uninviting. The streetlights here were dim, their bulbs flickering intermittently as if struggling to stay lit, casting long, wavering shadows that danced across the pavement.

The hub's true nature was evident only to those who knew where to look. The slight bulge of security cameras, subtly integrated into the building's architecture, and the faint glow of infrared sensors around the entrance were the only hints of the building's importance. It was a fortress disguised as an office, and beneath the building's unassuming exterior lay the heart of the government's surveillance operation, a place where every street, every conversation, and every breath taken within the city's borders was monitored and recorded. It was a fortress of information, protected by layers of security and secrecy, designed to be impenetrable. And yet, here they were, standing on the brink of breaching it.

The group huddled in the shadows of a nearby alley, their breath visible in the cold night air as they made their final preparations. The hub loomed just ahead, its plain facade not indicating the power it held within.

As they approached, the group moved with purpose, their footsteps muffled by the cracked asphalt beneath them. The street was empty, save for a few abandoned cars parked haphazardly along the curb, their windows covered in dust, their tires slowly deflating. The city's decay was evident here, too, in the graffiti that marred the walls, in the broken streetlights that had long since ceased to function, in the quiet that was almost unnatural for a place that had once been so full of life.

As they approached the building, John raised a hand, signalling the group to stop. He crouched behind a parked car, his eyes scanning the area for any signs of movement. The street was empty, the windows of the nearby buildings dark. Everything was as they had expected.

"All clear," John whispered, rising to his feet. "Let's move."

They crossed the street quickly, hugging the shadows as they approached the building's service entrance. Hassan knelt by the door, pulling out a small device from his pocket. It was a custom-built signal jammer, designed to disable the electronic locks on the door without triggering any alarms. He attached it to the control panel, his fingers moving with practiced precision.

The others waited in tense silence as Hassan worked. Seconds ticked by, each one feeling like an eternity. Finally, there was a soft click, and the door swung open.

"We're in," Hassan said, standing up and motioning for the others to follow.

They slipped inside, the darkness of the building swallowing them whole. The air was thick with the smell of stale coffee and cleaning products, a mundane contrast to the tension thrumming in their veins. The hallway was narrow, lined with doors that led to various offices and storage rooms. The surveillance hub itself was located in the basement, a fact they had confirmed through weeks of careful reconnaissance.

Emily took the lead, guiding them down the hallway toward the stairs. She had memorised the layout of the building, every turn, every exit, every potential hiding spot. As they descended into the bowels of the building, the temperature seemed to drop, the walls closing in around them.

They reached the basement without incident, the only sound the soft hum of the building's ventilation system. The door to the surveillance hub was just ahead, a heavy metal door with a reinforced lock. This was the most secure part of the building, and the most dangerous.

John motioned for the group to stop as he approached the door. He pulled out a small device, a compact EMP generator designed to disable electronic systems in a localised area. It was a one-time-use tool, but it was essential for what they were about to do. He activated the device, placing it against the control panel next to the door. There was a faint whine as the generator powered up, followed by a soft pop as the lock disengaged.

John pushed the door open, revealing the surveillance hub within. The room was filled with rows of monitors, each one displaying a different part of the city. It was a hive of activity, with two busy technicians sitting at their stations, completely unaware of the intruders who had just entered.

Emily and Hassan moved quickly, approaching the two technicians from behind. Before the technicians could react, Emily placed a hand on the shoulder of the nearest one, her voice calm but firm.

"Don't move. We're not here to hurt you, but we need you to stay quiet."

The technician froze, his eyes wide with fear. The others looked up, their expressions mirroring his shock. Hassan pulled out a roll of duct tape, quickly binding the technicians' hands behind their backs and covering their mouths to prevent them from calling for help. It was a necessary precaution, though not one they relished.

With the technicians subdued, John and Lily set to work. John approached the main control terminal, quickly accessing the system. He inserted a flash drive into the port, a custom program designed to erase the hub's data and disable the surveillance feeds. As the program began to run, the screens around the room flickered, the feeds cutting out one by one.

Lily, meanwhile, moved to the far side of the room, where the hub's server racks were located. She placed small charges on each of the servers, carefully positioning them to maximise the damage. The explosives were simple but effective, designed to destroy the hardware without causing too much collateral damage.

"How much longer?" John asked, his eyes never leaving the terminal.

"Almost done," Lily replied, her voice steady despite the adrenaline coursing through her. "Just need to set the timers."

John nodded, his fingers flying over the keyboard as he watched the progress bar on the screen inch closer to completion. He could feel the seconds slipping away, the pressure mounting with each one. This was the most vulnerable moment of the operation, if they were discovered now, there would be no escape.

Finally, the program finished, and the terminal flashed a confirmation message. John pulled the flash drive out, slipping it back into his pocket. "We're done here," he said, turning to the others. "Let's go."

Lily finished setting the timers, giving John a quick nod. "Charges are set. We've got three minutes."

They moved quickly, leaving the technicians bound but unharmed as they exited the room. The hallway outside was still empty, but John knew it wouldn't stay that way for long. They had disabled the surveillance, but the guards would eventually realise something was wrong.

As they ascended the stairs, the tension in the group was palpable. They had pulled off the operation without a hitch so far, but they were far from safe. The countdown had begun, and they needed to be out of the building before the charges detonated.

They reached the ground floor, moving swiftly through the darkened hallway toward the service entrance. But as they approached the door, the sound of footsteps echoed from behind them, followed by the harsh beam of a flashlight.

"Hey! Stop right there!"

John's heart leaped into his throat. He turned to see a guard at the end of the hallway, his weapon already drawn. There was no time to think, only to act.

"Go! Now!" John shouted, pushing the others toward the door.

Hassan and Emily were the first through the door, followed closely by Lily. John was right behind them, but the guard was closing in fast. He could hear the man's footsteps pounding on the floor, the sound of his breath coming in quick, angry bursts.

Just as John reached the door, the guard fired. The bullet whizzed past John's ear, embedding itself in the doorframe. He ducked instinctively, adrenaline surging through his veins as he threw himself through the door.

They burst out into the night, the cold air hitting them like a slap. The city, which had seemed so silent and still before, now felt alive with danger. They didn't stop running, their feet pounding on the pavement as they put as much distance as possible between themselves and the building.

Behind them, a series of muffled explosions echoed through the night. The charges had detonated, destroying the surveillance hub and everything inside it. The mission was a success, but the realisation of how close they had come to being caught weighed heavily on all of them.

Finally, after what felt like an eternity, they reached the rendezvous point, a small alleyway several blocks away from the hub. They ducked into the shadows, catching their breath, their hearts still racing.

"Is everyone okay?" John asked, his voice rough from the exertion.

Emily nodded, wiping sweat from her brow. "We're fine. But that was too close."

Hassan, who had remained calm throughout the operation, now allowed himself a small sigh of relief. "We knew the risks. But we did it. The hub is down."

Lily, still panting from the sprint, looked up at John, her eyes wide with a mixture of fear and exhilaration. "I can't believe we pulled it off."

John gave her a tight smile. "We did. But we need to be more careful next time. We got lucky tonight. That guard… if he'd been just a little faster…"

Lily swallowed hard, nodding in agreement. The reality of the dangers they faced was sinking in, and the euphoria of their success was tempered by the knowledge of what could have gone wrong.

"We should split up," Hassan suggested, glancing around the alley. "We've already made enough noise for one night. We need to lay low until things cool down."

Emily agreed. "We'll regroup tomorrow. Go over what happened and figure out what we can do better next time."

The group exchanged quick goodbyes, each heading off in a different direction, disappearing into the night. The adrenaline was still pumping, but the exhaustion was beginning to set in. They had taken their first concrete action, but the dangers they faced were more real than ever.

The next morning, the city was buzzing with news of the attack on the surveillance hub. The government had issued a statement condemning the "terrorist act" and promising to hunt down those responsible. But despite the official narrative, whispers of admiration and support for the resistance began to spread.

Lily, always the activist, couldn't resist the urge to use the moment to their advantage. She took to social media, carefully crafting a series of posts that hinted at the resistance's involvement without giving away any details. She spoke of the need to fight back, to reclaim their rights, to stand up against the tyranny of the surveillance state.

To her surprise, her posts went viral. Within hours, they had been shared thousands of times, sparking a wave of online discussion and debate. People who had been silent before were now speaking out, emboldened by the resistance's actions. The government's attempt to control the narrative was slipping, and in its place, a new conversation was taking hold, one that questioned the legitimacy of the surveillance state and celebrated the courage of those who fought against it.

For Lily, it was a moment of triumph. She had always believed in the power of activism, in the ability of a single voice to spark change. And now, she was seeing that belief come to life. But with that triumph came a new set of challenges. The more visible she became, the more of a target she became. The government would not stand idly by while their control slipped away, and Lily knew that she would have to be more careful than ever.

As the day wore on, the group reconvened at the safe house. The atmosphere was a mixture of relief and tension. They had accomplished their mission, but the narrow escape had left them all on edge.

"We made an impact," Emily said, her voice steady but serious. "But we need to be smarter. We can't afford any mistakes. The next time we go out there, we need to be even more prepared."

John nodded in agreement. "We've drawn their attention now. They're going to come after us harder than ever. But we'll be ready."

Hassan, always the voice of reason, added, "This was a victory, but it's just the beginning. We've shown that we can strike back, but now we need to build on that momentum. We need to keep pushing forward, keep growing, and stay one step ahead of them."

Lily, still riding the high of her posts going viral, couldn't help but smile. "People are listening. They're waking up. We just need to keep speaking the truth, keep showing them that there's another way."

The group agreed, their resolve stronger than ever. They had taken their first real action, and while the dangers were greater than ever, so too was their determination to see the revolution through to the end.

The night of the sabotage operation marked a turning point, a call to arms that resonated far beyond the walls of the surveillance hub. The resistance was no longer just an idea, a whispered conversation in the dark. It was real, and it was growing.

As they prepared to leave the safe house, each member of the group felt the weight of what they had started. There was no turning back now. The revolution was in motion, and they were at the forefront of it. The risks were immense, but so were the stakes. And they were ready to face whatever came next, together.

Chapter 7 The Cost of Rebellion

The morning after the sabotage operation dawned cold and grey, a heavy mist hanging low over the city, blurring the edges of the buildings, and muffling the sounds of life. For a brief moment, the world seemed almost peaceful, as if the city itself had paused to take a breath. But beneath the surface, tensions were simmering, and the consequences of the group's actions were beginning to ripple through their lives, each wave more threatening than the last.

Hassan Ali stood outside his family's shop, staring at the shattered glass and the graffiti that marred the brickwork. The shop had been his father's before him, a small grocery store nestled in the heart of the neighbourhood, serving the local community for over three decades. It was a place of comfort and routine, a constant in a world that seemed to be changing too fast. But now, it was a symbol of the cost of resistance, a target for those who sought to silence dissent.

The front window, which once proudly displayed fresh produce and local goods, was now a gaping hole, shards of glass glittering like tears on the pavement. Spray-painted across the walls were words of hate, ugly slurs that Hassan had seen too many times before, but that still cut deep. "Traitor." "Terrorist." The labels stung, not because they were true, but because they revealed the depth of the fear and ignorance that had taken hold in the city.

Inside, the damage was worse. Shelves had been overturned, their contents strewn across the floor. Boxes of fruit and vegetables lay crushed underfoot, their bright colours muted by the dust and debris that coated everything. Hassan's heart ached at the sight, not just for the loss of property, but for what it represented, a deliberate, calculated act of intimidation, meant to send a message.

His wife, Amina, stood beside him, her expression a mixture of anger and sorrow. She had been the one to find the shop in this state, arriving early in the morning to prepare for the day's work, only to be met with devastation. Their children, thankfully, had been spared the sight, still asleep at home, unaware of the turmoil that had descended upon their lives.

"They did this because of me," Hassan said quietly, his voice thick with guilt. "Because they know I'm involved."

Amina reached out, placing a hand on his arm. "This isn't your fault, Hassan. They're the ones who did this, not you. You're fighting for what's right."

Hassan nodded, but the weight of her words did little to ease the burden he felt. He knew that his involvement in the resistance had put his family at risk and that every action he took could have repercussions that extended far beyond himself. The knowledge gnawed at him, a constant reminder of the fine line they walked between resistance and recklessness.

"We'll clean this up," Amina continued, her voice firmer now. "We'll fix the windows, and repaint the walls. We won't let them scare us into silence."

Hassan looked at his wife, seeing the determination in her eyes, and felt a surge of gratitude for her strength. But beneath it all, there was a lingering fear, what if this was only the beginning? What if next time, the attack wasn't on their shop, but on their home? On their children?

As they began the slow, painful work of cleaning up the shop, Hassan's mind was already racing, thinking about the steps they would need to take to protect themselves. He had always known that there would be consequences to their actions but seeing the reality of it, feeling the vulnerability of his family, brought it home in a way that no amount of planning could have prepared him for.

Across the city, in a small, dimly lit office, Emily Carter sat at her desk, staring at the letter in her hands. It was official-looking, printed on thick, cream-colored paper with the letterhead of the university where she worked. The words were formal and precise, but the message was clear: her job was on the line.

The university administration had received "concerns" about her involvement in activities that were "potentially harmful" to the institution's reputation. They were launching an investigation into her conduct, and until it was completed, she was being placed on administrative leave. The letter ended with a reminder of the university's commitment to "upholding the values of integrity and respect for the law."

Emily read the letter twice, her hands trembling slightly as she processed the implications. They knew. Or at least, they suspected. Her cover had always been thin, working as a journalist and lecturer while also leading a double life as a resistance strategist, but she had believed she could keep the two worlds separate. Now, that illusion was shattered.

The threat to her job was more than just a financial blow. Teaching and writing had been her lifeline, a way to channel her energy and passion into something constructive, something that made a difference. Losing that would mean losing a part of herself, a part that she wasn't sure she could afford to give up.

But there was more at stake than just her career. The investigation meant scrutiny, scrutiny that could uncover her involvement in the resistance, that could lead to arrests, to trials, to the exposure of everything they had worked so hard to protect.

She tried to steady her breathing, to think rationally about her options. She could deny everything, cooperate with the investigation, and hope that it all blew over. But that would mean abandoning the cause, distancing herself from the very people she had inspired, and leaving them to face the consequences alone. Or she could double down, continue her work in the shadows, and hope that the university's probe didn't dig too deep.

Neither option was without risk. As much as she wanted to believe that she could navigate this crisis without compromising her values, the reality was that she was being forced to choose between her safety and her commitment to the movement.

Her thoughts drifted to the manifesto she had written, the words that had sparked a new wave of resistance, that had given people hope. Those words had power, but they also carried a cost, a cost that she was now being asked to pay.

As she sat there, the weight of her choices pressing down on her, Emily realised that the moral clarity she had once felt was beginning to erode. The lines between right and wrong, between courage and recklessness, were blurring. And in their place was a growing sense of fear, fear that she might not be strong enough to carry the burden she had taken on.

The sound of footsteps in the hallway snapped her out of her reverie. She quickly folded the letter and slipped it into her desk drawer, forcing herself to focus on the task at hand. There would be time later to grapple with the consequences of her actions, to decide what her next move would be. For now, she had to keep going, keep fighting, even as the ground beneath her feet began to crumble.

John Mason sat alone in his small apartment, the dim light from a single lamp casting long shadows across the room. The air was heavy with the smell of tobacco, the ashtray on the table overflowing with the remnants of his cigarettes. His military jacket, worn and frayed at the edges, lay draped over the back of a chair, a silent reminder of the life he had tried to leave behind.

But the past had a way of catching up, no matter how fast or how far you ran.

The operation at the surveillance hub had been a success, but it had also stirred up memories that John had spent years trying to bury. The precision, the tension, the split-second decisions, it had all brought him back to the battlefield, to the moments when lives hung in the balance and the weight of command felt like a crushing force on his chest.

He had been a soldier for most of his adult life, a leader of men, a protector of his country. But the things he had seen, the things he had done in the name of duty, had left scars that no amount of time could heal. The faces of the men he had lost, the orders he had given that led to their deaths, haunted his dreams and his waking moments alike.

And now, as he sat in the silence of his apartment, those ghosts were more present than ever.

He reached for the bottle of whiskey on the table, pouring himself another drink. The alcohol burned as it went down, but it did little to dull the memories that crowded his mind. He had been a good soldier, but that had come at a cost, a cost that he was only now beginning to fully understand.

The resistance had given him a new purpose, a new mission. But with it came the same burdens, the same responsibilities, the same fears. The people he was leading now, they weren't soldiers. They were civilians, ordinary people who had been pushed to the brink by a system that had failed them. And if he made the wrong call, if he led them into a situation they couldn't handle, it would be on him.

The weight of that responsibility was suffocating. And in the quiet of his apartment, with nothing but his thoughts for company, John wondered if he was truly capable of leading them, of protecting them, of seeing this fight through to the end.

He downed the rest of his drink, the liquid burning a path to his stomach. He knew he couldn't afford to dwell on these doubts, that he needed to stay strong, to stay focused. But the past was relentless, and it demanded to be reckoned with.

His phone buzzed on the table, breaking the silence. John glanced at the screen, seeing Emily's name flash across it. He hesitated for a moment before picking up, steeling himself for whatever news she had to share.

"Emily," he said, his voice rough. "What's going on?"

"I just got a letter from the university," Emily replied, her voice tense. "They're launching an investigation into my conduct. It's only a matter of time before they start digging into everything, my work, my connections, the resistance."

John closed his eyes, the weight of the situation pressing down on him even more. "This doesn't sound good Emily. They're not just sniffing around, they're out for blood. What are you going to do?"

"I don't know," Emily stared at the letter and admitted. "I can't abandon the movement, but I also can't afford to get caught. If they find out what we're really doing, it's over." She bit her lip and trembled. "Part of me wants to fight it, to stand my ground and refuse to let them push me out. But..." Sighing, continued, "The other part of me knows that's exactly what they're counting on. If I resist, they'll dig deeper, and sooner or later, they'll find something."

"Look," John said firmly, "They're already suspicious, which means they're looking for any excuse to make an example out of you. If they connect the dots between you and the resistance…"

Emily closed her eyes and, almost in a whisper "I've tried so hard to keep those worlds separate, to be careful. But maybe I wasn't careful enough. Maybe I was naive to think I could balance both without one spilling over into the other."

"You're not naive, Emily." John quickly cut in. "You're brave. You've been walking a tightrope, trying to do what's right without losing everything in the process. That takes guts. But now, they've pushed you into a corner."

Emily gave a bitter laugh. "Brave" doesn't feel like the right word right now. More like reckless. I knew the risks, John, and I still kept pushing. And now, it's not just my job on the line, it's the entire movement."

"We knew this would happen eventually." John said softly, although he felt his heart beating quickly in his chest. " We always knew the day would come when they'd start closing in. The question is, what are we willing to sacrifice to keep going?"

Emily looked around her office and her eyes came to rest on the photograph of her parents, taken at the time of her graduation, what now felt a million years ago. She sighed, "That's the thing, I don't know. I've spent years building my career, believing I could use it to make a difference, to change things from the inside. But now I'm starting to wonder if that was just a convenient excuse to avoid facing the reality that real change means real risk. And real loss."

"You've made a difference, Emily. You've inspired people, given them hope. The manifesto, what you've written, it's already changing the way people think. But you're right. Real change…" John searched for words, "it's messy. It's dangerous. And it doesn't come without a cost."

"I just… I don't want to lose everything." Her voice trembled, "I don't want to lose who I am in the process. But every time we take another step forward, it feels like I'm losing a piece of myself, like I'm becoming someone I don't recognise."

After a pause, John said steadily, with conviction, "Maybe that's part of the process. Maybe it's about becoming who we need to be to do what has to be done. But it doesn't mean you have to lose yourself completely. You're still you, Emily. The things that matter to you, that make you who you are, they're still there, even if they get a little lost along the way."

"I want to keep fighting, John. I do. But I'm scared. Not just for myself, but for everyone else, Hassan, Lily, you. What if I'm the weak link?" A sob broke from Emily, "What if I'm the one who brings everything crashing down?"

"You're not the weak link, Emily. You're the glue holding this whole thing together. Without you, we wouldn't have gotten this far." John paused, "But I get it, fear is a part of this. It's what keeps us sharp, what keeps us alive. We just can't let it paralyse us."

"Easier said than done" Emily responded quietly.

"Yeah, I know. But we're in this together. Whatever you decide, we'll figure it out," John said, trying to sound more confident than he felt. "We've come this far. We're not going to let them take us down now."

Emily smiled to herself. "Thanks, John. I needed to hear that."

"Anytime," John replied, smiling. " We're all walking a fine line here, but we're not walking it alone."

They talked for a while longer, going over the details of their next steps, trying to find a way forward that wouldn't expose them or the people they were trying to protect. The conversation was lighter but with the unspoken fears that neither of them wanted to acknowledge.

When they finally hung up, John was left alone with his thoughts once more. The room seemed even darker now, the shadows closing in around him. He stared at the empty glass in his hand, the weight of everything he had done, and everything he had yet to do, pressing down on him like a leaden blanket.

He knew that the road ahead was only going to get harder, that the cost of rebellion would continue to rise. But there was no turning back. The past might haunt him, but it was the future that demanded his attention, that required him to keep moving, to keep fighting.

As he set the glass down and stood up, John felt the familiar weight of his military jacket on his shoulders. He slipped it on, the worn fabric comforting in its familiarity. He might not have all the answers, but he knew one thing for certain, he couldn't afford to give up. Not now, not ever.

With that resolve in mind, he grabbed his keys and headed for the door. The city outside was still shrouded in mist, but John knew that the real storm was just beginning. And he would be ready for it.

The next few days passed in a blur of tension and uncertainty, as the group grappled with the fallout from their actions. Hassan worked tirelessly to repair the damage to his shop, but the unease in the neighbourhood lingered, a constant reminder of the threat that hung over them. Emily kept a low profile, avoiding the university as much as possible while she waited for the investigation to unfold. And John buried himself in preparations for their next move, trying to stay one step ahead of the ghosts that haunted him.

But despite the challenges, there was also a growing sense of determination among them, a recognition that they were in too deep to turn back now. The cost of rebellion was high, but so were the stakes, and each of them was willing to pay the price, whatever it might be.

They met again at the safe house. As the group gathered around the table, the atmosphere was thick with the unspoken burdens they each carried. The silence that greeted them as they entered the room was not one of discomfort but of mutual understanding. Each member of the group was acutely aware of the risks they were taking, the sacrifices they had already made, and the sacrifices yet to come. But there was also a sense of solidarity, of a bond that had been forged in the fire of resistance. They had become more than just allies; they were a family of sorts, united by a shared purpose and the knowledge that they were all in this together.

John took his usual seat at the head of the table, his presence steady and grounding. He had a way of filling the room without saying a word, his quiet strength a source of comfort to the others. Emily sat beside him, her eyes scanning the maps on the wall, her mind already turning over the next steps they needed to take. Hassan moved to the stove, pouring hot water from the kettle into a teapot, the simple act a calming ritual that helped him focus. Lily, ever the restless one, perched on the edge of her chair, her fingers tapping lightly on the table, the energy inside her barely contained.

"We've all made sacrifices," Hassan said, his voice steady but tinged with sadness. "But we can't lose sight of why we're doing this. The cost is high, yes, but the cost of doing nothing is even higher."

Emily nodded, her expression resolute. "We've started something that can't be undone. We have to see it through, for ourselves, for the people who are counting on us."

John looked around the room, seeing the resolve in their faces, and felt a surge of gratitude for the people he was fighting alongside. They were more than just comrades, they were a family, bound together by a shared purpose, a shared struggle.

"We'll get through this," John said, his voice firm. "But we have to be smart, and we have to stay strong. We've come too far to let fear or doubt stop us now."

Lily, who had been uncharacteristically quiet, finally spoke up, her voice soft but filled with conviction. "We're making a difference. People are listening, they're waking up. We just have to keep going."

They talked late into the night, discussing their plans, their strategies, and the steps they would take to protect themselves and their movement. There was no room for error, no room for hesitation. But there was also no room for defeat.

As they parted ways, each of them returned to their lives with a renewed sense of purpose, a recognition that the cost of rebellion was one they were willing to bear. The path ahead was treacherous, but it was also the only path they could take.

And so, they prepared to face the challenges that lay ahead, knowing that the fight was far from over, but also knowing that they would face it together, no matter the cost.

Chapter 8 A Growing Flame

The flame of revolution, once a small flicker in the dark, was beginning to spread. What had started as a handful of determined individuals operating in the shadows was now igniting pockets of resistance across the country. The original group's actions, their manifesto, and the successful sabotage of the government's surveillance hub had resonated far beyond the city's limits. In towns and cities hundreds of miles away, people were taking up the cause, inspired by the defiance of a few to challenge the oppressive grip of the government.

It began with whispers, passed in hushed conversations in backrooms and basements, in the quiet corners of pubs and community centres. People were starting to ask questions, starting to wonder if they too could stand against the tide of authoritarianism that was sweeping over the country. And soon, those whispers grew into something more, a collective murmur of dissent that could not be ignored.

The garage was tucked away at the end of a narrow alley, hidden behind a row of modest terraced houses that all looked the same under the grey, overcast sky. The town itself was a patchwork of history and industry, where red-brick buildings from the Victorian era stood beside the more functional, utilitarian structures of the 20th century. The air carried the faint scent of smoke from nearby factories, mingling with the earthy smell of rain-soaked pavement.

To the casual observer, the garage was just another forgotten corner of the town on the outskirts of Manchester. A place where an old car might be kept, or where someone stored their unused belongings. The paint on the garage door was chipped and peeling, revealing the bare wood underneath, and the concrete floor outside was cracked and uneven, with weeds poking through in places. A single, flickering bulb above the door cast a weak circle of light, barely visible in the encroaching dusk.

But inside, the garage told a different story.

The space was small and cramped, barely large enough to fit the old wooden table that dominated the centre of the room. Around it, a mismatched collection of chairs had been gathered, some scavenged from the nearby junkyard, others borrowed from parents or friends who didn't ask too many questions. The walls were lined with faded posters from decades past, their edges curling, and their colours dulled with age. Images of defiant workers, protest marches, and political slogans in bold lettering stared down at the room's occupants, a silent reminder of struggles that had come before.

Stacks of yellowing newspapers and old magazines were piled haphazardly in the corners, their pages brittle and worn. Headlines from a different time screamed out about scandals and crises long forgotten, but the spirit of resistance they captured had not faded. A broken radio, long past its prime, sat on a dusty shelf, its dials twisted and useless. The garage was a place where the past and present met, a shrine to the defiance that had simmered under the surface of society for years.

The light inside the garage was dim, provided by a few bare bulbs strung from the ceiling. They cast a warm, golden glow that softened the harsh lines of the space, creating deep shadows in the corners. The air was thick with the scent of oil and grease, mixed with the faint, lingering odour of cigarette smoke. A small space heater in the corner buzzed quietly, fighting a losing battle against the chill that seeped in through the gaps in the walls.

The group of young activists gathered around the table were young, their faces lit by a mixture of determination and uncertainty. They were dressed in a blend of old coats, hoodies, and worn jeans, clothes that were practical, unremarkable, and meant to blend in rather than stand out. Each of them bore the marks of the town they had grown up in, calloused hands from part-time jobs, dark circles under their eyes from long nights spent studying or working, and the quiet resilience that came from knowing the world wasn't fair but choosing to fight against it anyway.

Alex, the unspoken leader of the group, leaned forward on the table, his eyes glinting with a mix of excitement and resolve. His hair was tousled, his clothes slightly rumpled, but there was an energy about him that drew the others in. The garage was his uncle's, and it had become their unofficial headquarters, an unlikely war room for a group of young people ready to take on the world.

Sarah sat beside him, her fingers drumming lightly on the table's surface. She was the group's voice, a journalist by training who had been forced to abandon her dreams of working for a major newspaper after the government's crackdown on independent media. Her sharp eyes missed nothing, and her voice had a way of cutting through the noise, bringing clarity to the most chaotic of situations. A notebook lay open in front of her, filled with scribbled notes and ideas, the ink smudged from countless revisions.

Across the table, Liam adjusted his glasses, the lenses reflecting the dim light. He was the planner, the one who saw patterns where others saw only chaos. His laptop sat open beside him, its screen displaying a map of the town, marked with red dots and lines, possible targets, escape routes, and safe houses. He had spent hours poring over it, analysing every detail, every potential risk, until the plan was as solid as it could be.

The others, Mia, a local artist with a flair for creating the striking posters that had begun appearing around town; Ben, a factory worker who knew the backstreets and shortcuts better than anyone; and Olivia, a student who had recently been expelled for organising protests at her school, sat in a loose circle around the table, each one contributing their skills and knowledge to the cause.

Despite the seriousness of their discussions, there was an undercurrent of camaraderie, a shared understanding that they were all in this together. The garage, with its worn walls and makeshift furniture, had become more than just a meeting place. It was a symbol of their commitment, a space where they could speak freely, plan their actions, and share their fears and hopes without judgment.

As they talked, the sounds of the town drifted in through the thin walls, the distant rumble of a passing train, the murmur of voices from a nearby pub, the occasional bark of a dog. But inside the garage, the focus was singular, the atmosphere charged with the anticipation of what was to come.

They had watched from the sidelines for too long, feeling helpless as the government tightened its grip on the country. But now, inspired by the courage of those who had taken the first steps in the capital, they were ready to do more than just watch. The garage, once just a dusty, forgotten space, had become the heart of their resistance, a place where ideas were forged into plans, and plans into action.

And as they huddled together in the dim light, surrounded by the remnants of past struggles, they knew that the road ahead would be difficult, that the risks were great. But they also knew that they were part of something larger, something that could not be easily extinguished. The flame of resistance had reached their town, and they were ready to fan it into a blaze.

"We can't just sit here and wait for things to get better," said Alex, a university student with a fiery spirit and a quick mind. He leaned forward, his hands resting on the makeshift table that had been set up in the centre of the garage. "The government isn't going to stop on its own. We have to make them stop."

The others around the table nodded in agreement. They had all seen the changes in their town, the increased police presence, the surveillance cameras that had appeared on every street corner, the sense of fear that had begun to permeate even the most mundane aspects of life. But they had also seen something else: the courage of those who were fighting back, the sense that perhaps, just perhaps, they could do the same.

"We're not alone in this," said Sarah, a local journalist who had been documenting the government's crackdown on dissent. "There are others out there, people like us, who are starting to push back. We can connect with them, learn from them, build something together."

And so, in that small garage, a new cell of the resistance was born. They began to organise, to reach out to others in their community, to build a network of like-minded individuals who were ready to take a stand. They knew the risks, they had seen what had happened to those who had been caught, but they also knew that the alternative, doing nothing, was no longer an option.

As the days passed, more and more people joined their cause. Teachers, factory workers, shop owners, and students, each brought their skills, their own stories, their reasons for joining the fight. And with each recruit, the flame of rebellion grew stronger.

Similar scenes were playing out in other towns and cities across the country. In Birmingham, a group of disillusioned factory workers, tired of the government's broken promises and stagnant wages, began meeting in secret to discuss how they could disrupt the machinery of the state. In Glasgow, a network of community organisers started to coordinate protests and acts of civil disobedience, challenging the government's control over their city.

And in the rural areas of the north, farmers who had been squeezed by oppressive land policies began to form their resistance, using their intimate knowledge of the land to outmanoeuvre the authorities.

The original group in the capital watched with a mixture of pride and anxiety as the movement began to spread. They had always hoped that their actions would inspire others, but the speed with which the flame of rebellion was catching on took even them by surprise. It was exhilarating, but it was also dangerous. The more people who joined the cause, the more difficult it would be to remain hidden, to avoid the watchful eyes of the government.

Emily spent her days working tirelessly to keep the network connected, coordinating between the different cells, and ensuring that information flowed smoothly and securely. She had become the heart of the movement, her words and actions guiding the disparate groups that were now part of their resistance. But with each new message, each new report of another cell forming, she felt the weight of responsibility pressing down on her. The stakes were higher than ever, and any mistake could be catastrophic.

John, meanwhile, focused on preparing the original group for the challenges ahead. He knew that the government would not sit idly by as the resistance grew, they would strike back, harder, and more ruthlessly than before. And so, he intensified their training, drilling them in self-defence, in guerrilla tactics, in the art of staying one step ahead of their enemies. But even as he pushed them to their limits, he could not shake the feeling that they were on the brink of something much larger than any of them had anticipated.

The government, for its part, was not blind to the growing tide of rebellion. Reports of dissent, sabotage, protests, and strikes were coming in from all corners of the country. The Prime Minister, a man known for his hardline stance on law and order, was growing increasingly frustrated with the situation. He had underestimated the resistance, dismissed them as a fringe group that would soon burn out. But now, it was clear that they were becoming something far more dangerous.

In response, the government escalated its surveillance efforts, deploying new technologies to monitor communications, track movements, and identify those who were involved in the resistance. Drones patrolled the skies over major cities, their cameras scanning the streets below for any sign of trouble. New laws were passed, granting the authorities even greater powers to detain and interrogate suspected dissidents without trial. And in the dead of night, raids on the homes of known activists became a common occurrence, the knock on the door a prelude to a life torn apart.

But the resistance was not so easily crushed. They adapted to the new reality, learning to communicate in ways that eluded the government's prying eyes. They used coded language, encrypted messages, and dead drops to pass information between cells. They moved their meetings to ever-changing locations, never staying in one place long enough to be found. And they continued to strike back, targeting the very systems that the government relied on to maintain control.

It was in this atmosphere of tension and escalating conflict that Tom Harper emerged as a new figure in the resistance, a man whose name would soon become known to every member of the movement.

Tom had once been a rising star in the government, a charismatic politician with a reputation for being both charming and ruthless. He had been a loyal servant of the state, defending its policies with fervour and ambition. But over time, the cracks in the system had begun to wear on him. He had seen the corruption, the lies, the way the government's promises of security and prosperity had been nothing more than a veneer to cover the rot beneath.

Disillusionment had set in slowly, eroding the foundation of his beliefs until there was nothing left to support the weight of his conscience. He had tried to convince himself that he could change things from within, that he could reform the system, make it better. But the more he tried, the more he realised that the system was beyond saving.

And so, one night, Tom walked away. He left behind his cushy office, his carefully crafted image, his place at the heart of power. He disappeared from public view, retreating into the shadows, where he could finally see the truth of what was happening in his country. It was there, in the darkness, that he found the resistance.

It didn't take long for Tom to make his mark. His knowledge of the government's inner workings, his understanding of its strengths and weaknesses, made him an invaluable asset. He knew how the machine operated, how it thought, how it would respond to the growing threat of rebellion. And he knew how to exploit its vulnerabilities.

Tom's arrival brought a new energy to the movement. He was a man who had once been part of the very establishment they were fighting against, and yet he had turned his back on it, choosing to stand with the people instead. His speeches, delivered in secret meetings and distributed through underground channels, were electrifying. He spoke with passion and conviction, his words resonating with those who had felt powerless for so long.

"We stand at the edge of a precipice," Tom would say, his voice carrying the weight of his own transformation. "We can either fall into the abyss, surrendering to the forces that seek to control us, or we can rise. We can take back what is ours, claim the future that has been stolen from us. But we cannot do it alone. It will take all of us, united in purpose, to ignite the flame of revolution and keep it burning."

The people listened, and they were moved. Tom's charisma, his ability to articulate the anger and frustration that so many felt, made him a natural leader. But he was also pragmatic, understanding that words alone were not enough. He worked tirelessly to organise the resistance, to connect the different cells, to ensure that they were all working toward the same goal.

Under Tom's guidance, the resistance began to coordinate their efforts on a national scale. They planned larger operations, targeting key infrastructure and government installations. They used their growing numbers to stage simultaneous protests and strikes across multiple cities, overwhelming the authorities and forcing them to spread their resources thin. And they continued to recruit, drawing more and more people into the movement as the government's heavy-handed tactics only served to alienate the populace further.

But even as the resistance grew, so too did the dangers they faced. The government was becoming increasingly desperate, resorting to ever more brutal methods to maintain control. And within the resistance, there were whispers of dissent, of disagreements over strategy, of fears that they were moving too fast, too recklessly.

Tom was not immune to these challenges. He knew that his sudden rise to prominence had made him a target, both within the government and within the resistance itself. Some distrusted him, who saw him as an outsider, a former member of the very regime they were fighting against. But Tom was determined to prove himself, to show that he was committed to the cause, even if it meant putting himself at risk.

As the chapter drew to a close, the movement was at a crossroads. The flame of rebellion had spread, lighting fires of resistance across the country. But with that growth came new challenges, new dangers, and new questions about the future. The original group, now joined by Tom, stood at the centre of it all, aware that the decisions they made in the coming days would shape the course of the revolution.

The government was tightening its grip, but the resistance was adapting, growing stronger, and more united. The battle lines were being drawn, and the fight was far from over. The flame had been lit, and now it was up to them to ensure that it continued to burn, no matter the cost.

PART II

The Rising Tide

Chapter 9 The Rising Tide

The movement had taken on a life of its own. What had begun as a small, tight-knit group of determined individuals was now a sprawling network of cells, spreading out across the UK like veins carrying blood to every corner of the nation. It was a thrilling, heady time, each day brought new reports of actions taken, of recruits joining the cause, of government forces caught off guard by the audacity of their resistance. But with that growth came new challenges, new dangers that threatened to unravel everything they had worked so hard to build.

The setting sun cast a golden hue over the city, its rays filtering through the grime-streaked windows of the abandoned warehouse that had become one of the resistance's central meeting points. The air inside was thick with dust and the lingering scent of engine oil, a reminder of the building's past life as a factory. Long-forgotten machinery stood like silent sentinels in the corners, their rusted gears, and belts untouched by time. The space was vast and echoing, but tonight, it was filled with the low murmur of voices, the sounds of a movement trying to figure out how to steer the ship they had set in motion.

John Mason stood at the head of a makeshift table, an old workbench that had been dragged to the centre of the room. Around him, the core group had gathered, Emily, Hassan, Lily, and a handful of new faces that had been vetted and brought into the fold. But where once there had been a sense of unity, tonight there was tension, a palpable unease that crackled in the air like static before a storm.

"We've got more people joining every day," Emily was saying, her voice steady but tinged with concern. "That's a good thing, but it's also making it harder to keep things under wraps. We've had close calls, too many of them. If we're not careful, the whole thing could blow up in our faces."

Hassan, who was leaning against the wall with his arms crossed, nodded in agreement. "She's right. The more people we bring in, the harder it is to maintain security. We need to start thinking about tighter protocols, stricter vetting, and maybe even compartmentalising information so that not everyone knows everything."

"But we can't just stop growing," argued Lily, who was sitting cross-legged on the floor, her face flushed with the fervour that had come to define her involvement in the movement. "We need numbers. The more people we have, the stronger we are. If we get too paranoid, we'll stagnate."

John listened to the exchange in silence, his eyes flicking from one speaker to the next. The room felt claustrophobic, the walls pressing in on him as the voices rose and fell. He couldn't shake the feeling that something was off, that there was a current of discord running just beneath the surface, threatening to pull them all under.

"We're not talking about stopping growth," he said finally, his voice cutting through the noise. "But we do need to be careful. The government's stepping up its surveillance, drones, informants, and even infiltrators. We can't afford to be reckless."

The others fell silent, their eyes on John. He could see the weight of his words settling over them, the realisation that they were no longer just a small band of rebels playing a dangerous game. They were a movement now, with all the risks and responsibilities that entailed.

"Which brings us to the next point," John continued, his gaze shifting to Emily. "Strategy. We've had some success with our current approach, but we need to decide where we go from here. Do we keep up with the smaller actions, chipping away at the system bit by bit, or do we escalate? Start hitting bigger targets, making a real statement?"

Emily sighed, running a hand through her hair. "I've been thinking about that. There's a growing sentiment among some of the cells that we need to step up our game, show the government that we're not just a nuisance, but a real threat. But..."

"But what?" Lily pressed, leaning forward, her eyes bright with anticipation.

"But," Emily continued, "I'm worried about the consequences. If we escalate, we risk not only more lives but also losing the moral high ground. Right now, we still have a lot of public support. People are behind us because they see us as standing up for what's right. But if we start using violence indiscriminately, that could change. We could lose everything we've built."

The room fell into a contemplative silence, the weight of the decision before them hanging heavy in the air. It was Hassan who broke the silence, his voice measured and calm.

"Emily's right. We need to be strategic about this. Violence can be a tool, but it's a double-edged sword. If we wield it carelessly, it could turn against us. We need to focus on symbolic targets, things that hit the government where it hurts but don't alienate the public."

"Symbolic targets don't win wars," John muttered under his breath, but loud enough for the others to hear. He was tired of the endless discussions, the debates that seemed to go in circles. Every day, the stakes were getting higher, the dangers more immediate, and yet they were still debating strategy as if they had all the time in the world.

Lily caught his tone and jumped in. "We've been too cautious," she said, her voice rising. "We need to show the government that we're serious. That we're willing to do whatever it takes to win. They're not going to back down just because we hit a few symbols. They need to know we're a real threat."

"And what do you suggest, Lily?" Hassan asked, his tone neutral but with a hint of challenge. "Blowing up a government building? Assassinating a politician? Where does it end?"

"It ends when we win," Lily shot back, her eyes flashing with defiance.

The tension in the room was thick now, the divide between caution and aggression widening with every word. John could feel the group fracturing, the unity that had once held them together splintering under the weight of their growing numbers and differing opinions.

"Enough," John said, his voice low but firm. "This isn't getting us anywhere. We need to remember why we're doing this. It's not about revenge. It's about making things better, about giving people a chance to live in a country that doesn't treat them like enemies. If we lose sight of that, we're no better than the people we're fighting against."

His words hung in the air, a reminder of the line they had drawn for themselves, the line that separated them from the government they opposed. But even as he spoke, John couldn't shake the feeling that the line was becoming increasingly blurred.

Later that night, after the others had left, John remained in the warehouse, the silence around him a stark contrast to the heated discussion that had taken place just hours earlier. The dim light from the single bulb overhead cast long shadows on the walls, turning the machinery into hulking shapes that loomed in the darkness.

He lit a cigarette, the ember flaring in the gloom, and took a long drag. His thoughts were a tangled mess of doubts and fears, each one gnawing at him with increasing ferocity. He had never been one to shy away from danger, his years in the military had hardened him, and made him accustomed to the reality of conflict. But this was different. This wasn't a battlefield with clear enemies and objectives. This was a war of ideas, of strategies, of shadows and whispers.

And it was in the shadows that John sensed the greatest danger. The movement was growing too fast, too uncontrolled. He could feel it slipping out of his grasp, becoming something that he didn't fully understand, something that could turn on them if they weren't careful.

But there was something else, too. A feeling that had been growing in the back of his mind, a nagging suspicion that he couldn't shake. Someone in the group was hiding something. He couldn't pinpoint who, or what, but the signs were there, small things, inconsistencies in stories, a stray look, a comment that didn't quite add up. The more he thought about it, the more certain he became.

There was a traitor in their midst.

The thought chilled him, sending a shiver down his spine. He had seen what betrayal could do, how it could tear apart even the most disciplined units, how it could turn comrades into enemies overnight. And in a movement as fragile as theirs, a single betrayal could be catastrophic.

But how could he bring it up without sowing more discord? The group was already on edge, their differing opinions on strategy threatening to split them apart. If he voiced his suspicions now, it could push them over the edge, and lead to paranoia and infighting that would do more damage than any government crackdown.

He took another drag on his cigarette, the smoke curling up into the rafters, and exhaled slowly. No, he couldn't say anything, not yet. He needed to be sure. He needed to gather more evidence, to figure out who it was before making any accusations. But he also couldn't afford to wait too long. The clock was ticking, and every day they were vulnerable.

John crushed the cigarette under his boot and stood up, his mind made up. He would keep his suspicions to himself, for now. But he would watch, and he would wait. And when the time came, he would act.

As he walked out of the warehouse into the cool night air, the city around him silent and still, John knew that the real battle was just beginning. The movement had grown beyond anything they had imagined, but with that growth came new challenges, and new threats. And if they weren't careful, the very thing they had built could be their undoing.

The rising tide of rebellion was unstoppable, but it was also unpredictable. And in the days to come, they would need to navigate its treacherous waters with more caution than ever before.

In the days following the tense meeting in the warehouse, the challenges of maintaining secrecy became increasingly apparent. The city was under constant surveillance, with drones hovering in the skies like mechanical vultures, their cameras sweeping the streets for any sign of dissent. The government had ramped up its efforts to root out the resistance, deploying new technologies and tactics that made it harder for the movement to operate undetected.

The safe houses that had once felt secure now seemed vulnerable, their locations known to more people than ever before. The network of cells that had been their strength was now a potential liability, each new member a possible point of failure. The very growth that had given them hope now threatened to expose them.

Emily spent hours each day sifting through reports, trying to keep track of the expanding network. She communicated with the various cells using encrypted messages, constantly changing codes and protocols to stay ahead of the government's efforts to infiltrate their communications. But despite her best efforts, there were slip-ups, meetings that were nearly compromised, members who were arrested under suspicious circumstances, and plans that leaked before they could be executed.

The sense of unease grew with each passing day. The resistance was becoming too large to manage, too unwieldy. The very thing they had worked so hard to create was slipping out of their control, and there was no way to pull back without losing momentum.

The internal debates over strategy became more heated as the days went on. The group met in different locations each time, trying to stay ahead of the government's surveillance. One night, they gathered in the basement of an old church, the air thick with the scent of damp stone and burning candles. The dim light flickered across their faces, casting deep shadows that made them look older, wearier than they were.

The arguments played out much the same each time, Lily pushing for more aggressive action, Hassan cautioning restraint, Emily torn between the two, and John watching, listening, his mind elsewhere. The tension was palpable, the room crackling with the energy of unresolved conflict.

In one particularly heated meeting, Lily slammed her fist on the table, her voice rising in frustration. "We're running out of time! The government is tightening the noose around our necks, and we're just sitting here debating tactics! We need to hit them hard, make them realise we're not going to back down!"

Hassan, ever the voice of reason, responded calmly but firmly. "And if we do that, what happens next? The government will come down on us even harder. We'll lose the support of the people, and without that, we're finished. This isn't just about making a statement, it's about winning."

Emily's gaze shifted between the two, her doubts reflected in the lines of worry on her face. "We can't afford to lose public support," she said quietly. "But we can't afford to do nothing, either."

The room fell silent as the weight of the decision settled over them once again. John remained quiet, his thoughts turning inward, focusing not on the debate at hand, but on the growing suspicion that gnawed at him.

John's paranoia deepened with each passing day. He started seeing threats in every shadow, every glance, every word left unspoken. He began conducting his investigation, quietly questioning members of the group, cross-referencing their stories, and looking for inconsistencies. He spent hours poring over the details of their recent operations, trying to identify where they might have been compromised.

One night, he found himself in a small, windowless room in a rundown tenement building on the outskirts of the city. The air was stale, and the walls were covered in peeling wallpaper that had once been floral but was now just a faded, mottled pattern. The only light came from a single, naked bulb hanging from the ceiling, casting a harsh, unforgiving glow over the room.

John sat at a rickety table, a stack of documents in front of him. His eyes were bloodshot, his hands trembling slightly as he sifted through the papers. He knew he was on the verge of something, that he was close to uncovering the truth. But he also knew that once he did, there would be no turning back.

As he worked, the doubts and fears that had been building inside him began to take on a life of their own. He could no longer tell if he was being rational if the things he was seeing were real or just the product of his growing paranoia. But he couldn't stop. He had to know. He had to protect the movement, no matter the cost.

The sense of isolation was overwhelming. He couldn't trust anyone, couldn't confide in anyone, not even Emily. The burden of suspicion was his alone to bear, and it was slowly eating away at him.

Chapter 10 Operation Unity

The storm had been brewing for weeks, each day adding to the growing sense of urgency and resolve within the resistance. The movement had spread across the country like wildfire, igniting a fierce determination in the hearts of those who had suffered under the government's oppressive regime. But as the resistance grew, so did the risks. The time had come for a decisive strike, a coordinated action that would send a message to the government and the world that the resistance was not just a scattered collection of cells but a unified force with the power to disrupt the system.

Operation Unity was born from that need. It was ambitious, audacious, and dangerous, a plan that would require precision, courage, and sacrifice. The objective was simple in its concept but complex in its execution: to target key infrastructure across the UK, bringing government operations to a grinding halt, if only for a moment. The success of the operation depended on the flawless coordination of multiple cells, each tasked with a specific target, each moving in perfect synchrony with the others.

The basement of an old, disused library had become the nerve centre for the operation. The building, with its cracked stone facade and ivy-covered walls, stood on the outskirts of a small town, its once-grand structure now forgotten by the world. Inside, the air was thick with the scent of dust and old paper, a quiet testament to the knowledge that had once been housed within its walls. The basement, accessed by a hidden stairway behind a set of rotting bookshelves, was cold and dimly lit, the only light coming from a few strategically placed lanterns that cast long shadows on the walls.

In the centre of the room stood a large, rectangular table, its surface covered with maps, diagrams, and notes. A map of the UK dominated the space, its surface dotted with pins and lines that connected the various targets. Around the table, the core group, John, Emily, Hassan, Lily, and several key members of the other cells had gathered. Their faces were tense, their expressions grim, as they reviewed the final details of the plan.

John stood at the head of the table, his gaze fixed on the map. He had been the driving force behind the operation, pushing for a coordinated strike that would show the government just how vulnerable it was. But now, as the moment of action drew near, the weight of responsibility pressed heavily on his shoulders.

"Everyone knows their targets," John began, his voice steady but with an edge of tension. "We hit them simultaneously, no margin for error. Timing is everything. If one cell is delayed, the whole operation could be compromised."

Emily nodded, her eyes scanning the map. "We've planned for every contingency, but we need to be prepared for the unexpected. If something goes wrong, we abort. No unnecessary risks."

Lily, who had been pacing the room, stopped and turned to face the group. "And what if the unexpected happens to all of us? We need to be ready to adapt, to improvise if we have to. We can't let this fail."

Hassan, ever the voice of caution, leaned forward, his fingers tracing the lines on the map. "We've accounted for as much as we can, but we're dealing with a fluid situation. Once we're in the field, things will change. We have to trust our people, trust that they'll know what to do if the plan goes sideways."

John looked around the table, meeting the eyes of each person in turn. They were ready. They had to be.

"We go in at 0100 hours," John said, his voice firm. "Synchronise your watches. We'll be in constant communication but keep chatter to a minimum. Remember, the success of this operation depends on our ability to strike quickly and disappear before they know what hit them."

There was a moment of silence as the gravity of the situation sank in. Then, one by one, they nodded, a silent agreement that they were ready to face whatever came next.

The night was thick with anticipation, the kind of night where even the shadows seemed to hold their breath. The moon, usually a sentinel in the sky, was hidden behind a blanket of thick, roiling clouds, casting the land below into an abyss of darkness. The world was shrouded in an inky blackness that swallowed everything, leaving only the faintest outlines of trees and buildings as mere silhouettes against the void.

The air was dense and heavy, pressing down on the earth like a tangible weight. It carried the scent of rain, sharp and metallic as if the atmosphere itself was charged with the electricity of the coming storm. The first tentative drops began to fall, gentle at first, like nature testing the waters before unleashing its full force. Each droplet seemed to echo in the silence, a subtle reminder of the impending deluge.

Across the country, in towns, cities, and the quiet, forgotten corners of rural landscapes, the members of the resistance moved with the precision of shadows. There was no idle chatter, no unnecessary noise, just the sound of soft footsteps on damp ground, the rustle of clothing as figures darted from cover to cover, and the muted clinks of weapons being checked one last time.

In the urban sprawl of London, the city that never truly slept, the usual cacophony of nightlife was eerily absent. The streets, normally alive with the hum of cars, the chatter of pedestrians, and the distant wail of sirens, were now deserted as if the city itself was holding its breath. The tall, imposing buildings loomed like silent sentinels, their windows dark and empty, watching over the grid of streets that spread out like a web.

In the East End, where John Mason led his team, the narrow alleyways twisted and turned in a maze of brick and cobblestone, the walls damp from the persistent drizzle. The fog had rolled in from the river, thickening the air and reducing visibility to just a few feet. Streetlamps struggled to penetrate the gloom, their weak, yellow light casting long, distorted shadows that danced and flickered with every movement.

The resistance members moved with a practiced ease, their senses heightened by the adrenaline coursing through their veins. Every creak of a floorboard, every distant sound, was analysed and dismissed in an instant, their minds focused solely on the task ahead. The city, usually so familiar, now felt like an alien landscape, its comforting chaos replaced by an unsettling quiet.

In the countryside, where the land stretched out in vast, open expanses, the darkness was even more profound. Fields that by day were a patchwork of green and gold were now a uniform black, their boundaries invisible in the night. The trees, stripped of their colour, stood like skeletal figures, their branches swaying gently in the wind. The rain fell more heavily here, pattering against the leaves and the earth, creating a steady rhythm that was both calming and ominous.

The resistance cells in these rural areas moved through the darkness with the confidence of those who knew the land intimately. They navigated by memory, their paths through fields and woods as familiar as the streets of a city to an urban dweller. But tonight, even they were cautious, their usual routes feeling fraught with unseen dangers.

In small villages and towns, where everyone knew each other by name, the sight of strangers moving through the streets would have been cause for alarm. But the resistance members were careful, sticking to the shadows, avoiding the pools of light cast by the occasional porch light or street lamp. They knew that here, a single misstep could lead to discovery and discovery to disaster.

The rural safehouses, usually secluded farmhouses or barns, were dimly lit, the windows covered to prevent any light from escaping. Inside, the atmosphere was tense, the air thick with the smell of damp wood and hay, mixed with the sweat of nervous anticipation.

Weapons were laid out on tables, their cold metal gleaming in the low light, while maps and radios were spread across makeshift command centres.

Back in the cities, the resistance teams approached their targets with a sense of grim determination. Each group had its mission, each person their role, and there was no room for doubt. The buildings they were targeting, government offices, data centres, and substations, were all heavily guarded, their security designed to withstand any attack. But the resistance had planned for this, had studied every detail, and now, in the thick of the night, they moved with the confidence that comes from preparation.

In Birmingham, where Emily led her team, the air was thick with the smell of industry, oil, metal, and the faint tang of burning rubber from a distant factory. The city's industrial heartland, a sprawling complex of factories and warehouses, was their target. The group moved silently through the industrial park, their footsteps muffled by the wet concrete. The buildings towered over them, their darkened windows like empty eyes watching their every move.

The rain intensified, the droplets now heavy and persistent, drumming on the rooftops and the streets with a steady beat. The sound masked their movements, the perfect cover for their approach. Emily's heart raced as they neared their target, the weight of responsibility pressing down on her. She knew that the success of the operation rested on their ability to remain undetected until the last possible moment.

In Manchester, where Hassan's team prepared to strike, the city was a maze of narrow streets and alleys, each one a potential trap. The power substation they were targeting was nestled in the outskirts, surrounded by tall fences, and barbed wire. The rain here was a downpour, soaking through their clothes and turning the ground into a slick, muddy mess. But they pressed on, their eyes fixed on the prize.

The darkness was both an ally and an enemy. It concealed them from the watchful eyes of the government's security forces, but it also hid dangers they couldn't see, traps, patrols, and the ever-present threat of betrayal. The tension was a living thing, coiling around their chests, making it hard to breathe.

But beneath the fear, beneath the tension, was a sense of purpose that drove them forward. They were fighting for something larger than themselves, something worth the risks they were taking. As they moved through the night, the resistance members knew that they were not alone, that across the country, in towns, cities, and rural areas alike, others were doing the same, each one playing their part in the grand plan that would shake the foundations of the government.

The night was dark, the land blanketed in shadow, but the resistance was a spark in that darkness, a spark that, if nurtured, could grow into a flame, a fire that would burn away the old and make way for the new.

In London, the city that had become the epicentre of the resistance, John led a small team through the narrow, winding streets of the East End. The target was a government data centre, a nondescript building nestled between a row of abandoned warehouses. It was a critical node in the government's surveillance network, a place where vast amounts of data were processed and stored, data that the government relied on to monitor and control the population.

The streets were eerily quiet, the usual sounds of the city muffled by the thick fog that had rolled in from the Thames. The only light came from the occasional streetlamp, its yellow glow barely penetrating the darkness. The team moved like shadows, their footsteps silent on the wet pavement.

As they approached the data centre, John signalled for the team to halt. They crouched in the shadows of a nearby building, their eyes on the target. The data centre was surrounded by a high fence topped with barbed wire, and security cameras were mounted at regular intervals along the perimeter. A single guard stood at the entrance, his breath visible in the cold night air.

John checked his watch. 0055 hours. Five minutes to go.

He turned to the team, his voice a whisper. "We take out the cameras first. Ben, you're on the fence. Olivia, you've got the guard. On my mark."

The tension was palpable as they waited for the signal. John's heart raced, his mind running through the plan one last time. There was no room for error.

00:59 hours.

John took a deep breath, his hand hovering over the radio clipped to his belt. He pressed the button.

"Go."

The team sprang into action. Ben, a former electrician, quickly disabled the cameras with a small device he had rigged up, the lights on the cameras blinking out one by one. Olivia, who had been trained in close combat, moved swiftly toward the guard, a stun gun in hand. She reached him just as he turned to see what was happening, the electric shock sending him crumpling to the ground without a sound.

John and the others moved to the fence, cutting through the wire with practiced efficiency. Within moments, they were inside the compound, moving toward the entrance of the building.

In Manchester, another team led by Hassan was targeting a power substation, a critical piece of infrastructure that supplied electricity to a large part of the city. The substation was heavily guarded, with armed personnel patrolling the perimeter and guard towers at each corner.

Hassan's team approached the substation from the rear, using the cover of darkness and the dense trees that surrounded the area. The plan was to disable the security systems and take out the guards silently before planting explosives on the main transformers.

As they reached the outer fence, Hassan signalled for the team to split into two groups. The first group, led by Sarah, would take out the guards in the towers, while Hassan's group would disable the security systems.

The operation began smoothly. Sarah's group moved with precision, silencing the guards one by one with suppressed weapons. Hassan, meanwhile, accessed the security control panel, bypassing the alarms and cameras with the skills he had honed in his previous life as a university professor with a penchant for hacking.

But as they moved deeper into the substation, things started to go wrong.

A guard, returning from a patrol, stumbled upon one of the bodies before it could be hidden. His shout of alarm echoed through the night, and within seconds, the entire substation was lit up with floodlights. The element of surprise was gone.

"Abort! Abort!" Hassan shouted into his radio, but it was too late. The guards were already mobilising, and the team found themselves in a firefight, outnumbered and outgunned.

Hassan made a split-second decision. "Plant the charges! We'll cover you!"

The team moved with frantic speed, setting the explosives even as bullets whizzed past them. Hassan and Sarah provided cover fire, their hearts pounding with the knowledge that they might not make it out alive.

Finally, the charges were set. "Fall back!" Hassan ordered, and the team retreated, detonating the explosives as they ran. The explosion rocked the substation, sending a massive fireball into the sky and plunging the surrounding area into darkness.

But the cost was high. As they regrouped at the rendezvous point, they realised that two members of the team were missing, Ben and Olivia, who had been providing cover during the retreat. They were later confirmed to have been captured by government forces.

In Birmingham, the story was much the same. Emily's team had been tasked with sabotaging a communications hub, a critical link in the government's command-and-control network. The plan was to disable the satellite uplinks, severing the government's ability to coordinate its response to the other attacks.

The team had infiltrated the building without incident, using forged credentials to bypass security. But as they were planting the devices on the uplinks, they were discovered by a maintenance worker who raised the alarm.

Emily's heart sank as she heard the sound of approaching footsteps and the clatter of boots on metal stairs. They were trapped, with no clear way out.

"Get those charges set!" she shouted, drawing her weapon, and taking up a defensive position at the door.

The team worked with desperate speed, their hands shaking as they finished wiring the explosives. But as they moved to retreat, the door burst open, and a squad of government soldiers stormed in, weapons raised.

A firefight erupted, the confined space amplifying the sound of gunfire to a deafening roar. Emily fought with everything she had, but it was clear they were outmatched. One by one, her team members fell, and soon she was the only one left.

With no other options, Emily detonated the charges, the explosion ripping through the building and sending the satellite dishes crashing to the ground. She managed to escape in the chaos, but her team was lost, the cost of the operation weighing heavily on her as she fled into the night.

In the days following the operation, the resistance was reeling. The coordinated strike had succeeded in its objectives, government operations were severely disrupted, key infrastructure was destroyed, and the government's ability to maintain control was shaken. But the victory came at a steep price.

Across the country, cells reported heavy losses. Several members had been killed in the fighting, while others had been captured and were now in the hands of the government, facing interrogation and possible execution. The blow to morale was significant, and the movement was left to grapple with the reality of what they had done and what they had lost.

John, Emily, Hassan, and Lily gathered in the basement of the old library once again, the atmosphere heavy with grief and exhaustion. The maps and diagrams from the operation were still spread out on the table, but now they were marked with the names of the fallen, a stark reminder of the human cost of their struggle.

"We did what we had to do," John said quietly, his voice rough with fatigue. "But we need to take stock of where we are now. We've dealt a blow to the government, but they'll come back harder. We need to be ready."

Emily nodded, her face pale and drawn. "We can't let their sacrifices be in vain. We have to keep going, keep fighting. But we need to be smarter, more cautious. We can't afford to lose more people."

Hassan, who had lost two of his closest friends in the operation, spoke up, his voice tinged with bitterness. "We knew this would happen. We knew there would be losses. But that doesn't make it any easier."

Lily, who had been uncharacteristically silent, finally spoke, her voice trembling with emotion. "We have to remember why we're doing this. It's not just about taking down the government. It's about building something better, something worth all of this."

The group fell into a sombre silence, each of them grappling with their thoughts, their own doubts. The operation had been a success, but at what cost? The weight of their decisions hung heavy in the air, a burden they would all carry with them as they continued the fight.

Chapter 11 The Enemy Within

The remnants of the warehouse were still smouldering when they arrived, the acrid smell of burned wood and melted metal hanging heavy in the air. The morning sun was struggling to break through the thick layer of smoke that covered the sky, casting an eerie, orange light over the scene. John Mason surveyed the damage with a grim expression, his hands clenched into fists at his sides. The warehouse had been one of their key supply depots, a vital link in the chain of their operations. Now, it was nothing more than a charred ruin.

"This wasn't an accident," John muttered, his voice tight with barely suppressed anger.

Beside him, Tom Harper, the disillusioned politician who had recently joined their cause, nodded in agreement, his sharp eyes scanning the area for any clues. "No, it wasn't," Tom replied, his tone measured but carrying an undercurrent of tension. "Someone knew exactly where to hit us, and when."

John shot him a sideways glance, suspicion flickering in his eyes. "And who do you think that someone is, Tom?"

Tom met John's gaze evenly, not flinching under the weight of the accusation. "I don't know, John. But I intend to find out."

Emily stood a few feet away, her brow furrowed in deep thought. She had been the one to discover the first signs, small inconsistencies, unusual movements of supplies, and now, this. The pieces were beginning to fit together in her mind, but the picture they formed was one she wasn't ready to face.

"There's more," Emily said, her voice cutting through the tension between the two men. "I found something in the records. Transactions that don't add up. Supplies that were meant for different cells but never made it. And now this... it's too much to be a coincidence."

Hassan, who had been quietly observing the scene, stepped forward, his usually calm demeanour showing signs of strain. "Are you saying we have a mole?"

Emily nodded slowly, her eyes filled with concern. "Yes. I'm almost certain of it. But I don't know who we can trust."

A heavy silence fell over the group, the weight of Emily's words sinking in. The possibility of a mole was a threat far greater than any external force. It was the kind of danger that could tear them apart from within, turning allies into enemies and friends into suspects.

John turned to face the others, his expression hardening into one of resolve. "We need to find out who it is. And quickly. We can't afford to have someone feeding information to the government. It's too dangerous."

Tom crossed his arms, his posture defensive. "And how exactly do you propose we do that, John? Start interrogating everyone? We're supposed to be fighting for something better, not turning into the very thing we're trying to destroy."

John bristled at Tom's tone, the tension between them flaring into open hostility. "We can't just sit around and do nothing, Tom. If there's a traitor among us, we need to root them out before they do any more damage."

"And what if you're wrong?" Tom shot back, his voice rising. "What if you accuse the wrong person? How much more damage will that do?"

Emily stepped between them, her presence a calming influence despite the turmoil she felt inside. "Enough," she said firmly. "This isn't helping. We need to stay focused. We'll figure this out, but we have to do it carefully. We can't afford to let this tear us apart."

The two men exchanged a tense look before reluctantly backing down. The air was thick with unspoken accusations, but for now, they were forced to put them aside.

"We'll start by reviewing everything we know," Emily continued, taking control of the situation. "Every movement, every transaction, every person who had access to this warehouse. We'll find the pattern, and that will lead us to the mole."

Hassan nodded in agreement, his analytical mind already turning over the possibilities. "I'll go through the records again, see if there's anything we missed. But we need to be discreet. If the mole realises we're onto them, they might do something drastic."

"Agreed," John said, his voice softer now, the anger in his eyes replaced by a steely determination. "We'll get to the bottom of this. No matter what it takes."

The safe house was a stark contrast to the destruction they had just witnessed. It was a small, nondescript apartment in a run-down building on the outskirts of the city. The paint on the walls was peeling, and the furniture was old and worn, but it was a safe place, a sanctuary where they could regroup and plan their next move.

The group gathered in the living room, the air heavy with the scent of stale coffee and the faintest hint of mildew. The windows were covered with thick curtains, blocking out the outside world and creating a sense of isolation. The only light came from a single lamp on the table, casting long shadows across the room.

Emily sat at the table, her laptop open in front of her, the screen displaying a series of spreadsheets and documents. Hassan stood beside her, his brow furrowed as he reviewed the information. John and Tom stood on opposite sides of the room, both men tense, their eyes never quite meeting.

"We need to go over everything," Emily said, her fingers tapping on the keyboard as she pulled up more data. "Every detail, no matter how small. We can't afford to miss anything."

Hassan leaned in, his eyes scanning the data with the precision of someone used to solving complex problems. "There's something here," he said, pointing to a line on the screen. "Look at this. A shipment of medical supplies meant for a cell in Leeds. It never arrived, but the records show it was signed for by someone named 'Webb.'"

"Webb?" John frowned, trying to place the name. "I don't remember anyone by that name in Leeds."

"Neither do I," Emily replied, her voice tight with tension. "But it's not just Leeds. There are other discrepancies. Supplies that went missing, and information that was leaked before it could be acted on. And every time, this 'Webb' shows up in the records."

Tom, who had been listening quietly, stepped forward, his expression sceptical. "So, we have a name. But how do we know it's not just a pseudonym? Someone could be using it to cover their tracks."

"That's a possibility," Hassan conceded, his voice calm and measured. "But it's a lead. And right now, it's the only one we have."

John nodded, his mind already working through the implications. "We need to find out who this 'Webb' is. If it's a real person, we track them down. If it's a pseudonym, we find out who's using it. Either way, we get answers."

Tom leaned back against the wall, his arms crossed, a hint of a smirk on his lips. "And what if it's someone in this room? How do we deal with that, John? Are you ready to start pointing fingers?"

John's eyes narrowed, his voice low and dangerous. "If it comes to that, yes. But I'd rather find the truth than start a witch hunt."

Emily intervened again, sensing the conversation was heading into dangerous territory. "We can't let this tear us apart. We need to work together and stay united. That's the only way we'll get through this."

The tension in the room was palpable, each person grappling with their own doubts and suspicions. The possibility of a mole had sown seeds of distrust, and those seeds were beginning to take root, threatening to undermine everything they had built.

Later that night, long after the others had gone to bed, Emily sat alone in the dimly lit living room, her laptop casting a pale glow on her face. The rest of the apartment was silent, the only sound the occasional creak of the old building settling into the night.

She had been combing through the records for hours, her eyes heavy with exhaustion, but she couldn't stop. There was something she was missing, something just out of reach, and she knew she had to find it before it was too late.

Her fingers moved across the keyboard, pulling up more files, more data. And then she saw it, a pattern she hadn't noticed before. It was subtle, almost imperceptible, but it was there. A series of communications, each one coded differently, but all sent from the same location.

Her heart skipped a beat as she realised what she was looking at. The communications had been sent from within their network, but the codes were ones they hadn't used in months. Someone had been sending messages to the government, and they had been doing it right under their noses.

But who? Who could it be?

Emily's mind raced as she tried to piece together the clues. The communications had been sent at irregular intervals, never from the same device, but always from the same location. And that location…

She froze, her breath catching in her throat. The location matched the safe house they were currently using.

Someone in their group was the mole.

Her first instinct was to wake the others, to confront them with what she had found. But she hesitated. What if she was wrong? What if the mole was expecting her to do exactly that, to reveal what she knew before she had all the answers?

No, she needed to be sure. She needed to find more evidence, to confirm her suspicions before making any moves. But the knowledge that the traitor was close, perhaps even in the next room, sent a chill down her spine.

She closed the laptop, her mind whirling with possibilities, and sat back in her chair, staring into the darkness. The betrayal was deeper than she had ever imagined, and the consequences of it could destroy everything they had worked for.

But she couldn't act yet. Not until she was certain.

As she sat there, the shadows of doubt and fear closing in around her, Emily knew that the days ahead would be the most dangerous yet. The enemy wasn't just outside their walls, it was within. And if they didn't act quickly, it would tear them apart from the inside.

Chapter 12 A Nation Divided

The United Kingdom was no longer a united entity. The fractures in its social and political fabric had deepened, splitting the nation into factions with competing loyalties and ideologies. The tension that had simmered for months had finally boiled over, spilling across the land, and engulfing the population in a conflict that showed no signs of abating.

London, once the beating heart of the country, was now a city at war with itself. The capital was divided into zones, each controlled by different factions. Some areas remained under strict government control, where the Union Jack still fluttered proudly over government buildings, and heavily armed soldiers patrolled the streets with an air of grim determination. These zones were bastions of the old order, where citizens who were loyal to the government hunkered down, fearful of the encroaching chaos but resolute in their belief that the government would prevail.

But just a few blocks away, the story was different. Entire neighbourhoods had fallen into the hands of the resistance, transformed into makeshift fortresses where the red, white, and blue of the Union Jack was conspicuously absent. Here, the graffiti-covered walls proclaimed messages of defiance: "FREEDOM OR

DEATH," "END THE TYRANNY," "A NATION FOR THE PEOPLE." Armed checkpoints, manned by young, determined resistance fighters, marked the boundaries of these liberated zones. The streets were lined with barricades made of abandoned vehicles and piles of debris, a stark contrast to the government-controlled areas where order still held.

The sky above London was a battlefield of its own, with drones from both sides constantly patrolling, their buzzing presence a reminder that surveillance was omnipresent. The city was a patchwork of competing ideologies, each side determined to outlast the other. The once-bustling metropolis had been reduced to a series of isolated enclaves, each clinging to its version of the truth.

In Manchester, the situation was even more dire. The city, historically a hub of industry and working-class resilience, had become a flashpoint in the conflict. The government had declared martial law, deploying military forces to crush the rebellion that had taken root in the city's sprawling suburbs. Tanks rumbled down the narrow streets, their treads chewing up the asphalt, while helicopters hovered overhead, their searchlights sweeping over the city like the eyes of a vengeful god.

The resistance, however, had not given up without a fight. They had turned the city into a fortress, using the industrial landscape to their advantage. Factories that once produced textiles and machinery had been repurposed into armouries and workshops, churning out weapons and supplies for the fight against the government. The towering smokestacks that had once symbolised the city's industrial might now stood as sentinels over a city under siege.

But the cost of resistance was high. Entire neighbourhoods had been reduced to rubble, their inhabitants forced to flee or live among the ruins. The government's relentless bombardment had taken its toll, and the people of Manchester were caught in a desperate struggle for survival. The city was divided into pockets of resistance and government control, with each side digging in for a long and brutal fight.

The local media had been co-opted by both sides, each broadcasting its own version of events. Government channels depicted the resistance as terrorists, hell-bent on destroying the country, while the resistance's underground broadcasts portrayed the government as a tyrannical regime clinging to power through violence and deceit. The truth, if it existed at all, was buried beneath layers of propaganda.

The rural areas of the UK, once idyllic landscapes of rolling hills, patchwork fields, and tight-knit communities, had become battlegrounds in their own right. The peacefulness that had once characterised the countryside was shattered, replaced by a landscape of tension, fear, and rebellion. The quaint villages and small towns that dotted the countryside were now divided, their populations forced to choose sides in a conflict that had seeped into every corner of the nation.

For many farmers and rural workers, the government had long been a source of frustration and resentment. Years of neglect, compounded by the economic devastation wrought by poor agricultural policies and the abrupt reintroduction of stringent EU regulations following Brexit, had pushed these communities to the brink. The subsidies and support systems that had once sustained British agriculture were slashed, leaving farmers struggling to make ends meet. The promised benefits of independence from the EU had never materialised, replaced instead by a tangle of red tape and restrictions that choked the life out of small farms.

The situation reached a boiling point when the government, desperate to reassert control over the faltering economy, began to enforce EU regulations with renewed vigour. Inspections became more frequent, and fines were levied for even the smallest infractions. Traditional farming practices that had been passed down through generations were suddenly deemed non-compliant, and the cost of upgrading equipment and facilities to meet the new standards was more than most small farmers could bear.

The final straw came when the government, under pressure to meet international trade obligations, began allowing large agribusinesses to buy up farmland at bargain prices, squeezing out smallholders and family farms. The land, once the backbone of rural life, was being consolidated into the hands of a few wealthy corporations, and the people who had worked it for generations were left with nothing.

In this climate of anger and desperation, many farmers and rural workers turned to the resistance as their only hope for survival. The countryside, far from being a bastion of government loyalty, became a hotbed of rebellion. Local militias formed, not to defend the government's interests, but to protect their land and way of life from further encroachment. These groups made up of farmers, labourers, and rural community members, were fierce and determined, their knowledge of the land giving them a strategic advantage over government forces unfamiliar with the terrain.

In the fields and valleys, where crops once grew in neat rows, barricades were erected, and the sound of gunfire echoed through the hills. Farmhouses, with their thick stone walls and secluded locations, became impromptu fortresses, offering shelter to resistance fighters and serving as command centres for the rural insurgency. The barns that had once housed livestock now stored weapons and supplies, hidden from the prying eyes of government patrols.

The local pubs and community centres, which had been the heart of rural social life, became places of clandestine meetings and planning sessions. Farmers who had once discussed the weather and the harvest now spoke in hushed tones about strategy and sabotage. The language of rebellion had taken root in the countryside, and it was spoken with the same passion and intensity that had once been reserved for the land itself.

The government, recognising the growing threat from these rural militias, attempted to crack down with force. But each raid, each act of repression, only served to deepen the resolve of the rural resistance. The farmers and workers who had once been the backbone of the nation's agriculture were now the backbone of the rebellion, and they fought with the ferocity of those who had nothing left to lose.

In contrast to the government's narrative, which painted the resistance as a lawless mob intent on destroying the country, the rural rebellion was driven by a deep sense of injustice and a desire to protect their way of life. These were people who had been pushed too far, who had seen their livelihoods destroyed by policies made in distant cities by politicians who had never set foot on a farm. Their fight was not just against a government, but against a system that had abandoned them.

As the rebellion spread, the countryside became a network of defiance. Villages that had once been loyal to the government began to shift their allegiance, their residents swayed by the stories of resistance fighters who came through, offering hope and a vision of a better future. The rural militias coordinated with the urban resistance, sharing resources and intelligence, and together they struck at the heart of the government's power.

The patchwork of loyalty and rebellion that defined the countryside was constantly shifting, but the momentum was clearly with the resistance. The government's attempts to quash the rebellion only fuelled it further, and the rural areas, once seen as peaceful refuges, were now among the fiercest battlegrounds in the fight for the nation's future.

In these fields, hedgerows, and hills, a new kind of patriotism was born, not one of flags and anthems, but of soil and sacrifice. The farmers and rural workers, once the forgotten backbone of the country, had become its fiercest defenders, fighting not just for themselves, but for the very soul of the nation.

The landscape itself had become a battleground. Fields that had once been green and fertile were now scarred by the tracks of military vehicles and the craters left by airstrikes. Farmhouses and barns had been converted into bunkers, and the rolling hills of the countryside were dotted with makeshift fortifications.

But the countryside also held a different kind of danger, one of mistrust and suspicion. In these close-knit communities, the fear of betrayal was ever-present. Neighbours who had known each other for generations now eyed one another with suspicion, wondering who might be collaborating with the government, who might be feeding information to the resistance. The social fabric of rural life, once so strong, was fraying under the strain of civil war.

The airwaves and the internet had become the new frontlines in the war for the nation's soul. Both the government and the resistance flooded the media with propaganda, each trying to sway public opinion to their side. The government's broadcasts were slick and professional, filled with patriotic imagery and stirring rhetoric about the need to restore order and protect the nation from the "anarchists and traitors" who sought to tear it apart. These messages were carefully crafted to appeal to the fears and anxieties of the population, painting the resistance as a lawless mob intent on plunging the country into chaos.

On the other hand, the resistance's media was raw and impassioned, broadcast from hidden locations, and spread through underground networks. Their messages were filled with stories of government brutality, images of bombed-out neighbourhoods, and testimonies from those who had suffered under the government's rule. The resistance's propaganda was designed to evoke anger and a sense of injustice, rallying people to their cause by highlighting the government's failings and the suffering of the people.

But the flood of information, much of it conflicting, left the public in a state of confusion. People didn't know who to trust, or what to believe. Families were divided, with some members supporting the government and others joining the resistance. Friendships were strained, and communities were torn apart by the competing narratives that filled the airwaves and the internet.

Amid this chaos, the resistance struggled to maintain public support. The government's smear campaigns were relentless, and every action the resistance took was twisted into something sinister. When the resistance bombed a government facility, the government portrayed it as an attack on innocent civilians. When the resistance freed prisoners from a government detention centre, the government claimed they had released dangerous criminals back onto the streets.

Emily Carter, who had become one of the key figures in the resistance's media efforts, found herself in a constant battle to control the narrative. She spent long hours in their underground studio, writing and recording messages, editing videos, and coordinating with their network of operatives to ensure their broadcasts reached as many people as possible. But it was an uphill battle, and she knew it.

"We're losing the public," Emily said one evening, her voice weary as she addressed the group in the safe house. The dim light of the room did little to soften the lines of exhaustion etched into her face. "The government is outmanoeuvring us. They've got the resources, the reach. People are scared, and fear is a powerful motivator."

John, who had been pacing the room, stopped, and turned to face her. His expression was one of frustration, but also determination. "We can't give up, Emily. We've got to keep pushing and keep getting the truth out there. People need to see what's happening."

"But how?" Hassan interjected, his tone thoughtful but tinged with concern. "Every time we make a move, they twist it against us. We're fighting a war on two fronts, one in the streets, and one in the minds of the people. And right now, we're losing the latter."

Tom, who had been sitting quietly in the corner, leaned forward, his voice cutting through the tension. "Maybe it's time we start thinking outside the box. The government has the upper hand because it control the traditional media, but the internet is still our battleground. We need to focus more on viral content, things that can't be ignored or twisted, videos that show the truth, uncensored and raw. We need to bypass the mainstream and go directly to the people."

Emily nodded, her mind already racing with possibilities. "We can do that. But it's going to be risky. We'll need to expose ourselves more and take greater risks to get the footage and stories we need. If we're caught…"

"We're already risking our lives every day," John said, his voice firm. "This is just another front in the war. We fight it the same way we fight everything else, with everything we've got."

The group fell into a contemplative silence, each member grappling with the enormity of the task before them. They were fighting not just for control of the country, but for control of the narrative, and that was a battle that would require all their ingenuity and resolve.

As the conflict dragged on, the divisions within the UK grew starker. In Scotland, an independence movement gained traction, fuelled by the desire to break away from the chaos engulfing the rest of the country. The Scottish Parliament, which had long been at odds with Westminster, declared its intention to hold an independence referendum, defying the government's attempts to maintain control. The streets of Edinburgh were filled with demonstrations, both for and against independence, as the nation teetered on the brink of its civil conflict.

In Wales, the situation was similarly tense. The Welsh Assembly caught between loyalty to the UK and the rising tide of nationalist sentiment, struggled to maintain order. The government's heavy-handed tactics only served to inflame tensions, and the resistance found fertile ground among the disillusioned and the disenfranchised. The valleys and mountains of Wales, once symbols of peace and beauty, now echoed with the sounds of conflict.

In Northern Ireland, the situation was even more precarious. The fragile peace that had been maintained since the Good Friday Agreement was shattered as old wounds were reopened. Sectarian violence flared up once more, with the resistance gaining support from those who had never fully trusted the government. The streets of Belfast were scenes of daily clashes, with the police and military struggling to maintain control.

But it wasn't just the outer regions that were feeling the strain. In the heart of England, in towns and cities that had once been bastions of loyalty to the government, cracks were beginning to show. The government's attempts to maintain order were increasingly seen as acts of repression, and the resistance found allies in unexpected places. The middle class, once a pillar of stability, began to fracture as people were forced to choose sides. The wealthy, isolated in their gated communities, clung to their privilege, while the working class, struggling under the weight of austerity and neglect, began to see the resistance as their only hope for a better future.

In the face of these growing divisions, the resistance found itself stretched thin. The more the country fractured, the harder it became to maintain cohesion within their own ranks. Each region had its priorities, and its battles to fight, and the resistance's leadership struggled to keep everyone on the same page.

John felt the strain acutely. As one of the key figures in the resistance, he was constantly traveling between different cells, trying to keep the movement unified. But it was becoming increasingly difficult. The cells in Scotland were focused on independence, while those in Wales were fighting against government repression. In the north of England, the fight was against economic inequality, while in London, the battle was for control of the capital.

"We're being pulled in too many directions," John said one evening, as he and Emily sat in a cramped, dimly lit room in yet another safe house. The walls were bare, the only furniture a battered old table and a few chairs. "We're losing sight of the bigger picture."

Emily nodded, her expression one of exhaustion. "I know. But what can we do? We can't ignore what's happening in these regions. If we don't support them, we risk losing their loyalty."

"We need to find a way to bring everyone together," John said, his voice laced with frustration. "We need a unifying message, something that cuts across all these divisions."

Tom, who had joined them after a long day of planning, leaned back in his chair, his expression thoughtful. "Maybe the problem is that we're trying to impose a single vision on a country that's no longer united. Maybe what we need to do is embrace the differences, give each region the autonomy to fight their own battles while still being part of the broader resistance."

John frowned, the idea not sitting well with him. "That sounds like a recipe for chaos."

"Maybe," Tom conceded. "But it's also how revolutions work. They're messy, they're chaotic, and they're driven by local needs and desires. We need to adapt to that reality, or we'll lose."

Emily sighed, rubbing her temples as she tried to make sense of it all. "I don't know. It feels like we're losing control."

"Maybe that's not a bad thing," Tom said quietly. "Maybe what we're seeing is the birth of something new, something that can't be controlled in the way we're used to."

John and Emily exchanged a look, both of them grappling with the enormity of what Tom was suggesting. The idea of letting go, of embracing the chaos, was terrifying. But it was also compelling.

Chapter 13 The Betrayal

The night was thick with anticipation, a suffocating heaviness that clung to the air like a damp shroud. The sky above East London was a swirling mass of dark, churning clouds, threatening to unleash a torrent of rain at any moment. The storm that had been brewing for hours seemed to mirror the tension that lay heavy on the city below. The wind, usually a restless companion in the capital, was conspicuously absent, leaving the air still and stifling as if the world itself was waiting for something to break.

In the labyrinth of narrow, winding streets and alleys that crisscrossed this forgotten corner of East London, the safe house stood, blending seamlessly into its surroundings. The building was old, its brickwork weathered by decades of neglect, the facade streaked with grime. It was the kind of place people walked past without a second glance, its anonymity its greatest defence. A crumbling relic of a bygone era, it had once been a warehouse, or perhaps a workshop, but no one could say for certain anymore. Now, it was a sanctuary of sorts, though the word felt hollow given the circumstances.

The streets around the safe house were eerily silent, the usual sounds of the city conspicuously absent. There were no distant shouts, no blaring car horns, no hum of traffic. Even the ever-present drone of airplanes flying overhead had fallen silent. The streetlights flickered weakly, their yellow glow struggling to penetrate the encroaching darkness. The pavement, slick with the promise of rain, gleamed under the sporadic light, casting long, distorted shadows that twisted and writhed like spectres. The silence was unsettling, the kind that made the hairs on the back of your neck stand on end.

The building itself was a fortress of secrets. From the outside, it appeared abandoned, the windows boarded up or covered in layers of dust and grime. A rusting fire escape clung precariously to the side of the building, its steps creaking ominously in the occasional gust of wind. The heavy wooden door at the front was weathered and splintered, barely holding together, but it was reinforced with steel on the inside, a barrier that had kept them safe so far.

Inside, the safe house was a stark contrast to the stillness outside. The basement, where the core group had gathered, was a small, dimly lit space, buried deep within the building's bowels. The air was thick with the scent of damp concrete and old wood, mingled with the acrid smell of cigarette smoke and the faint, lingering odour of sweat. The basement walls were bare brick, their rough surface cold to the touch. A few exposed pipes ran along the ceiling, occasionally dripping water onto the floor with a soft, echoing plop. The ceiling was low, just high enough for the tallest among them to stand without stooping, and the single, narrow staircase leading down to the room creaked underfoot.

The only light in the room came from a few scattered candles, their flames flickering as they cast long, wavering shadows on the walls. The candles sat in makeshift holders, empty cans, old bottles, and chipped ceramic bowls, their light barely enough to push back the darkness. The room's corners were swallowed by shadow, leaving the group huddled around the table in the centre, their faces illuminated by the soft, warm glow.

The table itself was a battered relic, its surface scarred by years of use. Deep gouges and scratches marred the wood, and one of the legs was propped up with a stack of old books to keep it from wobbling. Around it were mismatched chairs, some wooden, others metal, each one showing signs of wear. One of the chairs was missing a backrest, while another had a seat cushion so worn it was practically flat. Despite their condition, the chairs were a luxury compared to the sofa pushed against the far wall. The sofa, once upholstered in some long-faded fabric, was sagging in the middle, its springs shot, and its arms threadbare. It had seen better days, but for now, it was their only place to rest.

The room was cluttered with the detritus of their rebellion. Maps, dog-eared and creased, covered one end of the table, pinned down by empty mugs and half-burned candles. The maps were marked with a dizzying array of lines, circles, and notes scribbled in the margins, plans for operations, escape routes, and safe zones. Beside the maps, a pile of documents lay haphazardly, some stained with coffee rings, others torn at the edges. A few weapons were strewn across the table, their dark metal surfaces reflecting the candlelight, handguns, knives, and a couple of grenades, each within easy reach.

On the far wall, a large corkboard was covered in photographs, newspaper clippings, and handwritten notes connected by a web of red string. The faces of key government officials stared out from the photos, their eyes cold and unyielding, as if daring the group to come for them. Scrawled notes beside each photo listed names, locations, and details, information that had been painstakingly gathered over months of surveillance and reconnaissance.

In the corner of the room, an old radio sat on a rickety shelf, its antenna bent at an awkward angle. The radio was their lifeline to the outside world, a source of information, and a link to other cells across the country. It crackled intermittently with static, the faint voice of a resistance broadcaster cutting through every few minutes with updates and coded messages. The group listened intently to every broadcast, their ears attuned to the slightest change in tone, the subtlest hint of new danger.

The atmosphere in the room was heavy with tension, the air almost crackling with unspoken fears and anxieties. Each member of the group carried the weight of their decisions, their losses, and the knowledge that at any moment, the fragile security they had built could come crashing down. The candles flickered, casting long shadows across their faces, accentuating the lines of worry etched into their skin. Every creak of the building, every gust of wind outside, seemed to send a shiver down their spines, a reminder that they were never truly safe.

But despite the tension, there was also a sense of determination in the room, a resolve that had been forged in the fires of adversity. These were people who had been pushed to the brink, who had lost everything but their will to fight. The safe house, with all its flaws and imperfections, was more than just a hiding place, it was a symbol of their resistance, a testament to their refusal to give up in the face of overwhelming odds.

And so, as the storm gathered strength outside, threatening to unleash its fury on the city, the group huddled in the basement of the safe house, their minds focused on the task ahead. The night was dark and full of danger, but they were ready. Whatever happened, they would face it together, bound by a shared purpose and a common enemy.

The storm was coming, and they would be ready to meet it.

John stood at the head of the table, his eyes scanning the faces of his comrades. Emily, Hassan, Lily, and Tom were all there, their expressions grim and tired. The successes and failures of the last few months weighed heavily on them, but tonight, there was something else, an undercurrent of tension that none of them could shake.

Emily was the first to speak, her voice low and steady, but with a hint of unease. "We've been compromised. There's no other explanation for what happened last night."

Last night's operation, meant to disrupt a key government supply line, had gone disastrously wrong. They had walked into an ambush, barely escaping with their lives. Two of their best fighters, Sarah, and Ben, hadn't been so lucky. They were gone, and their loss hung over the group like a shroud.

Hassan, usually the voice of calm and reason, was visibly shaken. "The government knew we were coming. They were waiting for us. Someone must have tipped them off."

John's gaze hardened as he looked around the room, his mind racing. There was a traitor among them. They had suspected it for weeks, but now, after last night, there was no doubt. Someone had been feeding information to the government, someone who knew their every move.

"Who?" Lily's voice cut through the silence, sharp and angry. "Who betrayed us?"

Tom shifted uncomfortably in his seat, his eyes darting around the room as if looking for an escape. "We can't jump to conclusions. We need to think this through."

But John wasn't listening. His instincts, honed over years of military service, were screaming at him. Something wasn't right, and he knew it. He took a step toward Tom, his voice dangerously calm. "You were the last one to know the details of the operation, Tom. You were the one who suggested the route we took."

Tom's eyes widened, and he shook his head, his voice rising in panic. "Wait a minute, John. You don't think I had anything to do with this, do you? I've been with you since the beginning. Why would I betray you?"

John didn't answer immediately. He took another step closer, his eyes never leaving Tom's. The room was so silent that you could hear the distant rumble of thunder outside, the storm drawing nearer. "You tell me, Tom. Why would you?"

The others watched their expressions a mix of shock and suspicion. Emily's heart pounded in her chest. She had trusted Tom, had believed in him. But now, doubts were creeping in. There had been signs, small inconsistencies, things that hadn't added up. And then there was the pattern she had discovered, the coded messages that had been sent from within their network.

"Stop it," Emily said, her voice trembling with emotion. "This isn't helping. We need to stay focused."

But John wasn't backing down. He reached into his pocket and pulled out a small device, a voice recorder. "I found this in the warehouse," he said, holding it up for everyone to see. "It was hidden in a place only someone with inside knowledge would know about. I played it back. It's full of conversations we've had over the last few weeks. Every plan, every move."

Tom's face drained of colour. He opened his mouth to speak, but no words came out.

"How do you explain that, Tom?" John's voice was icy, each word laced with accusation. "How do you explain a recording device planted in one of our most secure locations?"

"I don't know," Tom stammered, his eyes darting from John to Emily to Hassan. "I swear, I don't know how it got there."

But John wasn't convinced. He pressed on, his voice growing louder. "I trusted you. We all trusted you. And now, because of you, Sarah and Ben are dead. How much did they pay you, Tom? How much did you sell us out for?"

Tom recoiled as if struck, his face contorting with a mix of fear and anger. "You don't understand. You don't know what they did to me."

For a moment, the room was silent, the weight of Tom's words hanging in the air.

"They got to me," Tom said, his voice barely above a whisper. "They threatened my family, my wife, my children. They showed me pictures, pictures of what they would do if I didn't cooperate. I had no choice."

Emily felt her heart sink as she listened to Tom's confession. She could see the pain in his eyes, the desperation. But it didn't make it any easier. "And so you betrayed us," she said softly, the hurt clear in her voice. "You chose them over us."

"I didn't want to," Tom pleaded, his voice breaking. "I tried to protect you. I gave them just enough to keep them off my back, but I didn't think they'd move so fast. I thought I could buy us more time."

"More time?" John's voice was venomous. "You think that justifies what you did? You think that excuses the fact that you've been leading them right to us this whole time?"

Tom shook his head, tears streaming down his face. "I'm sorry. I'm so sorry. But I had no choice. They would have killed my family."

"And what about us?" Lily's voice was fierce, her hands clenched into fists. "We're your family too, or did you forget that? Did you forget that we trusted you, that we put our lives in your hands?"

Tom's sobs filled the room, the sound of a man who had lost everything. "I was trapped. They had me trapped. Please, you have to believe me. I never wanted this to happen."

But the damage was done. The betrayal was out in the open, and there was no going back.

Just as the weight of Tom's confession settled over the group, a loud crash echoed through the building. The sound of splintering wood and shattering glass filled the air, followed by the unmistakable clatter of boots on the stairs.

The government had found them.

John's military instincts kicked in immediately. "We're under attack! Everyone, move!"

Chaos erupted as the group scrambled to gather their weapons and escape. The safe house, once their sanctuary, was now a death trap. The air was thick with the acrid smell of gunpowder as government forces stormed the building, their rifles blazing.

John fired back, his eyes scanning the room for any sign of an escape route. But the government forces were too fast, too well-coordinated. They had been waiting for this moment, and now they were closing in.

Emily grabbed Lily's arm, pulling her toward the back door. "We have to go, now!"

But before they could reach it, the door burst open, and a squad of soldiers poured in, cutting off their escape. Emily raised her weapon, her heart pounding in her chest, but she knew it was over. There were too many of them.

Across the room, John and Hassan fought desperately to hold their ground, but it was a losing battle. The soldiers were closing in from all sides, their numbers overwhelming. John fired one last shot before a bullet caught him in the shoulder, sending him crashing to the floor.

"John!" Emily screamed, but there was nothing she could do. She watched in horror as the soldiers closed in, her heart breaking as she realised they were out of time.

"Get down!" Hassan shouted, pulling Emily and Lily to the floor just as a grenade was tossed into the room. The explosion rocked the building, the force of it knocking them all back. The walls shook, debris rained down from the ceiling, and the lights flickered out, plunging the room into darkness.

When the dust settled, the safe house was a scene of devastation. The walls were pockmarked with bullet holes, the furniture reduced to splinters, and the air thick with smoke and the scent of blood. John lay motionless on the floor, his breathing shallow, blood pooling around him. Hassan was beside him, his face pale and ashen, struggling to stay conscious.

Emily's ears rang from the explosion, her vision blurred, but she forced herself to move. She crawled over to John, her hands shaking as she tried to stop the bleeding. "John, stay with me. Please, stay with me."

But John's eyes were unfocused, his skin cold and clammy. He managed a weak smile, his voice barely a whisper. "It's... okay... Emily..."

"No, it's not okay," Emily choked out, tears streaming down her face. "We need you. I need you."

But John's eyes fluttered shut, his breathing growing weaker. "You... can do this... without me..."

And then he was gone.

Emily let out a sob, her body shaking with grief. But there was no time to mourn. The soldiers were still out there, still searching the building. She had to get out, had to get Lily and Hassan to safety.

With one last look at John, she forced herself to her feet, grabbing Lily's hand and pulling her toward the back door. "We have to go. Now."

Hassan struggled to his feet, his face twisted in pain, but he managed to follow them. They stumbled through the debris-strewn hallway, the sound of soldiers shouting orders and boots thundering on the stairs growing louder behind them.

They burst through the back door, into the alleyway behind the building. The rain was pouring down, the storm finally breaking, drenching them in seconds. But they didn't stop. They ran, their feet pounding the wet pavement, their breath coming in ragged gasps.

They had lost everything. The safe house, their comrades, and John. But they couldn't stop now. They had to keep going, had to survive. The resistance depended on it.

But as they disappeared into the night, the realisation hit them like a cold, hard slap. They were fractured, broken, and betrayed. The future of the resistance was uncertain, and the trust that had bound them together had been shattered.

And as the storm raged on, the truth became painfully clear. They were no longer just fighting a government. They were fighting to keep their movement from tearing itself apart.

Chapter 14 The Darkest Hour

The betrayal had shattered them. The remnants of the resistance were scattered across the country like the pieces of a broken mirror, each fragment reflecting a different face of despair. The safe houses that had once been sanctuaries were now empty, their occupants forced into hiding by the ruthless efficiency of the government's crackdown. The safe house in East London, the heart of their operation, was nothing more than a pile of rubble, a tombstone for those who had fallen in the raid.

Emily Carter sat alone in a small, remote cottage nestled deep within the Scottish Highlands. The air was crisp and cold, the sky a dull grey, threatening snow. The landscape around the cottage was stark and unforgiving, rugged hillsides covered in heather and gorse, their jagged peaks hidden by low-hanging clouds. The wind whipped through the valleys, howling like a wounded animal, its mournful cry echoing through the silence of the deserted landscape.

The cottage itself was little more than a stone shack, its walls thick and sturdy, built to withstand the harsh elements. Inside, the only warmth came from a small, crackling fire in the hearth, casting flickering shadows across the rough wooden walls. The furniture was sparse, a single wooden chair, a small table, and a narrow bed covered with a threadbare blanket. A few scattered items lay on the table: a half-empty bottle of whiskey, a small transistor radio, and a crumpled map of the UK, marked with red circles around the few remaining safe zones.

Emily sat by the fire, staring into the flames, a glass of whiskey in her hand. Her once determined and resolute features were now etched with lines of exhaustion and grief. The firelight reflected in her eyes, which were filled with a deep, lingering pain, the kind that comes from losing not just friends, but hope. The silence of the mountains pressed in on her, amplifying the void she felt inside.

She had lost John, the man who had been her anchor, her partner in the fight. His death had left a gaping wound in the resistance and in her heart, one that she wasn't sure would ever heal. The weight of the losses, the betrayals, and the endless fight had worn her down, grinding away at her resolve until there was little left but a hollow shell. She had fought for so long, but now, she wasn't sure if she had anything left to give.

Her thoughts were interrupted by the soft crackle of the radio on the table. It was tuned to one of the resistance's hidden frequencies, the signal weak but just clear enough to make out the words.

"...contact in Birmingham. Potential recruits... Need to regroup..."

Emily listened, the words washing over her without much impact. She had heard similar messages over the past few days, but none had sparked the hope she so desperately needed. The resistance was trying to rebuild, to find its footing after the devastating losses they had suffered, but without John, it felt like trying to navigate in the dark.

As the message faded into static, Emily took a long sip of her whiskey, feeling the burn as it went down. She had thought of leaving, of walking away from the fight and finding some forgotten corner of the world to disappear into. But every time she considered it, John's face would come to her mind, his voice urging her to keep going, to not let his death be in vain.

A soft knock at the door broke the silence. She hesitated for a moment, her hand instinctively reaching for the pistol lying on the table. But then she remembered that the only person who knew where she was, the only one who could find her now, was Lily.

"Emily? It's me, Lily."

Emily exhaled slowly, placing the gun back on the table. "Come in."

Lily pushed open the door and stepped inside, the cold wind following her in before she quickly shut it behind her. She was bundled up in a thick coat, her cheeks flushed from the biting air, but the weariness in her eyes mirrored Emily's. She looked around the small cottage, taking in the sparse surroundings before meeting Emily's gaze.

"You found me," Emily said, her voice flat, devoid of emotion.

Lily gave a small, sad smile. "It wasn't easy. You're not exactly on the map."

Emily gestured to the chair across from her. "Sit."

Lily took a seat, the wood creaking under her weight, and for a moment, they sat in silence, the crackling fire the only sound in the room. Finally, Lily spoke, her voice low and hesitant. "Emily, I know it's hard. I miss him too. But we can't give up. We can't let what happened destroy us."

Emily looked at her, her eyes filled with a mixture of grief and determination. "It's not just about John, Lily. It's about everything. We've lost so much... so many people... and now we're scattered, broken. How do we keep going?"

Lily reached across the table, taking Emily's hand in hers. "We keep going because we have to. Because if we don't, then everything we've fought for, everything John gave his life for, will be for nothing."

Emily closed her eyes, feeling the tears welling up. She had been trying so hard to hold it together, to be strong for the others, but it was becoming harder with each passing day. "I don't know if I can do this without him, Lily. He was the one who kept us together."

"And now it's up to us to keep it together," Lily said firmly. "John believed in you, Emily. He believed in us. We have to honour that by continuing the fight."

Emily nodded, wiping away a tear that had escaped down her cheek. "You're right. We can't give up."

Lily squeezed her hand, offering a small, reassuring smile. "We'll get through this, Emily. We'll find a way."

A week earlier, Lily Thompson stopped what she was doing and looked down at her hands, they trembled slightly.

Lily Thompson had always been a fighter. From the moment she joined the resistance, she had thrown herself into the cause with a passion and energy that had inspired those around her. But now, alone in an abandoned warehouse on the outskirts of Birmingham, she felt the crushing weight of loneliness and fear pressing down on her.

The warehouse was cold and dark, the only light coming from a few bare bulbs hanging from the high ceiling. The vast space was filled with the remnants of its former life, rusted machinery, broken pallets, and piles of discarded materials. The air was heavy with dust, and the floor was covered in a thick layer of grime. The only sound was the distant hum of the city, muffled by the thick walls of the warehouse.

Lily had taken refuge here after the raid on the safe house. It wasn't much, but it was a place to hide, to regroup, and to plan her next move. She had managed to gather a few supplies, a sleeping bag, some canned food, and a laptop with a weak internet connection, but she knew it wouldn't be enough. She needed allies, people she could trust, to continue the fight.

She sat cross-legged on the floor, her laptop balanced on her knees, the screen casting a pale blue glow on her face. She had been reaching out to old contacts, trying to reestablish the network that had been shattered by the government's crackdown. It was slow going, and every message she sent was a risk, but she couldn't stop. The resistance needed to rebuild, and she was determined to make it happen.

Her fingers flew over the keyboard, typing out messages to people she hadn't spoken to in months, people who might be willing to join her in the fight. She knew she was taking a gamble, but it was a risk she had to take. The government had tried to break them, to scatter them to the winds, but Lily was determined to show them that the resistance was still alive, still fighting.

As she sent off another message, a wave of exhaustion washed over her. She hadn't slept properly in days, her mind too full of plans and fears to rest. But she couldn't afford to stop now. There was too much at stake.

Her thoughts drifted to John, to Emily, to the others who had survived the raid. She didn't know where they were if they were even alive, but she had to believe they were out there somewhere, fighting just like she was. The thought gave her strength and a renewed sense of purpose.

She would build something new, something stronger. She would find others who shared her vision, and who believed in the cause as much as she did. And together, they would continue the fight.

Lily closed the laptop and leaned back against the cold, hard wall, her eyes closing for just a moment. She was alone now, but she wouldn't be for long. The resistance was more than just a group of people, it was an idea, a belief in something better, something worth fighting for. And as long as that belief lived on, so would the resistance.

Emily and Lily travelled together after their meeting in the Highlands, finding temporary refuge in a secluded cabin nestled deep within the Lake District. The cabin was surrounded by dense woodland, the towering trees providing cover from prying eyes. The air was crisp and fresh, the scent of pine and earth filling their lungs as they made their way through the thick underbrush. The only sounds were the rustling of leaves in the wind and the distant call of a bird, the peace of the natural world a stark contrast to the turmoil they had left behind.

The cabin itself was small and rustic, its wooden walls weathered by years of exposure to the elements. Inside, it was cosy, with a small fireplace crackling in the corner, casting a warm glow over the worn wooden floors and simple furnishings. There was a small kitchen with a few basic supplies, a table with two chairs, and a bed tucked away in the corner, covered in a thick woolen blanket. It was a place of refuge, a moment of calm in the storm.

Emily sat at the table, a map spread out in front of her, her brow furrowed in concentration. Lily was by the fireplace, stirring a pot of soup that was simmering over the flames. The quiet between them was comfortable, a shared silence that spoke of understanding and unspoken fears.

As the soup bubbled, Lily walked over to the table, placing two bowls down, and sitting across from Emily. They ate in silence for a while, the warmth of the food a small comfort against the cold outside.

Finally, Emily broke the silence. "We need to regroup. Find out who's still with us, who we can trust."

Lily nodded, taking a sip of her soup. "I've been reaching out to people, trying to rebuild the network. It's slow, but we're making progress."

Emily's gaze remained fixed on the map, her mind working through the logistics. "We can't afford to stay in one place for long. The government's reach is too far. We need to stay mobile, keep ahead of them."

"I know," Lily agreed. "But we also need to find a way to rebuild trust, to show the others that we're still in this together."

Emily looked up at her, her expression thoughtful. "We've been through hell, Lily. We've lost so much. But you're right. We can't let that stop us. We need to keep going."

Lily reached across the table, taking Emily's hand in hers. "We'll get through this, Emily. We'll find a way."

Emily squeezed her hand, a small gesture of solidarity and hope. "We will."

As the news of the devastating raid on the London cell spread across the country, a wave of shock and sorrow swept through the ranks of the resistance. The loss of John and Hassan, two of the movement's most steadfast leaders, was a heavy blow, one that left many questioning the future of their cause. Whispers of despair and uncertainty echoed through the hidden networks, and for a brief moment, it seemed as if the flame of rebellion might flicker and die.

But in the hearts of the rebels scattered across the UK, that flame did not extinguish. Instead, it burned hotter, fiercer, fuelled by the memory of those they had lost and the injustice that had claimed them. In the streets of Manchester, in the alleys of Birmingham, in the quiet countryside of Wales and Scotland, people gathered in secret, their faces grim but determined. They mourned the fallen, but they did not allow grief to paralyse them.

John's name became a rallying cry, a symbol of their shared struggle, a reminder of the sacrifices that had already been made. The image of his unwavering resolve, of his unyielding courage, was etched into their minds, a beacon that guided them through the darkness. Hassan's quiet wisdom, and his strategic brilliance, were remembered with reverence, his teachings now guiding those who had once looked to him for leadership. The loss of these men was a wound that cut deep, but it was also a call to arms, a reason to fight harder, dig in, and refuse to back down.

In the cold, stone-walled cellars beneath pubs and in the hidden rooms of remote farmhouses, the resistance planned and prepared. The government had dealt them a cruel blow, but it had not broken them. Far from it. The attack on the London cell had only steeled their resolve. They knew the risks and understood the dangers better than ever before, but they also knew what was at stake. The oppression, the brutality, the lies, it all had to end. And they would be the ones to end it.

Across the country, messages were passed in code, supplies were hidden away, and alliances were forged. The cells that remained connected in a way that transcended geography, they were united by a shared purpose, a common enemy. And while the losses they had suffered were great, the cause was greater still.

There was fear, of course, fear of more betrayals, of further losses, of the uncertain future that lay ahead. But that fear was tempered by something stronger: hope. Hope that, despite the odds, they could still win. Hope that, even in the darkest of times, there was light to be found. And in that hope, they found the strength to carry on.

The fire in their hearts burned bright, a flame that refused to be snuffed out. It burned for John, for Hassan, for Sarah, for Ben, and for all those who had given their lives for the dream of a free and just nation. It burned for the people who had yet to join the fight, for the innocents caught in the crossfire, and for the future generations who would inherit the world they were struggling to build.

As the chapter closed on its darkest hour, it was clear that the resistance was far from defeated. They were battered, yes, scarred by loss and betrayal, but they were also unbroken. And as long as they remained unbroken, there was hope. Hope that one day, they would see the dawn of a new revolution, a dawn that John and Hassan had fought so hard to bring about.

And so, with heavy hearts and resolute minds, the rebels across the UK prepared for what was to come. The path ahead was fraught with danger, but they were ready to walk it. Together, they would continue the fight, driven by the fire in their hearts and the unshakable belief that, no matter how dark the night, the dawn would come.

Chapter 15 Regroup and Rebuild

The farmhouse was tucked away in the rolling hills of the Welsh countryside, far from the prying eyes of the government's surveillance networks. It was an old, sturdy building, its stone walls thick with age and weathered by centuries of wind and rain. The surrounding landscape was a patchwork of green fields, crisscrossed by dry stone walls and dotted with ancient trees. The air here was fresh and clean, carrying the scent of damp earth and pine, a stark contrast to the smoky, oppressive atmosphere of the cities.

Inside, the farmhouse was warm and inviting, a refuge from the outside world. The main room was centred around a large, open fireplace, the flames crackling and casting a warm glow over the wooden beams overhead. The furniture was simple but comfortable, a few armchairs, a long wooden table, and shelves lined with books and old trinkets. The walls were adorned with faded tapestries and paintings, relics of a time long past. In the corner, a small radio played softly, tuned to a local station that only broadcast static now, the result of government control over the airwaves.

The farmhouse had become the new heart of the resistance, a place where they could regroup and rebuild after the devastating losses they had suffered.

It was here, in this quiet, secluded spot, that the remaining members of the resistance had gathered to plan their next move.

Emily stood by the window, her gaze fixed on the horizon. The landscape outside was peaceful, almost idyllic, but she couldn't shake the feeling that it was only a matter of time before the government found them again. They had been lucky to escape the last time, but luck wouldn't hold forever. They needed a new strategy, something that would allow them to stay one step ahead of their enemies.

Behind her, Lily was seated at the long table, a map spread out in front of her. She was marking potential locations for new safe houses, her brow furrowed in concentration. Her energy and determination had been a driving force in the days following the raid, but even she was beginning to show signs of strain. The loss of John and Hassan had hit her hard, but she was determined not to let it break her.

As the door creaked open, Emily turned to see a small group of figures entering the farmhouse. They were the new core of the resistance, survivors from the various cells that had been scattered across the country. Each of them carried the weight of their losses, but there was also a fire in their eyes, a resolve that had only grown stronger in the face of adversity.

Among them was Hassan's younger brother, Aamir, a quiet, introspective man who had taken up his brother's mantle in the wake of Hassan's death. He had been a professor of political science before the crackdown, and his calm, analytical mind made him a valuable addition to the group. Beside him was Sarah, a former journalist who had narrowly survived the brutal raid on the London safe house. She had been on her way to a meeting outside the city when the attack occurred, her late departure from the safe house saving her life by mere minutes.

After the raid, Sarah had gone into deep hiding, moving from one safe location to another, using her extensive knowledge of the city's underbelly to stay one step ahead of the government forces. Despite the overwhelming loss and the guilt that gnawed at her for not being there when it all went down, Sarah didn't retreat. Instead, she used her time in hiding to reestablish communication lines with surviving members of the resistance and other disillusioned groups. Her sharp wit and deep connections within the media made her an invaluable asset in their fight to win hearts and minds. She crafted new narratives, disseminating them through underground channels and encrypted networks, ensuring that the truth of what had happened to their comrades in London would not be buried by government propaganda. Her efforts kept the spirit of the resistance alive, even as the group struggled to regroup and rebuild.

Emily greeted them with a nod, her expression serious. "Thank you all for coming. I know it's not easy to keep going after everything that's happened, but we need to regroup and rebuild. We owe it to those we've lost."

Aamir stepped forward, his voice steady despite the tension in the room. "Hassan believed in this movement, in all of us. He wouldn't want us to give up now. We have a responsibility to continue what he started."

Lily looked up from the map, her voice filled with determination. "We've been fighting in the shadows for too long. It's time we took our message to the people. If we can win their hearts and minds, we can build a movement that the government can't ignore."

Sarah nodded in agreement, her eyes bright with the fire of conviction. "We need to be smart about this. The government controls the media, but we have the internet and social media. We can reach people in ways they can't control. We need to show them the truth, the reality of what's happening."

Emily listened, her mind already racing with possibilities. She had always been the strategist, the one who could see the bigger picture, but the events of the past few weeks had shaken her confidence. Now, as she looked around the room at the faces of those who had survived, she felt a renewed sense of purpose. They had been dealt a devastating blow, but they were still standing. And as long as they were standing, they could fight.

"Lily's right," Emily said, her voice firm. "We need to start thinking bigger. We've been playing defence for too long, reacting to what the government does. It's time we took the initiative and started dictating the terms of this fight."

Aamir spoke up, his tone thoughtful. "We need to build alliances with other groups, people who are disillusioned with the government but haven't yet joined the resistance. There are plenty of them out there, but they're scared, unsure of who to trust. We need to reach out to them, show them that we're organised, that we're fighting for something real."

Sarah leaned forward, her eyes alight with the possibilities. "If we can bring those groups together, we'll be stronger, more united. We can coordinate our efforts, strike at the government from multiple fronts. They won't be able to stop us if we're spread out and working together."

Emily nodded, feeling the energy in the room begin to shift. This was what they needed, a new strategy, a new focus. They couldn't bring back those they had lost, but they could honour their memory by continuing the fight, by building something stronger, something that could stand against the government's tyranny.

"We'll start small," Emily said, her mind already working through the logistics. "We'll rebuild the core group, focus on security and secrecy. But at the same time, we'll reach out to other groups and build alliances. We'll create a network that the government can't break, no matter how hard they try."

Lily grinned a fierce determination in her eyes. "We'll make them regret ever thinking they could silence us."

As the meeting continued, the group began to outline their plans in more detail, the atmosphere in the farmhouse shifting from one of quiet reflection to a charged, almost electric energy. Aamir, usually so reserved, found himself speaking with a newfound urgency, his mind racing as he connected the dots between potential allies and the strategic locations where they could set up new safe houses. His voice, calm and measured, carried the weight of his brother's legacy, but now it was infused with a personal resolve, a determination to ensure that Hassan's death would not be in vain. He could feel the eyes of the group on him, and for the first time, he didn't shy away from their gaze. Instead, he embraced it, feeling a sense of responsibility that went beyond mere duty, it was personal, almost sacred.

Sarah, seated beside Aamir, felt a surge of adrenaline as she contributed to the discussion, her sharp mind cutting through the fog of uncertainty that had plagued them since the raid. Every idea she voiced, every plan she helped to craft, felt like a small victory against the despair that had threatened to consume them all. As she talked about the importance of controlling the narrative, of using the media to their advantage, she could feel the tension in her chest easing, replaced by a fierce determination. The guilt that had weighed on her since she narrowly escaped the raid began to dissipate, replaced by a clear sense of purpose. She wasn't just a survivor, she was a fighter, and this meeting was the first real step towards reclaiming what they had lost.

Lily, who had initially been wary of the newcomers, felt her scepticism melt away as the plans took shape. She had always been driven by passion, by a burning need to act, but now she felt something new, a sense of cohesion, of unity. As the group discussed potential allies, she could see the pieces of a larger puzzle falling into place, and for the first time since John's death, she felt truly connected to the cause again. The fear that had been gnawing at her was still there, but it was tempered by growing confidence in their ability to outmanoeuvre the government. Her heart pounded in her chest, but it wasn't just from fear, it was from the thrill of knowing they were on the brink of something significant.

Emily had been the driving force behind this meeting and listened to the others with a sense of quiet satisfaction. The farmhouse, once a place of solitude and retreat, was now alive with the buzz of ideas, of hope rekindled. She could see the fire returning to the eyes of her comrades and could feel the momentum building as they outlined their plans. The loss of John still hung heavy over her, but at this moment, she felt his presence, felt that he would be proud of what they were building. As the conversation turned to the logistics of setting up new safe houses, she found herself smiling, a small, private smile that spoke of hope, of belief in their cause. They weren't just surviving, they were planning, strategising, and fighting back.

The farmhouse, with its thick stone walls and cosy interior, had transformed from a place of quiet reflection into the heart of their renewed resistance. The air buzzed with ideas, with the energy of a group that had found its footing again. As they spoke, the lingering shadows of doubt and despair were pushed back, replaced by a light that shone brighter with each passing minute. They were no longer just a group of individuals bound by loss, they were a team, united by a common goal, a shared vision of a future worth fighting for. And in that farmhouse, amidst the flickering firelight and the hum of determined voices, the seeds of that future were sown.

As the hours passed and the fire burned low, Emily found herself standing by the window once more, looking out at the darkening landscape. The road ahead would be long and difficult, but for the first time in weeks, she felt a sense of optimism. They had been beaten down, but they were not defeated. They had lost much, but they had also gained something invaluable, a renewed sense of purpose, a deeper understanding of what they were fighting for.

The farmhouse would be their new base, their place to regroup and rebuild. From here, they would take the fight to the government, not with guns and bombs, but with ideas, with truth, with the power of the people. They would rebuild the resistance, stronger and more united than ever before.

As the first light of dawn began to creep over the hills, Emily turned away from the window, her mind set on the tasks ahead. The night had been long and dark, but now, a new day was beginning. And with it, a new chapter in their fight for freedom.

The resistance was far from over. It was reborn.

Chapter 16 The Government Counteroffensive

The city was a fortress now, its streets lined with armoured vehicles, its skies patrolled by drones that hovered like silent sentinels. The once-bustling metropolis, known for its vibrancy and diversity, had become a place of fear and oppression. The government's response to the growing rebellion had been swift and brutal, transforming the urban landscape into a battlefield where every citizen was a potential enemy. The air was thick with tension, the kind that made people walk faster, talk quieter, and glance over their shoulders with every step.

For those who still dared to walk the streets, there was an overwhelming sense of being watched, of being hunted. The government's surveillance apparatus had grown insidious, with cameras on every corner, drones hovering ominously overhead, and informants embedded in every neighbourhood. People no longer spoke freely, even in their own homes, for fear that a careless word might be overheard by the wrong person. Conversations were conducted in hushed tones, eyes darting nervously to the shadows, where danger seemed to lurk at every turn.

The public, though cowered and weary, still clung to a semblance of resistance, a quiet, smouldering defiance that refused to be fully extinguished. It was in the small acts of rebellion, the graffiti scrawled in hidden corners, the underground networks that persisted despite the risks, and the knowing glances exchanged between strangers in the streets. But these acts came at a cost. Trust, once the bedrock of the community, had eroded, replaced by suspicion and fear. Former neighbours, friends, and even family members were no longer safe confidants. The government's relentless propaganda machine had sown seeds of doubt, turning people against each other in a bid to root out dissent.

A heavy darkness had settled over the city, not just in the physical sense, but in the hearts of its inhabitants. The bright lights that once illuminated the skyline now seemed cold and distant, casting long shadows that only deepened the sense of isolation. The vibrant street markets, the lively cafés, and the bustling parks, all had been silenced, replaced by the echoing footsteps of soldiers and the constant hum of surveillance drones. Curfew had turned the city into a ghost town after dark, with only the brave or the desperate venturing out into the night.

Fear was a tangible presence, hanging over the city like a storm cloud, ready to unleash its fury at the slightest provocation. But beneath that fear, there was also anger, a deep, simmering rage that threatened to boil over at any moment. The government had underestimated the resilience of its people, mistaking their silence for submission. But in reality, every day of oppression only fuelled the growing resentment, the unspoken desire for freedom that had not yet been crushed.

The people endured, but it was a fragile endurance, one that could break or erupt into something far more powerful. The city was a powder keg, and the government's heavy-handed tactics were the spark that could set it all ablaze. For now, the streets remained quiet, the people subdued. But the resistance, though battered and bruised, still lived in the hearts of many. And as the government tightened its grip, it unwittingly sowed the seeds of its undoing.

In this city of shadows and whispers, where every corner could hold a threat, and every conversation could be a trap, the people waited. They waited for a sign, for a moment when they could rise up and reclaim what had been taken from them. The air was thick with tension, yes, but also with the potential for change, a change that, despite the government's best efforts, could not be held back forever.

Martial law had been declared overnight, with a curfew imposed from dusk till dawn. The once lively streets were now deserted after dark, the silence only broken by the occasional roar of military vehicles patrolling the neighbourhoods. The familiar landmarks, cafés, shops, and parks had been transformed into checkpoints, their entrances guarded by soldiers with cold eyes and fingers resting lightly on the triggers of their rifles.

The government's crackdown was not confined to the cities alone. Across the country, from the rural farmlands to the coastal towns, the iron fist of the regime was felt. Communication networks were heavily monitored, travel restricted, and any sign of dissent was met with immediate and ruthless suppression. The rebellion that had once inspired hope now faced the full might of a government determined to crush it at any cost.

Beneath the streets of the city, hidden from the prying eyes of the government, the core group of the resistance had gathered in a makeshift bunker. The bunker was an old Cold War relic, long abandoned and forgotten until it was rediscovered by the resistance. It was a cold, damp place, with low ceilings and narrow passageways that seemed to close in on you the deeper you went. The walls were lined with rusting metal and exposed wires, the floor a patchwork of cracked concrete and dirt. The only light came from a series of dim, flickering bulbs strung haphazardly along the ceiling, casting long shadows that danced with every movement.

Inside, the atmosphere was thick with tension. The group had grown smaller in recent weeks, their numbers dwindling as more and more of their comrades were captured or killed. Those who remained were tired, worn down by the relentless pressure of a fight that seemed increasingly futile. Resources were scarce, their supply lines cut off by the government's new tactics, and the isolation they felt was suffocating. But despite the odds, the fire of resistance still burned within them, fuelled by the knowledge that surrender was not an option.

Emily stood at the centre of the room, her face illuminated by the dim light of a map spread out on the table before her. The map was marked with red circles, each one representing a location that had fallen to the government's forces. She traced the lines with her finger, her expression grim as she took in the extent of the damage. The government was closing in, and they were running out of time.

"We can't keep this up," Aamir said, his voice heavy with exhaustion. He was seated on a metal chair, his hands clasped tightly in his lap. The calm, analytical demeanour that had once defined him was now frayed at the edges, worn down by the relentless strain of their situation. "They're picking us off one by one. If we don't find a way to regroup, to reconnect with the other cells, we'll be next."

Lily, seated across from him, nodded in agreement. Her usual fire was tempered by the weight of the recent losses, but it still flickered in her eyes. "We need to get out of the city. It's too dangerous here.

They know we're still active, and they won't stop until they've wiped us out."

Emily looked up from the map, her gaze moving from Aamir to Lily and then to the others in the room. "We can't abandon the city," she said, her voice firm. "It's the heart of the rebellion. If we lose it, we lose everything. But we need to be smart about this. We can't keep fighting the way we have been. They've adapted to our tactics, and we're too exposed."

Sarah, who had been leaning against the wall, her arms crossed over her chest, spoke up. "We need to rethink our approach. The public executions are meant to instil fear, to make people think twice about supporting us. But we can turn that against them. We need to show the people what the government is doing and expose their brutality for what it is. If we can win back the hearts and minds of the people, we can create the kind of pressure the government can't ignore."

The mention of the public executions hung heavy in the air, a grim reminder of the government's ruthless tactics. It was a clear message, resist, and you will pay the price. But it was also a gamble, one that the group knew could backfire on the regime if they played their cards right.

"Public support is key," Aamir agreed, his voice regaining some of its usual steadiness. "But we're running out of resources. We can't keep relying on the same strategies. We need to find new allies and new ways to get supplies. And we need to be prepared for the worst."

Emily nodded, her mind already racing with possibilities. "We'll have to decentralise, spread out into smaller, more mobile units. We'll set up new safe houses outside the city, places they won't expect us to be. And we'll start focusing on guerrilla tactics, hit-and-run operations that keep them off balance."

The group exchanged glances, each of them understanding the gravity of what Emily was proposing. It was a risky plan, one that would require them to abandon the safety of the city and venture into the unknown. But it was also their best chance of survival.

"We'll need to stay in constant communication," Lily said, her voice laced with determination. "We can't afford to lose contact with each other. If they manage to cut us off, we're done for."

Sarah uncrossed her arms and stepped forward. "I'll work on reestablishing our networks. We still have contacts in the media, people who can help us get our message out. We need to show the people that we're still fighting, that we haven't given up."

Aamir nodded, the wheels in his mind already turning. "I'll reach out to the remaining cells, see who's still active and willing to join forces. We can't do this alone. If we're going to survive, we need to be united."

Emily looked around the room, at the faces of those who had become her family in this fight. They were tired, yes, but they were also resolute. The government might have launched a major operation to crush them, but they hadn't succeeded yet. And as long as there was breath in their bodies, they wouldn't give up.

"We've faced worse," Emily said, her voice firm. "And we've come through it. We'll come through this too. But we need to stay focused, stay strong. The government is scared, they know they're losing control. That's why they're lashing out. But that fear is a weakness, and we can use it against them."

The group nodded in agreement, the tension in the room easing slightly as they absorbed Emily's words. They knew the road ahead would be difficult, but they also knew they had no other choice. They were the resistance, and they would keep fighting, no matter the cost.

The square had once been a place of celebration, a gathering spot for festivals, concerts, and protests. But now, it was a place of fear. The government had chosen it as the site for their public executions, a brutal display meant to crush the spirit of the rebellion once and for all.

The stage was set in the centre of the square, flanked by soldiers in full combat gear. The air was thick with tension, the crowd that had been forced to gather there was silent and grim. The government had made it clear, attendance was mandatory, and anyone who refused would be arrested on the spot.

Emily, hidden among the crowd, watched with a mixture of rage and sorrow as the condemned were brought onto the stage. They were rebels, captured in the recent crackdown, their faces bloodied and bruised but defiant. The government wanted to make an example of them, to show the world that resistance was futile.

But as Emily watched, something unexpected happened. The crowd, which had been cowed into silence, began to stir. Whispers spread through the ranks, and soon those whispers grew louder, turning into a low, rumbling murmur. The people were beginning to resist, not with violence, but with their voices, their refusal to be silenced.

As the first rebel was led to the noose, a shout rang out from the crowd. "Down with the government!" It was quickly followed by another, and then another, until the square was filled with the sound of defiance. The soldiers tensed, their hands hovering over their weapons, but the crowd was undeterred. They had seen enough, endured enough, and they would not be silenced any longer.

Emily felt a surge of hope as she watched the scene unfold. The government had miscalculated. In their desperation to crush the rebellion, they had only strengthened it. The public executions, meant to instil fear, had instead ignited a fire that would not be easily extinguished.

The government's counteroffensive had begun, but so too had the next phase of the resistance. The road ahead would be long and fraught with danger, but as Emily looked around at the faces of those who stood with her, she knew one thing for certain, they would not go quietly.

The rebellion was far from over. It was only just beginning, a phoenix rising from the ashes of the fire that had sought to consume it. What the government had failed to understand was that in their attempt to stamp out the flames of dissent, they had only served to ignite a greater blaze. The loss, the pain, and the devastation, it had not weakened the resolve of those who fought for freedom. Instead, it had forged them into something stronger, more resilient, more determined.

Like embers smouldering beneath the surface, the spirit of the rebellion had not been extinguished. It had merely gone underground, waiting for the right moment to surge back into the open. Now, that moment was at hand. The attempts to crush them had only stripped away the fear and uncertainty, leaving behind a core of unwavering conviction. Those who remained were battle-hardened, tested by fire, and united in their purpose like never before.

The rebellion was no longer just a scattered collection of cells fighting a losing battle. It was becoming an unstoppable force, growing in strength and numbers as word spread of the atrocities committed by the regime. Every act of oppression, every public execution, every draconian measure only served to draw more people to the cause, to fan the flames of resistance. In the dark corners of the city, in the hidden enclaves of the countryside, and in the hearts of ordinary citizens who had once been too afraid to act, the rebellion was rekindling.

It was a movement reborn, rising with a ferocity that the government could no longer contain. The rebels were no longer just defending themselves, they were preparing to strike back, to take the fight to those who had tried to crush them. Their resolve was no longer simply to survive, but to win, to reclaim their country from the hands of tyranny.

The rebellion was a living, breathing entity now, fed by the collective will of those who refused to be silenced. It was a force of nature, unstoppable and inevitable, growing stronger with each passing day. The government's grip was slipping, and they knew it. What they had thought was the end was only the beginning of something far more powerful.

The rebellion was not just surviving, it was thriving, transforming into a force that would rise above the ashes, brighter and more determined than ever before. And as it grew, it became clear that this was not just a battle for survival; it was a fight for the very soul of the nation. A fight that the rebellion, now reborn and reinvigorated, was prepared to see through to the end.

Chapter 17 Turning the Tide

The prison was a grim, hulking structure of concrete and steel, a fortress designed to hold those deemed too dangerous to roam free. It loomed over the surrounding neighbourhood, its tall, barbed-wire fences casting long shadows across the abandoned streets. The building itself was a testament to the government's iron grip, a place where the voices of dissent were silenced behind thick walls and locked gates.

Inside, the atmosphere was suffocating, the air heavy with the stench of fear and despair. The cells were cramped, dark, and cold, and their occupants were left to rot in isolation. The guards, dressed in black uniforms and armed to the teeth, patrolled the corridors with an air of smug authority. This was a place where hope came to die, where the government kept its most dangerous enemies under lock and key, far from the eyes of the public.

But tonight, the rebellion had other plans.

Across the street, on the rooftop of an old, crumbling building, Emily crouched low behind the parapet, her eyes fixed on the prison fortress. The night was cool, a light breeze rustling through her hair as she adjusted her earpiece and checked her watch. The plan was set, and every detail was meticulously mapped out. Now, all that was left was to execute it.

Around her, the rest of the team was in position. Lily, nimble and focused, was stationed on the fire escape, her eyes scanning the streets below for any sign of movement. Sarah was in a nearby alleyway, ready to coordinate the escape route once the prisoners were free. And Aamir, calm and collected, was positioned at the building's entrance, prepared to create a diversion if necessary.

"Everyone in position?" Emily's voice was barely above a whisper as she spoke into her earpiece.

"Ready," came Lily's response, her voice tight with anticipation.

"Standing by," Sarah added, her tone calm but tinged with tension.

"All set," Aamir confirmed, his voice steady as always.

Emily took a deep breath, her heart pounding in her chest. This was it, the moment they had been preparing for. If they succeeded tonight, it would be a major victory for the rebellion, a chance to strike a blow against the government and boost the morale of their dwindling forces. If they failed… she pushed that thought aside. Failure was not an option.

"On my mark," she said, her voice firm. "Three… two… one… go."

Inside the prison, the power suddenly cut out, plunging the building into darkness. The guards, momentarily disoriented, fumbled for their flashlights, their confusion evident in the scattered beams of light that flickered across the walls. It was the opening the rebels had been waiting for.

Emily moved swiftly, her steps silent as she navigated the darkened corridors of the prison. The air was thick with the stench of damp concrete and despair, a suffocating reminder of the countless souls who had been trapped within these walls. Every creak of the floor beneath her feet, every distant clatter of metal against metal, sent a jolt of anxiety through her, but she pushed it down, focusing on the task at hand. She had memorised the layout of the prison over weeks of preparation, tracing the blueprints in her mind until they became second nature. Every twist and turn, every hidden corner and locked door was etched into her memory, a mental map that she now followed with unwavering determination.

She approached the first checkpoint, where a pair of guards stood, their postures rigid, their weapons at the ready. Her heart pounded in her chest, the familiar surge of adrenaline sharpening her senses. There was no room for hesitation. With a breathless precision, Emily launched into action. She moved like a shadow, quick and lethal, her body a blur as she closed the distance between herself and the guards. One guard barely had time to register her presence before she struck, a swift blow to his throat rendering him unconscious before he could even cry out. The second guard turned, eyes wide with shock, but Emily was already upon him, her movements fluid and practiced. In a matter of seconds, both guards were down, their weapons lying useless on the cold, hard floor.

"Checkpoint one clear," she whispered into her earpiece.

Above Emily's head, Lily, moving through the ventilation ducts above, dropped silently into the control room. She quickly disabled the remaining security systems, her fingers flying over the keyboard with practiced ease. The monitors that lined the walls flickered off, their screens going black one by one.

"We're in," she reported, a hint of triumph in her voice.

Emily stood there for a moment, her breath coming in quick, controlled bursts. The danger wasn't over, but she allowed herself a fleeting sense of satisfaction, her training had not failed her. But there was no time to dwell on it. She had to keep moving. Every second counted.

The corridors stretched on, a labyrinth of despair that seemed to twist and turn endlessly. Emily's senses were on high alert, every shadow and distant sound a potential threat. The prison was a place of horror, and she could feel its weight pressing down on her as she moved deeper into its belly. She had been in many dangerous situations before, but this felt different. The stakes were higher, the cost of failure unimaginable. The lives of her comrades depended on her, and that knowledge spurred her forward, pushing aside the nagging doubts that whispered in the back of her mind.

Finally, she reached the cell block where the rebels were being held. The doors were heavy, reinforced steel, with small, barred windows that offered only the faintest glimpse of the suffering within. Emily's heart clenched as she approached the first door. She had known these people, fought alongside them, shared hopes, and fears with them. To see them now, reduced to this, was almost too much to bear. But she couldn't afford to let emotion cloud her judgment. They needed her to be strong, to be the leader they could rely on.

She found the control panel for the cell doors, her fingers moving deftly over the buttons. Each door unlocked with a heavy click, the sound echoing ominously through the corridor. As the first door creaked open, Emily braced herself, unsure of what she would find.

The figure inside was huddled in the corner, barely recognisable as the person she had once known. Their clothes were torn, their skin bruised and pale from the lack of sunlight. The eyes that met hers were hollow, filled with a mixture of fear and disbelief. For a moment, Emily struggled to find her voice, the sight of her comrade in such a state nearly overwhelming her. But she couldn't afford to falter.

"It's me," she whispered, her voice hoarse with emotion. "We're getting you out of here."

The rebel blinked as if trying to comprehend her words. Slowly, they rose to their feet, every movement betraying the pain they were in. Emily reached out, steadying them as they stumbled forward. The sight of their broken body, their spirit hanging by a thread, filled her with a cold fury. This was what the government had done, reduced brave fighters to shells of their former selves.

She moved quickly to the next cell, the process repeating itself. Each time, she was met with the same heartbreaking sight, comrades who had been battered, starved, and left to rot. But there was also something else, a flicker of hope that reignited in their eyes as they realised they were not alone, that they were being rescued. Emily spoke to each one, her voice firm but gentle, urging them to hold on, to keep moving.

"Stay with me," she said, her tone both commanding and comforting. "We're almost out. Just a little further."

Some were too weak to walk on their own, and Emily found herself supporting them, half-carrying those whose legs could barely hold them up. She felt their weight, the physical and emotional burden of their suffering, and it fuelled her determination. She wouldn't let them down. She couldn't.

The group moved slowly through the corridors, Emily leading them with a fierce resolve. The fear that had gnawed at her earlier was still there, but now it was tempered by a burning sense of purpose. These were her people, and she would see them to safety, no matter the cost. She whispered words of encouragement as they moved, urging them to keep going, to not give up. Every step forward was a victory, every door they passed was a testament to their will to survive.

The exit was in sight now, just a few more steps. The sounds of the approaching guards grew louder, but Emily didn't let it shake her. They were so close. She could feel the tension in the air, the desperation of those around her. But she also felt something else, a rekindling of the spirit that had brought them all together in the first place. Even in their weakened state, the rebels held on to the hope that had sustained them through their darkest hours.

"We're almost out," Emily said, her voice a mix of urgency and determination.

As they reached the final door leading to the outside, Lily rejoined them, having secured the control room. They pushed through the door, emerging into the cool night air just as the first government vehicles arrived on the scene.

As they burst through the final door and into the cool night air, Emily felt a surge of relief wash over her. But she didn't allow herself to relax, not yet. They were free of the prison, but the danger was far from over. The vehicles were waiting, engines running, and she quickly helped the rebels into the vans, urging them to move as quickly as they could.

"You're safe now," she repeated, more for herself than anyone else. "We've got you."

Sarah, waiting in the alleyway, caught sight of the first group of prisoners being led out by Emily. They were gaunt, their eyes hollow from weeks of confinement, but there was a spark of hope in their expressions as they realised they were being rescued.

"Come on," Sarah urged them, guiding them toward the waiting vehicles. "We've got you."

Aamir, who had been monitoring the outside perimeter, suddenly spotted a convoy of government vehicles approaching. His heart skipped a beat, but he remained composed. He quickly relayed the information to the others.

"We've got company," he warned. "Move fast."

Emily, now leading the last group of prisoners through the prison's back corridors, quickened her pace. The sound of boots on the ground echoed ominously through the halls. The government was closing in.

"We need to go, now!" Sarah called out, helping the prisoners into the waiting vans. The engines roared to life, and within seconds, they were speeding away from the prison, the sound of sirens growing fainter in the distance.

As the last of the rebels climbed into the van, Emily took one final look at the prison. The dark, oppressive structure loomed behind them, but it no longer had power over her. They had done it, they had struck a blow against the government and reclaimed some of their own. It was a small victory, but a victory, nonetheless.

She climbed into the van, the door slamming shut behind her as they sped away into the night. The faces of the rescued rebels, filled with a mixture of exhaustion and hope, were a reminder of what they were fighting for. Emily knew that the road ahead would be difficult, and that there would be more battles to come. But tonight, they had turned the tide, and for the first time in a long while, she allowed herself to believe that they could win this war.

The escapees were taken to a hidden warehouse on the outskirts of the city, a safe house that had been prepared in advance. The warehouse was a large, cavernous space, filled with crates and equipment that the rebellion had managed to gather over the months. It was dimly lit, with a few scattered lights casting long shadows across the concrete floor.

Inside, the atmosphere was a mix of relief and tension. The rescued prisoners, though free, were still visibly shaken, their eyes darting nervously around the unfamiliar space. Emily, Lily, Sarah, and Aamir gathered them together, offering water and blankets, doing their best to provide some comfort after the ordeal they had endured.

One of the prisoners, a man in his late forties with a grizzled beard, looked up at Emily with a mixture of gratitude and disbelief. "I didn't think anyone was coming for us," he said, his voice hoarse. "Thank you."

Emily nodded, her expression softening. "We don't leave our own behind. You're safe now."

As the group began to settle in, Aamir pulled Emily aside, his expression serious. "We have to move them soon. The government will be looking for them, and it won't take long for them to figure out where we took them."

Emily nodded in agreement. "We'll split them up, send them to different safe houses. We can't risk keeping them all in one place."

At that moment, the door to the warehouse creaked open, and a figure stepped inside. The group tensed, but Emily quickly recognised the newcomer, a tall man in a government uniform, his face partially hidden by the shadow of his cap.

"Lieutenant James?" Emily asked, her voice filled with cautious surprise.

The man stepped forward, removing his cap to reveal a head of greying hair and a face lined with weariness. "It's me," he confirmed, his voice low. "I couldn't stay with them any longer. I've seen what they do... what they're planning to do. It's wrong, all of it. I want to help you."

The group exchanged glances, a mix of suspicion and hope flickering in their eyes. Aamir stepped forward, his expression unreadable. "Why now? Why turn against them after all this time?"

Lieutenant James looked down, his shoulders slumping slightly. "I've seen too much. The executions, the torture... it's not what I signed up for. I can't be a part of it anymore. I want to make it right if I can."

Emily studied him for a long moment before nodding. "If you're serious about this, we can use your help. But know this, if you betray us, you won't get a second chance."

James met her gaze with unwavering resolve. "I understand. I'm here to help."

Later that night, Emily, Aamir, Lily, and Sarah gathered in a small apartment that served as one of their safe houses. The room was sparsely furnished, with only a few chairs, a table, and a single lamp providing light. The atmosphere was tense, the events of the night still fresh in their minds.

"We did it," Lily said, breaking the silence. There was a note of disbelief in her voice as if she was still processing the reality of their success. "We did it."

Sarah smiled, though it was tinged with exhaustion. "We're not done yet. But this... this was a win. We needed that."

Emily leaned back in her chair, her mind already working on their next move. "We've shown them that we're not finished. The public is starting to see the truth, and now we have someone on the inside. This could be the turning point."

Aamir, always the strategist, nodded thoughtfully. "We have momentum now. But we need to be careful. The government will strike back harder than ever. We have to be ready."

They all knew he was right. The government would not take this loss lightly, and there was still a long road ahead. But for the first time in weeks, they felt a sense of hope, a belief that, against all odds, they could turn the tide in their favour.

The rebellion was far from over. But tonight, they had taken a step forward, a step that could change everything. The victory was small, but it was significant. And as they sat in that dimly lit apartment, the weight of their actions settling over them, they knew that they had reignited something powerful, a belief in their ability to win, to make a difference.

The tide was beginning to turn, and with it, the possibility of a new dawn.

Chapter 18 A New Dawn

The warehouse stood on the edge of the city, once a forgotten relic of industrial decline, now repurposed into the nerve centre of a growing movement. The early morning light streamed through the dusty, cracked windows, casting long rays that danced across the concrete floor. The air was filled with the hum of activity, people moving in and out, plans being whispered, maps being unfurled on makeshift tables. The warehouse was alive with the energy of a revolution rekindled, a place where hope had been reborn from the ashes of despair.

Emily stood near one of the tables, her eyes scanning the map before her. It was marked with red and blue lines, and arrows indicating the flow of resources, potential targets, and areas of government control. But the lines had begun to blur, the map no longer a representation of a city under siege, but of a city being reclaimed, one piece at a time. The rebellion had found its footing again, and the mood inside the warehouse reflected this new sense of purpose.

John, though no longer physically present, had left behind a legacy that was impossible to ignore. His leadership, his determination, had become the backbone of the resistance. In his absence, Emily had stepped into the role he had once filled, her resolve hardening with each passing day. She was no longer just a strategist, a voice of reason, she was a leader, one who carried the weight of the movement on her shoulders.

Across the room, Lily was deep in conversation with a group of young recruits. Her energy was infectious, and her passion was undeniable. She had grown from the fiery idealist she once was into a true leader, someone who inspired others to take up the cause. The recruits hung on her every word, their eyes wide with admiration and determination. Lily had a way of making people believe, of giving them the courage to fight back against the darkness that had enveloped their lives.

Aamir, ever the strategist, approached Emily with a quiet intensity. He placed a hand on her shoulder, drawing her attention away from the map. "We're ready," he said, his voice low but steady. "The cells are organised, the recruits are trained, and the support base is growing every day. We've made contact with several disillusioned groups within the government. They're willing to help us from the inside."

Emily nodded, a small smile playing at the corners of her lips. "Good. We need all the help we can get. The government won't go down without a fight, but if we strike decisively, we can end this once and for all."

Aamir's gaze drifted to the map, his mind already working through the logistics of what was to come. "We'll need to coordinate our efforts carefully. The final action has to be precise and calculated. We can't afford any mistakes."

Emily's eyes hardened with resolve. "There won't be any. We've come too far to fail now."

Later that day, Emily and Lily found a quiet corner of the warehouse to talk, away from the hustle and bustle of the main operations. The room was small, with only a single window that let in a narrow beam of light. Dust motes floated lazily in the air, the only movement in an otherwise still space. The walls were bare, save for a few tattered posters from a bygone era. It was a stark contrast to the activity outside, a moment of calm before the storm.

Emily sat on the edge of a wooden crate, her hands folded in her lap. Lily leaned against the wall, her arms crossed, her expression thoughtful. There was a heaviness in the air, a weight that both women felt but neither spoke of directly.

"He would be proud of you, you know," Lily said, breaking the silence. Her voice was soft, almost reverent.

Emily looked up, her eyes meeting Lily's. There was no need to ask who she was referring to. John's absence was a constant presence in their lives, a void that could never be filled. But his spirit lived on in the choices they made, in the steps they took toward victory.

"I hope so," Emily replied, her voice tinged with sadness. "I just want to make sure we don't waste what he gave us. We have to see this through, for him, for everyone we've lost."

Lily nodded a fierce determination in her eyes. "We will. We have to. There's too much at stake."

There was a pause, the weight of their conversation settling over them. Finally, Emily spoke again, her tone more resolute. "I need you to take on more responsibility, Lily. We're going to need every strong leader we have in the days ahead. The recruits look up to you, they trust you. And they'll follow you."

Lily's eyes widened slightly, a mix of surprise and pride flashing across her face. "You really think I'm ready for that?"

Emily gave her a small, encouraging smile. "I know you are. You've come a long way, Lily. You're not just a fighter anymore, you're a leader. And we need leaders now more than ever."

Lily straightened, her posture shifting from uncertainty to resolve. "I won't let you down. I won't let any of us down."

"I know you won't," Emily replied, her voice firm. "We're in this together. All of us."

As the day wore on, the core group gathered around a large table in the centre of the warehouse. The room was filled with the low murmur of voices, the shuffling of papers, and the occasional scrape of chairs against the concrete floor. The air was thick with anticipation, the gravity of their discussion palpable.

Emily, Aamir, Lily, and a few other key members stood around the table, the map of the city spread out before them. Red markers indicated their targets, key government buildings, communication hubs, and military installations. Blue markers represented their safe houses, supply lines, and known allies. The plan they were about to put into motion would be their most ambitious yet, a coordinated strike designed to cripple the government's ability to maintain control.

Emily took the lead, her voice calm but commanding. "We have to hit them where it hurts. If we can take out their communication hubs and cut off their supply lines, we'll throw them into disarray. The military installations are heavily fortified, but if we can disrupt their operations, even for a short time, it will give us the window we need to move on the government buildings."

Aamir nodded, his eyes scanning the map as he spoke. "Timing is everything. We'll need to coordinate with our allies inside the government to make sure they're in position to act when we do. If we can take out their leadership, even temporarily, it will send a shockwave through their ranks."

Lily chimed in, her tone decisive. "We'll need to make sure the public knows what's happening. If we can control the narrative, show them that we're not just rebels, we're the ones fighting for their freedom, it could turn the tide of public opinion in our favour."

Sarah, who had been quietly listening, leaned forward, her gaze intense. "I'll handle the media. We have contacts in the underground press who can get the message out quickly. If we do this right, it won't just be a victory on the battlefield, it will be a victory in the hearts and minds of the people."

Emily met each of their gazes in turn, her expression one of fierce determination. "This is it. Everything we've worked for, everything we've sacrificed, it all leads to this. We can't afford to hesitate. We have to be decisive, united, and unwavering in our resolve."

There was a collective nod of agreement, the room filled with the weight of their shared purpose. They knew the risks and understood the stakes, but there was no turning back now. The movement had emerged from the darkness stronger, more unified, and more determined than ever before.

As they finalised their plans, the atmosphere in the warehouse shifted from tense anticipation to a quiet, steely resolve. They were no longer a fragmented group of rebels fighting a losing battle. They were a force to be reckoned with, a movement poised to strike at the heart of a regime that had underestimated their strength.

Later, as dusk settled over the city, Emily found herself on the rooftop of the warehouse, looking out over the urban landscape. The city stretched out before her, a sprawling tapestry of concrete and steel, where the old and the new mingled in a chaotic yet somehow harmonious blend. The fading light of the day bathed everything in a warm, golden hue, casting long, slanting shadows that seemed to stretch out and touch the very edges of the horizon. It was a time of transition, where day met night, and the city seemed to hold its breath, suspended between the two.

The buildings that rose from the ground like monoliths were bathed in the soft glow of the setting sun, their harsh lines softened, their imposing structures rendered almost gentle in the twilight. These were the same buildings that had once inspired dread, symbols of a government that had ruled with an iron fist, their dark windows reflecting the cold, unfeeling nature of the power they represented. But now, as Emily gazed upon them, they no longer held the same sense of fear and oppression. Instead, there was a sense of vulnerability in their towering presence, as if the very foundations on which they stood were beginning to crumble.

From this vantage point, Emily could see the heart of the government's power, the tall, imposing structures that dominated the skyline. They had once seemed invincible, casting a shadow over the entire city, their presence a constant reminder of the regime's dominance. But now, in the light of the fading day, they looked different, less like fortresses of control, and more like relics of a bygone era, relics that were slowly being eroded by the tide of change that was sweeping through the streets below.

The city itself seemed to be transforming. The oppressive weight that had hung over it for so long, like a dark cloud blotting out the sun, was beginning to lift. There was a sense of release in the air, a collective exhale as the people who had endured so much began to feel the stirrings of hope once more. The heavy blanket of fear and dread was being peeled back, layer by layer, revealing the resilient spirit that had always been there, buried beneath the surface, waiting for the right moment to emerge.

The streets below, once silent, and empty under the watchful eyes of surveillance drones and patrols, were coming alive with movement and energy. Even from her high vantage point, Emily could sense the change. There was a new rhythm to the city, a pulse that beat stronger with each passing day. It was the heartbeat of a rebellion that refused to die, that had only grown stronger in the face of adversity.

As she stood there, taking it all in, Emily felt a sense of calm settle over her, a calm born not of resignation, but of determination. The city, her city, was waking up from a long nightmare, and she was a part of that awakening. The fear that had once gripped her, that had threatened to suffocate her and everyone she cared about, was dissipating, replaced by a steely resolve.

Those tall, ominous buildings on the skyline no longer held the dread they once had. They were no longer symbols of unassailable power, but rather, monuments to a regime that was losing its grip. They stood as reminders of what they were fighting against, but also of what they were fighting for, a future where those buildings would no longer cast such long shadows, where the light of day would shine freely on every corner of the city.

The black weight that had pressed down on the city was being ripped away, torn apart by the hands of those who had suffered under it for too long. The sun was setting, but Emily knew that it was also rising, bringing with it the promise of a new dawn. And as the last rays of daylight slipped below the horizon, she felt a surge of hope, a belief that they were on the brink of something extraordinary. The city was changing, and with it, the tide of history was turning in their favour.

Lily joined her, the two women standing side by side in silence for a moment, both lost in their thoughts.

"We're really going to do this," Lily said quietly, her voice filled with a mix of awe and determination.

Emily nodded, her gaze fixed on the horizon. "Yes, we are. And this time, we're going to win."

Lily looked over at her, a small smile playing at the corners of her lips. "John would be proud of you, Emily. Proud of all of us."

Emily's expression softened, a warmth spreading through her at the thought. "We're carrying on his legacy, Lily. And we're going to make sure it wasn't in vain."

The two women stood there for a long time, side by side in a shared silence that spoke louder than any words could. As the last light of day slowly surrendered to the encroaching night, the warm glow of the sun faded into deep purples and blues, casting the city in a soft, shadowed embrace. The world below seemed to hold its breath, the usual hum of life muted in the stillness of dusk. Yet, amidst the quiet, there was a palpable sense of anticipation, a feeling that something was shifting, like the first tremors before an earthquake.

Emily and Lily could feel it, a rising tide of resistance that surged through the city like a pulse, strong and undeniable. It was as if the city itself was coming alive, shaking off the chains that had bound it for so long. The atmosphere was electric, charged with the energy of countless lives converging on a single purpose. The people were no longer willing to bow under the weight of oppression; they were standing taller, their backs straightening as they prepared to reclaim what had been taken from them. The rebellion was no longer a flicker in the dark; it was a blaze, growing brighter and hotter with each passing moment, and the final battle was drawing near.

As Emily looked out over the skyline, she felt a mixture of emotions swirling within her. There was determination, fierce and unyielding, a resolve to see this through, no matter the cost. But there was also a flicker of fear, a small, quiet voice that whispered of the uncertainties that lay ahead. The coming battle would be the most difficult they had ever faced, a clash that would test their strength, their courage, and their unity. She knew the risks and understood the sacrifices that would be demanded of them. But she also knew that they had no choice. This was the moment they had been fighting for, the moment when they could finally strike at the heart of the regime that had cast such a long shadow over their lives.

Emily's thoughts drifted to those they had lost, John, Hassan, and so many others whose names were now etched into the fabric of their cause. Their absence was a wound that had not yet healed, a constant reminder of the price they had already paid. But it was also a source of strength, a reason to keep fighting. She could feel them with her, their spirits intertwined with her own, urging her forward. They had given everything for this, and she would not let their sacrifice be in vain.

Beside her, Lily was equally deep in thought. She had come so far, grown so much since the early days of the rebellion. The fiery idealism that had once driven her had been tempered by the harsh realities of their struggle, but it had not dimmed. If anything, it burned brighter now, fuelled by the experiences that had shaped her into the leader she had become. She felt a strange sense of calm as she looked out over the city, a calm that came from knowing they were on the right side of history. The fear was still there, lurking in the corners of her mind, but it was overshadowed by a sense of purpose so strong it was almost tangible.

Lily could feel the weight of the battle ahead, the enormity of what they were about to undertake. But with that weight came hope, a hope that was rooted in the belief that they could win, that they could bring about the change they had fought so hard for. The city below, once a symbol of the regime's unyielding power, now seemed different, less imposing, more vulnerable. It was as if the city itself was ready for change, ready to embrace the dawn that was coming.

The two women stood there, side by side, their gazes fixed on the horizon as night fully enveloped the city. The darkness was thick, but it did not feel oppressive. Instead, it felt like a prelude to something new, a canvas waiting to be painted with the colours of freedom. They could sense the countless lives connected to their own, the countless hearts beating in time with the rhythm of resistance. There was a unity now, a bond that could not be broken, and it filled them with a quiet confidence that they would prevail.

As the first stars began to twinkle in the sky, Emily and Lily shared a glance, a look of mutual understanding and shared resolve. The final battle was approaching, and it would be the culmination of everything they had endured, everything they had sacrificed. But it was also a new beginning, a chance to build a future free from the tyranny that had overshadowed their lives for so long. They were ready, ready to fight, ready to lead, and ready to win.

And as they turned to descend from the rooftop, back into the heart of the movement that had become their lives, they carried with them the knowledge that the dawn was coming. A new dawn, born from the fire of their rebellion, stronger and more brilliant than anything that had come before. And this time, they would not be denied.

The new dawn was breaking, not just for the movement, but for the nation. And as Emily and Lily stood on that rooftop, they knew that the future they had fought so hard for was within their grasp. All they had to do was reach out and take it.

Chapter 19 The Gathering Storm

The room was bathed in the cold, sterile glow of fluorescent lights, a sharp contrast to the warm hues of the sunset outside. The walls were lined with monitors displaying real-time feeds from surveillance drones, satellite imagery, and intercepted communications. A massive digital map of the city dominated one wall, its surface covered in flashing red and green markers that indicated areas of government control and suspected rebel activity.

Around the large, rectangular table at the centre of the room, a group of high-ranking officials and military leaders sat in tense silence. The air was thick with the weight of the decisions they were about to make, decisions that would determine the fate of the nation. General Webb, now fully in command of the government's military response, stood at the head of the table, his eyes hard as he surveyed the room.

Webb was a man who had built his career on decisive action and ruthless efficiency. Born into a family with a long military tradition, he had grown up steeped in the values of discipline, authority, and a deep-seated belief in the supremacy of order over chaos. From an early age, it was clear that Webb was destined for the military, and he had embraced that destiny with an unwavering focus. He excelled at the academy, rising quickly through the ranks due to his tactical brilliance, unyielding discipline, and a reputation for getting the job done, no matter the cost.

His early career had seen him posted to conflict zones around the globe, where he had earned a name for himself as a soldier who was not afraid to make hard decisions. Webb had a knack for quelling uprisings with a combination of military might and psychological warfare, using fear as a tool to maintain control. His methods were often brutal, swift crackdowns on dissent, public executions of rebel leaders, and a heavy reliance on surveillance and intimidation to keep the populace in line. But his superiors had always praised his results, caring little for how they were achieved.

When the situation in the UK began to deteriorate, and the government found itself increasingly challenged by a growing rebellion, Webb was the obvious choice to lead the military response. His track record of success in suppressing insurrections abroad made him the government's best hope for restoring order at home. But what they had failed to recognise, or perhaps chose to ignore, was that Webb's approach was one-dimensional. He knew only one way to deal with opposition: crush it completely, without regard for the long-term consequences.

As he stood at the head of the table, Webb exuded an air of absolute confidence. In his mind, the rebels were nothing more than a ragtag group of dissidents, a nuisance to be eradicated with the right application of force. He had overseen the introduction of martial law in major cities, transforming them into virtual war zones. He had ordered mass arrests, public executions, and a sweeping campaign of fear and repression designed to snuff out any flicker of resistance. To Webb, these were necessary actions, collateral damage in the pursuit of a greater good.

But in his single-minded focus on crushing the rebellion, Webb had failed to see the bigger picture. He did not realise that his heavy-handed tactics were fuelling the very fire he sought to extinguish. Every act of brutality, every life taken, every family torn apart by his orders only served to strengthen the resolve of the resistance and to draw more people to their cause. The more Webb tightened his grip, the more the people slipped through his fingers, rallying behind the rebels in their fight for freedom.

Webb's ego had grown in tandem with his power. He had come to see himself as the saviour of the nation, the one man who could restore order and lead the country back from the brink of chaos. His superiors had given him near-unlimited authority, and he wielded it with an iron fist, convinced that his way was the only way. To him, the government's survival depended on his ability to crush the rebellion swiftly and decisively, and he was determined to do just that, regardless of the cost.

But what Webb did not see, what his ego would not allow him to see, was that the government's position was far more precarious than he realised. The rebellion was not just a military threat; it was a symptom of a deeper, systemic failure. The government's inability to address the underlying issues of inequality, corruption, and repression had given rise to the very movement Webb now sought to destroy. And in his blind pursuit of victory, he was pushing the nation closer to a tipping point, where the people's anger and desperation would become unstoppable.

As Webb looked around the table, he saw only the faces of subordinates who would follow his orders without question, and who would carry out his plans with the same ruthless efficiency that had defined his career. He did not see the doubt in their eyes, the unease that had begun to take root as the situation spiralled further out of control. He could not hear the whispers of dissent among the ranks, the growing realisation that Webb's approach might be leading them all to disaster.

In his mind, the path forward was clear: strike hard, strike fast, and leave nothing standing in the wake of the military's advance. He was certain that with enough force, the rebellion would be broken, and order would be restored. But what Webb could not grasp was that his methods were not just a means to an end, they were accelerating the collapse of the very order he sought to preserve.

As he began to outline the details of the impending crackdown, Webb's voice was firm, his tone brooking no dissent. He was a man who believed in the power of control, in the idea that with enough discipline and force, any problem could be solved. But as the storm clouds gathered over the nation, it became increasingly clear that Webb's grip on the situation was not as strong as he believed. The rebellion was not weakening; it was growing stronger, fuelled by the very oppression that Webb had used to keep it at bay.

As the officials and military leaders listened to Webb's plans, some could not shake the feeling that they were standing on the edge of a precipice, being led by a man who could not see the ground crumbling beneath their feet.

"We've confirmed reports of increased rebel activity in the eastern districts," Webb said, his voice cold and authoritative. "They're mobilising, likely preparing for a large-scale offensive. We cannot afford to let them gain any more ground."

One of the ministers, a man with a narrow face and a nervous demeanour, spoke up. "What about the civilians in those areas? We've already had reports of collateral damage from previous operations. Public support is wavering."

Webb's gaze sharpened his tone cutting. "This isn't about public support anymore. It's about survival. If we don't crush this rebellion now, there won't be a government left to support. We need to act decisively. We target the known rebel strongholds, take out their leadership, and reassert control over the city. Any resistance is to be met with overwhelming force."

There was a murmur of uneasy agreement around the table. They all knew what Webb's plan entailed, martial law, mass arrests, and, if necessary, lethal force. But there was little room for dissent in a room filled with men and women who had long since traded their principles for power.

Webb turned back to the map, his finger tracing a line across the city. "We'll start with a sweep of the eastern districts. We have intel on several key rebel safehouses. We hit them hard, and we hit them fast. We can't give them time to regroup. Once we've secured the area, we'll move west, pushing them back to the outskirts. By the time we're done, there won't be a safe place left for them in this city."

As the officials began to discuss logistics and resource allocation, Webb's mind was already on the battlefield. He had spent his career suppressing uprisings and quelling dissent, but this was different.

The rebels were not just an enemy, they were a symbol of everything that had gone wrong with the regime he served. They were a mirror reflecting the corruption, the lies, the brutality. And now, they had to be shattered.

The atmosphere in the warehouse was a stark contrast to the cold, calculated efficiency of the government war room. The large, open space was filled with the sound of hurried footsteps, the rustle of papers, and the low murmur of conversation. Maps and plans were spread out across the tables, illuminated by the dim glow of overhead lights. The air was thick with tension, a tension born not of fear, but of anticipation.

Emily stood at one of the tables, surrounded by the core members of the resistance. Her face was set in a mask of determination, but there was a storm brewing beneath the surface, an internal conflict that threatened to pull her in two different directions. She had spent the day coordinating with their cells across the city, finalising the plans for their counterstrike. But even as she focused on the task at hand, her mind kept drifting to the letter she had received that morning, the one that now sat tucked away in her jacket pocket.

It had been from her mother, a simple letter written in her familiar, flowing script. It had been filled with words of worry, of love, of a plea for Emily to come home, to leave the rebellion behind before it was too late. The letter had been a stark reminder of everything she had left behind, her family, her old life, the future that had once seemed so certain. And now, as the final confrontation loomed, she found herself torn between the cause she had given everything for and the people she had once sworn to protect.

Lily approached, her steps light but purposeful. She had grown into her role as a leader, her once-youthful idealism now tempered by the realities of war. But her spirit had not dimmed; if anything, it burned brighter than ever. She could sense the turmoil in Emily, the tension that had been building ever since the letter had arrived.

"You've been quiet today," Lily said softly, her eyes searching Emily's face for answers.

Emily forced a smile, but it didn't reach her eyes. "Just a lot on my mind. A lot is riding on this."

Lily nodded, but she wasn't convinced. "Is it the letter?"

Emily hesitated, then sighed, her shoulders slumping slightly. "Yes. It's from my mother. She wants me to leave the rebellion, to come home. She's scared, and I don't blame her. But... I can't just walk away now. We're so close, Lily. We're on the brink of something huge, and I can't abandon it."

Lily's expression softened, a mix of understanding and concern. "I get it. I really do. But you need to be sure, Emily. This fight… it's bigger than all of us, but it's also deeply personal. We're all fighting for something, for someone. If you need to step back, we'll understand. No one will think less of you."

Emily shook her head, her resolve hardening. "I can't. If I leave now, it will be like admitting defeat. I've come too far to back down. But it's hard, knowing what I'm putting my family through. My mother, my sister… they've already lost so much. I don't want to be the reason they lose more."

Lily reached out, placing a comforting hand on Emily's arm. "Whatever happens, you won't be alone in this. We're in it together, all the way."

Emily looked into Lily's eyes and saw the strength there, the unwavering commitment that had carried them through so many dark days. It gave her the courage to push aside her doubts, and to focus on what needed to be done. She had made her choice, and she would see it through.

"Thank you," Emily said, her voice steadier now. "I needed that."

Lily smiled a small but genuine smile. "Anytime. Now, let's get to work. We have a city to take back."

As the night deepened, the city began to transform. Armoured vehicles rolled down the streets, their engines rumbling ominously in the silence. Soldiers in full combat gear moved in formation, their weapons at the ready, their faces hidden behind visors that reflected the cold light of the street lamps. Drones buzzed overhead, their mechanical eyes scanning the city below for any sign of resistance.

The crackdown had begun.

The once-vibrant neighbourhoods that had sheltered the rebellion were now battlegrounds. Doors were kicked in, homes were ransacked, and anyone suspected of harbouring rebels was dragged into the streets, their protests silenced by the butt of a rifle or the cold steel of handcuffs. The government was making its move, determined to crush the rebellion before it could strike.

But the resistance had not been idle. As the soldiers moved in, they were met with a fierce and organised defence. Barricades sprang up in the narrow streets, makeshift but effective. Rebels armed with whatever they could find, old rifles, Molotov cocktails, and even kitchen knives, fought back with a ferocity born of desperation and resolve. The city was a maze of narrow alleys and hidden passageways, and the rebels used every advantage they had, striking from the shadows, and then melting away into the darkness.

Emily led a small group through the chaos, her heart pounding in her chest as they navigated the labyrinthine streets. She knew the city better than most, every twist and turn etched into her memory from years of living and fighting in its shadows. The plan was to regroup at a designated safe house, where they would coordinate the next phase of their counterstrike. But the government's response had been swifter and more brutal than they had anticipated, and now they were on the defensive, trying to hold their ground as the city erupted into violence.

"We're almost there," Emily whispered to her group, her voice barely audible over the sounds of gunfire and shouting in the distance. "Just a few more blocks."

They moved quickly but cautiously, every shadow a potential threat. The city, which had once been their home, was now a battlefield, and they were caught in the middle of it. Emily's mind raced as she considered their options. The crackdown was more intense than they had expected, and the chances of pulling off their counterstrike were growing slimmer by the minute. But they had to try. They had to make a stand.

As they approached the safe house, a small, nondescript building tucked away in a quiet alley, Emily felt a flicker of hope. They had made it this far, and they would make it further. But as they rounded the corner, her heart sank. The safe house was already surrounded by government forces, the entrance blocked by a line of soldiers who were systematically searching the building.

"Damn it," Emily muttered under her breath, her mind racing as she weighed their options.

"What do we do?" one of the rebels asked, his voice tense with fear.

Emily took a deep breath, forcing herself to stay calm. "We retreat. We'll find another location to regroup. There's no point in trying to fight our way through them. We'll only get ourselves killed."

Reluctantly, the group began to backtrack, their movements careful and deliberate. They knew the city well enough to find another route, another place to hide, but the window of opportunity was closing fast. Emily's thoughts were a whirlwind of plans and contingencies, but no matter how she looked at it, the situation was dire.

Back at the warehouse, the remaining members of the resistance were preparing for the counterstrike. The tension in the air was palpable, every second ticking by like a countdown to the inevitable clash. They had worked tirelessly to coordinate their efforts, communicating with cells across the city and beyond, each one ready to strike at a moment's notice.

Lily paced the room, her mind racing with thoughts of Emily and the others who were out there, facing the full force of the government's crackdown. She hated being cooped up in the warehouse, hated the feeling of helplessness that gnawed at her insides. But she knew she had a role to play, and she had to stay focused.

Aamir approached her, his expression grim but determined. "The signal is ready. As soon as we get word from Emily, we'll launch the counterstrike."

Lily nodded, trying to keep her voice steady. "We'll show them that we're not going down without a fight."

Aamir placed a reassuring hand on her shoulder. "We've come too far to turn back now. We'll see this through, no matter what."

The two of them shared a moment of silent understanding, their eyes locking in a mutual promise. They were in this together, and they would fight with everything they had.

As they waited for the signal, the warehouse was a hive of activity. Weapons were distributed, final plans were reviewed, and messages were sent out to the other cells. The resistance was ready, but there was a tension in the air that couldn't be ignored, a tension that came from knowing that this was it, the moment they had been preparing for. The final confrontation was upon them, and everything was on the line.

As Emily and her group continued their retreat through the city streets, the weight of her personal crisis bore down on her like a leaden cloak. The letter from her mother was still tucked in her pocket, the words etched into her mind like a brand. Every step she took, every decision she made, was haunted by the thought of what she was sacrificing, not just her own life, but the safety and well-being of her family.

She had chosen this path, chosen to fight for something bigger than herself, but now, as the final battle loomed, she couldn't shake the feeling that she was abandoning the people who needed her most. Her mother's plea echoed in her mind, a voice of love and fear that tore at her heart.

"Emily," one of the rebels said, snapping her out of her thoughts. "We need to keep moving."

She nodded, her throat tight with emotion. "I know. Let's go."

But even as they moved through the darkened streets, Emily's mind was elsewhere, torn between the duty she felt to the rebellion and the love she had for her family. It was a choice she had hoped she would never have to make, but now it loomed before her like a shadow, inescapable and suffocating.

As they found another safe house and prepared to regroup, Emily's resolve hardened. She had made her choice, and she would see it through. But the weight of that choice, the knowledge of what it might cost her, settled deep in her chest, a pain that she knew would never fully go away.

Back at the warehouse, the signal finally came. A series of coded messages confirmed that the cells were in position, ready to launch the counterstrike. The room was filled with a sense of anticipation, of tension so thick it could be cut with a knife.

Lily took a deep breath, steeling herself for what was to come. "It's time."

Aamir nodded, his expression one of grim determination. "Let's do this."

As the final preparations were made, the warehouse became a flurry of activity. The tension that had been building all day now reached its peak, every heartbeat a countdown to the inevitable clash. The resistance had been preparing for this moment for so long, and now it was here, their time to strike back, to reclaim their city, their freedom.

Emily's voice crackled over the radio, steady and resolute. "This is it. No turning back. We're doing this for everyone we've lost, for everyone who's still fighting. Let's take our city back."

With those words, the counterstrike was launched. Across the city, rebel cells sprang into action, their movements coordinated and precise, the culmination of months of careful planning and preparation. It was a night that would be remembered for years to come, a turning point in the struggle for freedom.

The first target was the Central Command Station, a heavily fortified government installation that housed the regime's primary communications network. The building, a monolithic structure of steel and glass, had long been a symbol of the government's omnipresent surveillance. Its towering antennae loomed over the city, transmitting orders, and monitoring the populace with an unblinking eye. As the rebels moved in, the streets around the station were eerily quiet, the calm before the storm.

A team of rebels, led by a former military engineer named Marcus, approached the building under the cover of darkness. They were armed with explosives and a plan that hinged on perfect timing. Marcus, who had once served in the very army he now fought against, knew the building's weaknesses. As the team reached the perimeter, he gave the signal, and they planted charges at key structural points. The explosives were set to detonate in a precise sequence, designed to bring down the antennae and sever the station's link to the government's surveillance network.

As the final charge was placed, Marcus took a moment to survey the building, a structure he had once protected. The irony was not lost on him. With a final nod, he stepped back, and the team retreated to a safe distance. The explosions were deafening, a series of rapid, concussive blasts that lit up the night sky. The ground shook as the antennae buckled and collapsed, crashing into the building with a thunderous roar. Within moments, the station was engulfed in flames, the once-imposing structure reduced to a smouldering ruin.

But the night was far from over.

In the financial district, another group of rebels had set their sights on the Treasury Building, where the government's wealth was hoarded and controlled. This building was a fortress in its own right, guarded by heavily armed soldiers and protected by layers of security measures. Yet, the rebels knew that crippling the regime's financial power was essential to their cause.

A young woman named Clara, a former bank employee who had joined the rebellion after witnessing the regime's corruption firsthand, led this group. She had spent weeks studying the building's security protocols, identifying the weakest points in its defences. As her team approached, Clara's heart pounded in her chest, but her hands were steady. They infiltrated the building through a service entrance, moving with a quiet efficiency that belied the chaos they were about to unleash.

Inside, they planted devices designed to trigger a massive blackout across the financial network. The goal was not just to steal or destroy, but to undermine the government's ability to finance its war against the people. As the devices were activated, alarms blared, and the building's defences came to life. Soldiers poured into the corridors, but Clara and her team fought back with everything they had. Amid the firefight, Clara was hit, and a bullet tore through her shoulder. Despite the pain, she pressed on, determined to complete the mission.

With her good arm, Clara triggered the final device, sending a pulse through the system that plunged the Treasury's operations into chaos. Accounts were wiped, transactions were frozen, and the financial lifeblood of the regime was disrupted. As she and her team made their escape, Clara knew they had struck a critical blow. But the price had been high, several of her comrades had fallen, their sacrifice a sombre reminder of the cost of freedom.

Meanwhile, in the industrial sector, a group of rebels targeted the government's supply depots, where food, weapons, and medical supplies were stored for the military. These depots were the lifeline of the regime's forces, essential for maintaining control over the city.

The rebels knew that cutting off these supplies would weaken the government's ability to wage war.

A seasoned fighter named Javier led this group. A former dockworker, Javier had seen the suffering of his people firsthand, as government forces took everything they needed while leaving the citizens to starve. Tonight, he was determined to turn the tables. Under the cover of darkness, his team approached the largest depot in the sector. They were armed with little more than homemade explosives and a fierce determination.

As they reached the depot, Javier and his team moved swiftly, planting explosives along the fuel lines and storage tanks. The goal was to create a chain reaction that would destroy the entire facility in one fell swoop. As the last charge was set, they were discovered by a patrol. A firefight broke out, the sound of gunfire echoing through the night. Javier knew they were outgunned, but he refused to retreat. With bullets whizzing past him, he sprinted towards the control room, determined to detonate the charges manually if necessary.

He reached the room just as the patrol closed in. With a final, defiant shout, Javier slammed his hand down on the detonator. The explosion was instantaneous, a massive fireball that consumed the depot and everything around it. The blast could be heard for miles, a signal to the city that the rebellion was far from over. Javier's sacrifice ensured that the government's forces would be left scrambling for supplies, and their grip on the city weakened.

Across the city, similar scenes played out. Rebel cells struck at power plants, communication hubs, and military barracks. They knew that they were outnumbered and outgunned, but they fought with a ferocity that took the government forces by surprise. In a residential neighbourhood, a group of young rebels held off a government assault, buying time for their neighbours to escape. They fought from the rooftops and alleyways, using their intimate knowledge of the area to their advantage. When the soldiers finally overwhelmed them, the rebels had already done their job, the residents were safe, and the government had paid a heavy price.

In the old town district, a veteran rebel named Lucas led a daring raid on a government armoury. The plan was to seize weapons and distribute them to the unarmed civilians who were ready to join the fight. Lucas and his team moved with precision, taking out the guards and securing the weapons. But as they loaded the trucks, they were ambushed by a government squad. Outnumbered and with no way out, Lucas made the call to hold the line, allowing the trucks to escape. He and his team fought to the last man, their bodies found among the spent shells and broken weapons, a testament to their courage and dedication.

As the night wore on, the city became a battlefield, the streets filled with the sounds of gunfire, the cries of the wounded, and the defiant shouts of those who refused to surrender. The government installations that had once stood as symbols of the regime's power were now smouldering ruins, their destruction a rallying cry for the people. The rebellion, once confined to the shadows, had erupted into open warfare, and the city that had been under the regime's control for so long was now a crucible of resistance.

For every act of bravery, there was a sacrifice. For every victory, there was a loss. But the rebels knew that their actions were not in vain. They had struck a blow against the regime, one that would resonate throughout the country. The counterstrike had shown the world that the rebellion was not just a fleeting movement, it was a force to be reckoned with, a movement that would not be easily crushed.

And as dawn approached, the fires still burning across the city, the rebels knew that this was only the beginning. The government would strike back with all its might, but the rebellion was ready. The battle for the city, for the country, had truly begun, and there was no turning back.

As the resistance fought back, the government forces were caught off guard, their carefully laid plans thrown into disarray. The rebels were everywhere, striking from the shadows, using their knowledge of the city to outmanoeuvre the soldiers who had once seemed invincible.

In the midst of it all, Emily led her group with a fierce determination, her crisis pushed aside as she focused on the task at hand. The letter from her mother was still there, a reminder of the choice she had made, but now it was a source of strength rather than doubt. She was fighting for something bigger than herself, something that would outlast her, something that would bring freedom to those she loved.

As the night wore on, the tide of battle began to shift. The government forces were strong, but the resistance was stronger, fuelled by the fire of a cause that could no longer be contained. The city, once a fortress of oppression, was now a battlefield of liberation, and the outcome was far from certain.

But for the first time in a long time, there was hope.

The storm had gathered, the final confrontation had begun, and the fate of the nation hung in the balance. The resistance was ready, and they would fight with everything they had, knowing that the future was theirs to shape, if only they could seize it.

And as Emily looked out over the battlefield, she knew that no matter what happened, they would never give up. They had come too far and sacrificed too much. The final battle was here, and they were ready to face it, together.

Chapter 20 The Battle Begins

The night was thick with tension, the kind that made the air feel electric, every breath a struggle against the growing anticipation. Across the UK, a storm was gathering, not of nature's making, but one forged in the hearts of those who had finally been pushed too far. The resistance had planned for this moment, every detail meticulously thought out, every contingency considered. But no amount of preparation could erase the uncertainty that lay ahead. The first major battle of the Civil War was about to begin, and the outcome was anything but certain.

The streets of London, once teeming with life, now lay eerily quiet, as if the city itself was holding its breath. The distant rumble of military convoys echoed off the tall, grimy buildings, mingling with the occasional shout of a soldier or the crackle of a distant explosion. The government had fortified key areas, turning parts of the city into fortresses, but the rebels had their plans.

In an old, abandoned factory on the outskirts of the city, the core group of the resistance gathered. The building was a relic of the industrial age, its brick walls cracked and weathered, windows long since shattered. Inside, the air was thick with the scent of oil and rust, the remnants of machinery lying in silent disrepair. But tonight, the factory had a new purpose. It was the staging ground for the most ambitious operation the resistance had ever attempted.

Emily stood at the centre of the room, her eyes scanning the faces around her. These were the people she had come to rely on, those who had fought by her side, who had bled and sacrificed for the cause. Aamir, his face drawn with the weight of responsibility, was finalising the details with Sarah, who had survived the raid on the London safe house and had since become a key figure in forging alliances with other groups. Lily, her fiery red hair a stark contrast to the grim setting, was checking the equipment, her hands moving with practiced efficiency. They were ready, or as ready as they could be.

"The operation begins in fifteen minutes," Emily announced, her voice steady but low. "We've coordinated with cells across the country. This is it. We need to hit them hard and hit them fast, and we cannot afford to fail. Our target tonight is the Central Command and Control Centre. It's the heart of their military operations, and if we can take it, we'll cripple their ability to coordinate the crackdown."

A murmur of agreement rippled through the group, but there was no mistaking the gravity of the situation. They all knew the risks, the stakes. Failure tonight wouldn't just mean the loss of lives; it could mean the end of the rebellion itself.

As the clock struck midnight, the first wave of coordinated attacks began. In cities, towns, and villages across the UK, the resistance rose as one, their movements synchronised with military precision. Explosions rocked government buildings, power stations were sabotaged, and bridges were blown, severing critical supply lines. Chaos reigned as the government, caught off guard by the sheer scale of the operation, scrambled to respond.

In Manchester, the night was alive with tension as the rebels moved with swift precision. Their target was the main railway station, a vital transportation hub that had long been a lifeline for government forces, ensuring the smooth movement of troops, supplies, and weaponry across the region. The station, a sprawling complex of platforms, tracks, and towering signal boxes, was heavily guarded, but the rebels had been planning this operation for weeks.

Led by a former train conductor named Daniel, the rebel cell knew the station like the back of their hands. Daniel, who had once spent his days ensuring the safe passage of trains, now used his knowledge to bring the government's logistics to a grinding halt. As the team approached the station, Daniel felt a pang of nostalgia, he had walked these platforms countless times, but tonight, they were transformed into a battleground.

The rebels moved in silence, slipping past the perimeter guards with practiced ease. As they reached the control room, Daniel gave the signal, and the team burst in, taking the operators by surprise. The guards stationed within the building, young conscripts who had never seen combat, were overwhelmed by the sudden onslaught. Some dropped their weapons, hands raised in surrender, while others hesitated, fear and confusion etched on their faces.

But not all were willing to fight. One young soldier, no more than eighteen, looked into the eyes of the rebels and saw not enemies, but people, people like his own family, who had suffered under the same oppressive regime. When his commanding officer barked an order to open fire, the soldier lowered his rifle, refusing to shoot. The officer, enraged by what he saw as insubordination, drew his sidearm and aimed it at the soldier. But before he could pull the trigger, a rebel sniper took him down, the shot echoing through the control room.

The young soldier stood frozen, the horror of what had almost transpired sinking in. Daniel approached him, his voice calm but firm. "You don't have to fight us," he said. "You can join us. We're not the enemy."

The soldier, trembling, nodded slowly. He had seen enough, and in that moment, he made his choice. He dropped his rifle and joined the rebels, his resolve hardened by the events of the night. The station fell quickly after that, the rebels taking control of the main control room and severing the lines that connected Manchester to the rest of the country. As the last train ground to a halt on the tracks, Daniel looked out over the station, knowing that they had struck a significant blow to the regime.

In Birmingham, the scene was one of fire and fury. The rebels had set their sights on a government munitions depot, a heavily fortified complex where the regime stored its weapons and ammunition. The depot was surrounded by high fences, watchtowers, and guards armed to the teeth, but the rebels were undeterred. They knew that crippling the government's supply lines was essential to weakening their stranglehold on the country.

The attack was led by a woman named Priya, a former soldier who had defected to the resistance after witnessing the atrocities committed by the regime. Priya was a tactical genius, her mind a sharp weapon honed by years of military experience. As she and her team approached the depot, the night sky was clear, the stars shining down on them like silent witnesses.

Priya's team moved quickly, cutting through the fence, and neutralising the guards with ruthless efficiency. They reached the munitions storage area, where they planted explosives at strategic points, each device meticulously placed to maximise destruction. But as they worked, the alarm was raised, and the depot was soon swarming with soldiers.

A fierce firefight erupted, the night air filled with the sound of gunfire and the smell of cordite. Priya fought with a cold, controlled fury, her every shot precise and lethal. But the odds were against them, and as more government troops poured into the depot, it became clear that they were in danger of being overrun.

In the chaos, Priya spotted a group of soldiers hesitating at the edge of the battlefield. They were young, like the soldiers in Manchester, their faces pale with fear. Priya could see the doubt in their eyes, the realisation that they were fighting against their own people, that the enemy was not some faceless other but men and women who had once been their neighbours, their friends.

One of the soldiers, a lieutenant, lowered his weapon and called out to his men. "Enough!" he shouted. "We're killing our own! This isn't what we signed up for!"

His words hung in the air, a stark contrast to the violence around them. The soldiers hesitated, their loyalty to the regime wavering. But their commanding officer, a grizzled veteran of the regime's brutal campaigns, would not tolerate dissent. He ordered them to fire, to crush the rebellion without mercy.

But the soldiers refused. The lieutenant, emboldened by his decision, stepped forward, his voice carrying over the din of battle. "We didn't join the army to murder civilians. We're done with this."

The officer, his face twisted with rage, drew his weapon and aimed it at the lieutenant, but before he could pull the trigger, Priya's shot rang out, dropping him where he stood. The remaining soldiers, now free of their oppressive leader, threw down their weapons and joined the rebels, their hearts and minds finally won over.

The explosion that followed was heard and visible for miles, a fiery inferno that consumed the depot and sent shockwaves through the city. The rebels had succeeded but at a cost. As Priya and her team retreated, carrying their wounded, they knew that the battle was far from over. But the sight of the burning depot, the regime's munitions reduced to ashes, filled them with a renewed sense of purpose.

In Edinburgh, the resistance launched a daring raid on the military barracks, the nerve centre of the government's operations in Scotland. The barracks were heavily defended, a fortress of steel and stone that had withstood countless assaults. But the rebels had a secret weapon, a mole within the government's ranks who had provided them with detailed plans of the facility.

The attack was swift and brutal. The rebels infiltrated the barracks under the cover of darkness, using the element of surprise to their advantage. They moved through the corridors like shadows, their footsteps silent on the cold stone floors. As they reached the heart of the barracks, the sound of distant explosions reached their ears, other rebel cells were launching attacks across the city, sowing confusion and disorder among the ranks.

Inside the barracks, the soldiers were caught off guard, their usual discipline shattered by the sudden onslaught. Some fought back with desperate ferocity, but others, shaken by the realisation that the rebellion had reached their doorstep, hesitated. It was in this moment of chaos that the resistance struck, taking control of the command centre and disabling the barracks' defences.

But not all the soldiers were willing to stand down. In one wing of the barracks, a group of officers rallied their men, preparing to mount a counterattack. The rebel leader, an experienced veteran named Alistair, knew that they couldn't afford to be bogged down in a prolonged fight. He ordered his men to hold the line while he attempted to negotiate a surrender.

Alistair approached the officers with a flag of truce, his voice calm but firm. "We don't have to keep fighting," he said. "Your men are exhausted, and so are ours. Let's end this before more lives are lost."

One of the officers, a captain who had seen too much death in his years of service, nodded in agreement. But another, a hardliner who refused to see reason, drew his pistol and fired at Alistair. The bullet grazed his arm, but Alistair didn't flinch. Instead, he stared the officer down, his eyes filled with a steely determination.

"This is your last chance," Alistair said, his voice cold. "Surrender now, or you'll leave us no choice."

The tension was palpable as the two men faced off. But the captain, seeing the futility of further bloodshed, stepped forward and placed his hand on the hardliner's arm. "He's right," the captain said quietly. "This isn't our fight anymore."

With that, the remaining soldiers laid down their arms, their will to fight broken. The barracks fell without further bloodshed, the government's grip on Edinburgh slipping away. As the rebels secured the facility, Alistair knew that they had won a significant victory. But he also knew that the road ahead was long and fraught with danger.

But not all went as planned.

In Leeds, the night air was thick with tension as a rebel cell moved to take a police station. They had planned meticulously, their intelligence suggesting that the station was lightly defended, a perfect target for a quick strike. But what they didn't know was that their plans had been betrayed. Someone within their ranks had leaked their intentions to the authorities.

As the rebels approached the station, the trap was sprung. Floodlights blazed to life, illuminating the street as government soldiers emerged from the shadows, their rifles trained on the rebels. The air was filled with the deafening sound of gunfire as the soldiers opened fire, cutting down the rebels where they stood.

The night echoed with the screams of the wounded and the dying, the once-quiet street transformed into a war zone. The few survivors, realising that their mission had been compromised, fled into the darkness, their hearts heavy with the weight of failure. But even in their retreat, their resolve remained unbroken. They had lost the battle, but the war was far from over.

As the rebels scattered into the night, some of the government soldiers paused, their rifles lowered as they watched the fleeing figures. Doubt gnawed at them, had they just fought to protect the regime, or had they become pawns in a war they didn't understand? One soldier, a sergeant who had served for over a decade, felt a cold weight in his chest as he looked at the bodies of the rebels lying in the street. These weren't foreign invaders; they were his people, fighting for a cause they believed in.

The sergeant turned to his commanding officer, his voice thick with emotion. "Sir, is this really what we're fighting for? To gun down our own?"

The officer's response was a harsh bark of orders, but the seed of doubt had been planted. The sergeant lowered his rifle, the sense of duty that had driven him for years now in conflict with the growing realisation that the government he served might not be the righteous force he had always believed it to be.

That night, the rebellion gained more than just ground, it gained allies in the unlikeliest of places. Soldiers, once loyal to the regime, began to question their orders, their hearts heavy with the weight of the blood on their hands. The unity of the government's forces, once unshakable, began to crack, as the reality of the war they were fighting came into sharper focus.

The UK was descending into chaos, the carefully maintained order of the regime unravelling as the flames of rebellion spread. The battle had begun, and the outcome was anything but certain.

Back in London, the group prepared for their assault on the Central Command and Control Centre, a nondescript building that hid its importance behind a facade of anonymity. It was heavily fortified, surrounded by concrete barriers, and patrolled by armed guards. But Emily and her team had studied it for weeks, mapping out every entry point, every weakness.

As they approached the building under the cover of darkness, the city around them seemed to hold its breath. The distant sounds of battle reached their ears, but here, in the heart of the government's power, there was an eerie silence. The building loomed ahead, a symbol of the regime's might, but tonight, it would become a battlefield.

Emily led the way, her heart pounding in her chest. She knew what was at stake, and she couldn't afford to let doubt creep in. Behind her, Aamir, Sarah, and Lily moved with practiced ease, their every step deliberate, every action rehearsed. They reached the perimeter and split into two teams, each with a specific objective.

Aamir and Sarah would enter through the service entrance, disabling the building's security systems and creating a diversion. Emily and Lily would take the main entrance, their goal to reach the control room and seize the building's communications network.

As the teams moved into position, Emily took a moment to steady herself. This was it. The moment they had all been working towards. The fear was there, a cold knot in her stomach, but so was the resolve. She thought of John, of Hassan, of everyone they had lost, and it steeled her nerves. This was for them, for all of them.

With a nod, she gave the signal, and the operation began.

Aamir and Sarah moved swiftly, taking out the guards at the service entrance with silenced weapons. They entered the building, the hallways eerily quiet. As they approached the security room, Aamir's hands moved over the control panel with practiced skill, disabling cameras and alarms. But as they worked, the tension mounted. Every second felt like an eternity, every sound a potential threat.

In the main hall, Emily and Lily moved with equal precision. They encountered resistance, government soldiers who had been stationed there to protect the building, but the element of surprise was on their side. Emily's training kicked in, her movements swift and deadly as she took down the soldiers one by one. Lily, her face set in grim determination, covered her back, her rifle spitting bullets with deadly accuracy.

They reached the control room, the heart of the building. Inside, a handful of technicians were manning the consoles, their faces pale as they realised what was happening. Emily gave them one chance to surrender, her voice cold and commanding. When they hesitated, Lily fired a warning shot, and they quickly raised their hands in surrender.

As Emily and Lily secured the room, Aamir's voice crackled over the radio. "We're in. Security systems are down, but we've got company. Government reinforcements are on their way."

Emily cursed under her breath. They had anticipated this, but the timing was tighter than they'd hoped. "Hold them off as long as you can. We're securing the control room now."

But as they began to lock down the building's systems, the situation rapidly deteriorated. Outside, the sound of helicopters filled the air, their searchlights sweeping across the city. Government reinforcements were closing in, their response swift and overwhelming.

Aamir and Sarah fought valiantly, their position becoming increasingly precarious as more soldiers poured into the building. Sarah was hit, a bullet tearing through her side, but she refused to back down. She fired back with everything she had, her determination unshaken even as the blood seeped through her fingers.

Inside the control room, Emily and Lily worked frantically, trying to download critical data and seize control of the communications network. But the clock was ticking, and they knew their time was running out. The walls of the building began to shake as explosives detonated outside, the government forces attempting to breach the structure.

"We're out of time!" Lily shouted, her voice tinged with desperation.

Emily's mind raced. They had to make a choice, complete the mission or retreat. But even as she weighed their options, she knew the decision had already been made. "We hold our ground," she said, her voice resolute. "We don't leave until this is done."

But just as the final files were being transferred, the door to the control room burst open, and government soldiers stormed in. A firefight erupted, bullets ricocheting off the walls as the rebels fought for their lives. The room filled with the acrid smell of gunpowder, the chaos of battle drowning out everything else.

Emily took cover behind a console, her heart pounding as she returned fire. Lily was beside her, her face a mask of determination. But the odds were against them, and they both knew it. For every soldier they took down, more seemed to pour in, their numbers overwhelming.

A sudden explosion rocked the building, the force of it knocking Emily off her feet. The lights flickered and went out, plunging the room into darkness. For a moment, there was only the sound of laboured breathing, the distant rumble of the city in chaos.

But then, from the darkness, a voice crackled over the radio. It was Aamir, his voice strained but determined.

"We've done all we can. Fall back. We need to regroup."

Emily hesitated, her hand gripping the radio tightly. The mission wasn't complete, but the cost of staying was too high. With a heavy heart, she gave the order. "Fall back. Everyone, fall back."

They moved quickly, retreating through the darkened corridors, the sound of gunfire still echoing in the distance. The city was in chaos, the battle raging on all fronts. As they emerged into the night, the cold air hit them like a slap, the reality of their situation sinking in.

They had struck a blow, but victory was far from certain. The rebellion was in full swing, and the battle for the nation's future just beginning. As they disappeared into the shadows, Emily couldn't shake the feeling that the true cost of their fight had yet to be paid.

The city burned behind them, a landscape of destruction and defiance. The first major battle of the civil war had begun, but the outcome hung in the balance, teetering on the edge of uncertainty. And as they vanished into the night, the rebels knew that the fight was far from over.

Victory was uncertain, and the storm had only just begun.

PART III

Revolution's Dawn

Chapter 21 Aftermath

The city was a shell of its former self. Smoke hung heavy in the air, a grim reminder of the chaos that had unfolded just hours before. Buildings, once towering symbols of industry and progress, now stood as crumbling monuments to a battle that had scarred the heart of the nation. Streets that had been bustling with life were now littered with debris, shattered glass, broken bricks, and the remnants of hastily abandoned vehicles.

Amid this devastation, the silence was deafening. The occasional crackle of a distant fire, the groan of a collapsing structure, or the faint moan of the wounded were the only sounds that punctuated the stillness. It was as if the city itself was holding its breath, waiting for the next wave of violence to strike.

Emily stood on what remained of a once-bustling street corner, her eyes scanning the destruction with a numb detachment. She was covered in dust and grime, her clothes torn and bloodstained, though she couldn't tell if the blood was her own or someone else's. Her hands trembled slightly as she clenched them into fists, trying to ground herself in the moment.

The first major battle of the Civil War was over, but the cost had been staggering. They had lost so many, good people, brave fighters who had stood beside her, now reduced to names on a growing list of the dead. And yet, despite the carnage, there was a flicker of hope. They had won small victories, struck significant blows against the government's forces, and the morale of the survivors was cautiously optimistic. But Emily felt none of that hope. All she could see was the death, the destruction, the faces of those who would never see the dawn again.

Lily approached her, her face pale and drawn but her eyes still holding that spark of determination that had driven her from the beginning. "Emily," she said softly, placing a hand on her shoulder. "We need to regroup. We've got to count our losses and figure out our next steps."

Emily turned to look at her, blinking as if coming out of a daze. "How many?" Her voice was hoarse, barely above a whisper.

Lily hesitated, knowing the answer would cut deep. "Too many," she admitted. "But we also managed to hold key positions. We've hurt them, Emily. We've shown them we won't be crushed so easily."

The words were meant to comfort, but they rang hollow in Emily's ears. She nodded slowly, but her mind was elsewhere, lost in the chaos of the battle, the sound of gunfire, the screams, the sight of her comrades falling beside her. She could still feel the impact of the blast that had knocked her off her feet, the searing pain that had followed, and the frantic scramble to find cover as the world exploded around her.

"We need you, Emily," Lily pressed gently. "They need to see you're still standing, that you're still leading us."

Emily forced herself to meet Lily's gaze. There was no anger there, no frustration, only concern, and understanding. She nodded again, this time more firmly. "You're right. We can't afford to lose momentum now."

The group had set up a makeshift headquarters in the basement of a bombed-out building, its walls cracked and blackened by fire. The space was cramped and dimly lit, the only light coming from a few flickering candles and the occasional shaft of daylight that pierced through the cracks in the ceiling. The air was thick with the smell of smoke, sweat, and fear.

Around the room, survivors huddled together, tending to their wounds, cleaning weapons, or simply sitting in silence, their eyes vacant and hollow. The atmosphere was heavy with grief, but also with a quiet, simmering anger, a resolve that had only hardened in the face of the government's brutality.

As Emily entered the room, heads turned, and a hush fell over the group. She could see the mix of emotions on their faces, relief that she was still alive, gratitude for her leadership, and an unspoken question: What now?

She walked to the centre of the room, her steps slow and deliberate. "We've taken heavy losses," she began, her voice steady despite the turmoil inside her. "But we've also made progress. We've shown them that we're not going to back down, that we're willing to fight for our future, for our freedom."

There were murmurs of agreement, and nods of approval, but Emily could see the doubt lingering in some of their eyes. They were tired, scared, and unsure of what lay ahead. She needed to give them something to hold onto.

"We need to regroup," she continued. "We need to mourn our dead, and tend to our wounded, but we can't afford to stop. The government's grip is weakening, and the public is starting to see the truth. We need to capitalise on that, to reach out to those who are still on the fence, to show them that our cause is just, that we are fighting for all of us."

She looked around the room, meeting each gaze in turn. "I won't lie to you, this is only going to get harder. We're up against a regime that will stop at nothing to maintain its power. But we have something they don't, we have the truth on our side, and we have each other."

The room was silent for a moment, the weight of her words settling over them like a heavy blanket. Then, one by one, people began to nod, their expressions hardening with resolve. Emily felt a small surge of relief, she had reached them, at least for now.

Outside, the streets bore the heavy scars of the ongoing conflict, transforming London from a vibrant metropolis into a war-torn landscape reminiscent of the darkest days of the Blitz in 1940. The once grand and imposing buildings that lined the streets were now skeletal ruins, their facades blackened by fire and riddled with bullet holes. Windows, once reflective of the city's grandeur, were shattered, their jagged edges like broken teeth, while the walls that had once enclosed thriving businesses and bustling homes stood pockmarked and crumbling. The roads, which had once carried the lifeblood of the city, were now choked with debris, twisted metal, splintered wood, and the charred remnants of vehicles abandoned in the chaos. The occasional body, covered hastily with whatever was at hand, served as a grim reminder of the human cost of the battle that had raged through these very streets.

Yet, amidst this devastation, there was a spirit that refused to be extinguished, a resilience that echoed through the history of Londoners who had once faced a similar darkness. During the Blitz, when bombs rained down night after night, the people of London had stood strong, defiant in the face of terror. They had endured, finding strength in their unity and a shared determination to survive. That same spirit now pulsed through the veins of their descendants, a steely resolve that had been forged in the fires of past wars and was now rekindled in the fight against oppression.

Despite the ruins, there was movement on the streets, furtive, cautious, but unmistakably there. Small groups of civilians moved like shadows, their footsteps careful, their eyes darting nervously as they navigated the debris-strewn roads. They kept to the alleys and backstreets, avoiding the more heavily patrolled areas where government forces still held sway. The soldiers, once confident in their dominion over the city, now patrolled with a new sense of unease, their eyes scanning the surroundings with an intensity that spoke of growing fear. They were acutely aware that the city was no longer theirs to control, that the enemy they faced was not just a band of rebels, but a city of people whose spirit had been awakened.

The fear that had once paralysed the populace was beginning to shift, transforming into something more dangerous for the regime, a simmering resentment that grew stronger with each passing day. Where there had once been whispered conversations in the safety of darkened rooms, now there were open glares at soldiers, graffiti scrawled on walls declaring support for the resistance, and small acts of defiance that signalled the changing tide. The city, once cowed into submission, was now a powder keg, and the people, who had suffered in silence for so long, were ready to explode.

Rumours spread like wildfire, fuelled by the desperation and hope that gripped the city. These whispers moved faster than the government could contain them, jumping from person to person, block to block. Stories of the government's brutality, of mass arrests, of families torn apart, of civilians gunned down in the streets, circulated with growing ferocity. But alongside these tales of terror were the stories of the resistance's small victories. News of successful raids, of supply lines cut, of government forces ambushed and defeated in skirmishes, spread with a fervour that brought with it a glimmer of hope.

More than anything, it was the rumours of soldiers who had refused to follow orders, who had turned their guns on their officers rather than slaughter their fellow citizens, that sent shockwaves through the city. These stories were whispered in hushed tones in crowded rooms, spoken with a mix of awe and disbelief. Could it be that the very forces sent to crush the rebellion were beginning to doubt their mission? The implications were staggering, and the government knew it. The regime's grip on power was loosening, and the more it tightened its hold, the more people slipped through its fingers.

For the government forces still stationed in the city, these rumours were a source of growing dread. They had once viewed the rebels as a ragtag group of dissidents, easily crushed under the heel of their superior numbers and firepower. But the events of recent days had shaken that belief. The rebels had proven themselves to be more than just a nuisance, they were a force to be reckoned with, driven by a cause that made them fight with a ferocity that the soldiers could not match. There was a new respect among the ranks, begrudging though it was, for the bravery and tenacity of the rebels. But with that respect came fear. Fear that the war was not as easily won as they had been led to believe, fear that they were on the wrong side of history, and fear that they might soon find themselves facing a mutiny within their own ranks.

The effects of these rumours were not lost on the government itself. In the halls of power, where once there had been only certainty and control, there was now a palpable sense of unease. Reports of soldiers questioning their orders, of defections, and of growing civilian support for the rebellion were met with increasing desperation. The regime's propaganda machine worked overtime, churning out stories of rebel atrocities, of a lawless mob threatening to tear the country apart. But even these efforts were starting to falter, as the truth of the government's actions seeped through the cracks in their carefully constructed narrative.

The city, once a bastion of order, was now teetering on the edge of chaos. The battle lines were drawn, not just on the streets, but in the hearts and minds of the people. The government's forces, though still powerful, were beginning to waver, their unity fractured by the growing realisation that the rebellion might just succeed. And for the rebels, each new act of defiance, each small victory, was a step closer to the tipping point they had been working towards for so long.

London was a city on the brink, its future uncertain, its people caught between fear and hope. The flames of rebellion were spreading, and as the city smouldered in the aftermath of the battle, the question on everyone's mind was no longer if the rebellion would succeed, but when. The spirit of Londoners, once tested in the fires of the Blitz, was being tested again, and this time, they were determined to emerge victorious.

The rebellion was no longer just a fight for survival, it was a fight for the soul of the nation. And as the city prepared for the next battle, both sides knew that the outcome would determine the fate of the UK itself.

As the days wore on, Emily found herself increasingly haunted by the events of the battle. Nightmares plagued her sleep, vivid memories of the carnage replaying in her mind every time she closed her eyes. During the day, she forced herself to focus on the tasks at hand, coordinating with other cells, planning their next move, and rallying the survivors, but the weight of what she had seen, of the lives lost under her command, was becoming harder to bear.

One evening, as she sat alone in the makeshift headquarters, staring blankly at a map of the city, Lily approached her. "Emily," she said softly, pulling up a chair beside her. "You haven't been yourself lately."

Emily didn't respond at first, her eyes still fixed on the map. Finally, she sighed, running a hand through her dishevelled hair. "I keep seeing their faces," she admitted her voice barely above a whisper. "The ones we lost. The ones I couldn't save."

Lily reached out, placing a comforting hand on her arm. "You did everything you could. We all did. But this... this is war, Emily. We can't save everyone."

"I know that," Emily replied, her voice tinged with frustration. "But knowing it doesn't make it any easier. Every time I close my eyes, I see them. I hear them. And I wonder if I'm making the right choices if I'm leading us in the right direction."

Lily squeezed her arm gently. "You are, Emily. You're the reason we're still fighting, the reason we haven't given up. We believe in you, and we need you to believe in yourself."

Emily looked at her, searching Lily's eyes for the reassurance she so desperately needed. But the doubt lingered, a shadow that refused to be banished. "I'm trying," she said finally, her voice thick with emotion. "But it's hard, Lily. It's so damn hard."

Lily nodded, her expression softening with empathy. "I know it is. But you're not alone in this. We're all here, fighting with you. And together, we're going to see this through."

Emily managed a small, grateful smile. "Thank you, Lily. I don't know what I'd do without you."

Lily smiled back, a glimmer of hope in her eyes. "You'll never have to find out. We're in this together, until the end."

As the days passed, the public's sentiment began to shift. The government's heavy-handed response to the rebellion sparked outrage among the population, particularly in the aftermath of the battle. Reports of government atrocities, public executions, the massacre of civilians, and the crackdown on dissent, began to filter through the city, despite the regime's attempts to control the narrative.

People who had once been too afraid to speak out were now quietly voicing their anger, their discontent. Graffiti began to appear on the walls of the city, messages of defiance, of solidarity with the resistance. Small acts of sabotage, of civil disobedience, became more frequent as the people found their courage, their anger finally outweighing their fear.

The resistance took advantage of this growing unrest, reaching out to those who were willing to listen, and spreading their message of hope and freedom. Slowly but surely, public opinion began to turn against the government. The regime, once seen as unassailable, was now viewed as corrupt, brutal, and desperate. And as the people's anger grew, so too did their willingness to support the rebellion.

One evening, as Emily and Lily sat in the basement, pouring over reports from their various cells, Aamir entered the room, a newspaper clutched in his hand. "You need to see this," he said, his voice tinged with urgency.

He handed the newspaper to Emily, who scanned the front page. Her eyes widened as she read the headline: Government Brutality Exposed: Civilians Massacred in Crackdown on Dissent.

"They're finally seeing the truth," Emily murmured, her heart pounding in her chest. "People are starting to wake up."

Lily leaned over to read the article, a slow smile spreading across her face. "This could be the turning point," she said, her voice filled with hope. "If we can keep this momentum going, we might have a chance."

Emily nodded, a newfound determination settling over her. "We have to keep pushing, keep showing them that we're fighting for them, for all of us. This is our moment, Lily. We can't let it slip away."

Aamir, who had been listening quietly, spoke up. "The people are with us now, Emily. They're angry, and they're ready to fight. But we have to be smart about this. The government is going to come down on us harder than ever. We need to be prepared."

Emily looked at him, her resolve hardening. "We will be," she said firmly. "This isn't just about us anymore. It's about everyone who has suffered under this regime. We owe it to them to keep fighting, to see this through to the end."

As the days passed, the resistance began to regroup, their morale bolstered by the small victories they had won and the shifting tide of public opinion. They knew that the road ahead would be long and fraught with danger, but for the first time in a long while, there was a glimmer of hope.

Emily, though still haunted by the ghosts of the battle, found herself renewed by the support of her comrades, by the growing strength of the resistance.

She knew that the fight was far from over, but she was ready to face whatever came next.

As the sun set over the battered city, casting long shadows over the ruins, the resistance gathered together, their resolve stronger than ever. They had suffered heavy losses, but they had also found new allies and new strength. The battle had taken its toll, but it had also shown them that they were not alone, that the people were with them.

The rebellion was no longer a distant dream, it was a reality, a force that could no longer be ignored. And as they prepared for the next phase of their fight, they knew that they were on the right side of history.

The aftermath of the battle had tested them, but it had also forged them into something stronger, something unbreakable. The government had underestimated them, but they would not make that mistake again.

The rebellion was far from over. It was only just beginning, a realisation that settled deep within the hearts of those who had risen against the oppressive regime. The battle they had fought, the blood that had been spilled, and the lives that had been lost were but the first sparks of a fire that was now raging uncontrollably across the nation. What had started as a desperate act of defiance, a flicker of resistance in the face of overwhelming odds, had grown into a movement that could no longer be contained. The people, once silenced by fear, had found their voices, and those voices were now a thunderous roar that echoed through the streets, across the countryside, and into the very halls of power.

The scars of the recent battle were still fresh, the wounds both physical and emotional, but from the ashes of destruction, a new resolve had been forged. The rebels, battered but unbroken, knew that the fight ahead would be long and arduous, and that they would face countless more trials and tribulations. Yet, there was a new strength in their ranks, a unity born of shared sacrifice and a shared vision of a future free from tyranny. They had tasted the bitterness of loss, but they had also glimpsed the sweetness of victory, however small it might have been. And it was that taste that brief moment of triumph, that fuelled their determination to keep fighting, to keep pushing forward no matter the cost.

Across the country, in cities, towns, and villages, the seeds of rebellion were taking root. Ordinary men and women, once passive in their acceptance of the regime's cruelty, were now stepping into the light, joining the ranks of the resistance. They were driven by a deep-seated anger, a righteous fury that had been simmering for years, now unleashed in a wave of defiance that was spreading like wildfire. The government, once so confident in its control, was beginning to feel the heat, its iron grip slipping as the cracks in its foundation grew wider with each passing day.

This was not the end; it was the dawn of something greater. The rebellion was evolving, growing in strength and in numbers, its reach extending far beyond the initial pockets of resistance. It was a movement that could no longer be ignored, no longer dismissed as the actions of a fringe group. It was the voice of a nation rising up against oppression, demanding justice, demanding freedom, demanding change. And that voice was becoming impossible to silence.

The government's response, brutal and unyielding, had only served to fan the flames. Each act of repression, each public execution, each crackdown on dissent was met with renewed determination, with a resolve that hardened in the face of adversity. The rebels knew that the road ahead would be paved with hardship and that the regime would not go down without a fight. But they also knew that they were not alone. The tide was turning, and with it came the realisation that the power of the people, once awakened, was a force that could not be easily subdued.

The rebellion was far from over. It was only just beginning, and with it came the promise of a new dawn, a dawn that would be fought for in the streets, in the fields, in the very hearts of those who had taken up the mantle of resistance. It was a dawn that would come at a great cost, but it was a cost that they were willing to pay, for they knew that the fight for freedom was a fight worth waging. The rebellion was the spark that would ignite a revolution, and as the embers of that revolution began to glow brighter, they knew that the time for change had finally arrived. The battle had begun, and with it, the journey towards a new future, a future that they would build with their own hands, no matter the sacrifices that lay ahead.

Chapter 22 The Silent Resistance

The streets of London, once alive with the loud clamour of protest and the thunder of battle, had grown eerily quieter in recent weeks. But this newfound silence was deceptive, a thin veneer that barely masked the seething undercurrent of rebellion that now pulsed through the veins of the city. The cacophony of shouts, gunfire, and the pounding of boots on cobblestone had been replaced by a different kind of noise, one that was far less obvious but infinitely more dangerous to the regime. This silence was not the quiet of defeat, but rather the hushed whispers of a movement that had gone underground, adapting, and evolving to survive in the shadows. The rebellion had entered a new, more insidious phase, one where overt confrontations were set aside in favour of covert tactics, sabotage, espionage, and propaganda. The resistance had learned that to fight in the open was to invite annihilation; to fight in the shadows was to endure.

As the city settled into the predawn hours, draped in the soft grey light that heralded the coming day, figures moved with the quiet precision of ghosts through the labyrinthine streets. These were the rebels who had chosen a different path in the struggle for freedom, trading rifles and barricades for the tools of stealth and subversion. They were no longer the masses who had marched openly through Trafalgar Square or clashed head-on with riot police on Westminster Bridge. They were now the silent warriors of the resistance, slipping in and out of the darkened alleyways, their faces obscured by hoods and masks, their identities hidden even from each other.

In these early morning hours, the city itself seemed to hold its breath, as if aware that something significant was unfolding beneath its surface. The rebels worked in teams, each group with a specific mission, their operations carefully coordinated to strike at the heart of the regime's infrastructure. They moved with purpose, each step calculated, each action deliberate. Some carried small, inconspicuous packages, homemade explosives that would later be placed at critical junctures in the city's power grid or transportation network. Others wielded laptops and portable devices, their screens flickering with lines of code as they hacked into government communication systems, planting viruses that would disrupt the flow of information, creating confusion and mistrust within the ranks of the authorities.

But it wasn't just about destruction; it was about dismantling the very foundations of the government's power. In the stillness of the night, rebels pasted subversive posters onto walls, slipped leaflets under doors, and sent out clandestine broadcasts that spread messages of defiance and hope. These were the tools of propaganda, carefully crafted to chip away at the regime's control over the population. The messages were simple but powerful images of government atrocities, calls to action, and reminders that the people were not alone in their struggle. Each piece of propaganda was a spark, igniting the embers of rebellion in the hearts of those who had not yet taken up the cause.

The silence of the city was deceptive because it was pregnant with potential, with the anticipation of what was to come. The government's forces, still patrolling the streets in their armoured vehicles, were unaware of the shifting tides beneath their feet. They saw the quiet as a victory, a sign that they had finally crushed the rebellion. But in truth, it was the calm before the storm, a storm that would come not with a roar, but with the calculated precision of a thousand tiny cuts, each one weakening the regime's grip on power.

For the rebels, this new phase of the war was one of patience and strategy. It required a different kind of courage, the courage to fight without recognition, and to carry out missions that would never be celebrated with public acclaim. It was a war of attrition, where every act of sabotage, every piece of misinformation spread, was a small victory that chipped away at the foundations of tyranny. The rebels knew they were outnumbered and outgunned, but they also knew that their strength lay in their ability to adapt, to become something the government could not easily crush.

In the soft grey light of dawn, as the city slowly came to life, the rebels melted back into the shadows, their work done for the night. The explosives were in place, the systems had been breached, and the propaganda had been distributed. Now, they would wait, watching from the safety of their hidden lairs as the government scrambled to respond to the chaos that would soon unfold. The silence of the city was no longer just the absence of sound, it was the sound of resistance, of a movement that had found a new way to fight, a way that was as effective as it was invisible.

As the first rays of the sun broke over the horizon, casting long shadows across the city, the quiet streets of London held within them the promise of what was to come. The rebellion was not defeated; it was evolving, growing stronger with each passing day. The silence was not the end. it was the beginning of something far more powerful, something that the government, for all its might, would be unable to stop. The rebellion had found a new voice, and it was speaking through the silence, louder and more potent than ever before.

Lily had become a linchpin in this new form of warfare. She had always been tech-savvy, but the war had honed her skills into something lethal. Her small, makeshift command centre was set up in a hidden basement beneath an old, nondescript building on the outskirts of London. The room was dimly lit by the glow of multiple computer screens, the soft hum of electronics a constant background noise. Papers with hastily scrawled notes were pinned to the walls, maps with markings crisscrossed the tables, and in the centre of it, all was Lily, her fingers dancing across a keyboard as she orchestrated a campaign of digital warfare.

Her eyes were sharp with focus, her mind always a step ahead, calculating, planning, and executing a war that was fought in the shadows of the internet. She had become a ghost in the government's systems, slipping in and out without a trace, leaving behind a trail of confusion and disarray. Through carefully crafted leaks, she exposed the government's darkest secrets, hidden atrocities, financial corruption, and the inner workings of their oppressive machine. She manipulated the flow of information, turning the government's tools against them, and sowing discord and doubt among the population.

But it wasn't just about hacking into systems. Lily understood the power of narrative, of shaping public opinion. She coordinated with underground media outlets, ensuring that the truth of the rebellion's cause reached the masses, bypassing the government's censorship. She knew that winning the hearts and minds of the people was as crucial as any battle fought with guns and bombs.

One evening, after hours of relentless work, Emily found Lily hunched over her computer, the blue light casting a pale hue over her face. The room was cluttered, a testament to the whirlwind of activity that had become Lily's life. Emily approached her quietly, sensing the weight of the burden Lily carried.

"Lily," Emily said softly, pulling up a chair beside her, "you've been at this non-stop. You need to take a break."

Lily shook her head, not tearing her eyes away from the screen. "I can't, Emily. We're so close. The people are starting to see the truth. They're questioning everything. We can't let up now."

Emily placed a hand on Lily's arm, her voice gentle but firm. "I know how important this is. You're doing incredible work. But you can't do it alone. We need you to stay sharp, to stay strong. Pushing yourself to the brink won't help anyone."

Lily finally looked up, her eyes tired but filled with determination. "I just... I can't stop thinking about all the lives at stake. If I make one mistake, if I miss something, it could mean the difference between victory and defeat. I can't live with that on my conscience."

Emily sighed, understanding the pressure Lily was under. She had felt it herself, the crushing weight of responsibility. "We're all carrying that burden, Lily. But we're in this together. You're not alone, and you don't have to do everything by yourself. Lean on us. Trust us."

Lily hesitated, then nodded slowly. "You're right. I just... I don't want to let anyone down."

"You won't," Emily assured her. "You're one of the strongest people I know. And what you're doing here, it's making a difference. The people are listening, they're rising up. And it's because of you."

Lily's shoulders relaxed slightly, and she allowed herself a small, weary smile. "Thanks, Emily. That means a lot."

They sat in companionable silence for a moment, both feeling the gravity of the fight ahead. The battle wasn't just physical, it was a war for the soul of the nation, fought in the shadows, in the hearts and minds of the people.

Meanwhile, in a small town outside the capital, Hassan's community had become a refuge for those who had nowhere else to turn. His brother Aamir, who had taken over the leadership role in the town after Hassan's death, had quietly transformed the area into a haven for rebels and civilians alike. The town was a peaceful, unassuming place on the surface, but beneath that calm exterior, it was a hub of resistance activity.

The streets of the town were lined with modest homes, their gardens neatly kept, giving no outward sign of the turmoil that gripped the rest of the country. But within these homes, plans were being made, supplies were being stockpiled, and lives were being saved. The town's people were fiercely loyal to the resistance, their trust in Aamir and his vision unwavering. They had seen the horrors of the regime firsthand, and they were determined to fight back in whatever way they could.

In a secluded house at the edge of town, where the dense woods met the open fields, Aamir sat with a group of rebel leaders, their faces illuminated by the soft, flickering glow of a single lantern. The house, once the quiet retreat of a local farmer long gone, had now become a sanctuary for the resistance, a place where plans were hatched in secret and the future of the rebellion was shaped. The air inside was thick with the scent of damp earth and aged wood, a comforting contrast to the tension that gripped their hearts.

The room they occupied was small, its walls lined with worn, peeling wallpaper that spoke of a simpler time, now long forgotten. A battered, old table dominated the centre of the room, its surface scarred with the marks of countless gatherings like this one. The table was cluttered with maps, documents, and hastily scribbled notes, each piece of paper representing another piece of the complex puzzle they were trying to solve. Around the table, the leaders huddled close, their expressions set with determination, their voices hushed as they exchanged ideas and debated strategies.

The furniture in the room was sparse and functional, with a few mismatched chairs, each more unsteady than the last, and a single armchair pushed into a corner, its upholstery frayed and faded. The floorboards creaked with every movement, a reminder of the age and fragility of the house itself, yet it had stood through the years, much like the resolve of the rebels who now sought refuge within its walls.

Aamir, seated at the head of the table, exuded a calm authority that belied the storm of emotions swirling within him. His face, usually so composed, now bore the faint lines of worry and fatigue, though his eyes were sharp, focused. He scanned the maps laid out before him, topographical charts of the region, detailed layouts of government installations, and a series of red X's marking key targets that had either been hit or were next on the list.

The rebel leaders who sat with him were a diverse group, each bringing their unique strengths to the table. There was Zara, a former military strategist who had defected to the resistance, her sharp mind constantly assessing risks and potential gains; beside her sat Elias, a burly man with a heart as fierce as his appearance, a former miner turned rebel commander whose knowledge of the underground tunnels crisscrossing the area was invaluable. Next to Elias was Marah, a schoolteacher in her previous life, now an expert in covert communications, her quiet demeanour masking a relentless drive to see the rebellion succeed. And there was Rafik, a young engineer who had become the go-to person for anything related to explosives and sabotage, his eyes always alight with ideas on how to strike back at the regime.

As they spoke in low tones, their discussions were marked by a sense of urgency tempered with caution. Every decision they made here could mean the difference between life and death, not just for themselves but for the countless others who relied on their leadership. The room buzzed with quiet intensity, the sound of their voices mingling with the rustling of paper and the occasional clink of a glass as someone took a sip of the strong, bitter coffee that kept them alert through the long night.

Aamir listened carefully to each of them, weighing their words with the gravity they deserved. His role, now that his brother Hassan was gone, was not just to lead but to inspire confidence, to keep the flame of resistance burning brightly even when the darkness seemed overwhelming. He knew that every plan they made had to be both bold and measured, for they could not afford reckless mistakes, not when the stakes were this high.

The maps and documents on the table told a story of a rebellion that had been forced to adapt, to evolve from the open defiance of the early days to the clandestine warfare that now defined their struggle. They spoke of supply routes that needed to be secured, of safe houses that needed to be fortified, of recruits who needed to be trained in the arts of sabotage and survival. They highlighted the locations of government patrols and checkpoints, the weak points in the regime's defences, and the areas where the resistance could strike without risking too many lives.

As the leaders discussed their next move, the lantern light flickered, casting long shadows on the walls, the shadows of people who had been pushed to the brink but refused to break. Aamir felt the weight of the responsibility on his shoulders, but he also felt the strength of the people around him. They were not just rebels; they were a family bound together by a common cause, by a shared dream of a future free from tyranny. And as they planned, there was an unspoken understanding that no matter what came next, they would face it together.

The room, though small and worn, was alive with the pulse of resistance. Every whispered word, every nod of agreement, every mark on the map was a testament to their resolve, to their refusal to surrender. This house at the edge of town was more than just a meeting place, it was a beacon of hope in a world that had tried to snuff out that very hope. As the night wore on, as their plans began to take shape, the sense of purpose in the room grew stronger, filling the space with a quiet but unbreakable resolve.

They knew that what they were doing was dangerous and that the government would stop at nothing to crush them if they were discovered. But they also knew that they had come too far to turn back now. The rebellion was in their blood, in their bones, and it was this shared purpose that would carry them through whatever lay ahead. In this small, secluded house, on this cold, quiet night, the seeds of their next move were being sown, and with them, the promise of a new dawn for the resistance.

Aamir spoke in measured tones, his calm demeanour a steadying force in the room. "We've managed to establish a network of safe houses throughout the region," he explained. "But the government's surveillance is getting tighter. We need to be even more careful, and more discreet. Every move we make is being watched."

Zara, one of the leaders, nodded in agreement. "We've been hearing reports of increased patrols in the area. They're looking for us, for any sign of resistance. If they find out what we're doing here, it could mean the end of everything we've built."

Aamir's expression was serious, but there was a spark of determination in his eyes. "That's why we need to stay one step ahead. We need to keep our operations small and keep our communications secure. And we need to continue supporting Lily and her work. The information war is just as important as the physical one."

The group nodded in agreement, their resolve unshaken despite the risks they faced. They knew that their work was dangerous, and that the government would stop at nothing to crush them if they were discovered. But they also knew that their fight was just, that they were on the right side of history.

The town itself had become a symbol of quiet defiance, a place where the rebellion simmered just beneath the surface, ready to burst forth at any moment. On the surface, it appeared to be nothing more than an idyllic rural community, a scattering of quaint, thatched-roof cottages with well-tended gardens, narrow lanes winding between them, and a small town square where the local grocer and butcher still greeted their customers by name. The scent of fresh-baked bread often wafted from the bakery, mixing with the earthy smell of the nearby fields, while children laughed and played in the streets, their carefree shouts a stark contrast to the tension that lingered in the air.

But to the trained eye, to those who knew where to look, the town told a different story. This was not a place untouched by the conflict; rather, it was a bastion of quiet resistance, a stronghold of those who refused to bow to the regime's oppressive rule. The town's unassuming exterior was a carefully maintained façade, masking the determination and courage of its inhabitants.

Behind the closed doors of the town's homes, the reality of the resistance was far more evident. In living rooms that once hosted family gatherings, tables were now strewn with blueprints and maps, carefully marked with the locations of government patrols and potential targets. In the basements and attics of these homes, weapons were being assembled with the meticulous precision of those who knew their lives, and the lives of others, depended on their craftsmanship. Firearms were cleaned and loaded, explosives were carefully wired and hidden away, and knives were sharpened, all in preparation for the day when the resistance would need to rise once more.

The town's seemingly ordinary shops and businesses played their part as well. The local mechanic's garage was more than just a place for oil changes and tire rotations; it was a covert workshop where vehicles were modified to outrun government patrols and smuggle weapons across the countryside. The grocer's backroom, typically reserved for surplus stock, had been converted into a storage space for medical supplies, ready to treat the wounded when the time came. Even the bakery, with its inviting display of pastries and bread, harboured a secret, a hidden compartment in the back where coded messages were baked into loaves, ready to be delivered to nearby resistance cells under the guise of innocent commerce.

The townspeople themselves, outwardly polite and reserved, were the lifeblood of this hidden network. They had become adept at masking their true intentions, their conversations filled with coded language that to an outsider might seem like nothing more than casual chatter. A discussion about the weather might be about the timing of the next supply drop, while a comment on the quality of the bread could be a signal that the coast was clear for a meeting. The children, too, played their part, their games of hide-and-seek serving as a cover for the delivery of messages and small packages. They moved through the town with an innocence that belied the critical roles they played in maintaining the lines of communication between the resistance fighters.

In the evenings, when the sun dipped below the horizon and the town was bathed in the golden glow of lanterns and hearth fires, the true spirit of the resistance came alive. Gatherings were held in the larger homes, where townsfolk crowded into kitchens and sitting rooms, their voices low but filled with determination. They spoke of the latest developments, shared news from other resistance groups, and strategised their next moves. It was in these meetings that plans were made, plans that would later unfold in the dead of night, when the town's quiet streets became the pathways of revolution.

And yet, for all their activity, the townspeople never forgot the importance of maintaining the illusion of normalcy. They went about their daily lives with the same routines they had always followed, tending to their gardens, visiting the market, and attending Sunday services at the local church. But beneath the surface, they were always vigilant, always ready. The town's quiet defiance was not born of recklessness but of necessity. They knew that one misstep could bring the full force of the regime down upon them, and so they moved carefully, methodically, always one step ahead of the authorities.

The town had become a symbol not just of resistance, but of resilience, a place where the fight for freedom had been woven into the very fabric of everyday life. It was a living, breathing example of what could be accomplished when people came together with a shared purpose when they refused to be cowed by fear or oppression. As the war raged on, the town's quiet defiance would continue to be a beacon of hope for all those who dared to dream of a future free from tyranny.

In the basement of the town's church, a group of volunteers worked tirelessly, preparing supplies for the rebels who passed through on their way to the front lines. The air was thick with the smell of fresh bread and the sound of quiet determination. Every loaf of bread, every bandage, every piece of equipment they prepared was a small act of rebellion, a defiance of the regime that had taken so much from them.

The church itself had become a sanctuary, a place where rebels could rest and regroup before heading back into the fray. The pews, once filled with worshippers, now held the weary bodies of those who had given everything for the cause. The walls, once adorned with religious icons, now bore the marks of a different kind of faith, a faith in the rebellion, in the belief that they could build a better world.

But with each act of defiance, the risks grew greater. The town's people knew that it was only a matter of time before the government's gaze turned toward them. They had heard the stories of what had happened to other towns, of the brutal crackdowns, the mass arrests, the executions. But they also knew that they could not back down. They had made their choice, and they would stand by it, no matter the cost.

Later that night, as the town settled into a tense silence, Aamir and Zara walked through the quiet streets, their footsteps muffled by the soft dirt road. The night was cool, the sky clear and filled with stars, a stark contrast to the turmoil that simmered beneath the surface.

"I worry about the people here," Zara admitted, her voice barely above a whisper. "They've put so much faith in us, in this cause. But what if we can't protect them?"

Aamir looked up at the stars, his expression thoughtful. "We can't protect them from everything," he said quietly. "But we can give them something to believe in. Something worth fighting for."

Zara sighed, her shoulders heavy with the weight of responsibility. "I just don't want to see more innocent people get hurt."

"Neither do I," Aamir replied, his voice firm. "But this isn't just about us anymore. It's about everyone who has been hurt, who has suffered under this regime. If we give up now, then all of that suffering, all of those lives lost, will have been for nothing."

Zara nodded, a new resolve settling over her. "You're right. We can't stop now. We have to keep going, no matter the risks."

As they continued their walk, the town around them seemed to take on a new significance, a symbol of everything they were fighting for. The people here had shown incredible courage and had risked everything for a chance at a better future. And Aamir knew that he could not let them down.

The silent resistance was growing, spreading through the cracks of a regime that was beginning to crumble. And as the night wore on, the stars above them shining brightly in the darkness, Aamir and Zara knew that they were part of something much larger than themselves. They were part of a movement that would not be silenced, a force that would continue to grow until it could no longer be ignored.

The rebellion was far from over. It was evolving, adapting to the challenges it faced, and finding new ways to strike back at the forces that sought to oppress them. And in the small town that had become a beacon of hope for so many, the spirit of resistance burned brightly, a flame that would not be extinguished.

The silent resistance had found its voice, and it was only growing louder, a voice that spoke not with the sound of gunfire or the clash of steel, but with the quiet, unyielding force of a people united in their defiance. It was the whisper of secrets shared in darkened rooms, the clandestine meetings held in the dead of night, and the coded messages passed between allies. It was the graffiti scrawled on the walls of once-quiet towns, the flyers that appeared overnight, and the murmurs of rebellion that spread from one corner of the country to the other.

This voice, though hushed at first, was becoming a roar. It was the sound of pens scratching out the truth in underground newspapers, of radios crackling to life with forbidden broadcasts, and of the click of keys as hackers like Lily unleashed waves of information that shattered the government's stranglehold on the narrative. It was the voice of the people, rising through the cracks of a society that had tried to silence them, each word, each act of defiance, adding to the chorus that would no longer be ignored.

And as the voice grew louder, it became a beacon of hope for those who had once felt isolated and powerless. It reached into the hearts of the oppressed, giving them the strength to stand up, to fight back. It was the voice that told them they were not alone, that their struggle was part of something much larger, an unstoppable movement that was sweeping across the nation.

The government, once so confident in its ability to control and suppress, was beginning to feel the effects of this rising tide. They could no longer dismiss the resistance as a mere nuisance, a fleeting problem to be solved with brute force. The voice of the silent resistance was everywhere, in every city and town, in every home where the truth was spoken in whispers. It was in the eyes of the soldiers who began to question their orders, in the doubt that crept into the minds of the officials who had once believed in the regime's invincibility.

The louder this voice grew, the more it resonated with those who had yet to take a stand. It was a call to action, a reminder that the power of the people, when united, was greater than any force of oppression. It echoed through the corridors of power, a haunting refrain that no wall or barrier could keep out.

The silent resistance had found its voice, and that voice was a force of nature, relentless, unstoppable, and growing with each passing day. It was the voice of a nation waking up from a long nightmare, ready to reclaim its future. It was the voice of justice, of freedom, of a hope that could not be crushed.

And as it grew louder, it carried with it the promise of change. The rebellion was no longer a distant dream; it was a reality, a movement that had gained momentum and would not be silenced. The voice of the silent resistance was not just a cry for help; it was a declaration of war, a battle cry that would lead them to victory.

The silent resistance had found its voice, and it was a voice that would echo through history, a voice that would be remembered as the sound of a people who refused to be broken. It was a voice that would carry them through the darkest of times, a voice that would inspire generations to come. And as it grew louder, it became clear that this was only the beginning. The fight for freedom had truly begun.

Chapter 23 Love and War

The night was unusually still, a heavy, expectant silence that seemed to settle over the farmhouse like a shroud. The resistance members huddled together in the dimly lit room, their faces bathed in the soft, flickering glow of candles scattered around the rough-hewn table. Shadows danced across the walls, elongating the figures seated around the room, making the space feel both intimate and claustrophobic. The scent of wax and the faint, lingering aroma of burnt wood from the fireplace mingled with the cool, earthy smell that seeped in from the fields outside, creating an atmosphere that was both comforting and suffocating.

Outside, the wind whispered through the ancient oak trees that surrounded the farmhouse, their branches creaking and swaying like old sentinels standing guard over this last bastion of resistance. The wind carried with it the distant sounds of a world that had been forever altered by conflict, a world that was now a fractured mosaic of fear, defiance, and loss. Occasionally, the distant echo of gunfire or the rumble of military vehicles would punctuate the stillness, a grim reminder that the war was never far away, even in this remote corner of the countryside.

Inside, the air was thick with unspoken words, the tension palpable as the rebels navigated the delicate balance between their duty to the cause and the personal connections that had formed within their ranks. The flickering candlelight highlighted the lines of exhaustion etched into their faces, the weariness that came not just from physical fatigue but from the emotional toll of the choices they had been forced to make. Each of them carried their burdens, silent and heavy, the weight of past decisions and future uncertainties pressing down on their shoulders.

The silence in the room was oppressive, broken only by the occasional rustle of paper as someone shifted in their seat or the soft murmur of a whispered conversation. There was a sense of waiting, of anticipation, as if the night itself was holding its breath, unsure of what the dawn would bring. They had fought and bled together, their lives intertwined by the shared struggle, yet now, in this quiet moment, the distance between them felt vast, each of them lost in their thoughts, their fears.

The tension was not just from the war outside but from the complex web of relationships that had developed within the group. Bonds had been formed in the crucible of battle, forged by shared pain and mutual reliance, but those same bonds were now being tested by the weight of leadership, by the demands of a conflict that asked more of them than they had ever imagined. The personal had become inextricable from the political, and the lines between love and duty, between friendship and command, had blurred in ways that none of them had anticipated.

The room itself, with its low, wooden beams and thick, stone walls, seemed to close in around them, the space both a refuge and a prison. The farmhouse had once been a place of safety, a sanctuary from the chaos of the outside world, but now it felt like a pressure cooker, the air heavy with the unresolved tensions that simmered just beneath the surface. The crackle of the fire in the hearth was a poor comfort, the warmth it provided doing little to ease the chill that had settled in their hearts.

As the night wore on, the resistance members remained huddled together, their eyes reflecting the flickering flames as they grappled with the dual realities of war and personal connection. The silence between them spoke louder than words, a shared understanding of the sacrifices that had been made and the ones yet to come. In that stillness, each of them was alone with their thoughts, but they were also bound together by the invisible threads of loyalty, love, and a common purpose that kept them moving forward, even when the path ahead seemed impossibly dark.

Emily sat alone in a corner, her back against the rough wooden wall, her eyes fixed on the flames dancing in the hearth. The warmth from the fire did little to thaw the chill that had settled in her bones. Her mind was a whirlwind of conflicting emotions, a constant battle between the roles she had chosen and the unexpected feelings that had taken root in her heart.

Across the room, Aamir was deep in conversation with another member of the group, but Emily could feel his presence like a magnet pulling her attention. Over the past few months, they had grown closer, their connection forged in the crucible of shared grief and responsibility. Aamir had become a steady presence in her life, his quiet strength a source of comfort in the chaos. But with that closeness came a tension that neither of them could ignore, a tension that threatened to unravel everything they had fought for.

She knew that the feelings she had for Aamir were dangerous, a distraction that could compromise their mission. They both carried the weight of leadership, and their decisions affected not just themselves, but the lives of everyone who had placed their trust in them. Yet, despite her best efforts to remain detached, she found herself drawn to him in ways she hadn't expected.

Emily's thoughts were interrupted by the sound of Aamir's voice, low and steady as he spoke to the others. His words were measured, filled with the wisdom and caution that had made him such an invaluable leader. She admired his ability to remain calm under pressure, to see the bigger picture when everything around them seemed to be falling apart. But tonight, as she listened to him speak, she couldn't shake the feeling that their growing closeness was complicating everything.

A few feet away, Lily sat at the kitchen table, her hands wrapped around a steaming mug of tea. Her gaze was distant, her thoughts consumed by her internal struggle. Like Emily, Lily had always been fiercely dedicated to the cause, her passion for justice burning brightly in everything she did. But recently, that fire had been clouded by a different kind of intensity, one that had nothing to do with the war they were fighting.

Lily was torn between two men, both of whom had come to mean more to her than she was willing to admit. There was Rafik, the engineer with a sharp mind and a fierce loyalty to the resistance. He was the kind of person who always knew what needed to be done and was willing to do whatever it took to achieve their goals. With Rafik, everything felt clear and straightforward; their connection was based on mutual respect and a shared sense of purpose.

But then there was Daniel, the quiet, introspective recruit who had quickly proven himself in the field. Daniel was different, his presence brought a sense of calm that Lily hadn't realised she needed. He had a way of seeing through her defences, of understanding the parts of her that she usually kept hidden from the rest of the world. Their connection was more subtle and less defined, but it was powerful in its own way.

Lily sighed, her heart heavy with the weight of her dilemma. She cared deeply for Rafik, but her feelings for Daniel were growing stronger with each passing day. The war had taken so much from her already, and the thought of losing either of them or worse, hurting them, filled her with a deep sense of unease. She had always prided herself on her ability to stay focused, to keep her emotions in check for the sake of the mission. But now, she found herself questioning whether that was even possible.

As the night wore on, the members of the resistance began to drift off to their respective corners of the farmhouse, seeking what little rest they could find before the next day's challenges. Emily remained by the fire, her thoughts still tangled with the complexity of her feelings for Aamir. She knew she couldn't afford to let those feelings interfere with her role as a leader, but the thought of pushing him away filled her with a sense of loss that she wasn't ready to confront.

She was so lost in thought that she didn't hear Aamir approach until he was standing beside her. "Emily," he said softly, his voice breaking through the fog of her thoughts.

She looked up at him, surprised to see the concern in his eyes. "Aamir," she replied, her voice betraying the uncertainty she felt.

He took a seat beside her, their shoulders nearly touching as they both stared into the fire. For a moment, neither of them spoke, the silence between them filled with the unspoken tension that had been building for weeks.

"You seem...distant tonight," Aamir finally said, his tone gentle but probing.

Emily hesitated, unsure of how to put her feelings into words. "I've just been thinking," she admitted. "About everything that's happened, everything that's still to come."

Aamir nodded, his gaze fixed on the flames. "It's a lot to carry," he said quietly. "For both of us."

She turned to him, searching his eyes for the reassurance she desperately needed. "I don't want to make a mistake, Aamir. Not when so many people are depending on us."

"You won't," he replied, his voice filled with quiet conviction. "You've led us this far, and you've done it with courage and strength. We all have faith in you."

Emily felt a pang of guilt at the comfort his words brought her, knowing that the feelings she had for him complicated everything. "It's just...sometimes I wonder if we're doing the right thing. If we're making the right choices."

Aamir reached out, gently taking her hand in his. "We're doing the best we can, Emily. That's all anyone can ask of us."

She looked down at their intertwined hands, the warmth of his touch a stark contrast to the cold fear that gripped her heart. "But what if...what if our feelings get in the way? What if they cloud our judgment?"

Aamir's expression softened, and he squeezed her hand reassuringly. "We're human, Emily. We're allowed to have feelings, even in the midst of all this. But we can't let them control us. We have to stay focused on the mission, on what's at stake."

Emily nodded, though the conflict within her was far from resolved. "I care about you, Aamir," she said quietly. "More than I should."

"And I care about you," he replied, his voice filled with sincerity. "But we both know what we need to do. We can't let our personal feelings interfere with the cause."

It was the truth, and Emily knew it. But that didn't make it any easier to accept. "You're right," she said, her voice tinged with sadness. "We have to stay strong. For everyone."

Aamir smiled gently, though his eyes reflected the same sadness she felt. "We will. Together."

As the first light of dawn began to creep through the windows, the farmhouse settled into an uneasy quiet, the members of the resistance lost in their thoughts. The war had tested them in ways they had never imagined, stripping away their defences and forcing them to confront the rawest parts of themselves. And yet, for all the personal struggles they faced, they remained united in their cause, bound together by a shared sense of purpose that transcended their individual lives.

Lily, too, grappled with the choices she had to make. The connection she felt with both Rafik and Daniel was undeniable, but the path forward was anything but clear. The war had taken so much from her already, and the thought of losing either of them or worse, making the wrong choice, weighed heavily on her heart.

As the sun rose over the farmhouse, casting its first light across the weary faces of the rebels, they steeled themselves for what lay ahead. The war had tested them, pushed them to their limits, but it had also forged them into something stronger, something more resilient. And as they prepared to face the battles to come, they did so with the knowledge that whatever happened, they would face it together, united in their cause, and bound by the unbreakable ties of love and war.

Chapter 24 The Government's Last Gamble

The air in the command centre was thick with tension, the hum of machinery and the low murmur of voices underscoring the sense of urgency that permeated the room. General Webb stood at the head of the operations table, his eyes fixed on the large digital map that displayed the latest intelligence on the rebellion's movements. Around him, a cadre of high-ranking officers and government officials waited in grim silence, their faces etched with the strain of the impossible task before them.

For months, the government had been losing ground, its once unassailable authority eroded by a series of humiliating defeats at the hands of the rebels. Every tactical victory the resistance scored, no matter how small, had chipped away at the government's control, emboldening the population and sowing doubt among the military ranks. Now, with the rebellion gaining momentum and the cracks in the government's foundation growing wider by the day, Webb knew they were running out of time.

This was their last chance. The government's final gambit. Everything they had built, the power they had wielded for so long, teetered on the edge of a precipice. The rebellion once thought to be a minor nuisance, had grown into a force capable of toppling the very foundations of the state. The corridors of power were no longer filled with the confident footsteps of leaders certain of their control, but rather the hurried, nervous paces of those who knew they were running out of time. The streets they once commanded had turned hostile, the people they once ruled with ease now rose against them.

This final offensive wasn't just another military operation, it was a desperate attempt to cling to a crumbling empire. The government had thrown everything it had into this plan, mustering all its remaining resources, calling in every favour, and pushing its loyalists to the breaking point. It was a last-ditch effort to crush the rebellion, to smother the flickering flames of defiance before they erupted into an uncontrollable inferno that would consume the nation.

Every aspect of the operation had been meticulously planned, every variable considered, and yet there was an underlying fear that it wouldn't be enough. The rebellion had proven resilient, adapting and growing stronger with each attempt to stamp it out. It was as if the very act of oppression had become the rebellion's lifeblood, feeding its resolve and swelling its ranks.

And so, the government's final gambit was not just about military might. It was a psychological war, a bid to break the spirit of the resistance, to show them that the power of the state was absolute and unassailable.

It was an effort to sow fear, to turn the tide of public opinion back in their favour, to convince the wavering masses that standing against the regime was not only futile but suicidal.

But in the halls of power, behind the steely determination and the confident rhetoric, there was a gnawing uncertainty. The government knew that if this gambit failed, there would be no recovery. The regime had already been stretched to its limits, and this final push was draining the last of its reserves, military, economic, and moral. The officers and politicians who had once been so sure of their position now found themselves staring into the abyss, wondering if they were about to fall.

This was their last chance. The final gambit of a regime that had ruled through fear and control, now fighting to maintain a grip on a nation slipping through its fingers. If they succeeded, they might just crush the rebellion and restore order, but if they failed, they would plunge the country into chaos and seal their fate.

In the end, this gambit was not just a battle for control of the country, it was a battle for survival, for the very existence of the government itself. And with everything at stake, the tension was palpable, the stakes higher than they had ever been before.

"Operation Iron Fist," Webb began, his voice cold and commanding, cutting through the murmurs like a knife. "This is it. We've spent weeks amassing our forces, gathering intelligence, and planning this offensive. There is no room for error. We will strike hard, strike fast, and we will not stop until the rebellion is crushed."

The officers nodded, some with the conviction born of loyalty, others with a flicker of doubt in their eyes. Beneath the uniformed stoicism, a storm of conflicting emotions churned within them, hidden behind disciplined facades that had been honed over years of service. These were men and women who had dedicated their lives to the government, believing in the righteousness of their cause, in the necessity of order and control to maintain the fragile stability of the nation. They had risen through the ranks on the strength of their convictions, earning their positions through loyalty, skill, and a shared belief in the authority they served.

But now, as they listened to General Webb's bold proclamations, some of that conviction wavered. They had seen what the rebellion was capable of and witnessed the unexpected resilience and cunning of an enemy they had once dismissed as ragtag insurgents. What had started as small pockets of unrest had grown into a coordinated movement that had defied every attempt to crush it. The rebels had struck at the heart of the government's power, embarrassing them, eroding their control, and showing the world that the regime was not as invincible as it had once seemed.

The cost of underestimating this enemy was burned into their memories, the lives lost, the cities disrupted, the authority questioned. These were not just theoretical consequences; they were the realities these officers had faced in the field. They had seen comrades fall, witnessed the devastation of battles that should have been won easily, and felt the gnawing anxiety that came with each new report of rebel victories.

For some, loyalty remained unshaken. They believed in General Webb, believed in his ability to lead them to victory through sheer force of will and military might. They admired his decisiveness, his refusal to back down, and his commitment to crushing the rebellion no matter the cost. To them, Webb's confidence was a beacon in the storm, a reminder that they were fighting for a cause greater than themselves. They clung to the belief that, under his leadership, the government could still prevail and could still restore order to a nation on the brink of chaos.

But for others, doubt had begun to creep in, insidious and persistent. They questioned whether Webb truly understood the situation they were in, whether his relentless drive to win was blinding him to the realities on the ground. They had seen the cracks in the military's morale, heard the whispers of dissent among the ranks, and felt the growing disillusionment that had begun to spread like a virus. They wondered if Webb's unshakeable confidence was less a strength and more a dangerous hubris, a refusal to see that the tide was turning against them.

These officers knew that the stakes of this operation were higher than ever before. Webb had staked everything on this offensive, and failure was not an option. But in their private thoughts, some questioned whether it was already too late, whether the government's final gambit was doomed to fail not because of the rebels' strength alone, but because of the internal fractures that Webb refused to acknowledge.

As they looked at Webb, standing tall and resolute at the head of the table, they saw a man driven by an unyielding belief in his infallibility. He had risen to power on the back of his successes, his tactical brilliance, and his ruthless efficiency, and he had come to see himself as the embodiment of the government's will. To Webb, there was no room for doubt, no space for hesitation. Victory was the only acceptable outcome, and any price was worth paying to achieve it.

But for those officers who harboured doubts, who had seen the toll this war was taking not just on the country but on the very forces tasked with defending it, Webb's confidence felt increasingly disconnected from reality. They feared that his refusal to entertain the possibility of failure was leading them down a path from which there might be no return.

And yet, duty demanded their obedience. They had been trained to follow orders, to trust in the chain of command, to believe that those above them knew what was best. But as they nodded along to Webb's plans, as they steeled themselves for the battles to come, some could not shake the nagging fear that they were being led into a disaster of their own making.

In the silence that followed Webb's speech, the room was heavy with unspoken anxieties, with the weight of decisions that could not be undone. The officers would do their duty, but in the back of their minds, a question lingered: was this truly the path to victory, or were they marching headlong into their defeat?

The room fell silent as Webb outlined the plan, his voice unwavering as he described the massive military operation that would sweep across the country in a coordinated assault. Thousands of troops, backed by tanks, drones, and air support, would descend upon known rebel strongholds, obliterating their defences, and cutting off their supply lines. Major cities would be placed under strict martial law, with curfews enforced by heavily armed patrols. The goal was clear: annihilate the resistance, once and for all.

But as Webb spoke, the unease among the officers grew. They had been receiving reports, troubling reports, of growing dissent within their own ranks. Soldiers, once loyal to the regime, were beginning to question the orders they were given. The brutality of the government's tactics, the indiscriminate violence against civilians, and the relentless suppression of basic freedoms were wearing down the morale of the troops. Some had even refused to follow orders, leading to summary executions by their superiors, a fact that had spread like wildfire through the ranks.

There were whispers of desertion, of soldiers quietly slipping away in the dead of night to join the very rebels they were supposed to be fighting. The government's iron grip was beginning to loosen, not just among the civilian population, but within the military itself. And yet, Webb remained blind to these cracks, his focus singularly on the impending assault.

As the meeting adjourned, the officers dispersed, their faces a mix of determination and doubt. They knew the risks, but they also knew that they had no choice but to follow Webb's orders. The government was desperate, and desperate times called for desperate measures.

Outside the command centre, the military machine was in full motion. Troops were being deployed, convoys of armoured vehicles snaking through the streets, and the sky above buzzed with the constant drone of helicopters. The city had become a fortress, every street corner bristling with armed soldiers, every building a potential target.

But beneath the surface, there was a growing sense of unease, a silent tension that threaded its way through the ranks like a slow-acting poison. The soldiers, many of them young men and women who had enlisted out of a sense of duty, patriotism, or the desperate need for a steady pay check, were beginning to see the mission in a different light. What had once been a clear-cut battle to protect the nation had become something murkier, more troubling. The line between right and wrong, between protector and oppressor, had blurred.

The stories trickled down to them from the front lines, whispers of government-sanctioned brutality that made the blood run cold. There were tales of entire families wiped out in the name of maintaining order, of villages razed to the ground simply for harbouring suspected rebels. It wasn't just enemy combatants who were being targeted; it was anyone who stood in the way, anyone who dared to question the government's authority. These were not isolated incidents, but a pattern of violence that painted the government not as a force of protection, but as a tyrant lashing out in desperation.

These stories, once dismissed as rebel propaganda, became harder to ignore as the evidence mounted. Some soldiers had seen the atrocities firsthand, had witnessed the terrified faces of civilians as their homes were torn apart, and had heard the cries of children left orphaned by the government's iron fist. They had been told these measures were necessary, that the ends justified the means, but doubt began to creep in. What kind of victory was this, bought with the blood of innocents? What kind of order were they enforcing, when it demanded the annihilation of those they were supposed to protect?

And then there were the executions, the brutal, public punishments meted out to soldiers who hesitated, who questioned, who refused to carry out orders they knew in their hearts were wrong. These were not rebels; these were their own, their comrades, men, and women who had stood beside them in battle, who had shared in their victories and defeats. Seeing them executed for disobedience sent a chilling message: loyalty was not enough. Obedience was paramount, and dissent would not be tolerated.

In the barracks, the atmosphere had shifted. Where once there had been camaraderie, a shared sense of purpose, there was now a growing undercurrent of fear and mistrust. Conversations were held in hushed tones, eyes darting nervously to ensure they were not overheard. The soldiers spoke of the things they had seen, the orders they had been given, and the gnawing sense that something was deeply, fundamentally wrong.

Some spoke of leaving, of deserting before the operation began. They talked of slipping away in the dead of night, finding refuge with the rebels, or disappearing into the countryside where the government's reach was weaker. These were dangerous thoughts, treasonous even, but the seeds of doubt had been sown, and they were taking root.

Others remained loyal, clinging to the belief that they were still on the right side of history. They told themselves that the government's actions, no matter how harsh, were necessary to restore order, to bring peace back to a fractured nation. But even among the loyalists, the tension was palpable. They could feel the ground shifting beneath their feet, the foundation of their belief beginning to crack. The stories of brutality, the executions of their comrades, had left a mark, and the certainty they once felt was fading.

The barracks had become a place of quiet unrest. The soldiers moved through their routines with the same precision as always, but there was a hollowness to it, a sense of going through the motions. They followed orders because they had to because defiance meant death, but the spirit that had once driven them was waning. The government's authority, once unassailable, was crumbling before their eyes, and they all knew it.

Some tried to silence the doubts, to bury them beneath layers of discipline and duty. They repeated the slogans they had been taught, clung to the symbols of their allegiance, and focused on the tasks at hand. But the doubt was there, a constant whisper in the back of their minds, growing louder with each passing day. It was the whisper of a truth they could no longer ignore: that the government they served was not the protector they had believed it to be, but a force of oppression that was losing its grip on power.

And as the time for the operation drew near, that doubt became a heavy weight in their chests, a burden they carried with them as they prepared for battle. They knew that once the operation began, there would be no turning back. They would be forced to choose, between loyalty and conscience, between following orders and following their hearts. And for many, that choice would not be as simple as it once had been.

The rebellion was not just an external enemy; it was an idea, a question that had taken root in the minds of the soldiers themselves. And as they stood on the brink of the government's final gambit, they could feel the fragility of the order they had been sworn to protect. The authority of the government was crumbling, and in its place, something new was beginning to take hold, a growing sense of defiance, a quiet, simmering rebellion that was spreading through the ranks like wildfire.

Meanwhile, in a small, dimly lit room in the heart of the city, Emily sat hunched over a makeshift desk, her breath shallow and her pulse racing. The room, barely large enough to fit a single bed and a rickety table, was cloaked in shadows, the flickering candlelight casting long, ominous shapes against the cracked walls. The air was thick with the musty scent of dampness and decay, but Emily barely noticed. Her entire focus was on the worn piece of paper she held in her trembling hands, the ink smudged from the countless times she had unfolded and refolded it. The manifesto, the words she had poured her soul into, the rallying cry she had crafted with hope and desperation, had been discovered by the government.

A wave of cold dread washed over her, chilling her to the core. She had known the risks when she penned it, had understood that every word she wrote was a step further into dangerous territory. But she had never imagined this, never fully grasped the terrifying reality of what would happen if her words fell into the hands of those she had denounced. She could almost feel the cold, calculating eyes of the regime's enforcers scanning her words, dissecting them, twisting their meaning into something they could use against her.

Her manifesto, once a symbol of defiance, now felt like a noose tightening around her neck.

The manifesto had been meant for the people, a beacon of hope in the darkness, a rallying cry for those who had suffered under the oppressive weight of the government's rule. It spoke of freedom, of the fundamental human right to live without fear, of the duty to stand up against tyranny and injustice. She had written it with a fire in her heart, each word forged from the pain and anger of a people pushed too far. She had wanted to ignite that fire in others, to fan the embers of resistance into a blazing inferno that would burn away the corruption and cruelty of the regime.

But now, those words had become a death sentence. The government, with its iron grip on power, would stop at nothing to silence her. They would twist her words into treason, brand her as a dangerous radical, an enemy of the state. They would hunt her down, drag her before their kangaroo courts, and parade her as a cautionary tale, a grim reminder of what happens to those who dare to defy the might of the regime. Her thoughts raced, picturing the headlines, the propaganda that would follow: "Rebel Leader Exposed," "Traitor to the Nation Captured," and "Justice Served."

She could see it all so clearly, the cold, sterile courtroom, the faceless judges, the jeering crowd. They would strip away her dignity, and her humanity, and reduce her to a symbol of failure, of what happens when one stands against the machine. They would tear apart her manifesto, line by line, turning her words into weapons against her. They would make an example of her, hoping to crush the spirit of rebellion in one decisive, brutal act.

But more than the fear of her fate, what gnawed at Emily was the fear of what would happen to the movement she had helped build. Her manifesto had been a call to arms, a plea for justice, and now it was in the hands of the very people who would use it to destroy everything she and her comrades had fought for. The government would twist her message and use it to justify even harsher crackdowns and more brutal repression. They would use her words to stoke fear, to convince the undecided that the rebels were a threat that must be eliminated at all costs.

The thought was unbearable, and yet, beneath the dread, there was also a spark of defiance. They might capture her, might parade her through their courts and into a cell, but they could not erase the truth of what she had written. Her words were out there, in the hearts and minds of the people who had read them, who had been inspired by them. They could capture the author, but the ideas would live on. And if her capture became the catalyst for the final uprising, if her sacrifice ignited the flames of rebellion that would finally bring the regime to its knees, then perhaps it would all be worth it.

But for now, as she sat in that tiny room, alone with her fear and her thoughts, the weight of the situation pressed down on her like a crushing burden. She was being hunted, her name was on their lips, and every second brought them closer. She knew she had to move, had to disappear into the shadows, to find a way to survive long enough to continue the fight. But the fear, the bone-deep fear of what was to come, threatened to paralyse her.

Taking a deep breath, Emily forced herself to focus. She had to think clearly, to plan her next move. She couldn't afford to let the fear control her. She was not just running for her life, she was running for the lives of all those who believed in the cause, for the hope of a future free from tyranny. The government might have discovered her manifesto, but they had not yet won. The fight was far from over, and Emily knew she would do whatever it took to ensure that her words, her plea for justice, would not be silenced.

"They're coming for me," Emily whispered, her voice barely audible. Across the room, Lily looked up her expression a mix of concern and resolve.

"They'll have to go through us first," Lily replied, her voice steady. "We're not going to let them take you, Emily."

But Emily knew the danger was real, and it was only a matter of time before the government found her. She could feel the walls closing in, the weight of the impending manhunt pressing down on her. She had always known that this fight would come at a cost, but the reality of it was almost too much to bear.

"We need to retreat," Aamir said, his voice cutting through the tension. "Regroup, rethink our strategy. We can't face them head-on, not now."

Emily nodded, her mind racing as she tried to push aside the fear. They had to be smart and had to find a way to outmanoeuvre the government's forces. The rebellion had come too far to be crushed now.

But as they prepared to move, Emily couldn't shake the feeling that they were being watched, that the walls had ears, and that every step they took brought them closer to the edge of a precipice. The government's last gamble was in motion, and the rebels were running out of time.

The night was dark and oppressive as they slipped out of the safe house, their figures blending seamlessly into the inky shadows that clung to the narrow alleyways. The oppressive weight of the night bore down on them, a heavy blanket of dread that seemed to smother the very air they breathed. Every step was measured, every breath carefully controlled as they moved with the stealth of seasoned operatives, their eyes constantly scanning the surroundings for any sign of danger. The safe house, once a sanctuary, now felt like a distant memory, its relative safety replaced by the cold, unforgiving reality of the city-turned-war zone that awaited them outside.

The streets were a maze of destruction, the remnants of battle etched into the very fabric of the city. Buildings that once stood tall and proud now loomed like spectres, their facades pockmarked with bullet holes, their windows shattered and their foundations crumbling. The scent of smoke and burning debris hung thick in the air, mingling with the acrid stench of fear and desperation. The distant flashes of gunfire illuminated the sky intermittently, casting eerie, fleeting shadows that danced along the desolate streets. It was a city caught in the grip of violence, where every corner held the potential for death, and every sound could be the prelude to an ambush.

Emily's heart pounded in her chest, each beat a thunderous drum that seemed to echo through the night. Her nerves were frayed, but she forced herself to stay focused, to keep moving. There was no room for hesitation now, no room for fear. The world around them had descended into chaos, but they had a mission, and they would see it through, no matter the cost. Her mind was a whirlwind of emotions, a tempest of fear, determination, and the relentless drive to survive.

The memories of the day's events flashed through her mind, each one more harrowing than the last. She could still see the faces of those they had left behind comrades who had fought valiantly but had fallen in the face of overwhelming odds. The weight of their sacrifices pressed heavily on her shoulders, fuelling the fire that burned within her, the determination to make sure their deaths were not in vain.

They moved through the city with practiced precision, sticking to the shadows and avoiding the well-lit areas where patrols were likely to be. The soldiers that lined the streets were grim reminders of the government's tightening grip, their presence a constant threat that loomed over every step they took. The sound of boots on the pavement echoed faintly in the distance, a reminder that danger was never far away. Emily knew that one wrong move, one misstep, could mean the difference between life and death.

But it wasn't just the soldiers that haunted her thoughts. It was the oppressive silence that seemed to envelop the city, broken only by the occasional crack of gunfire or the distant wail of a siren. It was the eerie emptiness of streets that had once been filled with life, now reduced to nothing more than pathways of fear and destruction. The city felt like a living entity, wounded and angry, its once vibrant pulse now a faint, erratic beat that struggled to keep pace with the violence that had taken hold.

As they weaved through the labyrinth of darkened alleyways, the fear that gripped Emily threatened to overwhelm her, but she forced herself to focus on the task at hand. There was no time to dwell on the what-ifs, no time to second-guess their decisions. The government's forces were closing in, and the only way to stay ahead was to keep moving, to stay one step ahead of those who sought to silence them.

Each step they took was a step closer to their goal, but it was also a step further into the unknown. Emily's mind raced with possibilities, with the fear of what might happen if they were caught, but also with the hope that maybe, just maybe, they could make a difference. They had come too far to turn back now. The city might be a war zone, the streets lined with soldiers, but they were not alone. The resistance still had fight left in it, and as long as they were still standing, there was still hope.

The determination that fuelled Emily's every move was tempered by the very real fear that gripped her heart, but she refused to let it control her. The city around them was crumbling, but their resolve was not. As they moved through the shadows, her thoughts oscillated between the weight of what they had already lost and the hope of what they still had to fight for. This was a war, and she knew that there was no going back. The night was dark and full of danger, but they would not falter. They would keep moving, keep fighting, until the dawn broke and the darkness was finally driven away.

They reached a narrow alleyway, the walls pressing in on either side as they ducked behind a stack of crates. Emily's breath came in short, sharp gasps as she listened for the sound of approaching footsteps. But the night remained still, the only sound the distant rumble of tanks moving through the city.

"We're clear," Aamir whispered, his voice barely audible.

Emily nodded, her pulse racing as they moved forward. Every step was a gamble, every breath a risk. But they had no choice. The government was closing in, and they had to stay ahead of the storm.

As they continued their retreat, the weight of the government's offensive bore down on them, the sheer scale of the operation a testament to the regime's desperation. But even in the face of overwhelming odds, there was a flicker of hope, a small, stubborn flame that refused to be extinguished.

The rebellion was far from over. The fire was growing, spreading like a relentless wildfire across the landscape of a nation teetering on the edge. It was no longer just a flicker of defiance, hidden in the hearts of a few brave souls, it had become a blazing inferno, impossible to contain, powered by the anger and desperation of millions who had been pushed to the brink. What had once been a scattered, disjointed resistance was now a force to be reckoned with, its flames licking at the very foundations of the oppressive regime that sought to crush it.

The fire was growing in the hearts of those who had lost everything to the government's ruthless crackdowns, families torn apart, homes destroyed and lives shattered. It burned in the eyes of the soldiers who had begun to question the righteousness of their orders, the flickers of doubt in their minds igniting into something far more dangerous: a refusal to continue being pawns in a game of power and control. It spread in the whispers of rebellion that echoed through the streets and carried on the wind to every corner of the country. It took root in the minds of the oppressed, turning fear into resolve, and despair into determination.

Every act of resistance, no matter how small, added fuel to the fire. A protest in one town sparked another in the next; a single act of sabotage inspired others to follow suit. The government's efforts to stamp out the rebellion were like trying to extinguish a blaze with petrol, each crackdown, each act of brutality only served to fan the flames higher. The more they tried to silence the people, the louder their voices became, unified in a cry for freedom and justice.

The fire was growing in the stories of courage and sacrifice that spread like wildfire through the underground networks. Tales of rebels who had stood their ground against impossible odds, who had given their lives for the cause, became legends that inspired others to rise. It burned in the secret meetings held in the dead of night, where plans were made, alliances forged, and strategies devised to take the fight to the next level.

And as the fire grew, so did the sense of unity among the rebels. They were no longer just individuals fighting their own battles, they were a movement, a force of nature that was impossible to ignore. The fire connected them, gave them strength, and bound them together for a common purpose. It was the lifeblood of the rebellion, coursing through the veins of a nation that had been suffocated for too long.

The rebellion was far from over. The fire was growing, unstoppable, a force that would either consume the old order or be snuffed out in a final, desperate struggle. But one thing was certain: the flames would not die easily. They had been kindled by the pain and suffering of a people pushed too far, and they would continue to burn until justice was won, or until there was nothing left to burn. The fire was growing, and it was only a matter of time before it reached its peak, igniting a revolution that would change the course of history.

They would retreat, regroup, and rethink their strategy. But they would not give up. They would fight, and they would find a way to turn the tide once more.

Because the government had made its last gamble, and in doing so, had only fuelled the fire that burned in the hearts of those who refused to bow.

Chapter 25 The Underground

The air in the small, dimly lit room was thick with tension and the scent of damp earth, a pungent reminder of how far beneath the surface they had burrowed to escape the prying eyes of the regime. The underground chamber, nestled deep within a labyrinth of tunnels that had once served as forgotten service routes beneath the city, had become a sanctuary for the resistance, a place where the echoes of the world above seemed distant and unreal, like a fading memory of a life that once was.

The walls were rough-hewn, carved from the unforgiving stone that encased them, their surfaces jagged and uneven, bearing the marks of hasty excavation. Here and there, patches of exposed brick hinted at a time when these tunnels might have served a more mundane purpose, but now they had taken on a new life, their very existence a testament to the determination of those who refused to be crushed under the boot of tyranny. The ceiling hung low, close enough to brush the heads of the taller rebels, reinforcing the sense of confinement, of being pressed down by the weight of the earth above.

The light was sparse, provided by a few flickering lamps that had been carefully positioned around the room. Their glow was soft, almost feeble, casting long, wavering shadows that played across the walls like shadows of doubt and fear. The shadows moved with the slightest flicker of the flames, creating a sense of unease, as if the room itself was alive, holding its breath in anticipation of what might come next. In this space, every sound seemed amplified, the rustle of clothing, the murmur of voices, and the faint drip of water from some unseen source, all contributing to the atmosphere of secrecy that pervaded the room.

Despite the oppressive environment, there was an undeniable energy within those walls, a pulse that thrummed beneath the surface, matching the heartbeat of the resistance itself. It was the energy of survival, of resilience, of a cause that refused to die even in the face of overwhelming odds. The room was filled with people, some huddled in whispered conversation, others poring over maps and documents spread out on makeshift tables, but all shared the same steely resolve, a determination that had only grown stronger as the government's grip tightened.

This underground refuge was more than just a physical space; it was a symbol of the resistance's defiance, a place where their spirit could thrive away from the watchful eyes of their oppressors. Here, in the depths of the earth, they could plot and plan, rally and regroup, without fear of immediate reprisal. The walls, though cold and unyielding, provided a sense of security, a barrier against the chaos above. And yet, the very fact that they were forced to hide so deep underground was a constant reminder of the precariousness of their situation, a reminder that the world above was still under siege and that their fight was far from over.

In this place, time seemed to stand still, and the outside world was reduced to a distant hum that barely penetrated the layers of stone and earth. The rebels huddled together in their small, dimly lit sanctuary, knew that this was their last bastion, the heart of a movement that had spread across the nation like wildfire. It was here that they would make their stand, here that they would decide the fate of their cause. As they gathered in the flickering light, their faces drawn with exhaustion but their eyes burning with resolve, they knew that the resistance was not just surviving, it was thriving. The heartbeat of rebellion echoed through the tunnels, strong and steady, a rhythm that would not be silenced.

Emily stood at the head of a makeshift table, her gaze sweeping over the group assembled before her. They were a mix of hardened veterans and fresh faces, each with their own story, and their reasons for joining the fight. The underground network was a sprawling entity, a web of connections that reached into every corner of the city and beyond. It was a lifeline for the resistance, a place where information flowed, supplies were gathered, and plans were hatched in the dead of night.

To Emily's left stood Lena Rourke, a former MI5 operative who had turned against the government when she could no longer stomach the lies she was forced to uphold. Tall and lean, with sharp features and eyes that missed nothing, Lena had quickly become one of the most trusted leaders within the underground. Her knowledge of surveillance and counterintelligence was unmatched, and she had been instrumental in keeping the resistance one step ahead of the authorities. But beneath her steely exterior, there was a sense of weariness, a quiet sorrow that came from knowing too much, from seeing too many betrayals and losing too many friends.

Next to Lena was Tomasz Kowalski, a Polish immigrant who had made the UK his home years ago. His background in engineering made him invaluable to the resistance, particularly in the creation of devices that could disrupt government communication networks and sabotage their infrastructure. Tomasz had a broad build, his hands calloused from years of manual labour, but his eyes were soft, kind, reflecting a deep-seated belief in the cause. He had lost his wife to the government's crackdown on dissent, and since then, his resolve had hardened into something unbreakable. Yet, in quiet moments, the grief would surface, a shadow passing over his face.

At the far end of the table, almost hidden in the shadows, was Alia Zafar, a journalist who had gone underground after her exposés on government corruption made her a target. Alia was small in stature but had a presence that commanded attention. Her dark eyes were filled with a quiet intensity, and her words, when she chose to speak, were sharp and precise, cutting through the noise with the clarity of truth. Alia's network of contacts had been crucial in establishing connections with sympathisers abroad, and it was through her efforts that the resistance had begun to draw the attention of international allies.

The last new face was Dr. Raj Patel, a former surgeon who had turned his skills to treating the wounded among the resistance. With a calm demeanour and a steady hand, Raj had become the underground's lifeline, tending to injuries that would have been fatal without his expertise. He was older than most in the room, his hair peppered with grey, and his voice carried the weight of someone who had seen too much suffering. Raj had lost his family in the early days of the rebellion, a loss that had driven him to the underground, where he could channel his grief into saving others.

As Emily surveyed these new allies, she felt a surge of hope, a sense that, despite the losses they had endured, the resistance was growing stronger, more capable. They had not only survived the government's onslaught; they had adapted, learned, and evolved. But with that growth came new challenges, and new risks. The underground network was vast, but it was also vulnerable, and one misstep could unravel everything they had built.

"The government is getting desperate," Emily began, her voice low but firm. "Their crackdown is intensifying, and they're making fewer mistakes. We've seen an increase in surveillance, in raids, in arrests. We've all felt it. But that doesn't mean they're invincible. They're overextending themselves, and we need to exploit that."

Lena nodded, her gaze intense. "We've identified several key locations where the government is weakest. Supply depots, communication hubs, and even some of their more secure installations. They're vulnerable, but we need to be smart about how we hit them."

Tomasz leaned forward, his voice tinged with determination. "We've already been working on devices that can take down their systems, EMP generators, jammers, you name it. But we need more hands, more resources. We need to hit them hard, all at once, before they can regroup."

Alia spoke next, her tone measured. "Our international contacts are ready to help, but they need proof that we can succeed. We need a victory that will resonate, something that will show the world we're not just holding on, but that we're winning."

Emily nodded, considering their words. "Then we need to strike where it hurts the most. We target their supply depots, cut off their resources, and disrupt their communications. We make it impossible for them to maintain control. But we also need to think about the bigger picture. This isn't just about taking down the government, it's about winning the hearts and minds of the people. We can't just be the ones who destroy; we have to be the ones who rebuild."

Dr. Raj, who had been silent until now, spoke up. "And we have to be ready for the consequences. Every action we take will bring retaliation. We need to make sure we're protecting our own, that we're not sacrificing lives needlessly."

A murmur of agreement rippled through the room, and Emily felt a sense of unity among them, a shared purpose that bound them together. But she also knew the risks they were about to take. The government was on high alert, and any move they made could trigger a swift and brutal response.

"We'll need to be careful," Emily continued. "We'll plan every step meticulously, coordinate with our allies, and make sure we're ready for whatever comes next. This won't be easy, but it's our best chance to turn the tide in our favour."

The room fell into a tense silence as they absorbed the weight of what lay ahead. Each of them knew the stakes and knew that failure was not an option. But there was also a sense of resolve, a determination to see this through, no matter the cost.

Later that night, as the group began to disperse, Lena caught up with Emily in one of the narrow tunnels that led out of the underground chamber. The air was cool and damp, and their footsteps echoed softly against the stone walls.

"Are you sure about this?" Lena asked, her voice laced with concern. "These operations, they're dangerous. We could lose everything if we're not careful."

Emily paused, turning to face her. The flickering light from a distant lamp cast shadows across her face, highlighting the weariness in her eyes. "I'm sure, Lena. We don't have a choice. If we don't strike now, the government will tighten its grip even further. We've seen what they're capable of. We can't let them win."

Lena studied her for a moment, then nodded. "I trust you, Emily. Just… be careful. We've already lost too much."

With a faint smile, Emily reached out and squeezed Lena's arm. "I will. And we'll make sure this time, it's them who lose."

As they continued down the tunnel, Emily's mind was already turning over the details of the coming operation. The daring raid on the government supply depot would be their first major strike in this new phase of the rebellion. It would be risky, and there would be casualties, but it was a necessary step if they were to keep the movement alive.

The night of the raid was dark and moonless, the kind of night that swallowed sound and light alike, wrapping the world in a blanket of impenetrable blackness. It was as if the sky itself had conspired with the rebels, concealing their movements beneath its cloak of shadow. The air was thick with anticipation, a heavy stillness that pressed down on the city, muting even the distant hum of traffic. Not a single star pierced the inky sky, and the usual glow of the city lights was dimmed by the tension that hung in the air. It was the perfect cover for their operation, a night that seemed to hold its breath, waiting for something to happen.

For weeks, the underground network had been meticulously planning the raid, each detail carefully considered, each risk weighed against the potential reward. The depot was a high-value target, a nerve centre for the government's military operations, and its destruction would deal a significant blow to the regime's supply chain. The rebels had been patient, gathering intelligence with the precision of a surgeon.

They had studied the depot from every angle, noting the patterns of the guards, the timing of the shifts, the vulnerabilities in the security systems. Every detail had been recorded, analysed, and committed to memory.

Tomasz, the group's resident tech expert, had been the key to their plan. A wiry man with a sharp mind and a talent for electronics, he had spent countless hours developing a series of jammers and EMP devices that would disrupt the depot's security systems. His workbench had become a tangle of wires, circuits, and half-finished devices, the tools of his trade scattered in a chaotic array. But beneath the apparent disorder was a methodical mind, one that understood the intricacies of the technology they were up against.

The jammers were small, compact devices, easy to conceal and quick to deploy. They would scramble the depot's communication systems, cutting off any calls for reinforcements. The EMP devices were more powerful, designed to send a pulse that would fry the electronic circuits in the security cameras and disable the automated defences. Tomasz had tested each device rigorously, ensuring that they would work flawlessly when the time came. He knew that they would only have a small window of opportunity, a few precious minutes in which the depot would be vulnerable, and he had made sure that nothing would go wrong.

As the hour of the raid approached, the rebels moved into position, their footsteps silent on the damp pavement. The depot loomed ahead, a hulking silhouette against the dark sky, its high walls and barbed wire fences designed to keep out intruders. But tonight, those defences would be useless. The rebels had already infiltrated the perimeter, placing the jammers at strategic points around the facility. As they activated the devices, a soft hum filled the air, almost imperceptible, but enough to disrupt the depot's communication systems. The guards, unaware of the danger lurking in the shadows, continued their patrols, their radios now dead in their hands.

Tomasz's EMP devices were next, hidden in the underbrush near the main entrance. With a flick of a switch, the pulse was sent out, a silent wave of energy that swept through the depot, short-circuiting the security cameras, and leaving the facility blind. Inside, the automated defences went offline, the metal shutters that protected the entrances grinding to a halt. The rebels had their opening.

The team moved quickly, slipping through the gaps in the fences and making their way towards the depot's heart. The darkness was their ally, concealing their approach as they spread out, each member knowing their role by heart. The air crackled with tension, every breath taken in silence, every movement calculated to avoid detection. The ground beneath their feet was slick with rain, the damp earth absorbing the sound of their footsteps.

Inside the depot, the guards were growing uneasy, sensing that something was amiss. But before they could raise the alarm, the rebels struck. Silenced weapons took down the first wave of guards, their bodies crumpling to the ground without a sound. The team split up, each group heading towards their designated target. Explosives were placed on fuel tanks, ammunition caches, and supply trucks, the fuses set to ignite in a carefully timed sequence.

The depot was a labyrinth of storage rooms and loading bays, and the rebels navigated it with practiced ease, their training and preparation paying off. They moved like shadows, unseen and unstoppable, their hearts pounding in their chests. The tension was palpable, a tightness in the air that grew with each passing second. They knew that the clock was ticking, that they had only minutes before the guards would realise what was happening and the chaos would erupt.

But for now, everything was going according to plan. The explosives were in place, the jammers still humming softly, the EMP devices holding the security systems at bay. The depot was theirs, and in a few moments, it would be nothing but a smoking ruin. The rebels exchanged quick, determined glances, their resolve steeling for what was to come. This was it, the culmination of weeks of planning, the strike that would send a message to the government and ignite the flames of rebellion even higher.

As they prepared to withdraw, the first of the explosives detonated, a deafening roar that shook the ground beneath their feet. The night sky lit up with a flash of orange and red, the flames consuming the depot's fuel reserves and sending a plume of smoke into the air. The guards, now fully aware of the attack, scrambled in confusion, their shouts mingling with the crackle of gunfire as they tried to regain control.

But the rebels were already slipping away, melting back into the shadows from which they had emerged. The night had been their ally, and now it would be their refuge as they disappeared into the underground once more. The depot was in flames, the government dealt a heavy blow, and the rebellion was far from over. The fire that had been lit tonight would only grow, spreading through the city, through the country, until it consumed everything in its path.

As the team moved silently through the shadows, the weight of their mission hung heavily in the air. They had all been part of raids before, but this one felt different. There was a sense of finality, of a turning point. If they succeeded, it would be a major blow to the government's operations, but if they failed…

Emily pushed the thought from her mind, focusing instead on the task at hand. The depot loomed ahead, a massive structure surrounded by high fences and guard towers. Beyond the fence, rows of crates and containers stretched into the darkness, filled with weapons, ammunition, and supplies that the government relied on to maintain its stranglehold on the country.

Lena signalled for them to stop, her sharp eyes scanning the area for any sign of movement. When she was satisfied that the coast was clear, she nodded to Tomasz, who set to work on the jammers. The devices hummed to life, their frequencies cutting through the air like a knife, and within moments, the lights on the guard towers flickered and died.

"Now," Lena whispered, and the team moved forward, slipping through a gap in the fence that Tomasz had cut earlier. They spread out, each with a specific target in mind, working quickly and efficiently to plant explosives and disable key systems.

As they worked, Emily couldn't help but feel a surge of pride for the group she had helped build. They were more than just rebels; they were a force to be reckoned with, a testament to the power of resistance in the face of tyranny.

But as they planted the last of the explosives and prepared to retreat, a shout rang out from the far end of the depot, followed by the sharp crack of gunfire. The alarm had been raised, and within seconds, the depot was alive with the sounds of chaos, guards shouting orders, guns firing, and the deafening roar of explosions as the first of the charges detonated.

"Fall back!" Lena shouted, her voice cutting through the noise. "Get to the extraction point!"

The team moved as one, their training kicking in as they navigated the maze of crates and containers, dodging bullets and returning fire when necessary. But the element of surprise was gone, and the guards were closing in fast.

Emily could see the extraction point up ahead, a narrow alley that would lead them back to the safety of the underground tunnels. But as they neared the exit, Tomasz was hit, a bullet tearing through his side and sending him crashing to the ground.

"Leave me!" he gasped, clutching his wound. "Just go!"

"No," Emily said firmly, grabbing him under the arm and hauling him to his feet. "We don't leave anyone behind."

With Lena covering their retreat, Emily and another rebel managed to drag Tomasz to the extraction point, where Alia was waiting with a getaway vehicle. They piled in, slamming the doors shut as Lena dove into the back, and Alia hit the gas, speeding away from the depot just as the remaining explosives went off, lighting up the night sky with a brilliant flash of fire.

As they raced through the deserted streets, the sound of sirens growing fainter in the distance, Emily leaned back in her seat, her heart pounding with a mix of adrenaline and relief. They had done it. They had struck a blow against the government, and though the cost had been high, the victory was undeniable.

But as she looked around at the faces of her comrades, some of whom were wounded and bleeding, Emily knew that the fight was far from over. The government would retaliate, and the stakes would only get higher. They had won this battle, but the war was still raging, and the path ahead was fraught with danger.

Still, for the first time in a long while, Emily allowed herself a small glimmer of hope. They had shown the government that they were not beaten and that the resistance was still strong. As they disappeared into the shadows of the underground, Emily knew that they would continue to fight, no matter the cost. The fire of rebellion was burning brighter than ever, and nothing could extinguish it now.

Chapter 26 Betrayal and Loyalty

The night was cold, biting in a way that seeped through the thick walls of the underground safe house, turning the damp air into a near-tangible chill that clung to the skin. The warmth that once filled this hidden refuge, born from shared meals, whispered jokes, and the collective strength of a group united by a common cause, had evaporated, leaving behind an oppressive tension that pressed down on the room like a suffocating blanket.

This had been a place of sanctuary, where plans were made and victories, however small, were celebrated. Now, it felt more like a cage, its low ceilings and rough-hewn walls closing in on the rebels who sat or stood, scattered around the room, their faces etched with a mix of anger, disbelief, and hurt. The flickering candlelight only deepened the shadows, making the corners of the room seem to stretch into infinity, hiding secrets and fears that no one dared voice. The flames wavered, as if they, too, were uncertain of their place in this room where betrayal had cast its long, dark shadow.

The usual hum of quiet conversations that had always filled this space, the comforting background noise of murmured strategies, shared stories, and the occasional burst of laughter, was now replaced by a silence so thick it seemed to absorb sound, muting even the faintest of movements. It was the kind of silence that made the smallest noise, someone shifting in their seat, the creak of a chair, feel intrusive, breaking the fragile stillness that everyone seemed reluctant to disturb.

Shadows danced erratically on the stone walls, cast by the dim, trembling flames of the few candles that provided the only source of light. The shadows seemed almost alive, twisting and contorting as if reflecting the inner turmoil of the group, their shapes mirroring the doubt, the anger, and the fear that had taken root in the hearts of the rebels. The candles, normally a symbol of warmth and hope, now barely kept the darkness at bay, their light too weak to banish the growing sense of despair that pervaded the room.

The air was thick and heavy with the weight of unspoken words, accusations, confessions, and questions that no one dared ask. The tension was palpable, a living, breathing thing that coiled around each person, squeezing tight, making the room feel smaller, more suffocating with each passing moment. It was as if the betrayal that had been uncovered had not only shattered the trust within the group but had also tainted the very air they breathed, leaving a bitter taste in their mouths.

Betrayal, like a dark cloud, hung over them all, its presence inescapable, its effects far-reaching. It wasn't just the betrayal of one man; it was the betrayal of the belief that they were all in this together, that they could trust each other with their lives. Now, that belief lay shattered, the fragments cutting deep, leaving wounds that no one knew how to heal. The cold night outside seemed to have seeped into the very marrow of the safe house, turning it into a place of suspicion and fear, where once there had been unity and strength.

As the group sat in that cold, oppressive silence, each person grappled with their thoughts and their fears. The walls that had once felt like a protective barrier against the world above now felt like they were closing in, trapping them in a situation that had no easy answers, no clear path forward. And in the dim, flickering light, with shadows dancing like spectres on the walls, the rebels were left to confront the harsh reality that trusts, once broken, could never be fully mended.

Emily stood at the far end of the room, her arms crossed tightly over her chest. Her face, usually a mask of determination, was now etched with lines of worry and doubt. She stared at the floor, her mind racing, replaying the events that had led them to this moment. The discovery had been a shock, like a knife in the back from someone they had trusted, someone they had welcomed into their ranks as one of their own. The realisation that a mole had been among them all along, feeding information to the government, had sent ripples of fear and anger through the group.

In the centre of the room, seated on a rickety chair, was the accused, Jonas, a man who had fought alongside them for months. His hands were bound, his head hung low, the flickering candlelight casting eerie shadows on his gaunt face. He looked exhausted, his eyes hollow, as if the weight of his actions had drained the life from him. But there was also a stubbornness in his expression, a refusal to meet the eyes of those who now looked at him with a mix of disbelief and betrayal.

Lily paced the room, her steps quick and agitated, her usually calm demeanour shattered. "How could you do this, Jonas? How could you betray us like this?" Her voice was sharp, laced with the pain of betrayal. She had always been the optimist, the one who believed in the goodness of people, but, this had shaken her to her core.

Jonas didn't respond, his silence only fuelling the anger in the room.

Aamir, standing by the entrance, his face a mask of controlled anger, finally spoke. "We trusted you," he said quietly, his voice low but filled with a quiet intensity that made everyone in the room turn to look at him. "We brought you into our lives, into our fight, and you sold us out to the very people we're risking everything to defeat."

Emily closed her eyes for a moment, gathering her thoughts before she spoke. "We need to understand why, Jonas. We need to know what led you to this. Was it money? Threats? Were you coerced?"

Jonas finally looked up, his eyes meeting Emily's. There was a flicker of something, regret, maybe, or shame, but it was quickly buried under a layer of defiance. "You wouldn't understand," he muttered.

"Try us," Emily pressed, her voice steady, but there was an edge to it now, a hardness that hadn't been there before.

For a long moment, Jonas didn't speak. The silence in the room was suffocating, the tension thick enough to cut with a knife. When he finally did speak, his voice was barely above a whisper. "They had my family," he said, his words tumbling out in a rush as if he had been holding them in for too long. "They threatened to kill them if I didn't give them information. What was I supposed to do? Let them die?"

The words hung in the air like an unwelcome phantom, a chilling presence that refused to dissipate. The silence that followed was not one of relief, but of heavy contemplation, as each member of the group processed the gravity of what had just been revealed. The anger that had initially surged through the room, hot, raw, and all-consuming, began to ebb away, replaced by a swirling mix of emotions that was far more complex and difficult to grasp.

Pity seeped into the hearts of some, a reluctant empathy for the one who had betrayed them. It was the kind of pity born from the understanding that not all acts of betrayal are born from malice; sometimes, they are the desperate acts of a person cornered, afraid, or manipulated. The thought that one of their own had been so broken, so frightened, that they had turned against the very people who had fought alongside them was a bitter pill to swallow. It left a sour taste in the mouth, a discomfort that settled in the pit of the stomach.

Sorrow, too, wove its way through the room, a heavy, leaden feeling that pressed down on the chest and made it hard to breathe. It was the sorrow of loss, not just of the camaraderie they had shared, but of something deeper, something more fragile: the trust that had bound them together, the belief that they were all fighting the same fight, with the same conviction, the same courage. That belief had been fractured, and with it, a piece of their collective spirit seemed to have been lost.

But perhaps the most unsettling of all was the deep, gnawing uncertainty that began to take root. It was a creeping doubt that wormed its way into their minds, whispering insidious questions: If one among them could betray the cause, who else might falter? If the trust they had built could be shattered so easily, what else might crumble under the weight of fear and desperation? The certainty with which they had once faced the world, strong, united, unbreakable, now seemed a distant memory, replaced by the uneasy knowledge that nothing was as secure as they had once believed.

The room, once filled with the fire of righteous anger, now felt colder, as if the temperature had dropped along with the intensity of their emotions. Faces that had been flushed with fury now appeared drained, the fight in their eyes replaced by a flickering doubt. They exchanged glances, searching one another for reassurance, for some sign that they were not as lost as they felt. But the unease was mirrored back at them, a reflection of the inner turmoil that none of them could escape.

The weight of the betrayal, the pity for the betrayer, the sorrow for what had been lost, and the uncertainty of what lay ahead, all coalesced into a heavy, oppressive atmosphere that was almost tangible. The air in the room seemed thicker, harder to draw into their lungs as if the very act of breathing had become a laborious task.

And yet, amidst all these swirling emotions, there was also a fragile, tentative thread of something else, a faint glimmer of hope, perhaps, or the quiet resilience of those who had faced the worst and were still standing. It was faint, barely perceptible, but it was there, waiting to be grasped, nurtured, and fanned into a flame that might one day burn bright enough to chase away the shadows that had descended upon them.

But for now, in that moment, the group was left to sit with the heavy silence, the echoes of the words that had been spoken, and the crushing weight of the emotions that threatened to overwhelm them. It was a silence filled not with the absence of sound, but with the presence of everything they feared to confront.

Lily stopped pacing, her face softening as she looked at Jonas. "Why didn't you come to us? We could have helped you, protected them."

Jonas shook his head, a bitter smile on his lips. "You think you could have protected them? From them? You're all fighting a war you can't win, against an enemy that has more power, more resources, more everything. I didn't want to betray you, but they left me no choice."

Aamir's fists clenched at his sides, the anger in him barely contained. "And what about the lives you've endangered by betraying us? What about the people who trust us to protect them? How many of them will die because of what you've done?"

Jonas looked down again, unable to face the accusation in Aamir's words. "I didn't have a choice," he repeated, but the words sounded hollow, even to him.

Emily felt the room tilting on the edge of chaos, the emotions of the group ready to spill over into something they couldn't take back. She had to act, to steer them away from making a decision they might regret. "We're all angry," she said, her voice cutting through the tension. "And we have every right to be. But we need to think about what we do next. We can't let this destroy us."

"Destroy us?" Lily echoed, her voice thick with disbelief. "How can we come back from this? How can we ever trust anyone again?"

Aamir nodded in agreement, his gaze still fixed on Jonas. "She's right, Emily. Trust is the foundation of everything we do. Without it, we're nothing."

Emily took a deep breath, feeling the weight of her responsibility pressing down on her. "Trust is earned, and yes, it's fragile. But it's also necessary if we're going to win this fight. We can't afford to turn on each other, not now, not when the stakes are this high."

Jonas looked up at her, his eyes filled with a mixture of hope and fear. "What are you going to do with me?"

The room fell silent again as the question hung in the air, unspoken but present in everyone's mind. What do you do with a traitor? How do you balance justice with mercy in a world where every decision carries the weight of life and death?

Aamir spoke first, his voice hard. "He betrayed us. There has to be consequences."

"But what kind of consequences?" Lily countered, her voice tinged with sorrow. "Do we become the kind of people who execute someone for trying to save their family?"

Emily felt the group's eyes on her, waiting for her decision, for her to give them a direction in this moral quagmire. She knew that whatever she decided, would have lasting consequences for the group, for their trust in each other, and her leadership.

"We need to be better than the people we're fighting against," she said finally, her voice steady but soft. "Jonas will be exiled. He can't stay with us, not after what he's done. But we're not going to kill him. He'll have to live with what he's done, with the knowledge that he's betrayed the people who trusted him. That's punishment enough."

There was a murmur of agreement, though it was tinged with reluctance. The group was divided, but they trusted Emily's judgment, even if it wasn't the decision they had hoped for.

Jonas looked at her, his face a battlefield of conflicting emotions, each one vying for dominance. The struggle was palpable, a war waged silently behind his eyes, and the toll it had taken on him was evident in every line etched into his weary face. His shoulders, once broad and proud, now slumped as if the weight of his guilt had physically pressed them down, crushing the man he used to be.

Relief came first, surging through him in a way that was almost painful in its intensity. It was the relief of a man who had been carrying a burden too heavy to bear, finally able to lay it down, even if only for a moment. His chest heaved as he took in a deep, shuddering breath, the air rushing into his lungs like a drowning man gasping for air. Tears welled up in his eyes, unbidden and unstoppable, spilling over to carve tracks down his dirt-streaked cheeks. They were tears of relief, yes, but also of deep, soul-crushing sadness, sadness for what he had done, for what he had lost, for the man he had become.

He tried to speak, to say something, anything, to explain himself, to justify his actions, but the words caught in his throat, strangled by the lump of emotion that threatened to choke him. His lips trembled as they parted, but no sound came out, only a broken, anguished sob that echoed in the silence of the room. His hands, once steady and strong, now trembled violently as they hung limply at his sides, useless, powerless to undo the damage that had been done.

Anger flashed across his face, a brief but intense flare of self-loathing that twisted his features into a grimace of disgust. How had he allowed himself to fall so far? How had he betrayed everything he had once believed in, everyone he had once fought beside? The anger was directed inward, a burning hatred for his weakness, his cowardice, that had led him down this dark path. It seared through him, leaving behind a bitter taste in his mouth and a deep, gnawing ache in his chest.

And then, as quickly as the anger came, it was replaced by guilt, a pang of all-encompassing, suffocating guilt that wrapped itself around him like a heavy shroud. It was a guilt that went beyond mere remorse; it was the guilt of knowing that he had not just failed himself, but had failed those who had trusted him, who had looked to him as a comrade, a brother in arms. He could feel it in every beat of his heart, a relentless pounding that reminded him of the lives he had put in jeopardy, the trust he had shattered.

His legs threatened to give way beneath him, and he swayed slightly, catching himself on the edge of the table before he could collapse completely. The wood was rough beneath his fingers, grounding him in the present, in the reality of what he had done. His knuckles whitened as he gripped the edge, holding on as if it were the only thing keeping him from falling into the abyss of despair that yawned before him.

The tears continued to flow, hot and stinging, blurring his vision until all he could see was a hazy wash of light and shadow. He blinked rapidly, trying to clear them, but they kept coming, a relentless torrent that he could not stop. They were tears of sorrow, of shame, of the crushing realisation that he had lost everything, his loyalty, his honour, his place among the people he had once called friends.

He nodded slowly, his head dipping in a gesture of acceptance, of resignation. There was no escaping it now, no turning back the clock, no undoing the choices he had made. He had betrayed them, and in doing so, he had betrayed himself. The knowledge settled heavily on his shoulders, a burden that he would carry with him for the rest of his life, however long or short that might be.

Jonas knew that he had lost everything in the process, his comrades, his cause, his very sense of self. He was a man broken, hollowed out by his own actions, a shadow of the person he had once been. And as he stood there, tears streaming down his face, he knew that the only thing left for him was to face the consequences of his betrayal, to accept whatever fate awaited him, knowing that he had brought it upon himself.

As the room began to empty, each member lost in their thoughts, Emily felt a hand on her shoulder. She turned to see Aamir standing there, his eyes searching hers. "You did the right thing," he said quietly, though there was a trace of doubt in his voice.

"Did I?" Emily replied, her voice betraying the uncertainty she felt deep inside. "Sometimes I wonder if there is a right thing anymore."

Aamir squeezed her shoulder gently. "As long as we keep trying to do the right thing, that's what matters. That's what makes us different."

Emily gave him a small, grateful smile, though the doubt lingered. She knew that her leadership would be questioned and that this decision might have sown the seeds of dissent within the group. But she also knew that they had to hold on to their humanity, to the principles that had brought them together in the first place. Without that, they were no better than the regime they were fighting to overthrow.

As she watched Jonas being led away, his figure disappearing into the shadows of the tunnels, Emily felt a heaviness settle in her chest. Betrayal and loyalty are two sides of the same coin, each capable of tearing them apart or holding them together. She could only hope that they would find a way to balance the two, to survive the trials that lay ahead.

But in the back of her mind, a new fear had taken root. How many more betrayals would they face? How many more allies would they lose to fear, to desperation, to the lure of survival? The thought gnawed at her, even as she forced herself to push it aside.

They would have to rebuild trust, brick by brick, even as the world crumbled around them. And Emily knew that the hardest battles were yet to come, not just against the government, but within their own hearts.

Chapter 27 The Turning Point

The sun was setting over the city, casting a warm, amber glow over the crumbling buildings and scarred streets, bathing the shattered remnants of what had once been a thriving metropolis in a bittersweet light. The golden hues of the fading day mingled with the dark, jagged shadows of broken structures, creating an almost surreal landscape, one that bore witness to the relentless conflict that had torn through it, reshaping the very fabric of life. The city had been a battleground for so long that it was hard to remember a time when it wasn't; the memories of peace had become as distant as the sun sinking beyond the horizon.

The streets, once filled with the hustle and bustle of daily life, were now eerily quiet, haunted by the echoes of past skirmishes and the silent cries of lost souls. Buildings that had once stood tall and proud were now reduced to skeletal frameworks, their walls riddled with bullet holes, their windows shattered like the dreams of those who had once called them home. The air was thick with the lingering scent of smoke and dust, a constant reminder of the destruction that had swept through the city like a raging storm.

But tonight, as the sun dipped lower, there was a different kind of tension in the air, a tension that buzzed with the promise of change. It was subtle at first, a barely perceptible shift in the atmosphere, but it grew stronger with each passing moment, like the rising crescendo of an unseen orchestra. The rebels, scattered and battered by the relentless assaults of the government forces, were slowly coming back together, drawn by an unspoken understanding that their time had come.

Their numbers had dwindled over the years, worn down by the constant barrage of violence and fear, but now, new faces began to appear among the familiar ones. People who had once watched from the sidelines, paralysed by uncertainty or fear, were now stepping forward, driven by a newfound courage that had been kindled by the flame of hope. The ranks of the resistance were swelling with recruits, their spirits bolstered by the whispers of impending change that swept through the city like a refreshing breeze after a long, suffocating drought.

There was a spark in the eyes of the rebels that hadn't been there before, a spark of determination, of resilience. They had seen the worst that the regime could throw at them, and had faced down death and despair time and again, but they had emerged from the darkness stronger, more united in their purpose. The tide, which had once threatened to drown them in its relentless surge, was finally turning in their favour. They could feel it in the air, taste it in the wind, and see it in the way the setting sun painted the sky with the colours of fire and blood.

As the last rays of sunlight slipped below the horizon, giving way to the cool embrace of twilight, the city seemed to hold its breath, as if aware of the momentous events about to unfold. The rebels gathered in secret corners, basements, and back alleys, their whispers carrying the weight of their shared determination. They were battered, yes, but not broken. The fire that burned within them was brighter than ever, powered by the hope that their struggle had not been in vain.

Tonight, as the city stood on the brink of a new dawn, the rebels knew that they were not just fighting for survival anymore. They were fighting for victory, for the chance to rebuild their world from the ashes of the old. The setting sun was not just marking the end of another day, it was heralding the beginning of a new era. As darkness fell over the city, it was clear to all who walked its scarred streets that the fight was far from over. It was only just beginning.

In a hidden safe house deep within the city, the core members of the resistance had gathered once again. The room was dimly lit, the only light coming from a few flickering candles placed haphazardly on the table around which they sat. The atmosphere was thick with anticipation, the air charged with the knowledge that something monumental was about to happen.

Emily sat at the head of the table, her face illuminated by the soft glow of the candles. Her eyes were sharp, her expression focused, but there was a lightness in her that had been absent for too long, a hope that had been reignited in the wake of recent events. She looked around the table, taking in the faces of her comrades, each one etched with lines of fatigue but also with a new resolve.

To her right sat Aamir, his usually calm demeanour now tinged with a sense of urgency. He had been instrumental in forging new alliances, reaching out to disillusioned groups who had once been sceptical of the rebellion's chances. His efforts had paid off in ways none of them could have anticipated, and his presence at the table was a reminder of how far they had come.

Across from him, Lily leaned forward, her fingers tapping rhythmically on the table, a restless energy emanating from her. She had become a key figure in the information war, using her skills to hack into government networks, disseminate propaganda, and rally support. Her work had been crucial in spreading the message of the revolution, and the recent surge in public demonstrations was a testament to her effectiveness.

But it was the man seated next to Lily who commanded the most attention. General Marcus Hale, a high-ranking official within the government, had defected to the rebels just days earlier. His decision had sent shockwaves through both the government and the resistance, and his presence here, in this room, was nothing short of extraordinary.

Hale was a tall man, his broad shoulders giving him an imposing presence that had once commanded respect and even fear among those who served under him. In his prime, he had been the very embodiment of the regime's ideals, disciplined, unwavering, and utterly loyal. His neatly cropped hair had always been a symbol of his meticulous nature, a reflection of the order and precision with which he had approached his duties. But now, that hair was dishevelled, the sharpness of his once-pristine appearance dulled by the weight of disillusionment. The weariness in his eyes was unmistakable, a deep, penetrating fatigue that went far beyond physical exhaustion. It was the kind of weariness that came from a man who had spent years grappling with long-buried doubts, doubts that had finally clawed their way to the surface, refusing to be ignored any longer.

Hale's journey to this point had been a gradual, almost imperceptible descent into a chasm of moral ambiguity. He had grown up in a military family, the son of a decorated officer who had served the regime with distinction. From an early age, Hale had been taught the values of duty, honour, and loyalty. The regime was presented to him as a bastion of stability in a chaotic world, a force for good that protected the nation from external and internal threats alike. He had embraced this worldview wholeheartedly, entering the military academy with a sense of purpose and pride that had only grown stronger as he climbed the ranks.

His early career had been marked by success. He had excelled in tactical operations, leading missions that had neutralised insurgent threats with surgical precision. He was known for his strategic brilliance, his ability to outthink and outmanoeuvre enemies, and his unflinching commitment to the cause. Hale was a rising star, a man who seemed destined for the highest echelons of command.

But as he rose through the ranks, the nature of his assignments began to change. No longer was he dealing with clear-cut military operations against armed combatants. Instead, he found himself overseeing actions that targeted civilians, crackdowns on protestors, raids on communities suspected of harbouring dissenters, and operations that resulted in the disappearance of countless innocents. The regime's rhetoric remained the same, justifying these actions as necessary for national security, but the reality on the ground told a different story. Hale began to see the faces of those who were labelled as enemies of the state, ordinary men, women, and children whose only crime was being in the wrong place at the wrong time or daring to speak out against the growing tyranny.

The atrocities he witnessed began to eat away at the certainties that had once defined his life. He tried to rationalise the orders he was given, convincing himself that there was a greater good at stake and that the sacrifices were necessary to maintain order. But the more he saw, the harder it became to silence the voice of conscience that whispered in the back of his mind, questioning the morality of the regime he had devoted his life to serving.

It was during one particularly brutal operation that Hale reached his breaking point. He had been tasked with leading a raid on a small village rumoured to be a stronghold of rebel sympathisers. The orders were clear, take no prisoners, leave no witnesses. As he and his men stormed the village, the horror of what they were doing hit him like a tidal wave. The people they were gunning down were not combatants; they were farmers, children, the elderly, people who posed no real threat. As the screams of the dying filled the air, Hale froze, his rifle hanging limply in his hands as the truth finally pierced through the layers of indoctrination that had shielded him for so long.

In that moment, Hale saw the regime for what it truly was, a machine of oppression that crushed anything in its path to maintain power. The ideals he had once held dear were nothing more than lies, a veneer of righteousness that masked the rot at the core of the government. The realisation was like a knife to the heart, and for the first time in his life, Hale felt a deep, overwhelming sense of shame.

He tried to bury his doubts, to continue his duties as if nothing had changed, but the weight of what he had seen was too much to bear. Every order he followed, and every mission he led, only deepened the chasm between the man he had been and the man he was becoming. The faces of the innocent haunted his dreams, their cries for mercy echoing in his mind long after the battles had ended. Hale became withdrawn, his once commanding presence diminished as he struggled with the moral quagmire he found himself in.

It was in this state of inner turmoil that he began to secretly gather information, classified documents, intelligence reports, and anything that could expose the regime's crimes. He did it initially out of a vague sense of guilt, a need to atone for the blood on his hands, but as the rebellion gained momentum, Hale realised that he had a more urgent responsibility. The rebels were fighting for a cause that he had once believed in, a cause that had been twisted and corrupted by those in power. They needed the truth, and Hale knew he was the one who could give it to them.

Now, standing before the rebels, offering them the intelligence they had so desperately needed, Hale felt a strange mix of emotions. Relief, that he had finally chosen a side, the right side. Fear, for the consequences of his betrayal, not just for himself but for those who still served under him. And a simmering anger, directed not only at the regime but at himself, for having been blind to the truth for so long. The weariness in his eyes spoke volumes, a man who had seen too much, done too much, and was now trying to make amends for a lifetime of misplaced loyalty.

Hale knew that his decision to defect would likely cost him his life, but he had made peace with that. What mattered now was the fight ahead, the chance to help dismantle the very regime he had once helped build. The rebels looked at him with a mix of scepticism and hope, unsure of whether to trust him, but Hale was prepared to prove his loyalty through action. He had crossed a line from which there was no return, and for the first time in a long while, he felt a sense of clarity, a purpose that went beyond orders, beyond duty, to something far more profound: redemption.

"The government is on the brink," Hale began, his voice steady but carrying the weight of his confession. "They've lost control of the narrative, and they know it. Public support is crumbling, and the fear they've relied on for so long is no longer enough to keep the population in line. They're desperate."

A murmur of agreement rippled through the room, but it was tempered by the knowledge of the challenges that still lay ahead. Emily nodded for Hale to continue.

"Their stronghold," Hale continued, his eyes meeting each of theirs in turn, "is vulnerable. I've seen the reports, there's dissension within their ranks. Soldiers are questioning orders, and some have outright refused to fight. The chain of command is weakening, and morale is at an all-time low. If we strike now, we can turn that weakness into our advantage."

Emily exchanged a glance with Aamir, her mind racing as she processed this new information. They had been planning an assault on a key government facility for weeks, but this new intelligence could change everything. It wasn't just about attacking a stronghold anymore, it was about dealing a decisive blow to the regime, one that could cripple their ability to maintain control.

"We have to move quickly," Aamir said, his voice cutting through the room's tension. "If what Hale says is true, this is our chance to end this once and for all. But we need to be smart about it. We can't afford any mistakes."

Lily nodded, her gaze fixed on the map spread out on the table before them. "We'll need to coordinate with the other cells," she said, her fingers tracing the lines on the map that marked the locations of key government installations. "If we can hit multiple targets at once, it'll create chaos. They won't know where to focus their defences."

"Agreed," Emily said, her voice firm. "We'll need to be precise, surgical. This isn't just about brute force, it's about strategy. We've seen what they're capable of when they're cornered. We can't underestimate them."

Hale leaned forward, his expression serious. "I'll provide you with the intel you need," he said. "Security protocols, shift changes, weaknesses in their defences. But you need to understand, that once this starts, there's no going back. The government will throw everything they have at us."

"We're ready for that," Aamir replied, his tone resolute. "We've come too far to back down now."

Emily's gaze swept across the room, taking in the determined faces of her comrades. They had lost so much and sacrificed more than any of them had ever imagined, but they had also gained something invaluable, hope. The tide was turning, and for the first time in a long while, they could see a path forward.

"The uprisings are spreading," Emily said, her voice carrying the conviction of a leader who had finally found her footing. "People are rising up, not just here, but in cities across the country. They're fighting back, and they're looking to us for leadership. We can't let them down."

Lily's eyes sparkled with fierce determination. "We won't," she said. "This is it. The moment we've been fighting for."

There was a quiet, collective moment of understanding among them. The final assault would not be easy; it would come at a cost. But they were ready to pay that price. The time for hesitation was over. The rebellion, which had once seemed like a distant dream, was now a roaring fire that could no longer be extinguished.

As they continued to discuss the logistics of the upcoming operation, the tension in the room began to shift. It was no longer the tension of uncertainty, of fear, but the tension of anticipation, of readiness. Each of them knew their role, and each of them was prepared to do whatever it took to see this through.

The room, dimly lit and suffused with a sense of purpose, had become a war room. And as the candles flickered, casting long shadows on the walls, those within knew they were standing on the precipice of something monumental. The final battle was approaching, and they were ready to meet it head-on.

As the meeting came to a close, Emily stood and looked around at the faces of those who had become more than just comrades; they were her family. "This is our turning point," she said, her voice steady and sure. "We started this together, and we'll finish it together."

Aamir reached out, placing his hand on hers, a silent gesture of support. Lily followed suit, then Hale, and soon, all of them had their hands stacked together, a symbol of their unity, their resolve.

"For the people," Emily whispered, and the others echoed her words, their voices quiet but filled with the power of a promise made in blood and fire.

The path ahead was fraught with danger, every step a potential descent into chaos, but the flame of hope had been rekindled, burning brighter than ever before. The rebels could feel it in the air, a palpable shift that set their hearts pounding with a mixture of fear and determination. They had come so far, and endured so much, and now, standing on the precipice of what could be their final battle, the stakes had never been higher.

For years, they had fought in the shadows, waging a war of attrition against a seemingly insurmountable enemy. They had seen friends and comrades fall and had watched as entire communities were torn apart by the regime's ruthless grip on power. They had been hunted, beaten down, and nearly broken. But through it all, they had clung to the belief that change was possible, that a better future was within their grasp if only they dared to reach for it.

Now, that belief was more than just a flicker in the darkness. It was a blazing inferno, fired by the knowledge that they were no longer alone in their struggle. The tide was turning, and with each new defection, each small victory, the momentum was building. The people were beginning to rise, their voices no longer silenced by fear, and their actions no longer paralysed by despair. The government's once unyielding grip on the nation was slipping, and the rebels could sense the growing panic in their oppressors' ranks.

The final assault was coming, and with it, the chance to turn the tide once and for all. But they knew it wouldn't be easy. The regime would not go down without a fight, and the coming days would test them in ways they had never imagined. There would be bloodshed, sacrifice, and loss, more than they had already endured, but there would also be the possibility of victory, of finally breaking the chains that had bound them for so long.

As they prepared for the coming battle, the rebels found strength in one another, in the bonds that had been forged in the crucible of war. They had become more than just a group of fighters; they were a family, united by a common purpose, driven by a shared dream of freedom. And it was this unity, this unwavering resolve, that would carry them through the darkness and into the light.

The weight of what lay ahead was heavy, but it was a burden they were willing to bear. The flame of hope, once so fragile, now blazed with an intensity that could not be extinguished. It was a beacon, guiding them forward, illuminating the path that would lead them to either victory or defeat. But whatever the outcome, they knew one thing for certain: they would not go quietly into the night. They would fight with everything they had, for themselves, for their fallen comrades, and for the generations to come.

The final assault would be their defining moment, the culmination of all they had fought for. It was the moment when the rebellion would either triumph or be crushed under the weight of the regime's iron fist. But as they looked to the horizon, where the first light of dawn was beginning to break, they knew that they were ready. The path ahead was fraught with danger, but it was also paved with the possibility of a new beginning, a future where their children could live in a world free from tyranny.

And so, with their hearts full of hope and their spirits unbroken, the rebels steeled themselves for the battle to come. The flame of hope had been rekindled, burning brighter than ever, and they would carry it with them into the fray, lighting the way forward in the darkest of times. The final assault was coming, and with it, the chance to turn the tide once and for all, to seize their destiny and shape the future with their own hands.

And so, with the plan set and their resolve steeled for what lay ahead, the group disbanded, each member carrying with them the weight of what was to come. The night outside was still, but in the hearts of the rebels, there was a fire that nothing could quench. The revolution was no longer just a dream; it was a reality that would soon be written in the annals of history.

Chapter 28 The Final Push

The cold wind swept through the empty streets of the once-bustling city, carrying with it the echoes of a society teetering on the brink of collapse. The chill was sharp, biting through layers of clothing as if the city itself had turned against its inhabitants. The buildings, once proud symbols of industry and power, now stood as hollow sentinels, their glass facades cracked, and windows shattered. The skyscrapers that once touched the sky with optimism now loomed like tombstones, casting long, eerie shadows over the desolate streets below. Every corner of the city was marked by decay, graffiti-covered walls, the remnants of barricades, and the burnt-out shells of cars that littered the roads like the carcasses of some forgotten war.

This city, once the heart of a nation, had become a silent witness to the mounting tension that grew with each passing day. The streets, which had once echoed with the sounds of commerce and life, were now filled with an ominous quiet, broken only by the distant rumble of government patrols and the occasional crack of gunfire. The air was thick with the scent of smoke and dust, the acrid smell of destruction that clung to everything, a constant reminder of the battles that had raged through these streets.

But even within this desolation, a spark of hope flickered, small, but growing. It was a fragile thing, like the first green shoot pushing through the cracks of a barren landscape, but it was there, undeniable, and persistent. This hope was not born of naivety but of determination, forged in the fires of loss and tempered by the will to survive. It was the hope of a people who had been beaten down, only to rise again with renewed purpose.

In the depths of an abandoned warehouse on the outskirts of the city, this hope took form. The warehouse, once a hub of activity for goods that would never reach their destinations, had been reclaimed by the resistance. Long forgotten by the government, it now served as a sanctuary, a place where the flicker of rebellion could be nurtured into a blaze. The massive, corrugated metal doors had long since rusted in their tracks, giving the building a permanent aura of neglect, but inside, the space was alive with the hum of preparation.

The rebels, who had once been scattered and disorganised, now moved with a sense of purpose. They were no longer the disparate groups of idealists, students, and disillusioned citizens that had taken up arms in the early days of the conflict. They had evolved into something more, hardened fighters, strategists, and leaders, each one carrying the weight of the battles they had fought and the losses they had endured. The air inside the warehouse was thick with anticipation, a charged atmosphere that seemed to vibrate with the unspoken understanding that this could be their final stand.

The interior of the warehouse had been transformed from a derelict space into a makeshift command centre. Tables were covered in maps, blueprints, and communication devices, the tools of a war fought in shadows and back alleys. Weapons were stacked neatly against the walls, a stark contrast to the chaotic nature of the conflict outside. The rebels moved swiftly, their movements choreographed by months of practice and the knowledge that time was not on their side.

Every face in the room was etched with the hard lines of determination, their eyes reflecting the grim reality of their situation. There was no room for doubt here, no space for hesitation. Each person had a role to play, and they played it with the understanding that failure was not an option. The rebels had been pushed to the edge, but they had not broken. Instead, they had found strength in their unity, a shared belief that they could still win this fight, and that the sacrifices they had made had not been in vain.

Among them were those who had joined the cause early on, their resolve as unshakable as ever, and new recruits, young men and women who had come from all corners of the country, drawn by the promise of change. Their faces were a mix of fear and determination, the fire of idealism still burning brightly in their eyes, tempered by the knowledge of what lay ahead. They had come because they believed in something greater than themselves, something worth fighting for.

As the night deepened, the atmosphere inside the warehouse grew heavier, the silence punctuated only by the murmur of last-minute discussions and the occasional clatter of equipment being readied for the battle to come. Beneath the surface of activity, there was a shared understanding, a silent agreement that this was the moment they had been fighting for. Everything they had done, every life lost, every battle fought, had led them to this point.

This was it. The final push. The moment when hope would either triumph or be extinguished forever. And as they prepared to step into the fray once more, the rebels knew that whatever happened next, they had already made history. They had defied the odds, stood up against tyranny, and reignited the spark of resistance in a world that had seemed destined for darkness.

And now, as they gathered for what might be their last mission, that spark was about to become a flame.

Emily stood at the centre of the room, her eyes scanning the faces around her. These were her comrades, her family, each one hardened by the battles they had fought, but still carrying the scars of those they had lost. The reality of what lay ahead hung heavy in the air, but so too did the quiet determination that had kept them going through the darkest of times.

"We've come a long way," Emily began, her voice steady despite the turmoil in her heart. "Tonight, we stand together, not as individuals, but as one united force. This is our moment, the moment we've fought for, bled for, and lost so much for."

The room was silent, each person absorbing her words, the gravity of what she was saying settling deep within them. For many, this was the first time they had seen so many of their fellow rebels in one place, a testament to how far their movement had come, but also a stark reminder of the stakes.

Aamir, standing close by, stepped forward. "This isn't just about taking down a government," he said, his voice calm yet charged with emotion. "It's about reclaiming our lives, our futures. What we do tonight will echo through history. We fight not just for ourselves, but for those who can't, for those who've been silenced and oppressed."

Tomasz, the ever-practical tactician, nodded in agreement. "We've prepared as much as we can. Every cell is ready, every detail is accounted for. But remember, no plan survives first contact with the enemy. We'll need to be flexible, to adapt as the situation unfolds."

Lily, who had become a voice of hope within the group, spoke next. "No matter what happens tonight, know this: we have already won. We've shown the world that we won't be silenced, that we won't stand by while our freedoms are stripped away. And whatever the outcome, we've made our mark. They will remember us."

The warehouse fell silent once more as the weight of the moment pressed down on them. Each person knew that the odds were against them, that this could very well be the last time they stood together. Yet, there was no fear in their eyes, only resolve.

As the final preparations were made, Emily found herself drifting to the edges of the room, her presence there almost ghostly, as if she were a shadow observing from a distance. She watched the others engage in a ritual as old as war itself, saying their goodbyes. Each embrace was filled with a mix of desperation and affection, every clasped hand a silent promise that even if they were torn apart, they would always remain connected by the bond they had forged in the crucible of resistance.

Emily's eyes, usually so sharp and focused, softened as she took in the scene. There was a part of her that ached with every farewell, every whispered word of reassurance. The air was thick with emotion, so tangible she could almost reach out and touch it. Love, fear, and hope, all tangled together in a complex web of human connection that transcended the war they were about to wage. It was this connection, this deep-seated humanity, that made the fight worth it, but it was also what made it so excruciatingly difficult.

She was their leader now, and with that role came the burden of responsibility, a weight she had willingly shouldered, but one that sometimes felt impossibly heavy. She had to be strong for them, had to be the rock they could anchor to in the storm that was about to break. But as she watched her comrades, her friends, prepare for what might be their final mission, doubt gnawed at the edges of her resolve.

Her mind drifted back to the early days, to the time before the rebellion had become her entire world. She remembered the idealism that had driven her, the unshakable belief that they could make a difference, that they could bring about change. But the years had worn on her, had worn on all of them, and with each passing day, the cost of their fight had become more apparent. Friends lost, lives shattered, innocence sacrificed on the altar of necessity. She could still see the faces of those who had fallen, and hear their voices in her quiet moments, and it haunted her.

Emily wondered if she had done enough if the plans she had put in place were truly the right ones. The pressure of it all, the decisions she had to make, the lives that depended on those decisions, was almost unbearable. What if she had missed something? What if this final push, this desperate gamble for victory, ended in disaster? The thought twisted her insides, and for a moment, she was overwhelmed by a wave of fear so intense it threatened to paralyse her.

But then she forced herself to breathe, to focus. She had to trust in herself, in the work they had done. This wasn't just about tactics and strategy; it was about the people she had come to care for more deeply than she had ever thought possible. It was about the world they wanted to build, the future they were fighting for. She couldn't afford to let her doubts consume her, not now.

Emily's gaze swept over the room again, taking in the faces of those she had come to know so well. They believed in her and trusted her, and she couldn't let them down. The tears, the whispered words of encouragement and love, the steely determination in their eyes, all of it powered the fire within her. This was no longer just a rebellion; it was a fight for their very souls, for the right to live and love in a world that had nearly forgotten what those words meant.

Her memories flickered through her mind like a slideshow, moments of victory and loss, laughter and tears, all leading to this moment. She saw Aamir's face, his quiet strength giving her the courage to continue. She thought of Lily, of the bond they had formed, and the sacrifices each of them had made. And then there were the countless others who had joined their cause, whose lives were now intertwined with hers. She could not, would not, let them down.

As the group began to gather for the final briefing, Emily straightened, pushing her fears deep down where they couldn't reach her. This was the culmination of everything they had fought for. Every plan, every move, every sacrifice had led them here, to this moment. The outcome was uncertain, the path ahead fraught with danger, but Emily knew one thing with absolute clarity: they would give it everything they had.

The room began to quiet as the last goodbyes were spoken, and the rebels turned their attention to the task at hand. Emily stepped forward, her voice calm and steady as she began to speak, the weight of leadership sitting comfortably on her shoulders once more. She could feel the eyes of her comrades on her, the unspoken questions, the hopes they had placed in her. And in that moment, she knew that whatever happened next, they would face it together.

This was their fight, their cause, their moment. The fear was still there, lingering at the edges of her consciousness, but it was tempered by the fierce determination that burned within her. They were on the precipice of something monumental, and she was ready to lead them through it. As she looked around at the faces of those who had come to mean so much to her, Emily felt a surge of resolve. They had come too far to turn back now. The final push was here, and they would face it head-on, with all the courage and strength they could muster.

This was their last stand, their final push toward the dawn of a new day. And as Emily looked out over her comrades, she knew that no matter what happened, they had already won most importantly. They had stayed true to themselves, to each other, and to the cause they believed in. The rest, as always, was in their hands.

Aamir approached her, his expression serious. "Are you ready?" he asked, his voice soft.

Emily nodded, though the tightness in her chest betrayed her. "As ready as I'll ever be."

Aamir hesitated, his eyes searching hers. "Whatever happens tonight, I want you to know, "

"Don't," Emily interrupted, shaking her head. "Don't say it. Not now. We can't afford to think like that."

Aamir sighed, understanding. "You're right. But I need you to know that I'm with you, no matter what."

Emily met his gaze, her heart aching with the weight of unspoken words. "And I'm with you. Always."

As they stood there, the world around them seemed to blur, leaving only the two of them in a moment suspended in time. There was so much left unsaid, but they both knew there was no need for words. Their bond, forged in the crucible of war, was unbreakable.

Nearby, Lily stood in the dimly lit corner of the warehouse, her usual bright manner muted by the gravity of the moment. She had always been the optimist, the one who could find light even in the darkest of times. Her laughter was infectious, a balm for the group's weary souls, and her unwavering belief in their cause had carried them through more than one near defeat. But now, as the final hours before the assault ticked away, a shadow had fallen over her heart, one that even her unyielding positivity struggled to dispel.

Lily's thoughts were a whirlwind, her mind flickering between the mission at hand and the tangled emotions she had carefully tucked away for so long. She had developed deep feelings for two of her fellow rebels, both strong, courageous, and fiercely dedicated to the cause. With one, there was a sense of camaraderie that had blossomed into something more over the months they had fought side by side. They had a shared understanding, a bond forged in the fires of rebellion. With the other, the connection was different, more intense, a magnetic pull that left her breathless whenever they were near. It was a passion that scared her as much as it excited her, a raw and unfiltered emotion that she wasn't sure how to handle in a war.

She had always managed to keep her personal feelings separate from the mission. After all, there was no room for distractions when every decision could mean the difference between life and death. But as they stood on the brink of what could be their final battle, Lily found herself questioning whether she had made the right choice. What if this was it? What if she never got the chance to explore what might have been? The thought gnawed at her, an ache deep in her chest that she couldn't ignore.

Lily's gaze drifted across the room, settling on the two rebels who held pieces of her heart. One was busy adjusting his gear, the other deep in conversation with another member of the group. They were so focused, so determined, and the sight of them filled her with both pride and sorrow. She knew that she would fight alongside them with everything she had, but the knowledge that tonight might be the last time she saw them, might be the last time she felt the warmth of their presence, was almost unbearable.

She pressed her lips together, forcing herself to take a steadying breath. There was no time for uncertainty, no room for hesitation. She had to be strong and had to put the mission above all else. But the weight of unresolved emotions bore down on her like a physical force, making it hard to breathe. What if she never got the chance to tell them how she felt? What if they never knew the depth of her affection, the way she cherished every moment they had shared? The thought was suffocating, a bitter reminder of all the things war could take away from them.

As she stood there, lost in her thoughts, Lily clenched her fists at her sides, willing herself to focus. The mission was everything. It was what they had been fighting for, what they had sacrificed so much for. She couldn't let her emotions cloud her judgment, couldn't allow herself to be distracted when the stakes were so high. But the fear lingered, a cold dread that she might never find closure, that her feelings would remain unspoken, forever locked away in her heart.

She had always been the optimist, the one who believed in happy endings even when they seemed impossible. But tonight, the weight of reality pressed down on her, and for the first time, she wasn't sure if her optimism was enough. Could she set aside her emotions, and focus solely on the mission, when her heart was so conflicted? Or would her feelings for these two men, these two incredible souls who had become so important to her, be the thing that broke her resolve?

Lily shook her head, trying to clear her thoughts. This was not the time for doubt. They had a job to do, a mission that required every ounce of their strength and determination. She would push her feelings aside, bury them deep where they couldn't touch her, at least for tonight. But the knowledge that she might never get the chance to resolve those emotions, to see where those connections might have led, weighed heavily on her. It was a burden she would carry into battle, one more piece of armour to protect her fragile heart.

As the final preparations continued around her, Lily forced herself to smile, to be the beacon of hope her comrades needed her to be. But inside, she was anything but calm. Inside, she was a storm of conflicting emotions, a whirlwind of love, fear, and regret. And as she steeled herself for the fight ahead, she couldn't help but wonder if she would ever find peace, if she would ever get the chance to follow her heart.

As the time for the assault drew near, the rebels began to move out, their footsteps echoing through the warehouse like a drumbeat of destiny. The city outside was dark, the oppressive silence broken only by the distant hum of government patrols. The rebels moved like shadows, slipping through the streets with the stealth born of necessity.

Emily led the way, her heart pounding as she guided her team through the labyrinth of alleys and side streets. Every step brought them closer to their target, and with it, the realisation that this could be the end. But there was no turning back now. They had committed to this path, and they would see it through, no matter the cost.

As they approached the government stronghold, the tension in the air became almost palpable, a suffocating force that pressed down on them with every step. The night was thick with an oppressive silence, broken only by the distant hum of the city, now a city on the brink, teetering between the past it clung to and the uncertain future that loomed. The stronghold itself rose out of the darkness like a monolith, its silhouette sharp against the sky, a towering fortress of steel and concrete that seemed to reach out and touch the clouds.

Every inch of the structure exuded power and control. It was a place designed not just to protect, but to intimidate, to remind all who approached of the government's unyielding dominance. The walls were high and thick, lined with barbed wire and reinforced with layers of steel. Searchlights swept the grounds, their beams cutting through the night like knives, ready to expose any intruder who dared to come too close. Automated turrets and surveillance cameras dotted the perimeter, silent sentinels that watched and waited, ever vigilant for signs of dissent.

The rebels moved quietly, their breaths held as they approached the outer fence. The weight of the mission bore down on them, each one acutely aware of the stakes. This was no ordinary target; this was the heart of the regime, the nerve centre from which the government orchestrated its reign of terror. To take this stronghold would be to strike at the very core of their enemy's power, to cut off the head of the snake that had coiled itself around the nation.

But the stronghold's defences, though formidable, were not impenetrable. They had spent weeks gathering intelligence, poring over blueprints, and planning every detail of the assault. They knew where the weaknesses lay, the chinks in the armour that could be exploited. A single point of entry, a blind spot in the surveillance network, a guard shift that left a narrow window of opportunity, these were the threads they would pull to unravel the fortress's defences.

As they crouched in the shadows, waiting for the signal to move, the rebels exchanged glances, their eyes filled with a mix of fear and determination. They had come so far, fought so hard, and now they were on the brink of something monumental. The stronghold was more than just a building; it was a symbol of everything they were fighting against, the oppression, the brutality, and the suffocating control that had gripped their country for too long. To take it would be to shatter that symbol, to send a message to the government and the people alike that the tide had turned.

But the enormity of the task ahead weighed heavily on them. The stronghold was a fortress in every sense of the word, built to withstand any assault, to keep the outside world at bay. And yet, as they prepared to breach its walls, there was a sense of resolve among the rebels, a quiet understanding that this was their moment. They could not afford to fail. If they succeeded, they would cripple the government's ability to wage war, to oppress, to control. They would take away the regime's most powerful weapon, its ability to instil fear.

The tension mounted as the signal was given. The rebels moved with precision, their training and experience guiding their actions. They knew that once they were inside, there would be no turning back. Every step forward was a step deeper into the heart of the beast, and they could feel its pulse quicken as they drew closer. The air crackled with anticipation, with the electricity of a battle about to be joined.

And then, as they reached the outer gate, the first breach was made. The fence was cut, the alarm disabled, and they slipped through the opening like shadows. The stronghold loomed before them, its walls tall and foreboding, but the rebels pressed on, their hearts pounding with the knowledge that they were about to face the regime's full might. This was the final push, the moment they had been building toward for so long.

As they crossed the threshold into the stronghold's courtyard, the weight of what lay ahead settled over them like a shroud. But with it came a surge of adrenaline, a fierce determination that burned in their veins. They were no longer just rebels fighting against a faceless enemy; they were warriors on a mission, ready to do whatever it took to bring the regime to its knees.

This was their chance to cripple the government, to deliver a blow from which it might never recover. And as they moved deeper into the stronghold, the realisation struck them all: this was not just a battle for control of a building, it was a battle for the future of their country. The stronghold's walls might be high, and its defences might be strong, but the fire that burned within the rebels was stronger still. And with each step, they drew closer to the moment when that fire would ignite, consuming everything in its path.

The rebels spread out, taking their positions, each one a crucial piece in the puzzle of their assault. Emily glanced around at her comrades, her heart swelling with pride. They were ready, and so was she.

"On my signal," she whispered into her radio, her voice steady. "This is it. For everything we've fought for."

The final push had begun. The night was filled with the sounds of battle, gunfire, explosions, and the shouts of the wounded and the dying. But amidst the chaos, there was also hope, a belief that, against all odds, they could win this fight.

As the rebels surged forward, throwing everything they had into the fray, Emily knew that this was their moment of truth. The tide of war was turning, and with it, the future of their nation. But the cost would be high, and the road ahead was still shrouded in uncertainty.

Yet, for the first time in a long time, there was a light at the end of the tunnel. And no matter how dark the night became, they would keep moving forward, driven by the unshakable belief that freedom was within their grasp.

The final battle had begun, and with it, the dawn of a new era. It was a moment that had been years in the making, a crescendo of tension and conflict that had finally reached its breaking point. The air itself seemed to hum with the significance of the hour, a charged atmosphere that crackled with the weight of history being written in real time. Every rebel, every soldier, and every citizen caught in the crossfire could feel it, this was the moment that would define the future, not just for themselves, but for the generations to come.

The night sky, once serene, was now alight with the flashes of gunfire and the distant thrum of explosions. The world as they knew it was shattering, each detonation a hammer blow to the old order. The streets that had once been silent under the regime's oppressive grip were now alive with the sounds of battle, a chaotic symphony of resistance. The rebels, though outnumbered and outgunned, fought with a passion born of desperation and hope, their actions driven by a vision of a world free from tyranny.

As the conflict dragged on, it became evident that this was a fight for rebirth as much as survival. After years of unbridled dominance, the old world was collapsing due to its cruelty and corruption. Something new, fragile but full of promise, was struggling to take its place. The start of a new age wasn't simply a romantic idea; it was a real thing that was just waiting to be taken hold of.

For the rebels, this was a struggle waged with ideas as much as with guns. Every protest against the regime was a protest for justice, freedom, and the potential for a society free from terror. More than just a military conflict, the last fight represented the pinnacle of every act of resistance, every secret discussion held in the shadows, and every risk taken by those who dared to hope for a better world.

But the dawn of a new era was not guaranteed. The outcome of this battle would determine whether their hopes would be realised or extinguished. The rebels knew this as they pressed forward, every heartbeat a reminder of what was at stake. They had fought too long, sacrificed too much, to falter now. The path ahead was fraught with danger, but it was also lit by the faint, growing light of a new beginning.

The smoke and dust coming from the battlefield blended with the first rays of the morning as they peaked above the horizon. It was a daybreak unlike any other, signifying the beginning of a brand-new world forged in the furnace of revolution. The last fight had started, and with it the hope of a time when the oppressors would be lifted, and the people could live free once and for all. A new age was about to dawn, and the rebels, despite their wounds and losses, were prepared to fight to the death for it.

Chapter 29 The Battle for Freedom

The night had fallen like a shroud over the city, cloaking it in a silence that was almost unbearable in its intensity. But this silence was not one of peace, it was the tense, trembling quiet before the storm, a pause in which every breath was held, and every heart beat a little faster. The city, once vibrant and full of life, was now a dark and twisted battlefield, its streets lined with the remnants of a regime that had held power for too long. The sky, bruised and heavy with the promise of rain, seemed to mirror the turmoil below, where the final confrontation was about to unfold.

The rebels had gathered at the edge of the government stronghold, a massive fortress of steel and concrete that loomed ominously in the distance. The stronghold was an imposing structure, designed to intimidate and repel any who dared to challenge the regime's authority. Its walls were thick and unyielding, a seamless blend of metal and stone that rose high into the night sky, blocking out even the faintest glimmer of starlight. The sheer size of the fortress was daunting, a testament to the power that had been consolidated within its cold, grey walls.

But as the rebels stood at the brink of this formidable fortress, there was no hesitation in their eyes, only a fierce determination that burned brighter than the looming shadow ahead. Each of them carried the weight of years of struggle on their shoulders, the memories of friends lost, battles fought, and the countless sacrifices made along the way. Yet, it was not the past that drove them now, but the future they had fought so tirelessly for. This was their moment, the culmination of everything they had endured and everything they had dreamed of.

The ground beneath their feet was uneven, littered with the remnants of past skirmishes, scorched earth, twisted metal, and the occasional abandoned weapon, a silent testament to the battles that had been waged to bring them to this point. The air was thick with tension, charged with the anticipation of what was to come. It was as if the very earth itself was holding its breath, waiting for the clash that would determine the fate of a nation.

As the rebels prepared for the assault, they exchanged quiet glances, each one conveying a depth of understanding that words could never capture. There was a unity among them that transcended mere camaraderie; it was the bond forged in the fires of resistance, a shared belief in the possibility of a better world. The fortress ahead may have been a symbol of oppression, but to the rebels, it was also a symbol of the challenge they had chosen to face, a challenge they were ready to overcome.

The stronghold's defences were formidable, with watchtowers perched high above, their searchlights sweeping the surrounding terrain in search of any sign of movement. The entrance was guarded by heavily armed soldiers, their faces obscured by the cold, emotionless masks of their helmets. But despite the overwhelming odds, the rebels knew that this was their chance, perhaps their only chance, to strike at the heart of the regime.

For years, they had fought in the shadows, their efforts scattered and disjointed, but now, at this moment, they were united in purpose. This was not just a battle for survival; it was a battle for freedom, for the right to live in a world where fear no longer ruled their lives. The fortress may have stood as a monument to the regime's power, but the rebels had become a living testament to the power of hope and resilience.

In their minds, they knew the risks, the likelihood that not all of them would make it through the night. But as they stared down the fortress, there was no room for doubt, only the unshakable belief that their cause was just, that their fight was righteous. This was their moment to seize, the culmination of years of struggle, sacrifice, and unwavering belief in the possibility of a better world. The walls of the fortress, thick and unyielding, seemed almost insurmountable, but the fire in their hearts burned brighter still. This was their time, and they were ready to fight for the future they had always known was possible.

Emily stood at the forefront, her gaze fixed on the stronghold. Her mind was a whirlwind of thoughts and memories, of all they had endured to reach this point, of the friends they had lost along the way, and of the uncertain future that lay ahead. The weight of leadership pressed heavily on her shoulders, but so too did the weight of hope. This was their final push, their last chance to seize freedom from the jaws of tyranny. She glanced back at the group behind her, their faces illuminated by the dim light of the few torches they had dared to light. Each face told a story, of pain, of loss, but also of unwavering resolve.

Lily stood beside Emily, her usual bright demeanour now tinged with a solemnity that had come with the hard lessons of war. In the early days of the rebellion, she had been the beacon of hope, the one who always found a reason to smile, even in the darkest moments. But the years had worn on her, chiselling away at the naivety that had once shielded her from the brutal realities of their struggle. She had seen friends fall and witnessed atrocities that had shaken her to her core, and yet, through it all, she had clung to a fragile thread of hope. It was that hope that had carried her this far, that had kept her fighting even when everything seemed lost.

Now, as they stood on the precipice of the final battle, Lily felt the weight of all that had come before pressing down on her. The world they had known was crumbling, the future they had dreamed of seemed so close, yet so perilous. The optimism that had once been her shield was still there, but it was tempered by the knowledge of what they stood to lose. She had said her goodbyes and whispered words of love and resolve to those she cared about, knowing that they might be the last words she ever spoke to them. But she had also made peace with that possibility. For Lily, this fight was about more than just survival, it was about making sure that all the pain, all the sacrifice, had not been in vain. She stood ready, her heart full of quiet, determined hope, believing that somehow, they would make it through, that the dawn would break after the darkest night.

Aamir was there too, his presence a steadying force in the tumultuous sea of emotions that surrounded them. His face, often marked by a thoughtful intensity, was now a mask of quiet determination. The loss of his brother, Hassan, had been a devastating blow, one that had nearly broken him. But instead of crumbling under the weight of that grief, Aamir had allowed it to forge him into something stronger. Every decision he made, every plan he devised, was done with Hassan's memory in mind. He carried his brother's spirit with him, a silent vow to continue the fight Hassan had begun.

Aamir had become a cornerstone of the resistance, his sharp intellect, and strategic mind guiding their efforts with a precision that few others could match. He had earned the respect and trust of those around him, not just through his actions, but through the quiet strength he exuded even in the face of overwhelming odds. But tonight, as they prepared for what could be their final stand, Aamir knew that strategy alone would not be enough. The battle ahead would demand more than careful planning; it would require raw courage, the kind that compelled a person to stand their ground even when every instinct screamed to flee. It would require the willingness to lay everything on the line, to face the possibility of death with the knowledge that the fight for freedom was worth any sacrifice.

As Aamir looked around at the faces of his comrades, he felt a deep sense of resolve settle over him. This was not just about him or his brother anymore; it was about all of them, the living and the dead, the innocent and the guilty. It was about giving everything they had left to ensure that those who came after them would not have to live in fear. Tonight, Aamir was not just fighting for revenge or even for justice, he was fighting for a future that was free from the chains of oppression, for a world where the sacrifices they had made would not be forgotten.

The determination in his eyes mirrored that of the rebels around him, each one standing on the edge of the unknown, ready to face whatever came next. The air was thick with the shared understanding that they might not all make it through the night, but that didn't matter. What mattered was that they were here, together, united in purpose and in spirit. Aamir, like Lily, had reconciled himself to the possibility of death, but it was not fear that gripped him now, it was the fierce resolve to see this through to the end, to honour the memory of those who had fallen by continuing the fight they had begun.

As they stood together, Lily, Aamir, and Emily, all of them, felt the weight of the moment pressing down on them, but they also felt the strength that came from knowing they were not alone. This was their final push, the culmination of years of struggle and sacrifice, and they were ready to give everything they had to see it through. The fortress ahead might have been an imposing structure of steel and concrete, but the fire that burned within the hearts of the rebels was stronger and brighter, and it was that fire that would light their way in the darkness of the night to come.

The air was thick with tension as they approached the stronghold, their footsteps muffled by the soft earth beneath them. The silence was broken only by the distant rumble of thunder, a harbinger of the storm that was fast approaching. The plan had been carefully crafted, every detail meticulously considered. But as they neared the fortress, the enormity of what they were about to do settled over them like a heavy fog. This was it, their final stand.

The first shot rang out, shattering the silence and setting off a cascade of chaos. The rebels surged forward, their battle cries echoing off the cold, unforgiving walls of the stronghold. The government forces were ready, their defences formidable, but the rebels had one advantage: they were fighting for something greater than themselves. They fought with a ferocity born of desperation, of a need to see justice done, no matter the cost.

The battle quickly became a blur of movement and sound, the clashing of weapons and the shouts of combatants filling the air. The ground beneath them was soon stained with the blood of both sides, each drop a testament to the price of freedom. Emily fought with a singular focus, her every move calculated, her every strike aimed to disable rather than kill. She had long since come to terms with the necessity of violence in their struggle, but even now, she tried to spare those who stood against them, knowing that many were just as trapped by the regime as she once had been.

But this was not a battle they could win through sheer force alone. The government forces were well-equipped, their ranks bolstered by years of preparation for just such an uprising. The rebels, on the other hand, were a patchwork of civilians and soldiers, their weapons often outdated, their tactics improvised. Yet, what they lacked in resources, they made up for in heart. Each step they took was a step toward freedom, and that thought alone kept them moving forward, even as the odds stacked ever higher against them.

As the battle raged on, the rebels began to falter. The government forces, relentless in their defence, pushed them back, inch by inch. Key characters fell, brave souls who had fought so hard, who had believed so deeply in their cause. Their loss was felt keenly, a sharp stab of pain that threatened to overwhelm those who remained. But the rebels pressed on, driven by the memory of those who had given everything for this moment.

Emily found herself fighting side by side with Aamir, their movements synchronised, their bond forged in the crucible of war. She could see the pain in his eyes, the loss that he carried with him like a shadow. But she could also see the fire that still burned within him, a fire that would not be extinguished until justice was served.

Nearby, Lily fought with a desperation that bordered on recklessness. She had always been the heart of the group, the one who kept their spirits high, even in the darkest of times. But now, that light was flickering, her hope hanging by a thread. She had seen too much and lost too much, and the weight of it all was finally catching up with her. Yet, even now, she fought on, determined to see this through to the end.

The battle swung back and forth, each side gaining ground only to lose it again moments later. The rebels were relentless, their determination unwavering, but the government forces were equally resolute. It was a battle of wills as much as it was a battle of strength, and with each passing moment, the outcome became more uncertain.

As the night wore on, the rebels found themselves pushed back to the edge of the stronghold. They had come so far and fought so hard, but now it seemed as though victory was slipping through their fingers. Emily, battered and bruised, looked around at her comrades, seeing the exhaustion etched on their faces, the blood that stained their clothes, and the fear that flickered in their eyes. She knew they were close to breaking, that one more push could send them over the edge.

But just as all seemed lost, a new sound pierced the air, a sound that cut through the chaos like a blade through darkness. It was the sound of reinforcements, a roar of defiance that reverberated across the battlefield. The distant echoes of determined voices grew louder, the synchronised pounding of boots on the ground signalling the arrival of hope. The other rebel cells, scattered across the city and hidden in the shadows, had finally emerged from their positions, converging on the stronghold in a coordinated, desperate push.

They charged forward with a fierce resolve, their numbers swelling the ranks of the battered resistance. The sight of their comrades, surging into the fray with renewed energy, breathed life into those who had been on the verge of collapse. It was as if the very air had shifted, the oppressive weight of imminent defeat lifting, replaced by a collective surge of strength and unity. The fresh wave of fighters, their faces etched with determination, crashed into the government forces like a tidal wave, catching them off guard and forcing them to fall back.

The tide of battle shifted once again, the momentum swinging in favour of the rebels. For the first time in hours, the battered resistance began to push the government forces back, their advance slow but relentless. The sound of gunfire and explosions was now punctuated by the rallying cries of the rebels, their voices rising above the din, a chorus of hope and defiance. The once-unyielding walls of the government's defence began to buckle under the pressure, their lines thinning as they struggled to hold their ground.

The reinforcements fought with a tenacity born of desperation and unyielding belief in their cause. Among them were men and women who had seen their homes destroyed, their families torn apart by the very regime they now faced. They fought not just for survival, but for the chance to reclaim their lives, to build a future free from oppression. Each step they took pushed the government forces further back, the rebels' momentum growing with every inch gained.

Amid the chaos, a new sense of camaraderie emerged, binding the rebels together as they pressed forward. There was no distinction between the veterans who had been fighting since the beginning and the fresh recruits who had only just joined the cause. In that moment, they were all equals, united by a common purpose, their collective strength propelling them toward victory.

As the government forces continued to retreat, their once formidable defence now faltering, the rebels could feel the shift in the air, a palpable change that signalled the possibility of triumph. The stronghold, which had once seemed insurmountable, was now within reach, its defences crumbling under the weight of the rebels' determination. The realisation that they might succeed powered their efforts, their attacks growing more coordinated and precise.

For the first time in hours, a glimmer of hope shone through the darkness of the battle. The rebels, battered and bruised, were no longer on the defensive. They had taken the offensive, driving their oppressors back, inch by hard-fought inch. The outcome was still uncertain, but the tide had turned, and with it, the belief that they could, and would, emerge victorious.

With renewed energy, the rebels surged forward, their hope rekindled, their spirits lifted by the sight of their comrades joining the fray. The final push had begun, and this time, they would not stop until they had torn down the walls of oppression that had held them captive for so long.

As the first light of dawn began to creep over the horizon, casting a golden glow over the battlefield, the rebels fought with everything they had. The government forces, now on the defensive, began to falter, their once impenetrable defences crumbling under the weight of the rebels' resolve. The final battle had begun, and with it, the dawn of a new era.

In the end, it would not be weapons or tactics that decided the outcome of this battle. It would be the strength of their convictions, the belief that they were fighting for something greater than themselves. The rebels, united in their cause, fought with a ferocity that no amount of training or preparation could have anticipated. They fought for freedom, for justice, for the future they had dreamed of for so long. And as the sun finally rose over the city, its light banishing the shadows of the night, they knew that they were on the brink of something extraordinary, the beginning of a new chapter in the history of their nation.

The battle for freedom was far from over, but the rebels knew that they had taken the first step toward victory. The final push had begun, and with it, the dawn of a new era, a dawn that would be written in the blood and sweat of those who had fought so bravely, and who would continue to fight until the very end.

Chapter 30 Victory and Sacrifice

The first light of dawn crept over the horizon, casting a faint, golden hue over the battlefield that had, just hours before, been a maelstrom of violence and death. The soft glow of the rising sun seemed almost out of place against the backdrop of destruction, as if nature herself was attempting to heal the wounds inflicted upon the land. The once-proud government stronghold, a monolithic fortress of steel and concrete that had loomed over the city with an air of invincibility, now lay in shambles. Its towering walls, which had once symbolised the regime's unyielding power, were fractured and crumbling, unable to withstand the relentless force of the rebellion's final assault.

The great iron gates, which had stood as an impenetrable barrier against the outside world, now hung twisted and torn from their hinges, reduced to little more than jagged remnants of the oppressive force they had once represented. The courtyard beyond, where soldiers had once marched in rigid formation, was now a wasteland of debris, scattered weapons, the remnants of shattered vehicles, and the bodies of those who had fought with desperate fervour to defend the crumbling regime.

Smoke still billowed from the ruins, rising in thick, dark columns that twisted and curled in the morning air, mingling with the early morning mist that clung to the ground like a shroud. The acrid stench of burning metal, charred flesh, and explosives filled the air, a grim reminder of the ferocity of the battle that had raged through the night. The mist, once a symbol of quiet mornings and peaceful beginnings, now seemed to carry with it the ghosts of the fallen, swirling around the remnants of the stronghold as if mourning the loss of those who had perished in the fight.

The city beyond the walls was equally scarred by the conflict. Buildings that had once stood tall and proud were now hollowed shells, their facades blackened by fire, their windows shattered into jagged shards of glass. The streets, once bustling with life, were choked with debris, overturned cars, broken streetlights, and the remnants of hastily erected barricades. Here and there, the bodies of the fallen lay still, some draped in the tattered flags of the rebellion, others clad in the uniforms of the defeated regime.

As the light grew stronger, it illuminated the scene with an almost surreal clarity, highlighting the devastation that had been wrought in the name of freedom. The golden rays of the sun seemed to pierce through the smoke and mist, casting long shadows across the battlefield, where the lines between victory and defeat had been blurred by the bloodshed and sacrifice that had marked the night.

The stronghold, which had once been a symbol of fear and control, was now a graveyard of ambition, its ruins standing as a testament to the indomitable spirit of those who had dared to challenge the might of the regime. And yet, even in its destruction, there was a sense of finality, as if the collapse of the stronghold had brought with it the end of an era, an era defined by oppression, cruelty, and the relentless pursuit of power at any cost.

Now, as the first light of dawn crept over the horizon, it brought with it the promise of a new beginning. The rebellion had triumphed, but the cost had been immense, and the path forward was uncertain. The city, once a place of fear and despair, now stood on the brink of a new chapter, one that would be written by those who had survived the night and who now faced the daunting task of rebuilding what had been lost.

The golden hue of the sunrise bathed the ruins in a warm, almost ethereal light as if offering a glimmer of hope amidst the devastation. The battle was over, but the fight for the future was just beginning. The dawn of a new era had arrived, and with it, the opportunity to reshape the world in the image of those who had fought for its freedom.

The rebels, battle-worn and bloodied, stood scattered across the courtyard, their weapons clutched in exhausted hands. Their faces, streaked with dirt and the remnants of war, reflected a bittersweet mixture of triumph and sorrow. They had won, but the cost of their victory weighed heavily on their shoulders. For every cheer that echoed through the ruins, there was a cry of mourning for the comrades who had not lived to see this moment.

Emily stood on the edge of the shattered courtyard, her boots sinking slightly into the rubble beneath her feet as she surveyed the aftermath of the battle. The once-solid ground was now a chaotic jumble of broken concrete, twisted metal, and the remnants of the walls that had once surrounded the stronghold. She felt the cold, hard edges of debris through the soles of her boots, a stark reminder of the violence that had unfolded here just hours before.

Her gaze was fixed on the horizon, where the first light of dawn was beginning to break through the lingering darkness. The sun, slowly rising above the jagged skyline, cast a soft, golden glow across the battlefield, but its warmth did little to chase away the chill that had settled deep in her bones. The light felt almost mocking, a beautiful contrast to the devastation that lay all around her.

Emily's chest heaved with the exertion of battle, each breath a painful reminder of how close she had come to losing everything. The air she drew in was laced with the acrid scent of smoke and blood, and it burned her lungs with every inhale, yet she welcomed the discomfort, it was proof that she was still alive, capable of feeling, even after all she had endured. Her muscles ached, her limbs heavy and sluggish, as if the weight of the battle had settled into her very bones, making each movement a struggle.

The sun's rays touched her face, warming her skin but doing nothing to alleviate the coldness that had settled in her heart. She was alive, but the price of survival felt almost too great to bear. The weight of command, the crushing responsibility of leadership, bore down on her with an almost physical force. Every decision she had made, every order she had given, played over and over in her mind like a relentless tide, each one accompanied by the faces of those who had paid the ultimate price for her choices.

The lives lost under her watch pressed down on her, nearly crushing her spirit. She could see them in her mind's eye, men and women who had followed her into battle with unwavering trust, who had believed in her ability to lead them to victory. Some of them had been her friends, people she had laughed with, shared meals with, people she had come to love like family. And now they were gone, their bodies lying cold and still among the ruins of the stronghold, their voices silenced forever.

A knot of grief and guilt tightened in her chest, threatening to suffocate her. She had known, from the moment she had taken up the mantle of leadership, that losses were inevitable, that war demanded sacrifices. But nothing could have prepared her for the reality of it, for the sheer, overwhelming weight of knowing that every death, every shattered life, was in some way her responsibility.

She had made the hard decisions, the ones no one else wanted to make because she had believed in the cause and believed that the end would justify the means. But now, standing on the edge of the shattered courtyard, surrounded by the remnants of the battle, she found herself questioning everything. Was it worth it? Had the victory they had fought so hard to achieve truly been worth the cost?

The wind picked up, tugging at her hair and the tattered edges of her coat, as if urging her to move, to leave this place of death and destruction behind. But she couldn't. Not yet. She needed to stand here, to face the reality of what had happened, to acknowledge the lives that had been lost under her command. It was the only way she could honour them, the only way she could make sense of the pain that threatened to swallow her whole.

Her spirit, once so unyielding, felt fractured, like a piece of pottery that had been dropped one too many times. But even in her brokenness, there was a flicker of resolve, a small flame of determination that refused to be extinguished. She had led them this far, through hell and back, and she would not allow their sacrifices to be in vain.

As the sun continued its slow ascent, bathing the ruins in a warm, golden light, Emily took a deep breath and closed her eyes. She allowed herself a moment to grieve, to feel the full weight of the losses they had suffered. And then, with a resolve that was born out of both pain and hope, she steeled herself for what was to come. There was still work to be done, a future to be rebuilt, and she would carry the memory of the fallen with her, using it as a source of strength as she moved forward.

The weight of command might never leave her, but she would bear it. For them. For the future, they had all fought for. For the dawn that was finally breaking over a world that, despite everything, still held the possibility of a better tomorrow.

She turned her eyes away from the horizon, scanning the battlefield for familiar faces among the survivors. Each fallen body she passed filled her with a mixture of dread and hope, searching for those she had fought beside for so long. The ground was littered with debris, twisted metal, discarded weapons, and the bloodied remnants of a regime that had finally been toppled.

Lily approached her, her usual optimism muted by the gravity of their victory. The young woman had grown so much since the early days of the rebellion, her innocence slowly eroded by the harsh realities of war. Now, she stood beside Emily, her face etched with a solemnity that belied her years.

"We did it," Lily said, her voice hoarse from shouting orders during the battle. There was a tremor in her voice, a mix of relief and disbelief that it was finally over.

Emily nodded, unable to find the words to respond. She had dreamed of this day for so long, had fought and sacrificed everything for this moment, and yet now that it had arrived, it felt hollow. The victory had come at a cost she had never fully anticipated, a cost that was now laid bare before her in the form of fallen friends and comrades.

A few steps away, Aamir knelt beside a figure lying on the ground. His hands trembled as he gently cradled the head of a fallen comrade, a friend who had fought by his side through so many battles. The lifeless eyes of the man stared up at the sky, his sacrifice a stark reminder of the cost they had all paid. The loss of his brother, Hassan, had already been a wound that cut deep into Aamir's soul, and now this new loss threatened to reopen that scar, to overwhelm him with a grief that was almost too much to bear.

But even as the sorrow welled up inside him, threatening to drown him in its depths, Aamir felt a steely resolve harden within his heart. The memory of Hassan, of all they had shared, of the dreams they had fought for together, would not allow him to falter. Hassan's death had driven him to continue the fight with a renewed sense of purpose, to ensure that his brother's sacrifice, and the sacrifice of so many others, would not be in vain.

Now, as he held the head of his fallen friend, Aamir's face was a mask of quiet determination, mingled with the deep, aching sorrow that threatened to consume him. But he would not let it. He would carry on, for Hassan, for this fallen comrade, and for all those who had given their lives for the hope of a better future. With a final, silent promise to his friend, Aamir gently laid the man's head back down and rose to his feet, ready to face whatever came next.

As Emily approached, she saw the figure that Aamir was attending to, a figure that made her heart lurch in her chest. It was John. His body was still, his face pale and bloodied. A deep wound in his side bled slowly, a pool of crimson spreading beneath him. His breathing was shallow, each breath a ragged gasp as he fought to stay conscious.

"Aamir," Emily whispered, dropping to her knees beside him. The sight of him, so strong and steadfast throughout their journey, now reduced to this fragile state, sent a wave of grief crashing over her.

Aamir's eyes flickered open at the sound of her voice, and a faint smile touched his lips. "We did it, Em," he rasped, his voice barely more than a whisper. "We... won."

Emily nodded, tears welling in her eyes. "Yes, we won," she said, her voice thick with emotion. "But we're not done yet. You're not done yet. You have to stay with us, Aamir. We need you."

Aamir's smile faded, and a look of pain crossed his face. "I'm not sure... I can," he admitted, his hand weakly reaching for hers.

She took his hand, gripping it tightly. "You have to," she insisted, her voice breaking. "We've come this far because of you. You're the reason we're here. Don't leave us now."

But as she spoke, she could see the life slowly slipping from his eyes. The strength that had always defined him was ebbing away, leaving behind a man who had given everything for the cause he believed in.

Aamir watched in silence, his grief mirrored in Emily's. The battle might be won, but the cost had been more than they had ever imagined. And now, with John's life hanging by a thread, the victory felt incomplete, a hollow triumph overshadowed by the uncertainty of what would come next.

As the sun continued its ascent, the sounds of battle faded into an eerie silence. The government's forces had been routed, their stronghold taken, and their leaders either captured or dead. The regime that had ruled with an iron fist for so long had finally crumbled, its power shattered by the relentless force of the rebellion.

But the victory had come at a steep price. The country lay in ruins, its cities devastated, its people scarred by years of oppression and war. The collapse of the government had left a power vacuum, and the future was uncertain. Chaos reigned, and the hard-won freedom the rebels had fought for now hung in the balance.

As the rebels gathered around the fallen, a sense of unease settled over them. They had achieved what they had set out to do, but at what cost? The road ahead was fraught with danger, and the task of rebuilding a nation from the ashes of war would be no easy feat.

Emily rose to her feet, her eyes still fixed on John's pale face. "We have to move," she said, her voice steady despite the turmoil within her. "We need to get him to a medic, and we need to start organising. The fight isn't over, it's just beginning."

Lily and Aamir nodded, their resolve hardening in the face of the immense challenges ahead. They had fought for this moment, had sacrificed everything to see it through. And now, with the dawn of a new era on the horizon, they would do whatever it took to build the future they had dreamed of.

But as they moved to carry John to safety, the weight of their victory hung heavy in the air. The battle for freedom had been won, but the cost of that freedom was a burden they would carry with them forever. The government had collapsed, but the chaos it left in its wake was a new enemy they would have to confront, a challenge that would test the very limits of their strength and resolve.

As the rebels began to regroup, their eyes turned toward the future. The fight for freedom was far from over, but with John's fate uncertain and the country teetering on the brink of chaos, the path ahead was unclear. Yet, within that uncertainty, there was hope, a fragile, flickering hope that the sacrifices they had made would not be in vain.

The final push had brought them to the edge of victory, but it had also shown them the true cost of the struggle they had waged. As they prepared to face the challenges that lay ahead, they knew that the battle for freedom was not just about toppling a regime, it was about rebuilding a nation, piece by broken piece, and finding a way to heal the wounds that had been inflicted along the way.

Victory had come, but it had come at a price. And now, as the dawn of a new era broke over the horizon, the rebels stood on the precipice of a future they had fought so hard to create. a future that was theirs to shape, for better or for worse.

Chapter 31 A New Beginning

The city was a hushed ruin in the early morning light, its once-proud skyline now punctuated by the skeletal remains of buildings that had been reduced to rubble. Smoke still rose in thin tendrils from the remnants of the final battle, curling lazily into the sky as if reluctant to leave the scene of devastation. The streets, littered with debris and the remnants of hastily abandoned defences, were eerily silent. The war was over, but the scars it had left were deep and raw, etched into every corner of the city.

In the heart of this desolation, the resistance had gathered in what had once been the grand hall of the city's government building. Now, it was a cavernous, broken shell, a stark contrast to the opulence and authority it once represented. The high, vaulted ceilings, which had once echoed with the solemn voices of politicians and officials, were now cracked and crumbling, chunks of plaster littering the floor like the remnants of shattered ideals. The grandeur that had once symbolised power and control was reduced to rubble, a silent testament to the empire that had crumbled around it.

Shattered windows, once adorned with intricate stained glass depicting the city's history, now framed the hall with jagged edges, letting in beams of sunlight that slanted through the dusty air. The light cut through the gloom like the last vestiges of hope, illuminating the swirling motes of dust that danced in the air, remnants of the destruction that had torn through this place. The echoes of their footsteps, the soft shuffle of boots against the debris-strewn floor, seemed to resonate with the ghosts of the past, a haunting reminder of what had been lost in the pursuit of power and control.

The walls, once lined with the portraits of leaders and heroes long gone, were now bare, the paintings ripped down or burned in the fires of rebellion. The only artworks that remained were the scorch marks and bullet holes that pockmarked the walls, stark reminders of the fierce battles fought within these once-hallowed halls. The remnants of heavy wooden doors, now splintered and hanging off their hinges, bore the scars of countless breaches, their once-imposing presence now reduced to mere fragments of what they had been.

The grand hall, once a place of decisions that shaped the fate of a nation, now felt like a tomb, a place where the past lingered, a heavy presence that weighed down on those who stood within its walls. And yet, for the resistance fighters who had gathered here, this broken shell was not just a reminder of the losses they had endured; it was also a symbol of what they had overcome. The ruins of the government building were a testament to the fragility of power, and the fact that they now stood in this place, battered but unbroken, was a victory in itself.

As they moved through the hall, their voices low and hushed in reverence for the past and the future they were trying to build, the resistance members felt the weight of their responsibility more acutely than ever. They were the inheritors of a shattered world, but in the ruins of the old order, they saw the possibility of something new, something better. And as the sunlight filtered through the shattered windows, casting long shadows across the floor, they knew that their fight was far from over. This place, this grand hall now in ruins, was where the next chapter of their struggle would begin.

Emily stood at the front of the hall, a lone figure against the vast backdrop of the once-grand space, now reduced to rubble and memories. She surveyed the group of survivors who had fought beside her, their faces etched with lines of exhaustion, grime, and battle scars, yet lit with a fierce determination that refused to be extinguished. They were a ragtag assembly, a mix of seasoned fighters and those who had never imagined they would be thrust into the crucible of war. Each one bore the physical and emotional toll of the struggle, their bodies battered, their spirits tested to the very brink. Yet, against all odds, they had emerged from the fire, not unscathed, but unbroken.

The victory had been theirs, but it had come at a staggering cost, a cost that Emily felt with every beat of her heart, every breath she drew. The faces of those who had fallen flashed before her eyes, a haunting procession of friends, comrades, and leaders who had given everything in the name of freedom. Their absence left a gaping wound in the fabric of the resistance, a void that could never be filled. The weight of those losses pressed heavily on her shoulders, a burden that she carried alone, as the leader who had led them through the storm.

She could still hear their voices, the laughter that had once echoed through their camps, the whispered conversations shared in the dead of night, the cries of battle, and, finally, the silence that followed. The memories clung to her like shadows, a constant reminder of the price they had paid. Emily had never wanted this role, had never sought to be the one who others looked to for guidance and strength. But fate had a way of choosing its leaders, and now, standing at the forefront of this fractured assembly, she knew she could not falter.

Yet, as her gaze moved from one weary face to the next, she saw something in the eyes of those who remained that stirred something deep within her. It was a spark, faint but unmistakable hope. For so long, that glimmer of hope had been absent, snuffed out by the relentless onslaught of a regime that had seemed impossible to topple. But now, in the aftermath of their hard-won victory, that hope was rekindling, a fragile flame that flickered to life in the hearts of the survivors.

It was there in the way they stood, their postures not just of soldiers who had fought and bled together, but of individuals who had endured the worst and found within themselves the strength to continue. It was in the determined set of their jaws, in the unspoken understanding that, despite everything, they had achieved something monumental. They had struck a blow against tyranny, and though the cost had been high, they had shown that the power of the people could not be so easily extinguished.

Emily felt a surge of emotion rise within her, a mix of pride, sorrow, and an overwhelming sense of responsibility. These were her people, the ones who had entrusted her with their lives, their futures. And in their eyes, she saw the reflection of her resolve. They looked to her not just for leadership, but for a sense of direction, for the strength to carry on. She had guided them through the darkness, and now, as the first light of a new day filtered through the shattered windows, she knew that her task was far from over.

Hope, fragile and precious, was now theirs to nurture. It was a seed that needed to be tended, to be protected from the harsh realities that still loomed on the horizon. The battles they had fought were only the beginning, and the road ahead was fraught with uncertainty. But as long as that spark of hope remained, they had something to fight for, something to build upon.

Emily took a deep breath, feeling the weight of her role settle over her once more. The faces before her blurred for a moment as tears welled up in her eyes, but she blinked them away, steeling herself for what was to come. The time for mourning would come later. Now, there was work to be done, a future to be forged from the ashes of the past.

As she stepped forward to speak, the room fell silent. Her voice, though soft, carried the authority she had earned through hardship and sacrifice. "We've come so far," she began, her gaze sweeping over the faces before her. "And though the battle is over, our work has only just begun. We fought for a future where we could be free, and where our children could grow up without fear. Now, we have to build that future."

Her words resonated deeply with those who had lived through the revolution's darkest days. But even as she spoke, Emily couldn't ignore the new challenges that loomed on the horizon. The collapse of the government had left a power vacuum, and already, whispers of new factions rising to seize control were spreading like wildfire. These groups, each with their agendas, threatened to tear apart the fragile unity they had fought so hard to achieve.

Emily knew that if they were to succeed in rebuilding, they needed to move quickly to establish order. She turned her attention to the immediate tasks at hand, organising teams to clear the streets, restore basic services, and provide aid to the countless civilians who had been caught in the crossfire. But as she spoke, assigning roles and delegating tasks, she couldn't shake the feeling that the hardest battles were still ahead.

Later that day, as the sun began its descent toward the horizon, Emily found herself standing alone in what had once been the mayor's office. The room, once a symbol of authority and governance, was now a grim testament to the chaos that had swept through the city. Papers were scattered across the floor, their edges singed and torn, a chaotic jumble of bureaucracy reduced to debris. The heavy mahogany desk that had once dominated the space was overturned, its surface marred by deep gashes and the thick layer of dust that coated every inch of the room. The air was thick with the smell of smoke and decay, remnants of the battle that had ravaged this place.

Emily's gaze moved slowly across the room, taking in the signs of destruction, each broken object a reminder of the cost of their victory. The large windows that lined one wall were cracked and splintered, jagged shards of glass still clinging to the frames. They bore the scars of the explosion that had rocked the building during the final assault, the force of the blast etched into every fracture. Beyond the shattered panes, the city sprawled out before her, a landscape of devastation and hope intertwined.

Despite the chaos, there was a certain solemnity to the space, a heavy silence that seemed to hold the echoes of the decisions that had once been made within these walls. It was a room that had seen power wielded, often with a heavy hand, and now it was Emily who stood at the centre of it, the weight of responsibility pressing down on her with a force that threatened to buckle her knees. She was acutely aware that this was no longer just a fight for survival; it was a fight to rebuild, to restore, to heal.

She moved toward the window, her steps slow and deliberate, as if each one carried her deeper into the reality of the task ahead. The sun was beginning to set, casting long, golden shadows across the wreckage outside. The warm light filtered through the broken glass, creating a fractured pattern of brightness and shadow that danced across the floor. It was a strange juxtaposition, the beauty of the setting sun against the starkness of the ruined city.

As she stood at the window, looking out over the city that had once been her home, Emily felt a pang of sorrow, mingled with a quiet sense of pride. The streets, though littered with debris and marked by the scars of battle, were not empty. In the distance, she could see groups of people moving slowly through the rubble, their figures silhouetted against the fading light. They worked together, lifting the fallen bricks, clearing the remnants of what once was, and tending to the wounded who had not yet been evacuated. Their movements were purposeful, driven not just by necessity, but by a shared determination to rebuild what had been lost.

The sight filled her with a deep, quiet pride. These were her people, the ones who had stood beside her, who had fought and bled for the same dream. They had won the war, but now came the harder task: winning the peace. The battle had been fought with weapons and strategy, but the peace would be won with patience, resilience, and a commitment to a future that was still uncertain.

Yet, even as she felt that pride, it was tinged with a profound sense of anxiety. The peace that followed a war was always fragile, a delicate balance that could tip into chaos at the slightest provocation. She knew that the work of rebuilding was just beginning, and it would take all their strength, all their willpower, to preserve it. The factions that had united against a common enemy might now turn against each other, old grievances and new ambitions threatening to tear apart what they had fought so hard to achieve.

Emily's thoughts drifted to the faces of those she had lost along the way, friends, allies, and mentors who had believed in this cause with the same commitment she did. Their absence was a constant ache, a reminder of the price they had paid for this victory. And yet, their sacrifice had not been in vain. The city was still standing, and its people were still fighting, not with guns and bombs, but with the quiet, determined acts of rebuilding. They were clearing the debris, tending to the wounded, and beginning the slow, painful process of healing.

But there was so much more to do. The war had left the city in ruins, and the government that had once ruled with an iron fist had collapsed, leaving a power vacuum that could easily descend into anarchy. The survivors looked to her now, not just as a leader in battle, but as a beacon of hope in these uncertain times. She would have to guide them through this new phase, finding a way to bring together the disparate factions, to forge a new government from the ashes of the old, one that could truly serve the people it governed.

Emily's hands clenched into fists at her sides, the tension coiling in her muscles as she braced herself for the challenges ahead. The future was uncertain, and the road to true freedom would be long and fraught with danger. But as long as there was hope, as long as the sun continued to rise over the shattered city, there was a chance. And that was enough.

A knock at the door broke her reverie. She turned to see Lily standing in the doorway, her expression a mixture of relief and concern. "Emily, there's something you should see," Lily said, her voice hesitant.

Emily followed her out of the office and down the corridor to what had once been the council chamber. Inside, a group of people had gathered representatives from various factions that had emerged in the aftermath of the government's collapse. Some were familiar faces, allies who had fought beside them during the revolution. Others were new, leaders of groups that had risen to prominence in the chaos that followed the regime's downfall.

The tension in the room was palpable as the discussions began. Each faction had its vision for the future, and as the arguments grew more heated, it became clear that unity was far from guaranteed. Emily listened carefully, her mind racing as she tried to navigate the treacherous waters of post-war politics.

As the meeting continued, Emily's thoughts drifted to the people who weren't in the room, those who had given their lives for the cause. John, Aamir, Hassan... their absence was a gaping wound in her heart. But it was also a reminder of why they had fought, and why she had to keep fighting now. Their sacrifice could not be in vain.

Emily took a deep breath, steeling herself for what was to come. She had been a leader in war, but now she had to be a leader in peace, a role that, in many ways, was even more daunting. She knew that the choices she made in the coming days would shape the future of their fledgling nation and that the road ahead would be fraught with challenges. But as she looked around the room at the faces of those who had survived, those who had fought and bled for the dream of a better world, she felt a renewed sense of purpose.

"We've faced impossible odds before," Emily said, cutting through the heated debate. Her voice was calm, but there was an edge of determination that silenced the room. "And we came through stronger because we stood together. We can't let old divisions tear us apart now. We have to remember what we fought for, freedom, justice, and a future where everyone has a voice."

Her words hung in the air, and for a moment, the room was silent. Then, one by one, the leaders nodded in agreement. The tension began to dissipate, replaced by a sense of shared resolve. It was a small victory, but it was a start.

As the meeting adjourned, Emily stepped outside, breathing in the cool evening air. The city was quiet, the streets lit by the soft glow of lanterns as people went about their work, rebuilding their lives from the ashes. She walked through the streets, her mind heavy with the knowledge that the revolution was only the beginning. The real challenge lay in what came next.

She knew that the days ahead would be difficult, that new threats would emerge, and that the fight for a just and free society was far from over. But as she looked at the faces of the people she passed, faces filled with hope, determination, and a fierce will to live in a better world, she felt a spark of optimism. They had survived the storm, and now, together, they would build a new dawn.

The path forward would not be easy. There would be setbacks, conflicts, and sacrifices yet to come. But for the first time in a long time, Emily believed that they could make it. They had come too far, fought too hard, to let their dream slip away now. The future was uncertain, but it was theirs to shape.

And as the first stars began to appear in the night sky, Emily allowed herself a moment of quiet reflection. She thought of the friends she had lost, of the lives that had been forever changed by the revolution. Their memory would guide her, their legacy would live on in the world they were building. A new beginning was at hand, and with it, the promise of a better tomorrow.

The revolution had given them a chance, a chance to create something new, something lasting. And as Emily stood beneath the vast expanse of the night sky, she vowed that she would not let that chance slip through their fingers. Whatever challenges lay ahead, they would face them together, united in their shared vision of a world reborn from the ashes of the past.

Later that day, as the sun began its descent toward the horizon, Emily found herself standing alone in what had once been the mayor's office. The room, once a symbol of authority and governance, was now a grim testament to the chaos that had swept through the city. Papers were scattered across the floor, their edges singed and torn, a chaotic jumble of bureaucracy reduced to debris. The heavy mahogany desk that had once dominated the space was overturned, its surface marred by deep gashes and the thick layer of dust that coated every inch of the room. The air was thick with the smell of smoke and decay, remnants of the battle that had ravaged this place.

Emily's gaze moved slowly across the room, taking in the signs of destruction, each broken object a reminder of the cost of their victory. The large windows that lined one wall were cracked and splintered, jagged shards of glass still clinging to the frames. They bore the scars of the explosion that had rocked the building during the final assault, the force of the blast etched into every fracture. Beyond the shattered panes, the city sprawled out before her, a landscape of devastation and hope intertwined.

Despite the chaos, there was a certain solemnity to the space, a heavy silence that seemed to hold the echoes of the decisions that had once been made within these walls. It was a room that had seen power wielded, often with a heavy hand, and now it was Emily who stood at the centre of it, the weight of responsibility pressing down on her with a force that threatened to buckle her knees. She was acutely aware that this was no longer just a fight for survival; it was a fight to rebuild, to restore, to heal.

She moved toward the window, her steps slow and deliberate, as if each one carried her deeper into the reality of the task ahead. The sun was beginning to set, casting long, golden shadows across the wreckage outside. The warm light filtered through the broken glass, creating a fractured pattern of brightness and shadow that danced across the floor. It was a strange juxtaposition, the beauty of the setting sun against the starkness of the ruined city.

As she stood at the window, looking out over the city that had once been her home, Emily felt a pang of sorrow, mingled with a quiet sense of pride. The streets, though littered with debris and marked by the scars of battle, were not empty. In the distance, she could see groups of people moving slowly through the rubble, their figures silhouetted against the fading light. They worked together, lifting the fallen bricks, clearing the remnants of what once was, and tending to the wounded who had not yet been evacuated. Their movements were purposeful, driven not just by necessity, but by a shared determination to rebuild what had been lost.

The sight filled her with a deep, quiet pride. These were her people, the ones who had stood beside her, who had fought and bled for the same dream. They had won the war, but now came the harder task: winning the peace. The battle had been fought with weapons and strategy, but the peace would be won with patience, resilience, and a commitment to a future that was still uncertain.

Yet, even as she felt that pride, it was tinged with a profound sense of anxiety. The peace that followed the war was always fragile, a delicate balance that could tip into chaos at the slightest provocation. She knew that the work of rebuilding was just beginning, and it would take all their strength, all their willpower, to preserve it. The factions that had united against a common enemy might now turn against each other, old grievances and new ambitions threatening to tear apart what they had fought so hard to achieve.

Emily's thoughts drifted to the faces of those she had lost along the way, friends, allies, and mentors who had believed in this cause with the same fervour she did. Their absence was a constant ache, a reminder of the price they had paid for this victory. And yet, their sacrifice had not been in vain. The city was still standing, and its people were still fighting, not with guns and bombs, but with the quiet, determined acts of rebuilding. They were clearing the debris, tending to the wounded, and beginning the slow, painful process of healing.

But there was so much more to do. The war had left the city in ruins, and the government that had once ruled with an iron fist had collapsed, leaving a power vacuum that could easily descend into anarchy. The survivors looked to her now, not just as a leader in battle, but as a beacon of hope in these uncertain times. She would have to guide them through this new phase, finding a way to bring together the disparate factions, to forge a new government from the ashes of the old, one that could truly serve the people it governed.

Emily's hands clenched into fists at her sides, the tension coiling in her muscles as she braced herself for the challenges ahead. The future was uncertain, and the road to true freedom would be long and fraught with danger. But as long as there was hope, as long as the sun continued to rise over the shattered city, there was a chance. And that was enough.

Chapter 32 Revolution's Dawn

The air was thick with the scent of rain-soaked earth, mingling with the lingering smoke from the battle that had finally ended. The pungent aroma of charred wood and scorched metal hung in the atmosphere, a grim reminder of the destruction that had taken place. The once-grand city, a symbol of pride and power, now lay in ruins, reduced to rubble and ash. Streets that had once bustled with life were now eerily silent, save for the occasional crackling of embers that refused to die. Buildings that had once stood tall and imposing were now nothing more than skeletal remains, their facades crumbled and broken, casting long shadows in the dim light of dawn.

The early morning light, soft and tentative, began to creep over the horizon, casting the city in hues of pink, orange, and gold. It was a stark contrast to the devastation below as if nature itself was attempting to wash away the horrors of the night with the gentle touch of a new day. The sky, streaked with the soft hues of dawn, hinted at the promise of a new beginning, a fragile hope that clung to the survivors like a lifeline. But even as the light grew stronger, the weight of the past bore down on those who had lived through the night, a heavy burden that could not be easily shaken.

This was not the triumphant victory they had dreamed of. There were no cheers of celebration, no jubilant cries of joy. Instead, there was a solemn, almost reverent silence, as those who had survived the battle took stock of what they had gained and, more importantly, what they had lost. It was a victory, yes, but one that had been paid for in blood, sweat, and tears. The city, once a beacon of civilisation, was now a graveyard of dreams, its streets lined with the remnants of a society that had torn itself apart in the quest for freedom.

Yet, despite the devastation, there was a sense of hard-fought accomplishment, a blood-soaked claim to freedom that could not be denied. The rebels had won, but the cost had been high, and the road ahead was fraught with uncertainty. As the survivors stood amidst the ruins, their eyes turned to the future, knowing that the battle for their city was just the beginning of a much larger struggle. The ashes of the old world had given birth to something new, something fragile yet filled with potential. And as the first rays of sunlight began to break through the clouds, there was a collective sense of resolve, a determination to rebuild, to honour the sacrifices that had been made, and to forge a new path forward.

Emily stood at the centre of what remained of the city square, surrounded by the few who had survived. The ground beneath her feet was uneven, scarred by the blast that had torn through the area during the final assault. Around her, the buildings stood as hollow shells, their windows shattered, walls pockmarked with bullet holes. The silence was almost oppressive, broken only by the distant sound of footsteps and the occasional murmur of voices from those tending to the wounded or clearing debris.

The group that had once been a tight-knit band of rebels now felt diminished, not just in numbers but in spirit. They had lost so many along the way, each death a blow to their collective resolve. And yet, as Emily looked into the eyes of those who remained, Lily, Aamir, Tomasz, and a few others who had become the core of this resistance, she saw a glimmer of something more profound than mere survival. There was a quiet determination, a recognition that their fight was far from over. The battle had been won, but the war for a just and free society was just beginning.

As the first rays of sunlight pierced through the clouds, casting long shadows across the square, Emily felt a profound sense of both relief and responsibility. The golden light brought with it the promise of a new day, a new beginning, yet it also illuminated the harsh reality of their situation. The square, once a place of community and life, now bore the scars of battle, craters from explosions, bloodstains that had not yet dried, and the bodies of those who had fought and fallen for a cause they believed in. The sight was almost too much to bear, a visceral reminder of the price they had paid for this moment.

Emily's emotions were a tumultuous storm within her. Grief for those they had lost, for the friends and comrades who would never see this sunrise. Guilt, a gnawing sensation in the pit of her stomach, for the decisions she had made, the lives she had sent into the fray knowing not all would return. There was also a profound exhaustion that settled deep into her bones, the weight of leadership pressing down on her more heavily than ever before. But beneath it all, there was a spark of something else, determination, resolve, and a fierce, unyielding hope.

She knew they couldn't afford to linger in the past, to dwell on what had been lost. The future demanded their attention, their focus. The rebellion had won a significant battle, but the war was far from over. The city lay in ruins, its people weary and wounded, but alive. And it was up to her, and those who remained, to ensure that their sacrifices had not been in vain. Emily's heart ached with the enormity of the task ahead, but she also felt a surge of strength, a sense of purpose that pushed her forward.

As she took a deep breath, feeling the cool morning air fill her lungs, Emily steeled herself for what was to come. The trembling in her hands, the tightness in her chest, these were things she could not afford to show. Her people needed to see strength in her, needed to believe that she could guide them through the dark days that still lay ahead. She pushed down the fear, and the doubt, locking them away in the depths of her mind, and focused on the faces that looked to her for guidance.

Her voice, when she spoke, was steady, and firm, carrying with it the authority and conviction she had cultivated through years of struggle. Yet there was also warmth, a quiet compassion that acknowledged the pain they all shared, the bond that had been forged in the fires of revolution. Emily knew she had to be the one to lead them now, to channel their grief and anger into the resolve to rebuild, to create something new from the ashes of the old world. The future was uncertain, fraught with challenges and dangers, but it was theirs to shape, and she was determined to see it through, no matter the cost.

"We've come a long way," Emily began, her voice carrying over the stillness. "We've fought battles we never thought we could win. We've lost people we loved, people who believed in this cause as much as we do. But we're still here. And as long as we are, we have a responsibility to make sure their sacrifices weren't in vain."

Lily, standing beside her, nodded in agreement. Her usual bright manner was tempered by the gravity of the moment, but her eyes still held that spark of hope that had always defined her. "We have to rebuild," she said, her voice soft but resolute. "Not just the city, but the trust and unity we'll need to move forward. We can't let what happened to us tear us apart."

Aamir, his face lined with exhaustion and grief, spoke next. "We must stay vigilant. The government might be in ruins, but there are still forces out there that would see us fail. We can't afford to be complacent."

As if in response to his words, Tomasz stepped forward, holding a small device in his hand. His expression was grim, and there was an edge of urgency in his voice. "I think Aamir's right. We found this during our sweep of the government's command centre. It's a data drive, heavily encrypted, but I've managed to crack part of it. What I've seen so far... it's troubling."

Emily's heart sank. The victory they had achieved was fragile, and the last thing they needed was a new threat emerging from the ashes of the old regime. "What's on it?" she asked, her voice laced with apprehension.

Tomasz's gaze hardened as he answered. "It's a contingency plan. The government had a backup strategy in place, a network of loyalists embedded across the country, ready to destabilise any new order we try to establish. They've got caches of weapons, supplies, and most disturbingly, a plan to turn public sentiment against us by any means necessary. If we don't act quickly, everything we've fought for could be undone."

A murmur of concern rippled through the group. The idea that their hard-won freedom could be so easily threatened was almost too much to bear. But Emily felt a surge of resolve rise within her. They had faced overwhelming odds before, and they had prevailed. They could do it again.

"This isn't over," Emily said, her voice steady despite the gravity of Tomasz's revelation. "We've faced betrayal, loss, and nearly impossible challenges, and we're still standing. We'll deal with this, just as we've dealt with everything else. Together."

There was a moment of silence as her words sank in. Then, one by one, the others nodded, their faces set with renewed determination. They had pledged their lives to this cause, and they would see it through to the end, whatever that end might be.

As they began to discuss their next steps, Emily's thoughts drifted to the future. The challenges they faced were immense rebuilding a shattered society, dealing with the remnants of the old regime, and ensuring that the new order they fought to create was truly just and free. But for the first time in a long while, she felt a glimmer of hope.

The revolution had dawned, but the work of building a new world was just beginning. There would be more battles to fight, and more sacrifices to make, but Emily knew they were ready. They had to be.

As the meeting drew to a close, Emily stepped outside the crumbling government building. The sun was now fully risen, casting a warm, golden light over the city. Despite the destruction, there was a beauty to the scene, a sense of renewal in the air. The people who had fought so hard to free themselves from tyranny were now moving through the streets, beginning the work of rebuilding, brick by brick.

Emily watched them for a moment, a quiet resolve settling over her. There was much to do, and the road ahead would be long and difficult. But they were not alone. The people were with them, and as long as they stood united, there was nothing they couldn't achieve.

In the distance, she could hear the sounds of hammers striking metal, of voices calling out orders, of life slowly returning to the city. It was a new beginning, fraught with challenges but also filled with possibilities. The future was theirs to shape, and Emily knew they would not squander the chance they had fought so hard to earn.

The war was over, but the revolution had only just begun.

Author Biography

Served 23 years in the Royal Navy. Since leaving the navy, he has held senior roles in businesses and spent 5 years as a military trainer for the UAE's armed forces.

Married and living with his wife, Yvonne, in Derbyshire, this is his first serious foray into the world of writing.

And he likes it!

Printed in Great Britain
by Amazon